Every year the John W. Campbell Awards honor
the most promising new writers in SF, nominated
by the fans themselves.

The NEW VOICES series is the nominees' own
selections of their best and most adventurous work,
chosen especially for today's most eagerly-awaited
SF anthology . . .

NEW VOICES IV

"A FINE SHOWCASE FOR NEWER WRITERS!"
—*Seattle Times*

Berkley books edited by George R.R. Martin

NEW VOICES III: THE CAMPBELL AWARD NOMINEES

FOURTH ANNUAL VOLUME:

NEW 4 VOICES

THE JOHN W. CAMPBELL AWARD NOMINEES

**EDITED BY
GEORGE R.R. MARTIN**

BERKLEY BOOKS, NEW YORK

NEW VOICES IV

A Berkley Book / published by arrangement with
the author

PRINTING HISTORY
Berkley edition / August 1981

ISBN: 0-425-05033-5

A BERKLEY BOOK® TM 757,375

PRINTED IN THE UNITED STATES OF AMERICA

to the memory of Tom Reamy,
an eloquent new voice,
too soon silent.

CONTENTS

PREFACE

A literature is only as good as its new writers.

That proposition, in a nutshell, is what both the John W. Campbell Award and these anthologies are all about, so perhaps a few words of elaboration are in order. Certainly the new writers in a genre or subgenre are not the obvious signs of its health or lack thereof. Usually they are barely visible, down there on the bottom somewhere struggling for a little recognition, a larger advance, the next sale, whatever. Long-time professionals and established masters seem to dominate, and it is their books—not the efforts of the fledglings—that command the spotlight and prompt critics to make sweeping pronouncements about the vitality of the field.

But that's an optical illusion. If you really want to know how science fiction (or any branch of literature) is doing, don't look at the big names. Look at the new writers.

An established literary form has a certain amount of momentum, embodied in its long-time practitioners. A writer who has been writing SF for twenty years will likely as not continue to write it, no matter what shape the genre is in. He may get better or he may get worse; he may produce masterpieces or he may produce potboilers. But in any case, watching him will tell you little or nothing about the long-term prospects of the literature.

Watching the newcomers, however, can tell you an awful lot. A strong, healthy literature creates excitement, wins new readers, and *inspires many of those readers to write*. It makes it easy for neophytes to break into the professional ranks. It encourages innovation, diversity, new approaches. In short, a healthy genre is open and yeasty. If it doesn't seem to be . . . watch out.

If a literature has ceased to attract new writers at all, if all the by-lines have been around for years, if all the writers are grey and aging and prosperous—then what you have is a walking corpse. It may stroll around for ten or twenty more years, on momentum, but sooner or later it will be gone, with the last of its old masters.

If a literature becomes so competitive and in-bred that only a handful of newcomers can break in, and those usually the ones with some sort of professional contacts or "in,"—a head-start, so to speak—then what you have is the beginnings of a literary incest that will ultimately lead to loss of audience, fossilization, and decay.

If a literature encourages and rewards only those new writers who are turning out the product-as-before, rehashes of the things done by those who have come before them—then what you have is a genre on its way to becoming a commercial formula, a genre that has abandoned growth. Sales may hold up for years, so long as the formula satisfies public needs. But sooner or later times will change, the formula will become outmoded, and there will be nothing to take its place. Death comes quickly in such cases.

None of these are entirely hypothetical cases. The first case describes some of the difficulties of the western novel, a field dominated by its old-timers. One young writer of my acquaintance recently sold a western, and attended a conference of western writers. People kept asking him whose grandson he was, he said. Fortunately for western buffs, the genre seems to be opening up a bit, after a long hiatus.

The second case summarizes the plight of the so-called "literary novel," increasingly divorced from popular tastes, increasingly cliquish and without an audience, open to new talent only so long as the newcomer is someone's protege with the proper credentials in academia. No wonder critics fret about the novel being dead.

The third case fits several genres and subgenres, most notably the traditional gothic. Once a vital sort of literature, in the days of *Jane Eyre* and *Wuthering Heights*, the gothic became an almost total formula field, and sold wonderfully while the formula was popular. Today tastes have moved beyond it, and the gothic is withering on the vine while a new formula— the historical romance—gobbles up all its readers.

And SF? Where does SF fit in?

Fortunately, SF fits none of these cases. At least not yet. There are a number of reasons that might be offered for SF's peculiar immunity to these various literary diseases, but the most important, I think, is the field's hospitality to new writers of many different sorts.

That tradition can easily be seen to have started with John W. Campbell, Jr. Campbell edited *Astounding* (later *Analog*), the field's leading periodical, for more than thirty years, and during all of that long tenure he was constantly searching for new talent. He read every manuscript that came into the office personally, and he was famed for his long letters of advice and encouragement to aspiring unknowns. His efforts paid off. Most of the giants of SF today were Campbell discoveries. When he assumed command of *Astounding* in the late Thirties, he revolutionized the field by turning up such talents as Theodore Sturgeon, Isaac Asimov, Robert A. Heinlein, Lester del Rey, and A.E. van Vogt. Even writers already established, like Clifford Simak and Jack Williamson, fell under Campbell's spell and had their careers turned in new directions. Nor was Campbell ever satisfied. One stable of writers was not enough. When most of his discoveries went to war in 1941, he turned up others to take their place. He found yet others in the later forties, in the fifties, in the sixties. Gordon R. Dickson, Poul Anderson, Harry Harrison, Ben Bova, Stanley Schmidt, James Blish, even *Norman Spinrad*—all of them started with Campbell.

A.E. van Vogt, one of Campbell's earliest and most prominent discoveries, talks about that legendary editor and his influence on Van's career in the introduction that follows. Suffice it to say, then, that Campbell was, throughout his career, (in the words of Isaac Asimov) a patron saint of new voices in SF.

When he died in 1971, the publishers of his magazine, *Analog*, established a most appropriate memorial to his name: the John W. Campbell Award for the best new writer in SF. Given for the first time in 1973, the Campbell Award is controlled by the fans and readers, who first nominate the finalists from all those new writers who have appeared during the preceding two years, and then vote a winner from among the finalists. Like Campbell himself, the Campbell Award gives encouragement and recognition to the writers who are the cutting edge of the genre and its hope for tomorrow.

These anthologies have the same intent. Each volume is a showcase for one year's roster of Campbell Award finalists. Each nominee contributes an original, never-before-published story to the book. What you hold in your hand is a sampler of the most promising new talents in the field, writing at the top of their ability, in all their splendid diversity.

And—bearing in mind what I said earlier—what you have in hand is also, in a very real sense, an index of the health of the field.

The anthologies, previously titled *New Voices*, were initiated simultaneously with the Campbell Award itself, in 1973. However, the world of publishing can be a slow one at times, and because of a strange and boring series of delays, the anthologies are now running some five years behind the award. This fourth volume will probably appear in 1981. It contains stories by the five Campbell finalists of 1976, all of whom published for the first time in 1974–75. But this regrettable gap has its positive side. It gives us some perspective to look back on these writers, and this award, and to make a judgment on the vitality of SF.

Look at the contents page again. Look at the last page of this book, with its listing of Campbell winners and losers from 1973–1979. After you do, I think your judgment will agree with mine: science fiction in 1981 is still enormously healthy.

Some observations are beyond question. One: the field is wide open. Not only do new writers publish every day (hundreds of them broke in during the late Seventies), but *they are welcomed*. The ones that are good rise quickly. When a writer is first nominated for the Campbell, he or she is usually a beginner, with a handful of stories or perhaps a novel to their credit. Yet the field is such that many of these beginners have become major writers in a bare few years. Jerry Pournelle, the first Campbell Award winner, now commands six-figure advances for his books. Less than a decade ago no one had heard of him. John Campbell bought his first stories in 1971, just prior to his death. Campbell nominees, winners and losers both, regularly appear on the ballots for SF's top honors, the Hugo and Nebula, sometimes simultaneously with the Campbell nominations, usually a year or two later. Spider Robinson, the second Campbell winner, has won both Hugo and Nebula, as have two Campbell losers, John Varley and myself. Barry Longyear and Tom Reamy have both taken Nebulas; Joan Vinge and C.J. Cherryh have won Hugos. Others will soon join the list. The point is that recognition, awards, and money all come quickly in SF for a writer who does good work.

A second observation: the field is diverse. Not only is it drawing new writers, but it is drawing all *kinds* of new writers. Look at that list of nominees again. What do you see? Well, you have hard-nosed Heinleinesque storytellers like Pournelle and Chalker. You have fantasists like Stephen R. Donaldson and Elizabeth A. Lynn. You have hard-science speculators like Charles Sheffield and James P. Hogan and P.J. Plauger. You have horror story writers like Lisa Tuttle and Tom Reamy, each with a sure feel for character and place. You have humorists like Spider Robinson and Barry Longyear, and black humorists like George Alec Effinger. You get romanticism from Joan Vinge and myself, feminism from John Varley and Suzy McKee Charnas, avant-garde prose and character studies from Alan Brennert and Carter Scholz and Bob Thurston, you get hard science and soft science and no science, action-adventure and mood pieces and surrealism, and . . . well, you get the idea. If anyone can go through the list of Campbell finalists to date and find anything that all these writers have in common, they are a better person than I.

With the wonderful clarity of hindsight, it is easy to look back and see that SF is incredibly vital and thriving.

However, we ought not get complacent. Hindsight, remember, looks back. A literature must look forward. Looking forward, there are some definite dark clouds on the horizon. During the late Seventies, SF experienced the biggest boom in its history, a boom that helped—although it was by no means the only factor—in bringing in all this new talent, in encouraging the chaos of diversity. That boom crested early in 1980, and a decline began. How serious it will be and how long it will last, no one can be sure. But it is definitely on us. The test will be how the field responds to it.

New writers will bear the brunt of the decline. First novels will be harder to sell. So will second novels, for those whose first did not set the world afire. Big money and awards may not follow quite so closely on the heels of a first sale, even for the most talented. More starving in the garret may be necessary before the first blush of success.

Dangers are very real in this sort of scenario. If the hard times go on too long. If the competition becomes so intense that new writers are shut out or discouraged. If one strain of SF outsells the others so clearly that everyone starts writing that. Then, in time, we shall go the way of the western, the literary novel, the gothic.

To avoid that, it is vital that the field stay open, that it stay chaotic and diverse, that editors seek out new talent, that readers buy their books and awards voters remember their names. But I'm optimistic. The Campbell Award will help, and so, I hope, will these books. Besides, we have a tradition.

But only the future will tell.

Meanwhile, here in our fourth volume, let us go back to the 34th World Science Fiction Convention, held in Kansas City, Missouri on a sultry Labor Day weekend in 1976, when the nominees for the John W. Campbell Award were John Varley, M.A. Foster, Arsen Darnay, Joan D. Vinge, and Tom Reamy.

George R.R. Martin
Santa Fe, New Mexico
June, 1980

INTRODUCTION

The last letter I received from Campbell was when I sent him part of a novel. I evidently sent it to him early in 1970, for his reply was dated February 26, 1970.

What I submitted was the first third of *The Battle of Forever*. Ace Books had contracted for it during the editorship of Don Wollheim. My reason for submitting it to Campbell was that it was belatedly occurring to me that a magazine editor might be interested in serializing these new works of mine prior to paperback publication. In view of the paperback deadline, in this instance serialization would have to be quick.

Campbell returned the ms. with an accompanying letter, which opened: "I haven't a chance of using your novel—I'm stocked up through mid-1971 already!"

Next paragraph begins: "But I'm glad you're working yourself back into story-writing trim." (Because—third paragraph): "Yay, verily, the technology of writing has indeed changed over the near-20-years you've been out of it. Wonder how Michaelangelo would make out as a modern sculptor with an arc-welding machine? Or using an air-hammer to carve his stone?"

I have included paragraph three *in toto* because it is undoubtedly relevant to the stories in this collection. After all, in my time, although typewriters existed, if you made a mistake you corrected the error with an eraser. Today, I myself have only progressed to the IBM Correcting Selectric II. But such modern giants as Larry Niven, Jerry Pournelle, and David Gerrold use computerized typewriters. What would Michaelangelo have done with the compressed air brush?

In his letter about *The Battle of Forever*, Campbell goes on to say (paragraph four): "This one shows many of the old van Vogt touches, and has some highly interesting ideas. Some, I think, you carried a bit too far—I doubt that men would have taken the trouble to make *all* animal species intelligent. There'd be little point, because the inherent differences of the animals would have *had* to be almost totally suppressed in the process, or they'd never be able to live together in harmony . . ." Etc.

Paragraph five: "Think of intelligent rats and mice as electronic repairmen, and the hippos as civil engineers supervising irrigation and other waterways, beavers as erosion control supervisors, bears as forestry service specialists! Bears would also make great police, to handle emergencies!"

Paragraph six: "However—time makes our use of this one out of the question."

Paragraph seven: "But how about novelettes and shorts? You know we're paying five cents a word now for shorts (under 7500 words) because of the chronic shortage of that length." End of letter.

Over the years people have asked me what it was like to work for Campbell. Presumably, they meant that writing stories for him was "working" for him; and technically I have to disagree. During WW II the difference between an "author", defined in Canada as an employee of a publisher, and "professional free lance writer", which was given the same status under war time laws as doctors and lawyers, kept me out of the forced labor corps. So I have a stake in the meaning of the word "work" in relation to writers and their publishers.

But, of course, I know what the question means. And I have to say that at the time—back there in the 1940s—I didn't think about it. I took it for granted that someone in a New York editorial office read a portion of each story that came through the mail slot. Read enough of it, that is, to determine fairly the quality of every submission.

That's what happened to my work, both at MacFadden Publications when I submitted my first confession story in 1932, and at *Astounding* in 1938 when I sent in "Vault of the Beast," and then again in January, 1939, when I submitted "Black Destroyer."

It later developed that at *Astounding* Campbell himself read a portion of every story submitted. In my case, he read all the way through; and thus a new science fiction writer came into view from a far horizon—far, indeed, it was for a New York area dweller.

Picture that New York pulp publishing jungle in the 1930s!

Recently, we've had glimpses of what an "in" world it was in those days. In his autobiography, *The Way the Future Was*, Frederik Pohl describes how he became a science fiction editor at nineteen, and sold his own stories to the magazine under a pseudonym.

Everybody was half-starved; needed to sell his story right now so that his girl friend and he could eat. Thus if you belonged to a little group that had known the editor "when", your story was bought if it had any merit at all. But, contrariwise, there was no space available for outside writers. Other New York authors who were not part of the "in" group were equally ignored.

Just imagine a story arriving on that scene from faraway Winnipeg, Manitoba, Canada—which is where I lived in 1938 and most of '39. The hard part is to picture it even being read, let alone bought. That is, read by the editor.

The fact that Pohl had to pretend that someone else had written the stories he bought from himself tells us that the publisher was not part of the conspiracy. Because, naturally, publishers want to make money. So that was a pressure on editors to expand their horizons. Pohl, as we may observe, grew into his job. And later edited SF magazines that published superior stories. And himself wrote some of the best science fiction in the business.

I deduce from the treatment I received from Campbell on my early stories that this editor, beginning in 1937, built up the subsequent eminence of *Astounding* (now *Analog*) by invariably buying the best stories he could find from any source. Thus the publisher's relatives, and Campbell's own chums, waited in vain in his office for their inferior brain children to be accepted.

What Campbell's policy progressively established was that talent and craftsmanship are not a localized phenomena. Essentially, we observe, it took all of North America (if you count me in Canada) and Britain to keep science fiction growing. In my opinion, Campbell passed up a few good writers; but—to quote Adam (as I recall it)—no man is perfect.

Of course, there have always been those writers who, on selling a story or two, immediately move to a location near the publisher. Editors do call on such persons oftener than on those who remain at a distance.

A hack writer can make more money living in New York than he can living out in the sticks. Editors phone him, and say, "Joe, I need a 3000 worder by tomorrow to fill out my book. Got any ideas?" Or, "Peter, can you do an 18,000 word novelette by Wednesday? If so come over to the office and pick up an outline I have here." (This being Monday.)

There are tall tales of such New York writers sitting at a typewriter with the coffee pot on the stove, drinking black coffee all day and both nights, finishing that 18,000 worder.

The implications which I have taken from that last-ever Campbell letter to me tells me that the basic John W. Campbell, Jr. had not changed much between 1940 and 1970. Please note: he took the time to read 20,000 words of a story which, after he saw the accompanying letter, he realized he hadn't "a chance of using—"

And, more, he did his usual swift analysis of the material, and with that same editor's awareness as long ago, offered suggestions for improvement (some of which I used in the novel that I finally sent to Ace). I consider *The Battle of Forever* my farthest-out booklength (with *The Silkie* second farthest-out).

The fact that Campbell was, by February 1970, "stocked up" on serials "through mid-197*1* already" (the lone italic is his) also tells us that times have changed. In the 1940s booklengths were rare. I can't remember exactly but I would guess I sent *Slan* to Campbell no earlier than May, 1940. Serial publication started in September of that year.

Today, half a dozen paperback publishers put out four, five, or six SF novels a month. Each. Novelists seem to be growing in every bush; and, to judge by the shelf on shelf of science fiction, the U.S.A. all by itself has several hundred good writers. In 1940, by comparison, there was only a handful who could write a readable booklength.

Also more available currently is the writer who can turn out a good short length. Judging by the fact that the number of magazines continues to increase month after month, it appears that there is no longer, as in 1970, a "chronic shortage" of novelettes and shorts.

But what did Campbell mean when he said, "the technology of writing has indeed changed over the near-20-years you've been out of it"?

My initial comment on that: His 20-year estimate suggests that Campbell neither read nor even glanced at the opposition science fiction magazines. Because I essentially completed what I called my "study" of human behavior in 1961. And I had been busy a couple of years before that writing a double length mainstream novel titled, *The Violent Man*. This work was published by Farrar, Straus & Giroux in October 1962 as a hardcover, and it's had about nine paperback printings starting in 1963—the latest being from Pocket Books in '78.

Also, *IF Worlds of Science Fiction*, in 1963, printed a science fiction story of mine titled *The Expendables*. And in 1964 IF published the first of the "Silkie" novelettes. So my absence from the field was more like twelve years; and that doesn't take into account the Simon & Schuster publication of *The Mind Cage* in 1958.

Unquestionably, even during that period changes had taken place in the genre. My impression: there were many more poetic writers doing science fiction, and a surprisingly large number of women with lush, emotional styles—surprising because SF had been considered a male preserve—and of course there was the New Wave.

It also seemed to me that the action story played a progressively diminishing role during those years.

In my view, throughout the twelve-year period and since, American magazine science fiction featured primarily the works of writers who had been born into the English language, so to say. Stories continued to follow simple patterns of consecutive action and dialogue.

There continued to be no place, or only a rare place, for South American and European authors who, during that period—and actually always—wrote more in the literary tradition of Kafka and Hesse. More than a decade ago, Fred Pohl evidently felt strongly about this insular attitude. For he started a magazine titled—as I recall it—*International Science Fiction*. It was a short-lived venture. Which tells us that the change mentioned by Campbell was in the direction of popular mainstream, and not literary.

The reverse situation is not true. Many American and British writers are popular in France. Among super intellectuals the choice is Philip K. Dick. But French publisher J'ai Lu tells me that my books passed Ray Bradbury in sales five years ago, making me the top science fiction seller in the country of Jules Verne. (Since that's a vague claim, I'll just say that my share of French royalties in 1978, after three agents took their commissions, was over $26,000. If other SF writers made more than that, then J'ai Lu was doing one of those publicity things, for which I am not responsible.)

So all you new writers, you can see what you have to look forward to. But I seem to remember that it took a while. In my case, it was all by mail. No personal contact was involved.

Be persistent. And find a good editor.

I was. And did. And look what happened.

A.E. van Vogt

NEW
VOICES
4

THE **JOHN W. CAMPBELL**
AWARD NOMINEES

John Varley

was thrown out of my club last year, for conduct unbecoming a member.

The club is a rather exclusive one: the Hugo and Nebula Losers' Club, open only to those writers who are repeatedly nominated for SF's major awards and never manage to win them. The members are a tolerant albeit motley crew, but one thing they will not abide—winning. They even threw me out back in 1975, when one of my stories copped a Hugo, but I wrangled readmission the following year by losing two on a single night.

John Varley (Herb to his friends) was one of the club's most promising new members. He made a big splash by losing the Campbell Award twice, in 1975 and again in 1976, which no one had ever done before. Between 1976 and 1978, Herb set an amazing pace, losing four Hugos and two Nebulas. For a while it even looked as though he might wrest the club presidency away from founder Gardner Dozois by topping Gardner's loss record. Then, in 1979, Varley threw it all away. He published an incredible novella entitled "The Persistence of Vision" that totally destroyed his credibility as a loser by *winning Hugo, Nebula, and every other award in sight.*

Herb has managed to lose two more Nebulas since his 1979 sweep, and he has a couple of stories on the Hugo ballot as I write, but things will never be the same. Once you start winning, it is hard to stop. Most recently he won France's Prix d'Apollo. In a year or two he may need a new mantle for all these awards.

Truthfully, Varley came rather close to beginning his career on a winning note. Although he lost the Campbell Award twice, it was a close thing, especially the second time around. By 1976 Herb had already established an enviable reputation. In any other year, he might have been an odds-on favorite for the Campbell. But in 1976 he faced Tom Reamy, who had come just as far just as fast as Varley had. His narrow loss to Reamy was no disgrace. Four years later, from the vantage point of 1980, it is easy to see that Herb and Tom, emerging almost simultaneously, were perhaps the two most important new writers of the Seventies, although they had lots of talented competition.

John Varley the writer has already made important contributions to the genre. His Eight Worlds future history was the most strikingly original the field had seen in thirty years or more. His liberated and sometimes sex-changing protagonists helped destroy some of SF's hoariest sexist stereotypes, and his unique blend of innovative concepts, honest sexuality, and careful attention to human values set the tone for much of the SF of the past five years. On a couple of occasions I have heard people refer to "Varleyisms" in stories by other writers, a sure sign that Herb is already influencing the direction of the field.

Herb Varley the person is a tall (quite), quiet (quite) ex-Texan in his early thirties, presently living in Eugene, Oregon and writing full-time. He makes large demands on himself when writing, and is somewhat of a perfectionist. "I never seem to like my stories half as much as everyone else says they do," he confesses. He hates astrology. He also hates cars. "I buy them cheap, run them mercilessly until they fall apart, and leave them by the side of the road." He never changes his oil, because whenever he does his cars die. At heart a private person, he would rather readers concentrate on his work than on him.

The work, at this point, consists of more than twenty pieces of short fiction, compiled in two first-rate collections, The Persistence of Vision *(Quantum, 1978) and* The Barbie Murders *(Berkley, 1980), plus three novels.* The Ophiuchi Hotline *(Quantum, 1977), his first novel, is part of his famous Eight Worlds series.* Titan *(Berkley, 1979) and its sequel* Wizard *(Berkley, 1980) are two-thirds of a trilogy-in-progress, to be completed by* Demon, *still in Varley's typewriter. He is also at work on* The Gate, *a novel-length expansion of one of his short pieces, "Air Raid," and the basis for a major motion picture. It would be impossible in a few short words to do justice to this body of work; suffice it to say that it is impressive, for someone who has been around so short a time. No wonder he lost all those awards.*

"Blue Champagne," the novella that follows, is major Varley, as different as his Eight Worlds, as moving as "Persistence of Vision." Herb offers only one comment about it:"I'm a non-swimmer," he says. He is also a non-loser. If he keeps writing stories like this, he'll never get back into the club.

G R R M

BLUE CHAMPAGNE

John Varley

Megan Galloway arrived in the Bubble with a camera crew of three. With her breather and her sidekick she was the least naked nude woman any of the lifeguards had ever seen.

"I bet she's carrying more hardware than any of her crew," Glen said.

"Yeah, but it hardly shows, you know?"

Q.M. Cooper was thinking back as he watched her accept the traditional bulb of champagne. "Isn't that some kind of record? Three people in her crew?"

"The President of Brazil brought twenty-nine people in with her," Anna-Louise observed. "The King of England had twenty-five."

"Yeah, but only one network pool camera."

"So that's the Golden Gypsy," Leah said.

Anna-Louise snorted. "More like the Brass Transistor."

They had all heard that one before, but laughed anyway. None of the lifeguards had much respect for Trans-sisters. Yet Cooper had to admit that in a profession which sought to standardize emotion, Galloway was the only one who was uniquely herself. The others were interchangeable as News Anchors.

4

A voice started whispering in their ears, over the channel reserved for emergency announcements and warnings.

"Entering the Bubble is Megan Galloway, representing the Feelie Corporation, a wholly-owned subsidiary of GWA Conglom. Feeliecorp: bringing you the best in experiential tapes and erotix. Blue Champagne Enterprises trusts you will not impede the taping, and regrets any disturbance."

"Commercials yet," Glen said in disgust. To those who loved the Bubble—as all the lifeguards did—this was something like using the walls of the Taj Mahal for the Interconglomerate Graffiti Championship finals.

"Stick around for the yacht races," Cooper said. "They should have at least told us she was coming. What about that sidekick? Should we know anything about it if she gets into trouble?"

"Maybe she knows what she's doing," Leah said, earning sour looks from the other four. It was an article of faith that *nobody* on a first visit to the Bubble knew what they were doing.

"You think she'll take the sidekick into the water?"

"Well, since she can't move without it I sort of doubt she'll take it off," Cooper said. "Stu, you call operations and ask why we weren't notified. Find out about special precautions. The rest of you get back to work. A.L., you take charge here."

"What will *you* be doing, Q.M.?" Anna-Louise asked, arching one eyebrow.

"I'm going to get a closer look." He pushed off, and flew toward the curved inner surface of the Bubble.

The Bubble was the only thing Q.M. Cooper ever encountered which caught his imagination, held it for years, and did not prove a disappointment when he finally saw it. It was love at first sight.

It floated in lunar orbit with nothing to give it perspective. Under those conditions the eye could see the Earth or Luna as hunks of rock no bigger than golf balls, or a fleck of ice millimeters from the ship's window could seem to be a distant, tumbling asteroid. When Cooper first saw it the illusion was perfect: someone had left a champagne glass floating a few meters from the ship.

The constricted conic-shape was dictated by the mathematics of the field generators that held the Bubble. It was made of an intricate network of fine wires. No other configuration was possible. It was mere chance that the generator resembled the bowl and stem of a wine glass.

The Bubble itself had to be weightless, but staff and visitors needed a spin-gravity section. A disc was better than a wheel for that purpose, since it provided regions of varying gravity, from one gee at the rim to free-fall at the hub. The most logical place for the disc was at the base of the generator stem, which also made it the base of the glass. It was rumored that the architect of the Bubble had gone mad while designing it and that, since he favored martinis, he had included in the blueprints a mammoth toothpick spearing a giant green olive.

But that was only the station. It was beautiful enough in itself, but was nothing compared to the Bubble.

It floated in the shallow bowl of the generators, never touching them. It was two hundred million liters of water held between two concentric spherical fields of force, one of them one hundred meters in diameter, the other one hundred and forty. The fields contained a shell of water massing almost a million tonnes, with a five-hundred-thousand-cubic-meter bubble of air in the middle.

Cooper knew the relevant numbers by heart. Blue Champagne Enterprises made sure no one entered the Bubble without hearing them at least once. But numbers could not begin to tell what the Bubble was really like. To know that, one had to ride the elevator up through the glass swizzle stick that ended in the center of the air bubble, step out of the car, grab one of the monkeybar struts near the lifeguard station, and hold on tight until one's emotions settled down enough to be able to *believe* in the damn thing.

The lifeguards had established six classes of visitors. It was all unofficial; to BCE, everyone was an honored guest. The rankings were made by a guest's behavior and personal habits, but mostly by swimming ability.

Crustaceans clung to the monkeybars. Most never got their feet wet. They came to the Bubble to be seen, not to swim. Plankton thought they could swim, but it was no more than a fond hope. Turtles and frogs really could swim, but it was a comical business.

Sharks were excellent swimmers. If they had added brains to their other abilities the lifeguards would have loved them.

Dolphins were the best. Cooper was a dolphin-class swimmer, which was why he had the job of chief lifeguard for the third shift.

To his surprise, Megan Galloway ranked somewhere between a frog and a shark. Most of her awkward moves were the result of being unaccustomed to the free-fall environment. She had obviously spent a lot of time in flat water.

He pulled ahead and broke through the outer surface of the Bubble with enough speed to carry him to the third field, which kept air in and harmful radiation out. On his way he twisted in the air to observe how she handled the breakthrough. He could see gold reflections from the metal bands of her sidekick while she was just an amorphous shape beneath the surface. The water around her was bright aquamarine from the camera lights. She had outdistanced her crew.

He had an immediate and very strong reaction: what a ghastly way to live. Working in the Bubble was very special to him. He griped about the clients, just like everyone did, complained when he had to ferry some damn crustacean who couldn't even get up enough speed to return to the monkeybars, or when he had to clean up one of the excretory nuisances that got loose in surprising numbers when somebody got disoriented and scared. But the basic truth was that for him, it never got old. There was always some new way of looking at the place, some fresh magic to be found. He wondered if he could feel that way about it if he lived in the middle of a travelling television studio with the whole world watching.

He was starting to drift back toward the water when she burst free of it. She broke the surface like a golden mermaid, rising, trailing a plume of water that turned into a million quivering crystals as it followed her into the air. She tumbled in the middle of a cloud of water globes, a flesh and metal Aphrodite emerging from the foam.

Her mouthpiece fell from her lips to dangle from its airhose, and he heard her laugh. He did not think she had noticed him. He was fairly sure she thought she was alone, for once, if only for a few seconds. She sounded as delighted as a child, and her laughter went on until the camera crew came grumbling out of the water.

They made her go back and do it over.

*   *   *

"She's not worth the effort, Q.M."

"Who? Oh, you mean the Golden Gypsy."

"You want your bedroom technique studied by ninety million slobs?"

Cooper turned to look at Anna-Louise, who sat behind him on the narrow locker room bench, tying her shoelaces. She glanced over her shoulder and grinned. He knew he had a reputation as a star-fucker. When he first came to work at the Bubble he had perceived one of the fringe benefits to be the opportunity to meet, hob-nob with, and bed famous women, and had done so with more than a few. But he was long over that.

"Galloway doesn't make heavy-breathers."

"Not yet. Neither did Lyshia Trumbull until about a year ago. Or that guy who works for ABS . . . Chin. Randall Chin."

"Neither did Salome Hassan," someone chimed in from across the room. Cooper looked around and saw the whole shift was listening.

"I thought you were all above that," he said. "Turns out we're a bunch of feelie-groupies."

"You can't help hearing the names," Stu said, defensively.

Anna-Louise pulled her shirt over her head and stood up. "There's no sense denying I've tried tapes," she said. "The trans-sisters have to make a living. She'll do them. Wet-dreams are the coming thing."

"They're coming, all right," Stu said, with an obscene gesture.

"Why don't you idiots knock it off and get out of here?" Cooper said.

They did, gradually, and the tiny locker room at the gee/10 level was soon empty but for Cooper and Anna-Louise. She stood at the mirror, rubbing a lotion over her scalp to make it shine.

"I'd like to move to the number two shift," she said.

"You're a crazy loonie, you know that?" he shot back, annoyed.

She turned at the waist and glared at him.

"That's redundant and racist," she said. "If I wasn't such a sweet person I'd resent it."

"But it's true."

"That's the other reason I'm not going to resent it."

He got up and embraced her from behind, nuzzling her ear. "Hey, you're all wet," she laughed, but did not try to stop him, even when his hands lifted her shirt and went down under the waistband of her pants. She turned and he kissed her.

Cooper had never really understood Anna-Louise, even though he had bunked with her for six months. She was almost as big as he was, and he was not small. Her home was New Dresden, Luna. Though German was her native tongue, she spoke fluent, unaccented English. Her face would inspire adjectives like strong, healthy, glowing, and fresh, but never a word like glamorous. In short, she was physically just like all the other female lifeguards. She even shaved her head, but where the others did it in an attempt to recapture past glory, to keep that Olympic look, she had never done any competitive swimming. That alone made her unique in the group, and was probably what made her so refreshing. All the other women in the lifeguard force were uncomplicated jocks who liked two things: swimming and sex, in that order.

Cooper did not object to that. It was a pretty fair description of himself. But he was creeping up on thirty, getting closer every day. That is never a good time for an athlete. He was surprised to find that it hurt when she told him she wanted to change shifts.

"Does this have anything to do with Yuri Feldman?" he asked, between kisses.

"Is that his shift?"

"Are we still going to be bunkmates?"

She drew back. "Are we going to talk? Is that why you're undressing me?"

"I just wanted to know."

She turned away, buckling her pants.

"Unless you want to move out, we're still bunkmates. I didn't think it really meant a hell of a lot. Was I wrong?"

"I'm sorry."

"It's just that it might be simpler to sleep alone, that's all." She turned back and patted his cheek. "Hell, Q.M. It's just sex. You're very good at it, and so long as you stay interested we'll do just fine. Okay?" Her hand was still on his cheek. Her expression changed as she peered intently into his eyes. "It *is* just sex, isn't it? I mean—"

"Sure, it's . . ."

"If it *isn't* . . . but you've never said anything that would—"

"God, no," he said. "I don't want to get tied down."

"Me, either." She looked as if she might wish to say more, but instead touched his cheek again, and left him alone.

*   *   *

Cooper was so preoccupied that he walked past the table where Megan Galloway sat with her camera crew.

"Cooper! Your name is Cooper, right?"

When he turned he had his camera smile in place. Though being recognized had by that time become a rare thing, the reflexes were still working. But the smile was quickly replaced by a more genuine expression of delight. He was surprised and flattered that she had known who he was.

Galloway had her hand to her forehead, looking up at him with comical intensity. She snapped her fingers, hit her forehead again.

"I've been trying to think of the name since I saw you in the water," she said. "Don't tell me . . . I'll get it . . . it was a nickname . . ." She trailed off helplessly, then plunked both elbows on the table and put her chin in her hands, glowering at him.

"I can't think of it."

"It's—"

"Don't tell me!"

He had been about to say it was not something he revealed, but instead he shrugged and said nothing.

"I'll get it, if you'll just give me time."

"She will, too," said the other woman, who then gestured to an empty seat and extended a hand to him. "I'm Consuela Lopez. Let me buy you a drink."

"I'm . . . Cooper."

Consuela leaned closer and murmured, "If she doesn't have the goddam name in ten minutes, tell her, huh? Otherwise she won't be worth a damn until she gets it. You're a lifeguard."

He nodded, and his drink arrived. He tried to conceal his amazement. It was *impossible* to impress the waiters at the promenade cafes. Yet Galloway's party did not even have to order.

"Fascinating profession. You must tell me all about it. I'm a producer, studying to be a pimp." She swayed slightly, and Cooper realized she was drunk. It didn't show in her speech. "That devilish fellow with the beard is Markham Montgomery, director and talent prostitute." Montgomery glanced at Cooper, made a gesture that could have been the step-outline for a nod. "And the person of debatable sex is Coco-89 (Praisegod), recordist, enigma, and devotee of a religio-sexual cult so obscure even Coco isn't sure what it's about." Cooper had seen Coco in the water. He or she had the genitals of a man and the breasts of a woman, but androgynes were not uncommon in the Bubble.

"Cheers," Coco said, solemnly raising a glass. "Accly your am tance to deep make honored."

Everyone laughed but Cooper. He could not see the joke. Lopez had not bothered him—he had heard cute speeches from more rich, sophisticated people than he could count. But Coco sounded crazy.

Lopez lifted a small, silver tube over the edge of the table, squeezed a trigger, and a stream of glittering silver powder sprayed toward Coco. It burst in a thousand pinpoint scintillations. The androgyne inhaled with a foolish grin.

"Wacky Dust," Lopez said, and pointed the tube at Cooper. "Want some?" Without waiting for an answer she fired again. The stuff twinkled around his head. It smelled like one of the popular aphrodisiacs.

"What is it?" he asked.

"A mind-altering drug," she said, theatrically. When she saw his alarm she relented a little. "The trip is very short. In fact, I gave you such a little squirt you'll hardly notice it. Five minutes, tops."

"What does it do?"

She was eyeing him suspiciously. "Well, it should have done it already. Are you left-handed?"

"Yes."

"That explains it. Most of it's going to the wrong side of your head. What it does is scramble your speech center."

Montgomery roused himself enough to turn his head. He looked at Cooper with something less than total boredom. "It's like inhaling helium," he said. "You talk funny for a while."

"I didn't think that was possible," Cooper said, and everyone laughed. He found himself grinning reflexively, not knowing what was funny until he played his words back in his head and realized he had said something like "Pos that ib think unt I bull . . ."

He gritted his teeth and concentrated.

"I," he said, and thought some more. "Don't. Like. This." They seemed delighted. Coco babbled gibberish, and Lopez patted him on the back.

"Not many people figure it out that fast," she said. "Stick to one-word sentences and you're okay."

"The Wacky Dust scrambles the sentence-making capability of the brain," Montgomery said. He was sounding almost enthusiastic. Cooper knew from experience that the man was speaking of one of the few things that could excite him, that being his current ten-minute's wonder, the thing that everyone of any importance was doing today and would forget about tomorrow. "Complex thoughts are no longer—"

Cooper slammed his fist on the table and got the expected silence. Montgomery's eyes glazed and he looked away, bored by poor sportsmanship. Cooper stood.

"You," he said, pointing at all of them. "Stink."

"Quarter-meter!" Galloway shouted, pointing at Cooper. "Quarter-meter Cooper! Silver medal in Rio, bronze at Shanghai, fifteen-hundred meter freestyle, competed for United N.A., then for Ryancorp." She was grinning proudly, but when she looked around her face fell. "What's wrong?"

Cooper walked away from them. She caught him when he was almost out of sight around the curved promenade floor.

"Quarter-meter, please don't—"

"Don't me call that!" he shouted, jerking his arm away from her touch, not caring how the words came out. Her hand sprang back and poised awkwardly, each joint of her fingers twinkling with its own golden band.

"Mr. Cooper, then." She let her hand fall, and her gaze with it, looked at her booted feet. "I want to apologize for her. She had no right to do that. She's drunk, if you hadn't..."

"I no...ticed."

"You'll be all right now," she said, touching his arm lightly, remembering, and pulled it away with a sheepish smile.

"There are no lasting effects?"

"We hope not. There haven't been so far. It's experimental."

"And illegal."

She shrugged. "Naturally. Isn't everything that's fun?"

He wanted to tell her how irresponsible that was, but he sensed she would be bored with him if he belabored it and while he did not care if Montgomery was bored with him, he did not want to be tiresome with her. So when she offered another tentative smile, he smiled back, and she grinned, showing him that gap between her front teeth which had made a fortune for the world's dentists when one hundred million girls copied it.

She had one of the most famous faces in the world, but she did not closely resemble herself as depicted on television. The

screen missed most of her depth, which centered on her wide
eyes and small nose, framed by her short blonde curls. A faint
series of lines around her mouth betrayed the fact that she was
not twenty, as she looked at first glance, but well into her
thirties. Her skin was pale, she was taller than she seemed in
pictures, and her arms and legs were even thinner.

"They compensate for that with camera angles," she said,
and he realized she was not reading his mind but merely noticing where he was looking. He had given her a stock reaction,
one she got every day, and he hated that. He resolved not to
ask any questions about her sidekick. She had heard them all
and was surely as sick of them as he was of his nickname.

"Will you join us?" she asked. "I promise we won't mis-
behave again."

He looked back at the three, just visible at their table before
the curved roof cut off his view of the corridor promenade,
gee/1 level.

"I'd rather not. Maybe I shouldn't say this, but those are
pretty stock types. I always want to either sneer at them or run
away from them."

She leaned closer.

"Me too. Will you rescue me?"

"What do you mean?"

"Those three could teach limpets a thing or two about clinging. That's their job, but the hell with them."

"What do you want to do?"

"How should I know? Whatever people do around here for
a good time. Bob for apples, ride on the merry-go-round,
screw, play cards, see a show."

"I'm interested in at least one of those."

"So you like cards, too?" She glanced back at her crew.
"I think they're getting suspicious."

"Then let's go." He took her arm and started to walk away
with her. Suddenly she was running down the corridor. He
hesitated only a second, then was off after her.

He was not surprised to see her stumble. She recovered
quickly, but it slowed her enough for him to catch her.

"What happened?" she said. "I thought I was falling—" She
pulled back her sleeve and stared at the world's most complicated wristwatch. He realized it was some sort of monitor for
her sidekick.

"It isn't your hardware," he said, leading her at a fast walk.
"You were running with the spin. You got heavier. You should

bear in mind that what you're feeling isn't gravity."

"But how will we get away if we can't run?"

"By going just a little faster than they do." He looked back, and as he had expected, Lopez was already down. Coco was wavering between turning back to help and following Montgomery, who was still coming, wearing a determined expression. Cooper grinned. He had finally succeeded in getting the man's attention. He was making off with the star.

Just beyond stairwell Cooper pulled Galloway into an elevator whose door was closing. He had a glimpse of Montgomery's outraged face.

"What good will this do us?" Galloway wanted to know. "He'll just follow us up the stairs. These things are slow as the midtown express."

"They're slow for a very good reason, known as coriolis force," Cooper said, reaching into his pocket for his keys. He inserted one in the control board of the elevator. "Since we're on the bottom level, Montgomery will go up. It's the only direction the stairs go." He twisted the key, and the elevator began to descend.

The two "basement" levels were the parts of the Champagne Hotel complex nearest hard vacuum. The car stopped on B level and he held the door for her. They walked among exposed pipes, structural cables, and beams not masked by the frothy decorations of the public levels. The only light came from bare bulbs spaced every five meters. The girders and the curved floor made the space resemble the innards of a zeppelin.

"How hard will they look for you?"

She shrugged. "They won't be fooling around. They'll keep it up until they find me. It's only a question of time."

"Can they get me in trouble?"

"They'd love to. But I won't let them."

"Thanks."

"It's the least I could do."

"So my room is out. First place they'd look."

"No, they'd check my room first. It's better equipped for playing cards."

He was mentally kicking himself. She was playing games with him, he knew that, but what was the game? If it was just sex, that was okay. He'd never made love with a woman in a sidekick.

"About your nickname..." she said, leaving the sentence unfinished to see how he would react. When he said nothing, she started over. "Is it your favorite swimming distance? I seem to recall you were accused of never exerting yourself more than the situation required."

"Wouldn't it be foolish if I did?" But the label still rankled. It was true he had never turned in a decent time just swimming laps, and that he seldom won a race by more than a meter. The sports media had never warmed to him because of that, even before he failed to win the gold. For some reason, they thought of him as lazy, and most people assumed his nickname meant he would prefer to swim races of no more than a quarter of a meter.

"No, that's not it," was all he would say, and she dropped the subject.

The silence gave him time to reflect, and the more he did, the less happy he was. She had said she could keep him out of trouble, but could she? When it came to a showdown, who had more clout with BCE? The Golden Gypsy, or her producers? He might be risking a lot, and she was risking nothing at all. He knew he should ditch her, but if he spurned her now, she might withdraw what protection she could offer.

"I sense you don't care for your nickname," she said at last. "What should I call you? What's your real name?"

"I don't like that, either. Call me Q.M."

"Must I?" she sighed.

"Everybody else does."

He took her to Eliot's room because Eliot was in the infirmary and because Montgomery and company would not look for them there. They drank some of Eliot's wine, talked for a while, and made love.

The sex was pleasant, but nothing to shout about. He was surprised at how little the sidekick got in his way. Though it was all over her body, it was warm and most of it was flexible, and he soon forgot about it.

Finally she kissed him and got dressed. She promised to see him again soon. He thought she said something about love. It struck him as a grotesque thing to say, but by then he was not listening very hard. There was an invisible wall between them and most of it belonged to her. He had tried to penetrate it—not very hard, he admitted to himself—but a good ninety-nine percent of her was in a fiercely-guarded place he was sure he'd never see. He shrugged mentally. It was certainly her right.

He was left with a bad post-coital depression. It had not been one of his finer moments. The best thing to do about it was to put it behind him and try not to do it again. It was not long before he realized he was doing uncommonly well at that already. Reclining naked on the bed, gazing at the ceiling, he could not recall a single thing she had said.

What with one thing and another, he did not get back to his room until late.

He did not turn on the light because he did not want to wake Anna-Louise, and he walked with extra care because he was not balancing as well as he might. There had been a few drinks.

Still, she woke up, as she always did. She pressed close to him under the covers, her body warm and humid and musky, her breath a little sour as she kissed him. He was half-drunk and she was half-awake, but when her hands began to pull and her hips to thrust forward insistently he found to his surprise that he was ready and so was she. She guided him, then eased over onto her side and let him nestle in behind her. She drew her knees up and hugged them. Her head was pillowed on his arm. He kissed the back of her smooth scalp and nibbled her ear, then let his head fall onto the pillow and moved against her slowly for a peaceful few minutes. At last she stretched, squeezing him, making small fists, digging her toes into his thighs.

"How did you like her?" she mumbled.

"Who?"

"You know who."

He was pretty sure he could pull off a lie, because Anna-Louise couldn't be *that* sure, and then he frowned in the darkness, because he had never wanted to lie to her before.

So he said, "Do you know me that well?"

She stretched again, this time more sensually, to more of a purpose than simply getting the sleepiness out of her system.

"How should I know? My nose didn't give me a chance to find out. I smelled the liquor on your breath when you came in, but I smelled her on my fingers after I touched you."

"Come *on*."

"Don't get mad." She reached around to pat his buttocks and at the same time pressed herself back against him. "Okay, so I guessed at the identity. It didn't take much intuition."

"It was lousy," he admitted.

"I'm so sorry." He knew she really was, and did not know

if that made him happy or sad. It was a hell of a thing, he thought, not to know something as basic as that.

"It's a damn shame," she went on. "Fucking should never be lousy."

"I agree."

"If you can't have fun doing it, you shouldn't do it."

"You're one hundred percent right."

He could see just her teeth in the darkness; he had to imagine the rest of her grin, but he knew it well.

"Do you have anything left for me?"

"There's a very good chance that I do."

"Then what do you say we just skip the next part and *wake up*?"

She shifted gears so fast he had a hard time keeping up at first. She was all over him and she was one of the strongest women he knew. She liked to wrestle. Luckily, there were no losers in her matches. It was everything the encounter with Galloway had not been. That was no surprise; it *always* was. Sex with Anna-Louise was very good indeed. For that matter, so was everything else.

He lay there in the dark long after she had gone to sleep, their bodies spooned together just as they had begun, and he thought long and hard and as clearly as he could. Why not? Why not Anna-Louise? She could care if he gave her the chance. And maybe he could, too.

He sighed, and hugged her tighter. She murmured like a big, happy cat, and began to snore.

He would talk to her in the morning, tell her what he had been thinking. They would begin the uncertain process of coming to know each other.

But that he woke with a hangover, and Anna-Louise had already showered, dressed, and gone, and someone was knocking on his door.

He stumbled out of bed, and found it was her—Galloway. He had a bad moment of disorientation, wishing that her famous face would get back on the television screen where it belonged. But somehow she was in the room, though he did not recall standing aside to admit her. She was smiling, smiling, and talking so fast he could barely understand her. It was an inane rattle about how good it was to see him and how *nice* the room was. Her eyes swept him and the room from head to toe and corner to corner until he was sure she knew Anna-Louise better than he did himself, just from the faint traces she had left on the bare, impersonal cubicle.

This was going to be difficult. He closed the door and padded to the bed, where he sank down gratefully and put his face in his hands.

When she finally sat down he looked up. She was perched on the edge of the room's only chair, hands laced together on her knees. She looked so bright and chipper he wanted to puke.

"I quit my job," she said. It took a while for that to register. In time, he was able to offer a comment.

"Huh?" he said.

"I quit. Just said screw this and walked out. All over, ka-put, down the toilet. Fuck it." Her smile looked unhealthy.

"Oh." He thought about that, listening to the dripping of the bathroom faucet. "Ah . . . what will you do?"

"Oh, no problem, no problem." She was bouncing a little now. One knee bobbed in four-four time while the other waltzed. Perhaps that should have told him something. Her head jerked to the left, and there was a whine as it slowly straightened.

"I've had offers from all over," she went on. "CBS would sacrifice seven virgin vice-presidents on a stone altar to sign me up. NAAR and TeleCommunion are fighting a pitched battle across Sixth Avenue at this very moment, complete with tanks and nerve gas. Shit, I'm already pulling down half the GNP of Costa Rica, and they all want to triple that."

"Sounds like you'll do all right," he ventured. He was alarmed. The head movement was repeating now, and her heels were hammering the floor. He had finally figured out that the whining noise was coming from her sidekick.

"Oh, bugger them, too," she said, easily. "Independent production, that's for me. Doing my own thing. I'll show you some tapes. No more LCD, no more trendex. Just me and a friend or two."

"LCD?"

"Lowest common denominator. My audience. Eight-year-old minds in thirty-one-point-three-six-year-old bodies. Demographics. Brain-cancer victims."

"Television made them that way," he said.

"Of course. And they loved it. Nobody could ever under-estimate them, and nobody could ever give them enough crap. I'm not even going to try anymore."

She stood up, turned at the waist, and knocked the door off

its hinges. It clattered into the hallway, teetering around the deep dimple her fist had made in the metal.

All that would have been bizarre enough, but when the noise had finally stopped she still stood there, arm extended, fist clenched, half-turned at the waist. The whining sound was louder now, accompanied by something resembling the wail of a siren. She looked over her shoulder.

"Oh, darn it," she said, in a voice that rose in pitch with every word. "I think I'm stuck." And she burst into tears.

Cooper was no stranger to the ways of the super-rich and super-famous. He had thought he understood clout. He soon learned he knew nothing about it.

He got her calmed in a few minutes. She eventually noticed the small crowd that had gathered beyond the space where his door had been, whispering and pointing at the woman sitting on Cooper's bed with her arm stuck in an odd position. Her eyes grew cold, and she asked for his telephone.

Thirty seconds after her first call, eight employees of BCE arrived in the hallway outside. Guards herded the audience away and engineers erected a new door, removing two twisted hinges to do so. It was all done in less than four minutes, and by then Galloway had completed her second call.

She made three calls, none of them over two minutes long. In one, she merely chatted with someone at the Tele-Communion Network and mentioned, in passing, that she had a problem with her sidekick. She listened, thanked the person on the other end, and hung up. The call to GM&L, the conglom that owned Sidekick, Incorporated, was businesslike and short.

Two hours later a repairman from Sidekick knocked at their door. It was not until the next day that Cooper realized that the man had been on the Earth's surface when he got the call, and that his trip had involved a special ship boosting at one gee all the way and carrying no cargo but himself and his tool kit, which he opened and plugged into the wall computerminal before starting to work on the sidekick.

But in those two hours...

"If you'd like me to leave, I'll leave," she said, sipping her third glass of Cooper's wine.

"No, please."

She was still frozen like a frame from a violent film. Her legs worked and so did her right arm, but from her hips all the

way up her back and down her left arm the sidekick had
shorted out. It looked awfully uncomfortable. He asked if there
was anything he could do.

"It's okay, really," she said, resting her chin on the arm
that crossed in front of her.

"Will they be able to fix it?"

"Oh, sure." She tossed down the rest of the wine. "And if
they can't, I'll just stay here and you'll have a real conversation
piece. A human hat-rack." She picked up her shirt from the
couch beside her and draped it over her frozen arm, then smiled
at him. It was not a pretty smile.

He had helped her get the shirt off. It had been like undressing a statue. The idea had been to check the sidekick core
for hot spots and visible cracks, which would necessitate the
quick removal of the apparatus. It was clearly a prospect she
did not relish. But as far as he had been able to see the thing
was physically intact. The damage was on the electronic level.

It was the closest look he had taken yet at the technological
marvel of the age. Closer even than the night before when he
had made love to her, when manners had prevented him from
staring. Now he had a perfect excuse, and he used it.

When he thought about it, it was frightening that they could
pack so much power into a mechanism that, practically speaking, was hardly even there. The most massive part of the
sidekick was the core, which was segmented, padded in flesh-
toned soft plastic, and hugged her spine from the small of her
back to the nape of her neck. Nowhere was it more than three
centimeters thick.

Radiating away from the core was an intricate network of
gold chains, bands, and bracelets, making such a cunningly
contrived system that one could almost believe it was all decoration rather than the conductors for energizing fields that
allowed her to move. Woven belts of fine gold wire criss-
crossed like bandoliers between her breasts and just happened
to connect, via a fragile gold chain, with the sinuous gooseneck
that was concealed by her hair before it attached to the back
of the golden tiara that made her look like Wonder Woman.
Helical bands fashioned to look like snakes coiled down her
arms, biting each other's tails until the last ones attached to
thick, jewel-encrusted bracelets around her wrists, which in
turn sprouted hair-fine wires that transformed themselves into
finger rings, one for each joint, each inset with a single diamond. Elsewhere the effect was much the same. Each piece,

taken by itself, was a beautiful piece of jewelry. The worst that could be said about Megan Galloway in the "nude" was that she was ostentatiously bejeweled. If one didn't mind that, she was absolutely stunning: a gilded Venus, or an artist's fantasy Amazon in full, impractical armor. Dressed, she was just like anyone else, except for the tiara and the rings. There were no edges on her sidekick to savage clothes or poke out at unnatural angles. Cooper guessed this was as important to Galloway as was the fact that the sidekick was a beautiful object, and emphatically not an orthopedic appliance.

"It's unique," she said. "One of a kind."

"I didn't mean to stare."

"Heavens," she said. "You weren't staring. You are so pointedly *not* staring that your fascination must be intense. And no...don't say anything." She held up her free hand and waited for him to settle back in his chair. "Please, no more apologies. I've got a pretty good idea of the problem I present to somebody with both manners and curiosity, and it was shitty of me to say that about not staring. That puts you in the wrong whatever you do, huh?" She leaned back against the wall, getting as comfortable as she could while waiting for the repairman to arrive.

"I'm proud of the damn thing, Cooper. That's probably obvious. And of course I've answered the same questions so many times that it bores me, but for you, since you're providing me a refuge in an embarrassing moment, I'll tell you anything you want to know."

"Is it really gold?"

"Twenty-four carat, solid."

"That's where your nickname comes from, I presume."

She looked puzzled for a moment, then her face cleared.

"Touché. I don't like that nickname any more than you like yours. And no, it's no more correct than yours is. At first, *I* wasn't the Golden Gypsy. The sidekick was. That was the name of this model sidekick. But they've still only made one of them, and before long the name rubbed off on me. I discourage it."

Cooper understood that too well.

He asked more questions. Before long the explanations got too technical for him. He was surprised that she knew as much about it as she did. Her knowledge stopped short of the mathematics of Tunable Deformation Fields, but that was her only limit. TDF's were what had made the Bubble possible, since they could be made to resonate with particular molecular or atomic structures. The Bubble's fields were tuned to attract or repel H_2O, while the fields generated by Galloway's sidekick influenced gold, Au^{197}, and left everything else alone. She went on to tell him far more than he could absorb about the ways in which the fields were generated in the sidekick core, shaped by wave guides buried in the jewelry and deformated—"Physics terms are usually inelegant," she apologized,—to the dictates of nanocomputers scattered through the hardware, operating by a process she called "augmented neuro-feedback holistitopology."

"The English of which is . . ." he pleaded.

". . . that when I think of pressing the middle valve down, the music goes round and round and it comes out here." She held out her hand and depressed the middle finger. "You would weep to know how many decisions the core made to accomplish that simple movement."

"On the other hand," he said, and rushed on when he remembered what had happened to her other hand, "what goes on in my brain to do the same thing is complex, but I don't have to program it. It's done for me. Isn't it much the same with you?"

"Much. Not exactly. If they made one of these for you and plugged you in right now, you'd twitch a lot. In a few weeks you'd patty-cake pretty well. But in a year you'd not even think about it. The brain re-trains itself. Which is a simple way of saying you struggle day and night for six or seven months with something that feels totally unnatural and eventually you learn to do it. Having done it, you know that learning to tap-dance on the edge of a razor blade would be a snap."

"You say you've heard all the questions. What's your least favorite?"

"God, you're merciless, aren't you? There's no contest. 'How did you hurt yourself?' To answer the question you so cleverly didn't ask, I broke my fool neck when me and my hang-glider got into an argument with a tree. The tree won. Many years later I went back and chopped that tree down, which just *may* be the stupidest thing I ever did, not counting today." She looked at him and raised one eyebrow. "Aren't you going to ask me about that?"

He shrugged.

"The funny thing is, that's the question I *want* you to ask. Because it's tied up with what we did yesterday, and that's really what I came here to talk to you about."

"So talk," he said, wondering what she could have to say about it beyond the fact that it had been hideous, and demeaning to both of them.

"It was the worst sexual experience I ever had," she said. "And you bear zero percent responsibility for that. Please don't interrupt. There are things you don't know about.

"I know you don't think much of my profession—I *really* don't want you to interrupt, or I'll never get all this out. If you disagree you can tell me when I'm through.

"You'd be a pretty strange lifeguard if you were a fan of trans-tapes, or if you didn't feel superior to the kind of people who buy them. You're young, fairly well-educated and fairly articulate. You've got a good body and an attractive face, and the opposite sex neither terrifies nor intimidates you. You are out on the end of *all* the bell-curves, demographically. You are *not* my audience, and people who *aren't* my audience tend to *look down* on my audience, and usually on me and my kind, too. And I don't blame them. Me and my kind have taken what might have been a great art-form and turned it into something so exploitative that even Hollywood and Sixth Avenue gag at it.

"You know as well as I do that there are many, many people growing up now who wouldn't know an honest, genuine, self-originated emotion if it kicked them in the behind. If you take their Transers away from them they're practically zombies.

"For a long time I've flattered myself by thinking that I'm a little better than the industry in general. There are some tapes I've made that will back me up on that. Things I've taken a chance on, things that try to be more complex than the LCD would dictate. *Not* my bread-and-butter tapes. Those are as simple-headed as the worst hack travelogue. But I've tried to be like the laborers in other artistic sweatshops of the past. Those few who managed to turn out something with some merit, like some directors of Hollywood westerns which were never meant to be anything but crowd pleasers and who still produced some works of art, or a handful of television producers who . . . None of this is familiar to you, is it? Sorry, I didn't mean to get academic. I've made a study of it, of art in the mass culture.

"All those old art-forms had undergrounds, independents who struggled along with no financing and produced things of varying quality but with some *vision,* no matter how weird. Trans-tapes are more expensive than films or television, but there is an underground. It's just so far under it practically never comes to light. Believe it or not, it's possible to produce great art in emotional recording. I could name names, but you will not have heard of any of them. And I'm not talking about the people who make tapes about how it feels to kill somebody; that's another underground entirely.

"But things are getting tight. It used to be that we could make a good living and still stay away from the sex tapes. Let me add that I don't feel contempt for the people who make sex tapes. Given the state of our audience, it has become necessary that many of them have their well-worn jerk-off cassette so that when they get horny they know what to do with it. Most of them wouldn't have the vaguest notion otherwise. I just didn't want to make them myself. It's axiomatic in the trade that love is the one emotion that cannot be recorded, and if I can't have—"

"I'm sorry," Cooper said, "but I have to interrupt here. I've never heard that. In fact, I've heard just the opposite."

"You've been listening to our commercials," she reproved. "Get that shit out of your head, Cooper. It's pure hype." She rubbed her forehead, and sighed. "Oh, all right. I wasn't precise enough. I can make a tape of how I love my mother or my father or anybody I'm already in love with. It's not easy to do—it's the less subtle emotions that are more readily transed. But nobody has ever recorded the process of falling in love. It's sort of a Heisenberg Principle of transing, and nobody's sure if the limitation is in the equipment or in the person being recorded, but it exists, and there are some very good reasons to think nobody will *ever* succeed in recording that kind of love."

"I don't see why not," Cooper confessed. "It's supposed to be very intense, isn't it? And you said the strong emotions are the easiest to tape."

"That's true. But... well, try to visualize it. I've got my job because I'm best at ignoring all the hardware involved in transing. It's because of my sidekick; I mean, if I can learn to forget I'm operating *that*, I can ignore anything. That's why the nets scour the trauma wards of hospitals looking for potential stars. It's like... well, in the early days of sex research they had people fuck in laboratories, with wires taped to them. A lot of people just couldn't do it. They were too self-conscious. Hook most people up to a transcorder and what you get is, "Oh, how interesting it is to be making a tape; look at all those people watching me; look at all those cameras; how interesting, now I have to forget about them, I must forget about them, I just *must* forget—"

Cooper held up his hand, nodding. He was recalling seeing her burst from the water that first day in the Bubble, and his feelings as he watched her.

"So the essence of making a tape," she went on, "is the ability to ignore the fact that you're making one. To react just as you would have reacted if you *weren't* doing it. It calls for some of the qualities of an actor, but most actors can't do it. They think too much about the process. They can't be natural about it. That's my talent: to feel natural in unnatural circumstances.

"But there are limits. You can fuck up a storm while transing, and the tape will record how good everything feels and how goddamn happy you are to be fucking. But it all falls apart when the machine is confronted with that moment of first falling in love. Either that, or the person being recorded just can't get into the *frame of mind* to fall in love while transing. The distraction of the transer itself makes that emotional state impossible.

"But I really got off on a tangent there. I'd appreciate it if you'd just hear me out until I've said what I have to say." She rubbed her forehead again, and looked away from him.

"We were talking about economics. You have to make what sells. My sales have been dropping off. I've specialized in what we call 'elbow-rubbers.' 'You, too, can go to fancy places with fancy people. You, too, can be important, recognized, appreciated.'" She made a face. "I also do the sort of thing we've been making in the Bubble. Sensuals, short of sex. Those, frankly, are not selling so well anymore. The snob-tapes still do well, but everybody makes those. What you're marketing there is your celebrity, and mine is falling off. The competition has been intense.

"That's why I . . . well, it was Markham who talked me into it. I've been on the verge of going into heavy-breathers." She lifted her eyes. "I assume you know what those are."

Cooper nodded, remembering what Anna-Louise had said. So even Galloway could not stay out of it.

She sighed deeply, but no longer looked away from him.

"Anyway, I wanted to make something just a *little bit* better than the old tired in-and-outers. You know: Door-to-door salesman enters living room. 'I'd like to show you my samples, ma'am.' Woman rips open nightgown, 'Take a look at these samples, buster.' Fade to bed. I thought that for my first sex tape I'd try for something more erotic than salacious. I wanted a romantic situation, and if I couldn't get some love in it at least I'd try for affection. It would be with a handsome guy I met unexpectedly. He'd have some aura of romance about him. Maybe there'd be an argument at first, but the irresistible attraction would bring us together in spite of it, and we'd make love and part on a slightly tragic note since we'd be from different worlds and it could never...".

Tears were running down her cheeks. Cooper realized his mouth was open. He was leaning toward her, too astonished at first to say anything.

"You and me..." he finally managed to say.

"Shit, Cooper, *obviously* you and me."

"And you thought that... that what we did last night... did you really think that was worth a tape? I knew it was bad, but I had no inkling *how* bad it could be. I knew you were using me. Hell, I was using you, too, and I didn't like that any better. But I never thought it was so cynical—"

"No, no, *no, no, no!*" She was sobbing now. "It wasn't that. It was *worse* than that! It was supposed to be *spontaneous,* damn it! *I* didn't pick you out. *Markham* was going to do that. He would find someone, coach him, arrange a meeting, conceal cameras to tape the meeting in the bedroom later. I'd never really *know.* We've been studying an old show called *Candid Camera* and using some of their techniques. They're *always* throwing something unexpected at me, trying to help me stay fresh. That's Markham's job. But how surprised can I *be* when you show up at my table? Just look at it. In the romantic Bubble, the handsome lifeguard—*lifeguard,* for pete sake!— an Olympic athlete familiar to millions from their television sets, gets pissed at my rich, decadent friends... I couldn't have gotten a more clichéd script from the most drug-brained writer in Television City!"

For a time there was no sound in the room but her quiet sobs. Cooper looked at it from all angles, and it didn't look pretty from any of them. But he had been just as eager to go along with the script as she had.

"I wouldn't have your job for anything," he said.

"Neither would I," she finally managed to say. "And I *don't,* damn it. You want to know what happened this morning? Markham showed me just how original he really is. I was eating breakfast and this guy—he was a lifeguard—are you ready? He tripped over his feet and dropped his plate in my lap. Well, while he was cleaning me up he started dropping cute lines at a rate that would have made Neil Simon green. Sorry, getting historical again. Let's just say he sounded like he was reading from a script . . . he made that shitty little scene we played out together yesterday seem just wonderful. His smile was phoney as a brass transistor. I realized what had happened, what I'd done to you, so I pushed the son-of-a-bitch down into his french toast, went to find Markham, broke his fucking jaw for him, quit my job, and came here to apologize. And went a little crazy and broke your door. So I'm sorry, I really am, and I'd leave but I've busted my sidekick and I can't *stand* to have people staring at me like that, so I'd like to stay here a little longer, until the repairman gets here. And I don't have any notion of what I'm going to *do*."

What composure she had managed to gather fell apart once again, and she wept bitterly.

By the time the repairman arrived Galloway was back in control.

The repairman's name was Snyder. He was a medical doctor as well as a cybertechnician, and Cooper supposed that combination allowed him to set any price he fancied for his services.

Galloway went into the bathroom and got all the clean towels. She spread them on the bed, then removed her clothes. She reclined, face down, with the towels making a thick pad from her knees to her waist. She made herself as comfortable as she could with her arm locked in the way, and waited.

Snyder fiddled with the controls in his tool kit, touched needle-sharp probes to various points on the sidekick core, and Galloway's arm relaxed. He made more connections, there was a high whine from the core, and the sidekick opened like an iron maiden. Each bracelet, chain, amulet and ring separated along invisible join lines. Snyder then went to the bed, grasped the sidekick with one hand around the center of the core, and lifted it away from her. He set it on its "feet," where it promptly assumed a parade-rest stance.

There was an Escher print Cooper had seen called "Rind" that showed the bust of a woman as if her skin had been peeled off and arranged in space to suggest the larger thing she had once been. Both the inner and outer surfaces of the rind could be seen, like one barber-pole stripe painted over an irregular, invisible surface. Galloway's sidekick, minus Galloway, looked very much like that. It was one continuous, though convoluted, entity, a thing of springs and wires, too fragile to stand on its own but doing it somehow. He saw it shift slightly to maintain its balance. It seemed all too alive.

Galloway, on the other hand, looked like a rag doll. Snyder motioned to Cooper with his eyes, and the two of them turned her on her back. She had some control of her arms, and her head did not roll around as he had expected it to. There was a metal wire running along her scarred spine.

"I was an athlete, too, before the accident," she said.

"Were you?"

"Well, not in your class. I was fifteen when I cracked my neck, and I wasn't setting the world on fire as a runner. For a girl that's already too old."

"Not strictly true," Cooper said. "But it's a lot harder after that." She was reaching for the blanket with hands that did not work very well. Coupled with her inability to raise herself from the bed, it was a painful process to watch. Cooper reached for the edge of the blanket.

"No," she said, matter-of-factly. "Rule number one. Don't help a crip unless she asks for it. No matter how badly she's doing something, just don't. She's got to learn to ask, and you've got to learn to let her do what she *can* do."

"I'm afraid I've never known any crips."

"Rule number two. A nigger can call herself a nigger and a cripple can call herself a cripple, but lord help the able-bodied white who uses either word."

Cooper settled back in his chair.

"Maybe I'd better just shut up until you fill me in on all the rules."

She grinned at him. "It'd take all day. And frankly, maybe some of them are self-contradictory. We can be a pretty prickly lot, but I ain't going to apologize for it. You've got your body and I don't have mine. That's not your fault, but I think I hate you a little because of it."

Cooper thought about that. "I think I probably would, too."

"Yeah. It's nothing serious. I came to terms with it a long time ago, and so would you, after a bad couple of years." She still hadn't managed to reach the blanket, and at last she gave up and asked him to do it for her. He tucked it around her neck.

There were other things he thought he would like to know, but he felt she must have reached the limits of questioning, no matter what she said. And he was no longer quite so eager to know the answers. He had been about to ask what the towels on the bed were for, then suddenly it was obvious what they were for and he couldn't imagine why he hadn't known it at once. He simply knew nothing about her, and nothing about disability. And he was a little ashamed to admit it, but he was not sure he *wanted* to know any more.

There was no way he could keep the day's events from Anna-Louise, even if he had wanted to. The complex was buzzing with the story of how the Golden Gypsy had blown a fuse, though the news about her quitting her job was still not general knowledge. He was told the story three different times during his next shift. Each story was slightly different, but all approximated the truth. Most of the tellers seemed to think it was funny. He supposed he would have, too, yesterday.

Anna-Louise inspected the door hinges when they got back from work.

"She must have quite a right hook," she said.

"Actually, she hit it with her left. Do you want to hear about it?"

"I'm all ears."

So he told her the whole story. Cooper had a hard time figuring out how she was taking it. She didn't laugh, but she didn't seem too sympathetic, either. When he was through— mentioning Galloway's incontinence with some difficulty— Anna-Louise nodded, got up, and started toward the bathroom.

"You've led a sheltered life, Q.M."

"What do you mean?"

She turned, and looked angry for the first time.

"I mean you sound as if incontinence was the absolute worst thing you'd ever heard of in your life."

"Well, what is it, then? No big thing?"

"It certainly isn't to *that* woman. For most people with her problem, it means catheters and feces bags. Or diapers. Like my grandfather wore for the last five years of his life. The operations she's had to fix it, and the hardware, implanted and external . . . well, it's damn expensive, Q.M. You can't afford it on the money my grandfather was getting from the State, and Conglomerate health plans won't pay for it, either."

"Oh, so that's it. Just because she's rich and can afford the best treatment, her problems don't amount to anything. Just how would *you* like to—"

"Wait a minute, hold on..." She was looking at him with an expression that would not hold still, changing from sympathy to disgust. "I don't want to fight with you. I know it wouldn't be pleasant to have my neck broken, even if I was a trillionaire." She paused, and seemed to be choosing her words carefully.

"I'm bothered by something here," she said, at last. "I'm not even sure what it is. I'm concerned about you, for one thing. I still think it's a mistake to get involved with her. I like you. I don't want to see you hurt."

Cooper suddenly remembered his resolve of the night before, as she lay sleeping at his side. It confused him terribly. Just what *did* he feel for Anna-Louise? After the things Galloway had told him about love and the lies of the Transer commercials, he didn't know what to think. It was pitiful, when he thought about it, that he was as old as he was and hadn't the vaguest notion what love might be, and that he had actually assumed the place to find it, when the time came, was on trans-tapes. It made him angry.

"What are you talking about, hurt?" he retorted. "She's not dangerous. I'll admit she lost control there for a moment, and she's strong, but—"

"Oh, help!" Anna-Louise moaned. "What am I supposed to do with these emotionally stunted smoggies who think nothing is real unless they've been told by somebody on the—"

"Smoggies? You called me a racist when—"

"Okay, I'm sorry." He complained some more but she just shook her head and wouldn't listen, and he eventually sputtered to a stop.

"Finished? Okay. I'm getting crazy here. I've only got one more month before I go back home. And I do find most Earthlings—is that a neutral enough term for you?—I find them weird. *You're* not so bad, most of the time, except you don't seem to have much notion about what life is *for*. You like to screw and you like to swim. Even *that* is twice as much purpose as most sm—, Terrans seem to have."

"You . . . you're going?"

"Surprise!" Her tone dripped sarcasm.

"But why didn't you tell me?"

"You never asked. You never asked about a lot of things.

I don't think you ever realized I might like to tell you about my life, or that it might be any different from yours."

"You're wrong. I sensed a difference."

She raised an eyebrow and seemed about to say something, but changed her mind. She rubbed her forehead, then took a deep, decisive breath.

"I'm almost sorry to hear that. But I'm afraid it's too late to start over. I'm moving out." And she began packing.

Cooper tried to argue with her but it did no good. She assured him she wasn't leaving because she was jealous; she even seemed amused that he thought that might be the reason. And she also claimed she was not going to move in with Yuri Feldman. She intended to live her last month in the Bubble alone.

"I'm going back to Luna to do what I planned to do all along," she said, tying the drawstring of her duffel bag. "I'm going to the police academy. I've saved enough now to put me through."

"Police?" Cooper could not have been more astonished if she had said she intended to fly to Mars by flapping her arms.

"You had no inkling, right? Well, why should you? You don't notice other people much unless you're screwing them. I'm not saying that's your fault; you've been trained to be that way. Haven't you ever wondered what I was doing here? It isn't the working conditions that drew me. I despise this place and all the people who come to visit. I don't even like water very much, and I *hate* that monstrous obscenity they call the Bubble."

Cooper was beyond shock. He had never imagined anyone could exist who would not be drawn by the magic of the Bubble.

"Then why? Why work here, and why do you hate it?"

"I hate it because people are starving in Pennsylvania," she said, mystifying him completely. "And I work here, God help me, because the pay is good, which you may not have noticed since you grew up comfortable. I would have said rich, but by now I know what real rich is. I grew up poor, Q.M. Another little detail you never bothered to learn. I've worked hard for everything, including the chance to come here to this disgusting pimp-city to provide a safety service for rich degenerates, because BCE pays in good, hard GWA Dollars. You probably never noticed, but Luna is having serious economic troubles because it's caught between a couple of your corporation-states . . . Oh, forget it. Why worry your cute little head with things like that?"

She went to the door, opened it, then turned to look at him.

"Honestly, Q.M., I don't dislike you. I think I feel sorry for you. Sorry enough that I'm going to say once more you'd better watch out for Galloway. If you mess around with her right now, you're going to get hurt."

"I still don't understand how."

She sighed, and turned away.

"Then there's nothing more I can say. I'll see you around."

Megan Galloway had the Mississippi Suite, the best in the hotel. She didn't come to the door when Cooper knocked, but just buzzed him in.

She was sitting tailor-fashion on the bed, wearing a loose nightgown and a pair of wire-rimmed glasses and looking at a small box in front of her. The bed resembled a sternwheeler, with smoke and sparks shooting from the bedposts, and was larger than his entire room and bath. She put her glasses at the end of her nose and peered over them.

"Something I can do for you?"

He came around until he could see the box, which had a picture flickering dimly on one side of it.

"What's that?"

"Old-timey television," she said. "*Honey West*, circa 1965, American Broadcasting Company. Starring Anne Francis, John Ericson, and Irene Hervey, Friday nights at 2100. Spin-off from *Burke's Law*, died 1966. What's up?"

"What's wrong with the depth?"

"They didn't have it." She removed her glasses and began to chew absently on one rubber tip. "How are you doing?"

"I'm surprised to see you wear glasses."

"When you've had as many operations as I have, you skip the ones you think you can do without. Why is it I sense you're having a hard time saying whatever it is you came here to say?"

"Would you like to go for a swim?"

"Pool's closed. Weekly filtering, or something like that."

"I know. Best possible time to go for a swim."

She frowned. "But I was told no one is admitted during the filtering."

"Yeah. It's illegal. Isn't everything that's fun?"

*   *   *

The Bubble was closed one hour in every twenty-four for accelerated filtering. At one time the place had been open all day, with filtration constantly operating, but then a client got past the three safety systems to where he was aerated, churned, irradiated, centrifuged, and eventually forced through a series of very fine screens. Most of him was still in the water in one form or another, and his legend had produced the station's first ghost.

But long before the Filtered Phantom first sloshed down the corridors the system had been changed. The filters never shut down completely, but while people were in the pool they were operated at slow speed. Once a day they were turned to full power.

It still wasn't enough. So every ten days BCE closed the pool for a longer period and gave the water an intensive treatment.

"I can't believe no one even watches it," Megan whispered.

"It's a mistake. Security is done by computer. There're twenty cameras in here but somebody forgot to tell the computer to squeal if it sees anybody enter during filtration. I got that from the computer itself, which thinks the whole fuck-up is very funny."

The hordes of swimmers had been gone for over two hours, and the clean-up crew had left thirty minutes before. Megan Galloway had probably thought she knew the Bubble pretty well, on the basis of her two visits. She was finding out now, as Cooper had done long ago, that she knew nothing. The difference between a resort beach on a holiday weekend and on a day in mid-winter was nothing compared to what she saw now.

It was perfectly still, totally clear: a crystal ball as big as the world.

"Oh, Cooper." He felt her hand tighten on his arm.

"Look. Down there. No, to the left." She followed his pointing finger and saw a school of the Bubble goldfish far below the surface, moving like lazy submarines, big and fat as watermelons and tame as park squirrels.

"Can I touch it, daddy?" she whispered, with the hint of a giggle. He pretended to consider it, then nodded. "I almost don't want to, you know?" she said. "Like a huge field covered in new snow, before anybody tracks across it."

"Yeah, I know." He sighed. "But it might as well be us. Hurry, before somebody beats you to it." He grinned at her, and pushed off slowly from his weightless perch on the sundeck tier that circled the rim of the champagne glass.

She pushed off harder and passed him before he was halfway there, as he had expected her to. The waves made by her entry spread out in perfect circles, then he broke the surface right behind her.

It was a different world.

When the Bubble had first been proposed, many years before, it had been suggested that it be a solid sphere of water, and that nothing but weightlessness and surface tension be employed to maintain it. Both forces came free of charge, which was a considerable factor in their favor.

But in the end, the builders had opted for TDF fields. This was because while any volume of water would assume a spherical shape in free-fall, surface tension was not strong enough to keep it that way if it was disturbed. Such a structure would work fine so long as no swimmers entered to upset the delicate balance.

The TDF's provided the necessary unobtrusive force to keep things from getting messy. Tuned to attract or repel water, they also acted to force foreign matter toward either the inner or outer surfaces; and in effect, making things that were *not* water float. A bar of lead floated better than a human body. Air bubbles also were pushed out. The fields were deliberately tuned to a low intensity. As a result, humans did not bob out of the water like corks but slowly drifted toward a surface, where they floated quite high in the water. As a further result, when the pool was open it was always churned by a billion bubbles.

When Cooper and Galloway entered the water the bubbles left behind by the happy throngs had long since merged with one of the larger volumes of air. The Bubble had become a magic lens, a piece of water with infinite curvature. It was nearly transparent, with an aquamarine tint. Light was bent by it in enchanting ways, to the point that one could fancy the possibility of seeing all the way around it.

It distorted the world outside itself. The lifeguard station, cabanas, bar, and tanning chairs in the center were twisted almost beyond recognition, as if vanishing down the event horizon of a black hole. The rim of the glass, the deep violet field-dome that arched over it, and the circle of tanning chairs where patrons could brown themselves under genuine sunlight bent and flowed like a surrealist landscape. And everything, inside and outside the Bubble, oozed from one configuration to another as one changed position in the water. Nothing remained constant.

There was one exception to that rule. Objects in the water were not distorted. Galloway's body existed in a different plane, moved against the flowing, twisting background as an almost jarring intrusion of reality: pink flesh and golden metal, curly yellow hair, churning arms and legs. The stream of air ejected from her mouthpiece cascaded down the front of her body. It caressed her intimately, a thousand shimmering droplets of mercury, before it was thrashed to foam by her feet. She moved like a sleek aerial machine, streamlined, leaving a contrail behind her.

He customarily left his mouthpiece and collar-tank behind when he swam alone, but he was wearing it now, mostly so Galloway would not insist on removing hers, too. He felt the only decent way to swim was totally nude. He conceded the breathers were necessary for the crustaceans and plankton who did not understand the physical laws of the Bubble and who would never take the time to learn them. It was possible to get hopelessly lost, to become disoriented, unable to tell which was the shortest distance to air. Though bodies would float to a surface eventually, one could easily drown on the way out. The Bubble had no ends, deep or shallow. Thus the mouthpieces were required for all swimmers. They consisted of two semi-circular tanks that closed around the neck, a tube, a sensor that clipped to the ear, and the mouthpiece itself. Each contained fifteen minutes of oxygen, supplied on demand or when blood color changed enough to indicate it was needed. The devices automatically notified both the user and the lifeguard station when they were nearly empty.

It was a point of honor among the lifeguards to turn them in as full as they had been issued.

There were things one could do in the Bubble that were simply impossible in flat water. Cooper showed her some of the tricks, and soon had her doing them herself. They burst from the water together, described long, lazy parabolas through the air, trailing comet tails of water. The TDF fields acted on the water in their bodies at all times, but it was such a lackadaisical force that it was possible to remain in the air for several minutes before surrendering to the inexorable center-directed impulse. They laced the water with their trails of foam, be-spattered the air with fine mist. They raced through the water, cutting across along a radial line, building up speed until they emerged on the inner surface to barrel across the width of the Bubble and re-enter, swim some more, and come up outside in the sunlight. If they went fast enough their momentum would carry them to the dark sun-field, which was solid enough to stand on.

He had had grave misgivings about asking her to come here with him. In fact, it had surprised him when he heard himself asking. For hours he had hesitated, coming to her door, going away, never knocking. Once inside it hadn't seemed possible to talk to her, particularly since he was far from sure he knew what he wanted to say. So he had brought her here, where talking was unnecessary. And the biggest surprise was that he was glad. It was fun to share this with someone. He wondered why he had never done it before. He wondered why he had never brought Anna-Louise, remembered the revelation of her real opinions of the place, and then turned away from thoughts of her.

It was strenuous play. He was in pretty good shape but was getting tired. He wondered if Galloway ever got tired. If she did, she seemed sustained by the heady joy of being there. She summed it up to him in a brief rest period at the outer rim.

"Cooper, you're a genius. We've just hijacked a swimming pool!"

The big clock at the lifeguard station told him it was time to quit, not so much because he needed the rest as because there was something he wanted her to see, something she would not expect. So he swam up to her and took her hand, motioned toward the rim of the glass, and saw her nod. He followed her as she built up speed.

He got her to the rim just in time. He pointed toward the sun, shielding his eyes, just as the light began to change. He squinted, and there it was. The Earth had appeared as a black disc, beginning to swallow the sun.

It ate more and more of it. The atmosphere created a light show that had no equal. Arms of amber encircled the black hole in the sky, changing colors quickly through the entire spectrum: pure, luminous colors against the deepest black imaginable. The sun became a brilliant point, seemed to flare sharply, and was gone. What was left was one side of the corona, the halo of Earth's air, and stars.

Millions of stars. If tourists ever complained about anything at the Bubble, it was usually that. There were no stars. The reason was simple: space was flooded with radiation. There was enough of it to fry an unprotected human. Any protection that could shut out that radiation would have to shut out the faint light of the stars as well. But now, with the sun in eclipse, the sensors in the field turned it clear as glass. It was still opaque to many frequencies, but that did not matter to the human eye. It simply vanished, and they were naked in space.

Cooper could not imagine a better time or place to make love, and that is exactly what they did.

"Enjoyed that a little more, did you?" she said.

"Uh." He was still trying to catch his breath. She rested her head against his chest and sighed in contentment.

"I can still hear your heart going crazy."

"My heart has seldom had such a workout."

"Nor a certain quarter of a meter, from the look of things."

He laughed. "So you figured that out. It's exaggerated."

"But a fifth of a meter would be an understatement, wouldn't you say?"

"I suppose so."

"So what's between? Nine fortieths? Who the hell needs a nickname like 'Nine-fortieths-of-a-meter Cooper'? That is about right, isn't it?"

"Close enough for rock and roll."

She thought about that for a time, then kissed him. "I'll bet you know, *exactly*. To the goddam tenth of a millimeter. You'd *have* to, with a nickname like that." She laughed again, and moved in his arms. He opened his eyes and she was looking into them.

"This time I rock, and *you* roll," she suggested.

"I guess I'm getting older," he admitted, at last.

"You'd be a pretty odd fellow if you weren't."

He had to smile at that, and he kissed her again. "I only regret that we didn't get to see the sun come out."

"Well, I regret a little more than *that*." She studied his face closely, and seemed puzzled by what she found. "Damn. I never would have expected it, but I don't think you're really upset. For some reason, I don't feel the need to soothe your wounded ego."

He shrugged. "I guess not."

"What's your secret?"

"Just that I'm a realist, I guess. I never claimed to be superman. And I had a fairly busy night." He shut his eyes, not wanting to remember it. But the truth was that something *was* bothering him, and something else was warning him not to ask about it. He did, anyway.

"Not only did I have a rather full night," he said, "but I think I sensed a certain...well, you were less than totally enthusiastic, the second time. I think that put me off slightly."

"Did it, now?"

He looked at her face, but she did not seem angry, only amused.

"Was I right?"

"Certainly."

"What was wrong?"

"Not much. Only that I have absolutely no sensation from my toes to...right about here." She was holding her arm over her chest, just below her shoulders.

It was too much for him to take in all at once. When he began to understand what she was saying, he felt a terror beside which fear of impotence would have been a very minor annoyance.

"You can't mean...nothing I did had...you were faking it? Faking everything, the whole time? You felt—"

"That first night, yes, I was. Totally. Not very well, I presume, from your reaction."

"...but just now..."

"Just now, it was something different. I really don't know if I could explain it to you."

"Please try." It was very important that she try, because he felt despair such as he had never imagined. "Can you...is it all going through the motions? Is that it? You can't have sex, really?"

"I have a full and satisfying sex life," she assured him. "It's different than yours, and it's different from other women's. There are a lot of adaptations, a lot of new techniques my lovers must learn."

"Will you—" Cooper was interrupted by high-pitched, chittering squeals from the water. He glanced behind him and saw that Charlie the Dolphin had been allowed to re-enter the Bubble, signaling the end of their privacy. Charlie knew about Cooper, was in on the joke, and always warned him when people were coming.

"We have to go now. Can we go back to your room, and . . . and will you teach me how?"

"I don't know if it's a good idea, friend. Listen, I enjoyed it, I loved it. Why don't we leave it that way?"

"Because I'm very ashamed. It never occurred to me."

She studied him, all trace of levity gone from her face. At last, she nodded. He wished she looked more pleased about it.

But when they returned to her room she had changed her mind. She did not seem angry. She would not even talk about it. She just kept putting him off each time he tried to start something, not unkindly, but firmly, until he finally stopped pursuing the matter. She asked him then if he wanted to leave. He said no, and he thought her smile grew a little warmer at that.

So they built a fire in her fireplace with logs of real wood brought up from Earth. ("This fireplace must be the least energy-efficient heater humans have ever built," she said.) They curled up on the huge pillows scattered on the rug, and they talked. They talked long into the night, and this time Cooper had no trouble at all remembering what she said. Yet he would have been hard put to relate the conversation to anyone else. They spoke of trivia and of heartbreaks, sometimes in the same sentence, and it was hard to know what it all meant.

They popped popcorn, drank hot buttered rum from her autobar until they were both feeling silly, kissed a few times, and at last fell asleep, chaste as two eight-year-olds at a slumber party.

For a week they were separated only when Cooper was on duty. He did not get much sleep, and he got no sex at all. It was his longest period of abstinence since puberty, and he was surprised at how little he felt the lack. There was another surprise, too. Suddenly he found himself watching the clock while he was working. The shift could not be over soon enough to suit him.

She was educating him, he realized that, and he did not mind. There was nothing dry or boring about the things they did together, nor did she demand that he share all her interests. In the process he expanded his tastes more in a week than he had in the previous ten years.

The outer, promenade level of the station was riddled with hole-in-the-wall restaurants, each featuring a different ethnic cuisine. She showed him there was more to food than hamburgers, steaks, potato chips, tacos, and fried chicken. She never ate *anything* that was advertised on television, yet her diet was a thousand times more varied than his.

"Look around you," she told him one night, in a Russian restaurant she assured him was better than any to be found in Moscow. "These are the people who own the companies that make the food you've been eating all your life. They pay the chemists who formulate the glop-of-the-month, they hire the advertising agencies who manufacture a demand for it, and they bank the money the proles pay for it. They do everything with it but *eat* it."

"Is there really something wrong with it?"

She shrugged. "Some of it used to cause problems, like cancer. Most of it's not very nutritious. They watched for carcinogens, but that's because a consumer with cancer eats less. As for nutrition, the more air the better. My rule of thumb is if they have to flog the stuff on television it *has* to be bad."

"Is everything on television bad, then?"

"Yes. Even me."

He was indifferent to clothes but liked to shop for them. She did not patronize the couturiers but put her wardrobe together from unlikely sources.

"Those high-priced designers work according to ancient laws," she told him. "They all work more or less together— though they don't plan it that way. I've decided that trite ideas are born simultaneously in mediocre minds. A fashion designer or a television writer or a studio executive cannot really be said to possess a mind at all. They're hive mentalities. They eat the sewage that floats on the surface of the mass culture, digest it, and then get creative diarrhea—all at once. The turds look and smell exactly alike, and we call them this year's fashions, hit shows, books, and movies. The key to dressing is to look at what everyone else is wearing, then avoid it. Find a creative person who has never thought of designing clothes and ask her to come up with something."

"You don't look like that on television," he pointed out.

"Ah, my *dear*. That's my job. A Celebrity must be homogenized with the culture that believes she *is* a Celebrity. I couldn't even get *on* the television dressed like I am now; the Taste Arbiter would consult its trendex and throw up its hands and have a screaming snit. But take note; the way I'm dressed now is the way everyone will be dressed in about a month."

"Do you like that?"

"Better than I like getting into costume for a guest spot on the *Who's Hot, Who's Shit?* show. This way the designers are watching me instead of the other way around." She laughed, and nudged him with her elbow. "Remember drop-seat pajamas, about a year and a half ago? That was mine. I wanted to see how far they'd go. They ate it up. Didn't you think that was funny?"

Cooper did recall thinking they were funny when they first came around. But then, somehow, they looked sexy. Soon a girl looked frumpy without that rectangle of flannel flapping against the backs of her thighs. Later, another change had happened, the day he realized the outfits were old-fashioned.

"Remember tail-fins on shoes? That was mine, too."

One night she took him through part of her library of old tapes.

After her constant attacks on television, he was not prepared for her fondness, her genuine love, for the buried antiques of the medium.

"Television is the mother that eats its young," she said, culling through a case of thumbnail-sized cassettes. "A television show is senile about two seconds after the phosphor dots stop glowing. It's dead after one re-run, and it doesn't go to heaven." She came back to the couch with her selection and dumped them on the table beside the ancient video device.

"My library is hit-and-miss," she said, "but it's one of the best there is. In the real early days they didn't even save the shows. They made some films, lost most of those, then went to tape and erased most of them after a few years in the vault. Shows you how valuable the product was, in their own estimation. Here, take a look at this."

What she now showed him lacked not only depth, but color as well. It took him a few minutes to reliably perceive the picture, it was so foreign to him. It flickered, jumped, it was all shades of gray, and the sound was tinny. But in ten minutes he was hypnotized.

"This is called *Faraway Hill*," she said. "It was the first net soap. It came on Wednesday nights at 2100, on the DuMont Net, and it ran for twelve weeks. This is, so far as I know, the only existing episode, and it didn't surface until 1990."

She took him back, turning the tiny glass screen into a time machine. They sampled *Toast of the Town, One Man's Family, My Friend Irma, December Bride, Pete and Gladys, Petticoat Junction, Ball Four, Hunky & Dora, Black Vet, Kunklowitz, Kojak,* and *Koonz.* She showed him wonderfully inventive game shows, serials that had him deeply involved after only one episode, adventures so civilized and restrained he could barely believe they were on television. Then she went to the Golden Age of the Sitcom for *Gilligan's Island* and *Family Affair.*

"What I can't get over," he said, "is how *good* it is. It's so much better than what we see today. And they did it all with no sex and practically no violence."

"No nudity, even," she said. "There was no frontal nudity on network TV until *Koonz.* Next season, *every* show had it, naturally. There was no actual intercourse until much later, in *Kiss My Ass.*" She looked away from him, but not before he had caught a hint of sadness in her eyes. He asked her what was wrong.

"I don't know, Q.M. I mean...I don't know exactly. Part of it is knowing that most of these shows were panned by the critics when they came out. And I've showed you some flops, but mostly these were hits. And I *can't tell the difference.* They all look good. I mean, none of them have people you'd expect to meet in real life, but they're all recognizably human, they act more or less like humans act. You can care for the characters in the dramas, and the comedies are witty."

"So those critics just had their heads up their asses."

She sighed. "No. What I fear is that it's *us.* If you're brought up eating shit, rotten soyaloid tastes great. I really do think that's what's happened. It's possible to do the moral equivalent of the anatomical impossibility you just mentioned. I know, because I'm one of the contortionists who does it. What frightens me is that I've been kidding myself all along, that I'm *stuck* in that position. That none of us can unbend our spines any longer."

She had other tapes.

It was not until their second week together that she brought them out, rather shyly, he thought. Her mother had been a fanatic home vidmaker; she had documented Megan's life in fine detail.

What he saw was a picture of lower-upper class life, not too different in its broad outlines from his own upper-middle milieu. Cooper's family had never had any financial troubles. Galloway's was not fabulously wealthy, though they brought in twenty times the income of Cooper's. The house that appeared in the background shots was much larger than the one Cooper had grown up in. Where his family had biked, hers had private automobiles. There was a woman in the early tapes that Megan identified as her nurse; he did not see any other servants. But the only thing he saw that really impressed him was a sequence of her receiving a pony for her tenth birthday. Now there was class.

Little Megan Galloway, pre-sidekick, emerged as a precocious child, perhaps a trifle spoiled. It was easy to see where at least part of her composure before the Transer came from; her mother had been everywhere, aiming her vidcam. Her life was *cinema verité*, with Megan either totally ignoring the camera or playing to it expertly, as her mood dictated. There were scenes of her reading fluently in three languages at the age of seven, others showing her hamming it up in amateur theatricals staged in the back yard.

"Are you sure you want to see more?" she asked, for the third or fourth time.

"I tell you, I'm fascinated. I forgot to ask you where all this is happening. California, isn't it?"

"No, I grew up in *La Barrio Cercado, Veintiuno*, one of the sovereign enclaves the congloms carved out of Mexico for exec families. Dual United States and GWA citizenship. I never saw a real Mexican the whole time we lived there. I just thought I ought to ask you," she went on, diffidently. "Home vids can be deadly boring."

"Only if you don't care about the subject. Show me more."

Somewhere during the next hour of tapes, control of the camera was wrested from Megan's mother and came to reside primarily with Megan herself and with her friends. They were as camera-crazy as her mother had been, but not quite so restrained in subject matter. The children used their vidcams as virtually every owner had used them since the invention of the device: they made dirty tapes. The things they did could usually better be described as horseplay than as sex, and they generally stopped short of actual intercourse, at least while the tape was rolling.

"My god," Megan sighed, rolling her eyes. "I must have a million kilometers of this sort of kiddieporn. You'd think we invented it."

He observed that she and her crowd were naked a lot more than he and his friends had been. The students at his school had undressed at the beach, to participate in athletics, and to celebrate special days like Vernal Equinox and The Last Day of School. Megan's friends did not seem to dress at all. Most of them were Caucasian, but all were brown as coffee beans.

"It's true," she said. "I never wore *anything* but a pair of track shoes."

"Even to school?"

"They didn't believe in dictating things like that to us."

He watched her develop as a woman in a sequence that lap-dissolved her from the age of ten, like those magic time-lapses of flowers blooming.

"I call this 'The Puberieties of 2073,'" she said, with a self-deprecating laugh. "I put it together years ago, for something to do."

He had already been aware of the skilled hand which had assembled these pieces into a whole which was integrated, yet not artificially slick. The art learned during her years in the business had enabled her to produce an extended program which had entranced him far longer than its component parts, seen raw, could ever have done. He remembered Anna-Louise's accusations, and wondered what she would think if she could see him now, totally involved in someone else's life.

A hand-lettered title card appeared on the screen: "The Broken Blossom: An Act of Love. By Megan Allegra Galloway and Reginald Patrick Thomas." What followed had none of the smooth flow of what had gone before. The cuts were jerky. The camera remained stationary at all times, and there were no fades. He knew this bit of tape had been left untouched from the time a young girl had spliced it together many years ago. The children ran along the beach in slow-motion, huge waves breaking silently behind them. They walked along a dirt road, holding hands, stopping to kiss. The music swelled behind them. They sat in an infinite field of yellow flowers. They laughed, tenderly fondled each other. The boy covered Megan with showers of petals.

They ran through the woods, found a waterfall and a deep pool. They embraced under the waterfall. The kisses became passionate and they climbed out onto a flat rock where—coincidentally—there was an inflatable mattress. ("When we rehearsed it," Megan explained, "that damn rock didn't feel half as romantic as it looked.") The act was consummated. The sequence was spliced from three camera angles; in some of the shots Cooper could see the legs of one of the other tripods. The lovers lay in each other's arms, spent, and more ocean breakers were seen. Fade to black.

Galloway turned off the tape player. She sat for a time examining her folded hands.

"That was my first time," she said.

Cooper frowned. "I was sure I saw—"

"No. Not with me, you didn't. The other girls, yes. And you saw me doing a lot of other things. But I was 'saving' that." She chuckled. "I'd read too many old romances. My first time was going to be with someone I loved. I know it's silly."

"And you loved him?"

"Hopelessly." She brushed her eyes with the back of her hand, then sighed. "He wanted to pull out at the end and ejaculate on my belly, because that's the way they always do it on television. I had to argue with him for hours to talk him out of that. He was an idiot." She considered that for a moment. "We were both idiots. He believed real life should imitate television, and I believed it wasn't real unless it was *on* television. So I had to record it, or it might all fade away. I guess I'm still doing that."

"But you know it's not true. You do it for a living."

She regarded him bleakly. "This makes it better?"

When he did not answer she fell silent for a long time, studying her hands again. When she spoke, she did not look up.

"There are more tapes."

He knew what she meant, knew it would no longer be fun, and knew just as certainly that he must view them. He told her to go on.

"My mother shot this."

It began with a long shot of a silver hang-glider. Cooper heard Megan's mother shout for her daughter to be careful. In response, the glider banked sharply upward, almost stalled, then came around to pass twenty meters overhead. The camera followed. Megan was waving and smiling. There was a chaotic moment—shots of the ground, of the sky, a blurred glimpse of the glider nearing the tree—then it steadied.

"I don't know what was going through her mind," Megan said, quietly. "But she responded like an old pro. It must have been reflex."

Whatever it was, the camera was aimed unerringly as the glider turned right, grazed the tree, and flipped over. It went through the lower branches, and impaled itself. The image was jerky as Megan's mother ran. There was a momentary image of Megan dangling from her straps. Her head was at a horrifying angle. Then the sky filled one half of the screen and the ground the other as the camera continued to record after being flung aside.

Things were not nearly so comprehensive after that. The family at last had no more inclination to tape things. There were some hasty shots of a bed with a face—Megan, so wrapped and strapped and tucked that nothing else showed— pictures of doctors, of the doors of operating rooms and the bleak corridors of hospitals. And suddenly a girl with ancient eyes was sitting in a wheelchair, feeding herself laboriously with a spoon strapped to her fist.

"Things pick up a little now," Megan said. "I told them to start taping again. I was going to wow them. I was going to contrast these tapes with the ones they would make a year from now, when I was walking again."

"They told you you would walk?"

"They told me I would *not*. But everyone thinks they're the exception. The doctors tell you you'll regain some function, and hell, if you can regain some you can regain it all, right? You start to believe in mind over matter, and you're sure God will smile on you alone. Oh, by the way, there's trans-tape material with some of these."

The implications of the casual statement did not hit him for a moment. When he understood, he knew she would not mention it again. It was an invitation she would never make more directly than she had just done.

"I'd like to run them, if you wouldn't mind." He had hoped for a tone of voice as casual as hers had been, and was not sure he had pulled it off. When she looked at him her eyes were measuring.

"It would be bad form for me to protest," she said, at last. "Obviously, I want very much for you to try them. But I'm

not sure you can handle them. I should warn you,
they're—"

"—not much fun? Damn it, Megan, don't insult me."

"All right." She got up and went to a cabinet, removed a
very small, very expensive Transer unit and helmet. As she
helped him mount it she would not look into his eyes, but
babbled nervously about how the Feelie Corporation people
had showed up in the hospital one day, armed with computer
printouts that had rated her a good possibility for a future
contract with the company. She had turned them away the first
time, but they were used to that. Transing had still been a fairly
small industry at that time. They were on the verge of break-
throughs that would open the mass market, but neither Feeliecorp nor Megan knew that. When she finally agreed to make
some tapes for them it was not in the belief that they would
lead to stardom. It was to combat her growing fear that there
was very little she could do with her life. They were offering
the possibility of a job, something she had never worried about
when she was rich and un-injured. Suddenly, any job looked
good.

"I'll start you at low intensity," she said. "You don't have
a tolerance for transing, I presume, so there's no need for
power boosters. This is fragmented stuff. Some of the tapes
have trans-tracks, and others don't, so you'll—"

"Will you get on with it, please?"

She turned on the machine.

On the screen, Megan was in the therapy pool. Two nurses
stood beside her, supporting her, stretching her thin limbs.
There were more scenes of physical therapy. He was wondering
when the transing would begin. It should start with a shifting
of perspectives, as though he had (*The television screen expanded; he passed through the glass and into the world beyond.*) actually *entered*—

"Are you all right?"

Cooper was holding his face in his hands. He looked up,
and shook his head, realized she would misinterpret the gesture,
and nodded.

"A touch of vertigo. It's been a while."

"We could wait. Do it another time."

"No. Let's go."

*He was sitting in the wheelchair, dressed in a fine lace
gown that covered him from his neck to his toes. The toes were
already beginning to look different. There was no muscle tone*

in them. Most important, he could no longer feel them.

   He felt very little sensation. There was a gray area just above his breasts where everything began to fade. He was a floating awareness, suspended above the wheelchair and the body attached to it.

   He was aware of all this, but he was not thinking about it. It was already a common thing. The awful novelty was long gone.

   Spring had arrived outside his window. (Where was he? This was not Mexico, he was sure, but his precise location eluded him. No matter.) He watched a squirrel climbing a tree just outside his window. It might be nice to be a squirrel.

   Someone was coming to visit real soon. It would only be a few more hours. He felt good about that. He was looking forward to it. Nothing much had happened today. There had been therapy (his shoulders still ached from it) and a re-training session (without thinking about it, he made the vast, numb mittens that used to be his hands close together strongly— which meant he had exerted almost enough force to hold a sheet of paper between thumb and bunched fingers). Pretty soon there would be lunch. He wondered what it would be.

   Oh, yes. There had been that unpleasantness earlier in the day. He had been screaming hysterically and the doctor had come with the needle. That was all still down there. There was enough sadness to drown in, but he didn't feel it. He felt the sunlight on his arm and was grateful for it. He felt pretty good. Wonder what's for lunch?

   "You still okay?"

   "I'm fine." He rubbed his eyes, trying to uncross them. It was the transition that always made him dizzy; that feeling as though a taut rubber band had snapped and he had popped out of the set and back into his own head, his own body. He rubbed his arms, which felt as though they had gone to sleep. On the screen, Megan still sat in her wheelchair, looking out the window with a vague expression. The scene changed.

   He sat as still as he could so he wouldn't disturb the sutures in the back of his neck, but it was worth a little pain. On the table in front of him, the tiny metal bug shuddered, jerked forward, then stopped. He concentrated, telling it to make a right turn. He thought about how he would have turned right while driving a car. Foot on the accelerator, hands on the wheel. Shoulder muscles holding the arms up, fingers curled, thumbs . . . what had he done with his thumbs? But then he had them, he felt the muscles of his arms as he began turning the wheel. He tapped the brake with his foot, trying to feel the tops of his toes against the inside of his shoe as the foot lifted, the steady pressure on the sole as he pushed down. He took his right hand off the wheel as his left crossed in front of him . . .

On the table, the metal bug whirred as it turned to the right. There was applause from the people he only vaguely sensed standing around him. Sweat dripped down his neck as he guided the device through a left turn, then another right. It was too much. The bug reached the edge of the table and, try as he might, he could not get it straightened out. One of the doctors caught it and placed it in the center of the table.

"Would you like to rest, Megan?"

"No," he said, not allowing himself to relax. "Let me try it again." Behind him, an entire wall flashed and blinked as the computer found itself taxed to its limits, sorting the confusing neural impulses that gathered on the stump of his spinal cord, translating the information, and broadcasting it to the servos in the remotalog device. He made it start, then stopped it before it reached the edge of the table. Just how he had done it was still mostly mysterious, but he felt he was beginning to get a handle on it. Sometimes it worked best if he tried to trick himself into thinking he could still walk and then just DID it. Other times the bug just sat there, not fooled. It knew he could not walk. It knew he was NEVER going to—

A white-sheeted form was being wheeled down the corridor toward the door to the operating room. Inside, from the gallery, he saw them transfer the body onto the table. The lights were very bright. He blinked, confused by them. But they were turning him over now, and that made it much better. Something cool touched the back of his neck—

"A thousand pardons, sir," Megan said, briskly fast-forwarding the tape. "You aren't ready for that. *I'm* not ready for that."

He was not sure what she was talking about. He knew he needed the operation. It was going to improve the neural interfaces, which would make it easier for him to operate the new remotes they were developing. It was exciting to be involved in the early stages of . . .

"Oh. Right. I'm . . ."

"Q.M. Cooper," she said, and looked dubiously into his eyes. "Are you sure you wouldn't rather wait?"

"No. Show me more."

The nights were the worst. Not all of them, but when it was bad it was very bad. During the day there was acceptance, or some tough armor that contained the real despair. For days at a time he could be happy, he could accept what had happened, know that he must struggle, but that the struggle was worth it. For most of his life he knew that what had happened was not the end of the world, that he could lead a full, happy life. There were people who cared about him. His worst fears had not been realized. Pleasure was still possible, happiness could be attained. Even sexual pleasures had not vanished. They were different and sometimes awkward, but he didn't mind.

But alone at night, it could all fall apart. The darkness stripped his defenses and he was helpless, physically and emotionally.

He could not move. His legs were dead meat. He was repulsive, disgusting, rotting away, a hideous object no one could ever love. The tube had slipped out and the sheets were soaked in urine. He was too ashamed to buzz for the nurse.

He wept silently. When he was through, he coldly began plotting the best way to end his life.

She held him until the worst of the shaking passed. He cried like a child who cannot understand the hurt, and like a weary old man. For the longest time he could not seem to make his eyes open. He did not want to see anything.

"Do I . . . do I have to see the next part?" He heard the whine in his voice.

She covered his face with kisses, hugging him, giving him wordless reassurance that everything would be all right. He accepted it gratefully.

"No. You don't have to see anything. I don't know why I showed you as much as I have, but I can't show you that part even if I wanted to because I destroyed it. It's too dangerous. I'm no more suicidal now than anybody else, but transing that next tape would strip me naked and maybe drive me crazy, or anybody who looked at it. The strongest of us is pretty fragile, you know. There is so much primal despair just under our surfaces that you don't dare fool around with it."

"How close did you come?"

"Gestures," she said, easily. "Two attempts, both discovered in plenty of time." She kissed him again, looked into his eyes and gave him a tentative smile. She seemed satisfied with what she saw, for she patted his cheek and reached for the Transer controls again.

"One more little item," she said, "and then we call it a night. This is a happy tape. I think we could both use it."

There was a girl in a sidekick. This machine was to the Golden Gypsy what a Wright Brothers Flyer was to a supersonic jet. Megan was almost invisible. Chromed struts stuck out all over, hydraulic cylinders hissed. There were welds visible where the thing had been bashed into shape. When she moved, the thing whined like a sick dog. Yet she was moving, and under her own control, placing one foot laboriously in front of the other, biting her tongue in concentration as she pondered the next step. Quick cut to...

...next year's model. It was still ponderous, it poked through her clothes, it was hydraulic and no-nonsense orthopedic. But she was moving well. She was able to walk naturally; the furrows of concentration were gone from her brow. This one had hands. They were heavy metal gauntlets, but she could move each finger separately. The smile she gave the camera had more genuine warmth than Cooper had seen from her since the accident.

"The new Mark Three," said an off-camera voice, and Cooper saw Megan running. She did high kicks, jumped up and down. And yet this new model was actually bulkier than the Mark Two had been. There was a huge bulge on her back, containing the computers which had previously been external to the machine. It was the first self-contained sidekick. No one would ever call it pretty, but he could imagine the feeling of freedom it must have given Megan, and wondered why she wasn't playing the trans-track. He started to look away from the screen *but this was no time to worry about things like that. He was free!*

He held his hands before his face, turning them, looking at the trim leather gloves he would always have to wear, and not caring, because they were so much better than the mailed fists, or the fumbling hooks before that. It was the first day in the new sidekick, and it was utterly glorious. He ran, he shouted, and jumped and cavorted, and everyone laughed with him and applauded his every move. He was powerful! He was going to change the world. Nothing could stop him. Some day, everyone would know the name of Me(Q.M.)gan Gallo

(Cooper)way. There was nothing, nothing in the world he couldn't do. He would—

"Oh!" He clapped his hands to his face in shock. "Oh! You turned it off!"

"Sort of like coitus interruptus, huh?" she said, smugly.

"But I want more!"

"That would be a mistake. It's not good to get too deeply into someone else's joy or sadness. Besides, how do you know it stays that good?"

"How could it not? You have everything now, you—" He stopped, and looked into her face. She was smiling. He would come back to the moment many times in days to come, searching for a hint of mockery, but he would never find it. The walls were gone. She had showed him everything there was to know about her, and he knew his life would never be the same.

"I love you," he said.

Her expression changed so slightly he might have missed it had he not been so exquisitely attuned to her emotions. Her lower lip quivered, and sadness outlined her eyes. She drew a ragged breath.

"This is sudden. Maybe you should wait until you've recovered from—"

"No." He touched her face with his hands and made her look at him. "No. I could only put it into words just now, in that crazy moment. It wasn't an easy thing for me to say."

"Oh boy," she said, in a quiet monotone.

"What's the matter?" When she wouldn't talk, he shook her head gently back and forth between his hands. "You don't love me, is that it? I'd rather you came out and said it now."

"That's not it. I do love you. You've never been in love before, have you?"

"No. I wondered if I'd know what it would feel like. Now I know."

"You don't know the half of it. Sometimes, you almost wish it was a more rational thing, that it wouldn't hit you when you feel you can least cope with it."

"I guess we're really helpless, aren't we?"

"You said it." She sighed again, then rose and took his hand. She pulled him toward the bed.

"Come on. You're going to have to learn how to make love."

*   *   *

He had feared it would be bizarre. It was not. He had thought about it a great deal in the last weeks and had come up with no answers. What would she do? If she could feel nothing below the collarbone, how could any sexual activity have any meaning for her?

One answer should have been obvious. She still felt with her shoulders, her neck, her face, lips, and ears. A second answer had been there for him to see, but he had not made the connection. She was still capable of erection. Sensation from her genitals never reached her brain, but the nerves from her clitoris to her spinal cord were undamaged. Complex things happened, things she never explained completely, involving secondary and tertiary somatic effects, hormones, transferred arousal, the autonomic and vascular systems of the body.

"Some of it is natural adaptation," she said, "and some of it has been augmented by surgery and microprocessors. Quadraplegics could do this before the kind of nerve surgery we can do today, but not as easily as I can. It's like a blind person, whose senses of hearing and touch sharpen in compensation. The areas of my body I can still feel are now more sensitive, more responsive. I know a woman who can have an orgasm from having her elbow stimulated. With me, elbows are not so great."

"With all they can do, why can't they bridge the gap where your spinal cord was cut? If they can make a machine to read the signals your brain sends out, why can't they make one to put new signals into the rest of your body, and take the signals that come from your lower body and put them into..."

"It's a different problem. They're working on it. Maybe in fifteen or twenty years."

"Here?"

"More around here. All around my neck, from ear to ear...that's it. Keep doing that. And why don't you find something for your hands to do?"

"But you can't feel this. Can you?"

"Not directly. But nice things are happening. Just look."

"Yeah."

"Then don't worry about it. Just keep doing it."

*   *   *

"What about this?"

"Not particularly."

"This?"

"You're getting warmer."

"But I thought you—"

"Why don't you do a little less thinking? Come on, put it in. I want this to be good for you, too. And don't think it won't do something for me."

"Whatever you say. Oh, lord, that feels...hey, how did you do that?"

"You ask a lot of questions."

"Yeah, but you can't move any muscles down there."

"A simple variation on the implants that keep me from making a mess of myself. Now, honestly, Q.M. Don't you think the time for questions is over?"

"I think you're right."

"You want to see something funny?" she asked.

They were sprawled in each other's arms, looking at the smoke belching from her ridiculous bedposts. She had flipped on the holo generators, and her bedroom had vanished in a Mark Twain illusion. They floated down the Mississippi River. The bed rocked gently. Cooper felt indecently relaxed.

"Sure."

"Promise you won't laugh?"

"Not unless it's funny."

She rolled over and spread her arms and legs, face down on the bed. The sidekick released her, stood up, found the holo control, and turned off the river. It put one knee on the bed, carefully turned Megan onto her back, crossed her legs for her, then sat beside her on the edge of the bed and crossed its own legs, swinging them idly. By then he was laughing, as she had intended. It sat beside her and encased her left forearm and hand, lit a cigarette and placed it in her mouth, then released her hand again. It went to a chair across the room and sat down.

He jumped when she touched him. He turned and saw the thin hand on his elbow, not able to grasp him, not strong enough to do more than nudge.

"Will you put this out?" She inclined her head toward him. He carefully removed the cigarette from her lips, cupping his hand under the ash. When he turned back to her, her eyes were guarded.

"This is me, too," she said.

"I know that." He frowned, and tried to get closer to the truth, for his own sake as well as hers. "I hadn't thought about it much. You look very helpless like this."

"I *am* very helpless."

"Why are you doing it?"

"Because *nobody* sees me like this, except doctors. I wanted to know if it made any difference."

"No. No difference at all. I've seen you this way before. I'm surprised you asked."

"You shouldn't be. I hate myself like this. I disgust myself. I expect everyone else to react the way I do."

"You expect wrong." He hugged her, then drew back and studied her face. "Do you...would you like to make love again? Not this second, I mean, but a little later. Like this."

"God, no. But thanks for offering." When she was inside the sidekick again she touched his face with her be-ringed hand. Her expression was an odd mixture of satisfaction and uncertainty.

"You keep passing the tests, Cooper. As fast as I can throw them at you. I wonder what I'm going to do with you?"

"Are there more tests?"

She shook her head. "No. Not for you."

"You're going to be late for work," Anna-Louise said, as Cooper lifted one of her suitcases and followed her out of the shuttleport waiting room.

"I don't care." Anna-Louise gave him an odd look. He knew why. When they had been together he had always been eager for his shift to begin. By now he was starting to hate it. When he worked he could not be with Megan.

"You've really got it bad, don't you?" she said.

He smiled at her. "I sure do. This is the first time I've been away from her in weeks. I hope you aren't angry."

"Me? No. I'm flattered that you came to see me off. You...well, you wouldn't have thought of something like that a month ago. Sorry."

"You're right." He put the suitcase down beside the things she had been carrying. A porter took them through the lock and into the shuttle. Cooper leaned against the sign that an-

nounced "New Dresden, Clavius, Tycho Under." "I didn't
know if you'd be angry, but I thought I ought to be here."

Anna-Louise smiled wryly. "Well, she's certainly changed
you. I'm happy for you. Even though I still think she's going
to hurt you, you'll gain something from it. You've come alive
since the last time I saw you."

"I wanted to ask you about that," he said, slowly. "Why
do you think she'll hurt me?"

She hesitated, hitching at her pants and awkwardly scuffing
her shoes on the deck.

"You don't like your work as much as you did. Right?"

"Well . . . yeah. I guess not. Mostly because I'd like to spend
more time with her."

She looked at him, cocking her head.

"Why don't you quit?"

"What . . . you mean—"

"Just quit. She wouldn't even notice the money she spent
to support you."

He grinned at her. "You've got the wrong guy, A.L. I don't
have any objections to being supported by a woman. Did you
really think I was that old-fashioned?"

She shook her head.

"But you think money will be a problem."

She nodded. "Not the fact that she has it. The fact that you
don't."

"Come on. She doesn't care that I'm not rich."

Anna-Louise looked at him a long time, then smiled.

"Good," she said, and kissed him. She hurried into the
shuttle, waving over her shoulder.

Megan received a full sack of mail every day. It was the
tip of the iceberg; she employed a staff on Earth to screen it,
answer fan mail with form letters, turn down speaking en-
gagements, and repel parasites. The remainder was sent on,
and fell into three categories. The first, and by far the largest,
was the one out of a thousand matters that came in unsolicited
and, after sifting, seemed to have a chance of meriting her
attention. She read some, threw most away unopened.

The last two categories she always read. One was job offers,
and the other was material from facilities on Earth doing research into the nervous system. Often the latter were accompanied by requests for money. She usually sent a check.

At first she tried to keep him up on the new developments

but she soon realized he would never have her abiding and personal interest in matters neurological. She was deeply involved with what is known as the cutting edge of the research. Nothing new was discovered, momentous or trivial, that did not end up on her desk the next day. There were odd side effects: the Wacky Dust which had figured in their first meeting had been sent by a lab which had stumbled across it and didn't know what to do with it.

Her computer was jammed with information on neurosurgery. She could call up projections of when certain milestones might be reached, from minor enhancements all the way up to complete regeneration of the neuron net. Most of the ones Cooper saw looked dismal. The work was not well funded. Most money for medical research went to the study of radiation disease.

Reading the mail in the morning was far from the high point of the day. The news was seldom good. But he was not prepared for her black depression one morning two weeks after Anna-Louise's departure.

"Did someone die?" he asked, sitting down and reaching for the coffee.

"Me. Or, I'm in the process."

When she looked up and saw his face she shook her head.

"No, it's not medical news. Nothing so straightforward." She tossed a sheet of paper across the table to him. "It's from *Allgemein Fernsehen Gesellschaft*. They will pay any price . . . if I'll do essentially what I've been doing all along for Feeliecorp. They regret that the board of directors will not permit the company to enter any agreement wherein AFG has less than total creative control of the product."

"How many does that make now?"

"That you've seen? Seventeen. There have been many more that never got past the preliminary stage."

"So independent production isn't going to be as easy as you thought."

"I never said it would be easy."

"Why not use your own money? Start your own company."

"We've looked into it, but the answers are all bad. The war between GWA and Royal Dutch Shell makes the tax situation . . ." She looked at him, quickly shifted gears. "It's hard to explain."

That was a euphemism for "you wouldn't understand." He did not mind it. She had tried to explain her business affairs

to him and all it did was frustrate them both. He had no head
for it.

"Okay. So what do you do now?"

"Oh, there's no crisis yet. My investments are doing all
right. Some war losses, but I'm getting out of GWA. The bank
balance is in fair shape." That was another euphemism. She
had begun using it when she realized he was baffled by the
baroque mechanism that was *Gitano de Oro,* her corporate
self. He had seen some astounding bills from Sidekick, Inc.,
but if she said she was not hurting he would believe her.

She had been toying with the salt shaker while her eggs
benedict grew cold. Now she gave a derisive snort, and glanced
at him.

"The funny thing is, I've just proved all the theoreticians
wrong. I've made a breakthrough no one believed was possible.
I could set the whole industry on its ear, and I can't get a job."

It was the first he had heard of it. He raised one eyebrow
in polite inquiry.

"Damn it, Cooper. I've been wondering how to tell you
this. The problem is I didn't realize until something you said
a few days ago that you didn't know my transcorder is built
in to my sidekick."

"I thought your camera crew—"

"I know you did, now. I swear I didn't realize that. No,
the crew makes nothing but visual tapes. It's edited into the
trans-tape which is made by my sidekick. I leave it on all the
time."

He chewed on that one for a while, and frowned at her.

"You're saying you got love on tape."

"The moment of falling in love. I got it all."

"Why didn't you tell me?"

She sighed. "Trans-tapes have to be developed. They aren't
like viddies. They just came back from the lab yesterday. I
transed them last night, while you slept."

"I'd like to see them."

"Maybe someday," she hedged. "For right now, it's too
personal. I want to keep this just for myself. Can you understand that? God knows I've never sought privacy very hard in
my life, but this . . ." She looked helpless.

"I guess so." He considered it a little longer. "But if you
sell them, it'll hardly be personal then, will it?"

"I don't want to sell them, Q.M."

He said nothing, but he had been hoping for something a

little stronger than that. For the first time, he began to feel alarmed.

He did not think about money or about trans-tapes in the next two weeks. There was too much else to do. He took his accumulated vacation and sick leave and the two of them travelled to Earth. It might as well have been a new planet.

It was not only that he went to places he had never seen. They went there in a style to which he was not accustomed. It was several steps above what most people thought of as first class. Problems did not exist on this planet. Luggage took care of itself. He never saw any money. There was no schedule that had to be met. Cars and planes and hypersonic shuttles were always ready to whisk them anywhere they wanted to go. When he mentioned that all this might be costing too much she explained that she was paying for none of it. Everything was provided by eager corporate suitors. Cooper thought they behaved worse than any love-smitten adolescent. They were as demonstrative as puppies, and as easily forgiving when she snubbed them while accepting their gifts.

She did not seem afraid of kidnapping, either, though he saw little in the way of security. When he asked, she told him that security one kept tripping over was just amateur gun-toting. She advised him never to think of it again, that it was all taken care of.

"You wouldn't market that tape, would you?" There, he finally had it out in the open.

"Well, let me put it this way. When I first came to you, I was near a nervous breakdown from just thinking about going into the sex tape business. This is much more personal, much dearer to me than plain old intercourse."

"Ah. I feel better."

She reached across the bed and squeezed his hand, looked at him fondly.

"You really don't want me to market it, do you?"

"No. I really don't. The first day I saw you, a good friend warned me that if I got into bed with you my technique would be seen by ninety million slobs."

She laughed. "Well, Anna-Louise was wrong. You can put that possibility right out of your mind. For one thing, there were no vidicams around, so no one will ever see you making love to me. For another, they wouldn't use my sensations while

I'm making love if I ever got into the sex-tape business. Those are a little esoteric for my audience. That would all be put together in the editing room. There would be visuals and emotionals from me, showing me making love in the regular way, and there'd be a stand-in for the physical sensations."

"Pardon my asking," he said, "but wasn't your reaction that first day a little overblown, then?"

She laughed. "Much ado about nothing?"

"Yeah. I mean, it'd be your body on the screen—"

"—but I've already shown you I don't care about that."

"And if you were making love in the conventional way, you'd hardly be emotionally transported—"

"It would register as sheer boredom."

"So I presume you'd splice in the emotional track from some other source, too." He frowned, no longer sure of what he was trying to say.

"You're catching on. I told you this business was all fake. And I can't really explain why it bothers me so much, except to say I don't want to surrender that part of myself, even a little bit. I *taped* my first intercourse, but I didn't show it to anybody until you saw it. And what about you? You're worried that I might sell a tape of me falling in love with you. You wouldn't be on it at all."

"Well, it was something we shared."

"Exactly. I don't want to share it with anyone else."

"I'm glad to hear you don't plan to sell it."

"My darling, I would hate that as much as you would."

It was not until later that he realized she had never ruled out the possibility.

They went back to the Bubble when Cooper's vacation time was over. She never suggested that he quit his job. They checked into a different suite. She said the cost had little to do with it, but this time he was not so sure. He had begun to see a haunted expression around her eyes as she read letter after letter rejecting increasingly modest proposals.

"They really know the game," she told him bitterly, one night. "Every one of those companies will give me any salary I want to name, but I have to sign their contract. You begin to think it's a conspiracy."

"Is it?"

"I really don't know. It may be just shrewdness. I talk about how stupid they are, and artistically they live up to that description. Morally, there's not a one of them who wouldn't pay to have his daughter gang-raped if it meant a tenth-point ratings jump. But financially, you can't fault them. These are the folks who have suppressed the cures to a dozen diseases because they didn't cost enough to use. I'm speaking of the parent congloms, of course, the real governments. If they ever find a way to profit off nuclear war we'll be having them every other week. And they have obviously decided that television outside their control is dangerous."

"So what does it mean to you and me?"

"I got into the business by accident. I won't go crazy if I'm not working."

"And the money?"

"We'll get along."

"Your expenses must be pretty high."

"They are. No sense lying about that. I can cut out a lot, but the sidekick is never going to be cheap."

As if to underscore her words of the night before, the Golden Gypsy chose the next morning to get temperamental. The middle finger of Megan's right hand was frozen in the extended position. She joked about it.

"As they say, 'The perversity of the universe tends toward the maximum.' Why the *middle* finger? Can you answer me that?"

"I guess you'll have the repairman up here before I get back."

"Not this time," she decided. "It'll be hard, but I'll struggle through. I'll wait until we return to Earth, and drop by the factory."

She called Sidekick while he dressed for work. He could hear her without being able to make out the words. She was still on the phone when he came out of the bathroom and started for the door. She punched the hold button and caught him, turned him around, and kissed him hard.

"I love you very much," she said.

"I love you, too."

She was not there when he returned. She had left a tape playing. When he went to turn it off he found the switch had been sealed. On the screen, a younger Megan moved through the therapy room in her Mark One sidekick. It was a loop, repeating the same scene.

He waited for almost an hour, then went to look for her. Ten minutes later he learned she had taken the 0800 shuttle for Earth.

A day later he realized he was not going to be able to get her on the telephone. That same day he heard the news that she had signed a contract with TeleCommunion, and as he turned off the set he saw the trans-tape which had been sitting on top of it, unnoticed.

He got out the Transer she had left behind, donned the headset, inserted the cassette, turned on the machine. Half an hour later it turned itself off, and he came back to reality with a beatific smile on his face.

Then he began to scream.

They released him from the hospital in three days. Still numb from sedation, he went to the bank and closed his account. He bought a ticket for New Dresden.

He located Anna-Louise in the barracks of the police academy. She was surprised to see him, but not as much as he had expected. She took him to a lunar park—an area of trees with a steel roof and corridors radiating in all directions—sat him down, and let him talk.

". . . and you were the only one who seemed to have understood her. You warned me the first day. I want to know how you did that, and I want to know if you can explain it to me."

She did not seem happy, but he could see it was not directed at him.

"You say the tape really did what she claimed? It captured love?"

"I don't think anyone could doubt it."

She shivered. "That frightens me more than anything I've heard in a long time." He waited, not knowing exactly what she meant by that. When she spoke again, it was not about her fears. "Then it proved to your satisfaction that she really *was* in love with you."

"Absolutely."

She studied his face. "I'll take your word for it. You look like someone who would recognize it." She got up and began to walk, and he followed her. "Then I've done her an injustice. I thought at first that you were just a plaything to her. From what you said, I changed my mind, even before I left the station."

"But you were still sure she'd hurt me. Why?"

"Cooper, have you studied much history? Don't answer that. Whatever you learned, you got from corporate-run schools. Have you heard of the great ideological struggles of the last century?"

"What the *hell* does that have to do with me?"

"Do you want my opinions or not? You came a long way to hear them." When she was sure he'd listen, she went on.

"This is very simplified. I don't have time to give you a history lesson, and I'm pretty sure you aren't in the mood for one. But there was capitalism, and there was communism. Both systems were run, in the end, by money. The capitalists said money was really a good thing. The communists kept trying to pretend that money didn't actually exist. They were both wrong, and money won in the end. It left us where we are now. The institutions wholly devoted to money swallowed up *all* political philosophies."

"Listen, I know you're a crazy Loonie and you think Earth is—"

"Shut up!" He was caught off guard when she spun him around. For a moment he thought she would hit him. "Damn you, that might have been funny in the Bubble, but now you're on *my* territory and *you're* the crazy one. I don't have to listen to your smoggie *shit*."

"I'm sorry."

"Forget it!" she shouted, then ran her hand through her short hair. "Forget the history lesson, too. Megan Galloway is trying to make it as best she can in a world that rewards nothing so well as it rewards total self-interest. So am I, and so are you. Today or yesterday, Earth or Luna, it doesn't really matter. It's probably *always* been like that. It'll be that way tomorrow. I am *very sorry*, Q.M. I was right about her, but *she had no choice*, and I could see that from the start."

"That's what I want you to explain to me."

"If she was anybody but the Golden Gypsy, she might have gone with you to the ends of the world, endured any poverty. She might not have cared that you were never going to be rich. I'm not saying you wouldn't have had your problems, but you'd have had the same chance anyone else has to overcome them. But there is only one Golden Gypsy, and there's a reason for that."

"You're talking about the machine now. The sidekick."

"Yes. She called me yesterday. She was crying. I didn't know what to say to her, so I just listened. I felt sorry for her, and I don't even *like* her. I guess she knew you'd séek me out. She wanted you to hear some things she was ashamed to tell you. I *really* don't like her for that, but what can I do?

"There is only one Golden Gypsy. It is not owned by Megan Galloway. Rich as she is, she couldn't afford that. She leases it, at a monthly fee that is more than you or I will ever see in our lives, and she pays for a service contract that is almost that much money again. She had not been on television for over a month. Babe, it's not like there aren't other people who would like to use a machine like that. There must be a million of them, or more. If you ran the conglom that owned that machine, who would you rent it to? Some nobody, or someone who will wear it in ten billion homes every night, along with a promo for your company?"

"That's what they told her on the phone? That they were going to take the machine away."

"The way she put it was they threatened to take her *body* away."

"But that's not enough!" He was weeping again, and he had thought he was past that stage. "I would have understood that. I told her I didn't care if she was in a sidekick, in a wheelchair, in bed, or whatever."

"Your opinion is hardly the one that matters there," Anna-Louise pointed out.

"No, what I'm saying is, I don't *care* if she had to sign a contract she didn't like to do things she hates. Not if it means that much to her, if having the Golden Gypsy is that important. That wasn't enough reason to walk out on me."

"Well, I think she gave you credit for that much. She was less certain you'd forgive her for the other thing she had to do, which was sell the tape she made of her falling in love with you. But maybe she'd have tried to make you understand why she had to do that, too... except that wasn't her real problem. The thing is, *she* couldn't live with it, not with her betrayal of herself, if you were around to remind her of the magnitude of the thing she had sold."

He looked at it from all angles, taking his time. He thought it would be too painful to put into words, but he gave it a try.

"She could keep me, or she could keep her body. She couldn't keep both."

"I'm afraid that's the equation. There's a rather complex question of self-respect in there, too. I don't think she figured she could save much of that either way."

"And she chose the machine."

"You might have, too."

"But she *loved* me. Love is supposed to be the strongest thing there is."

"Get your brain out of the television set, Q.M."

"I think I hate her."

"That would be a big mistake."

But he was no longer listening.

He tried to kill her, once, shortly after the tape came out, more because it seemed like the right thing to do than because he really wanted to. He never got within a mile of her. Her security had his number, all right.

The tape was a smash, the biggest thing ever to hit the industry. Within a year, all the other companies had imitations, mostly bootlegged from the original. Copyright skirmishes were fought in Hollywood and Tokyo.

He spent his time beachcombing, doing a lot of swimming. He found that he now preferred flat water. He roamed, with no permanent address, but the checks found him, no matter where he was. The first was accompanied with a detailed royalty statement showing that he was getting fifty percent of the profits from sales of the tape. He tore it up and mailed it back. The second one was for the original amount plus interest plus the new royalties. He smeared it with his blood and paid to have it hand-delivered to her.

The tape she had left behind continued to haunt him. He had kept it, and viewed it when he felt strong enough. Again and again the girl in the wheezing sidekick walked across the room, her face set in determination. He remembered her feeling of triumph to be walking, even so awkwardly.

Gradually, he came to focus on the last few meters of the tape. The camera panned away from Megan and came to rest on the face of one of the nurses. There was an odd expression there, as subtle and elusive as the face of the Mona Lisa. He knew this was what Megan had wanted him to see, this was her last statement to him, her final plea for understanding. He willed himself to supply a trans-track for the nurse, to see with her eyes and feel with her skin. He could let no nuance escape him as she watched Megan's triumphant walk, the thing the girl had worked so long and hard to achieve. And at last he was sure that what the woman was feeling was an uglier thing than mere pity. That was the image Megan had chosen to leave him with: the world looking at Megan Galloway. It was an image to which she would never return, no matter what the price.

In a year he allowed himself to view the visual part of the love tape. They had used an actor to stand in for him, re-playing the scenes in the Bubble and in the steamboat-bed. He had to admit it: she had never lied to him. The man did not even resemble Cooper. No one would be studying his love-making.

It was some time later before he actually transed the tape again. It was both calming and sobering. He wondered what they could sell using this new commodity, and the thought frightened him as much as it had Anna-Louise. But he was probably the only spurned lover in history who knew, beyond a doubt, that she actually *had* loved him.

Surely that counted for something.

His hate died quickly. His hurt lasted much longer, but a day came when he could forgive her.

Much later, he knew she had done nothing that needed his forgiveness.

M.A. Foster

        and his singular fictions were introduced to the science fiction readership by the only genre editor who has ever seriously rivalled Campbell as a discoverer of new talent: Donald A. Wollheim of DAW Books and, for many years before that, of Ace. During the Fifties, Wollheim and his Ace Doubles published early works by Robert Silverberg, John Brunner, Harlan Ellison, and numerous others, including virtually all of Andre Norton and Philip K. Dick. Came the Sixties, and Wollheim began publishing unknowns like Samuel R. Delany, Roger Zelazny, and Ursula K. LeGuin. And in the Seventies, under his own DAW imprint, Wollheim has brought the field C.J. Cherryh, Tanith Lee, Jo Clayton, and M.A. Foster.
    The Warriors of Dawn (DAW, 1975) marked Foster's professional debut. It won him an immediate reputation and a devoted readership. Two sequels followed, developing and detailing the history and struggles of the Ler race that Foster had introduced so successfully in Warriors—The Gameplayers of Zan *(DAW,1977) and* Day of the Klesh *(DAW, 1979). After*

Klesh, *Foster left the Ler behind him. His fourth novel,* Waves *(DAW, 1980) strikes out in new directions, as does* The Morphodite, *his current novel-in-progress.*

The man behind the stories was born Michael Anthony Foster in Greensboro, North Carolina in 1939, and has lived a rather varied life. He served two stints in the Air Force, as an enlisted man from 1957–62 and an officer from 1965–76. In between he attended college, at Syracuse University, at the University of Maryland in Europe (Karamursel, Turkey), and at the University of Oregon, where he took his degree in 1964 with a major in Russian and Greek. His Air Force duties included intelligence, electronic warfare, cryptanalytics, and other subjects which he is "not encouraged to discuss in detail."

Mike is well-traveled, to say the least. Besides North Carolina, Oregon, New York, and Turkey, he has also lived in South Dakota, South Carolina, Texas, Florida, California, Japan, Korea, and Greece. Finally, however, he returned to Greensboro, where he now lives with his wife, two children, and three beagles in a "pleasant suburb somewhat out in the country." In between novels for DAW, Foster makes a living by selling welding supplies and driving a truck.

"Entertainment" is his first excursion into short fiction. He says of it, "Of all the critical comments I have seen directed at works of science fiction, the most amusing has always been the hoary old saw that accuses the author of scientific inaccuracy—this, may I add, after forty years of stories extolling faster than light spaceships, tractor beams, telepathy, time machines, galactic empires, and mutants of every possible sort. What we have in this portrayal is equally impossible according to engineers of the day, but we are much closer to the attitudes herein displayed than any of us would like to admit in public. And, may I add, much closer as well to attaining it." Foster goes on to add that, "All the artists (of various media) mentioned in the text are real world. The particular combinations may seem odd, or even obscure, to some, but of all available within the concept, the ones I use seem to me to fit the story best, as well as being common enough...(so)...most of them (will) be recognizable." Readers who like to search for secondary meanings may also be interested to know that the surnames of all the live characters are words in Turkish.

"Entertainment" is a splendid tour de force *of a novella,*

rich with fresh concepts, heady with originality, decadent as Moorcock and as slyly ironic as Vance ("I admit publicly to being a Vancian, certainly by choice and not by accident," Foster says), but for all that, uniquely Foster. Once you've read it, I suspect you'll join with me in hoping that Mike henceforth spends less time driving a truck, and more driving his typewriter.

G R R M

ENTERTAINMENT

by M. A. Foster

For Suzanne, who played Faero, or perhaps, vice-versa.

The whole secret is to know how to set about it, to be able to concentrate the mind on a single point, to obtain a sufficient degree of self-abstraction to produce the necessary hallucination and so substitute the vision of reality for the reality itself.

J. K. Huysmans, A Rebours, 1884

Cormen Demir-Hisar settled himself carefully in his contour chair, at first facing the door. He tipped it with his foot into a slow rotation to his left, to face the view-window, picked up the window control handset as he did, and dialed in the code setting for city-now, center reference this house in an unobtrusive corner of Crithote Hills, no magnification, normal spectrum, azimuth 090°, elevation sea level + 100 meters, pitch 0, roll 0. The south wall of the room, a slick grey surface, momentarily shimmered, trembled, and suddenly became transparent, just as if there had been no wall there, but a perfect window.

It was afternoon and the shadows were falling in long slants across the east, the direction he had chosen. He could see across the panorama of the city—a view of low, plain towers, pastel low domes, various foliage of carefully-tended trees: Umbrella Pine, Poinciana, Labernum, Giant Lagerstroemia, certain palms, Columnar Cypress. Beyond the city could be glimpsed the shimmer of the river through the foliage, and further still, beyond the river, the brown-gold hills and swales of the Dawnlands rolled away to the limits of vision. The sun illuminated everything with a clear golden late-afternoon light, and the sky was cloudless and cobalt-blue.

City-now. The real world, just as it came, a view to the east. He could have selected other scenes, some merely casually, as a curious excursion, others he called for again and again, so often that he had contracted to have special precoding for them so as to avoid the tiresome necessity of dialing in the entire reference code. Everest By Moonlight, Point Lobos Surf, Moorea Dawn, The Sea of Grass, Persepolis at Sundown, The Barque "Kurt" Going Around Cape Horn From East to West In a Squall. These and thousands more. But when he did his most serious work, he always preferred to have city-now, East, in the window. It seemed to help focus his attention.

For some time, Cormen had enjoyed a peculiar suspicion which he had learned from his wanderings around the city, and he cultivated it in a little notebook in which he had made a detailed series of notes and jottings, as well as crude but effective charts and maps of certain districts. "Cormen's Problem", as it was known, was familiar to the members of the circle in which he moved. In fact, if he had not been so effective with his productions and engaging in personality, they might even have considered him a bore.

It seemed, so his suspicion went, that the city was slowly shrinking, as evidenced by abandoned districts along the city edges. Beyond the empty houses were ruins, and beyond that, traces of foundations and street-lines. Moreover, it had recently dawned on him that there were no roads out of the city, although there were no restraints. One hardly noticed this—it was the norm. But like many an easy assumption, once broken, it became increasingly obvious.

Cormen's acquaintances were tolerant of his aberration, but generally unsympathetic. What he needed was proof, something he could demonstrate in black and white—and color, if required. Proof. But the City was reluctant, so it appeared, to give up its realities so easily. The Master Entertainment Center, MEC, would not answer direct queries about this, even though it would obediently show him presentations, pictorial or symbolic, as he required of the areas in question. But it was tiresome, detailed work, in which he had to proceed completely on his own.

Here was how it could begin; Cormen began arranging his notes in an order, from which supplementary instructions could be sent to MEC for additional information. Specificity, that was the word. But before he could properly begin, a soft belling chime from the communicator interrupted the flow of his thoughts.

The chime broke the silence of the house: a caller, requesting a contact. Cormen put his notes on the floor beside him and rotated the chair another 90° counterclockwise to face the reception-plate. He said, aloud, "Answer!"

The receptor, apparently an oval mirror, hung with its long axis parallel to the floor. It was mounted in an elaborate baroque gilt frame, ornamented with cherubs and garlands of flowers and cornucopia bearing streams of fruit. At the upper center of the frame, a red telltale shone; when Cormen spoke, it turned yellow, then green. The mirror surface flowed like smoke and cleared, to transmit an image of a pleasant garden adjacent to a rustic house, inhabited by a young woman of remarkable beauty who sat at an umbrella-covered table with a tall frosted glass close to hand. She was of no identifiable age, but tall, graceful, and possessed of a ripe, curved figure. Her complexion was a dark suntanned olive, with black hair cascading in waves and ripples down her shoulders. The face was aqualine, the eyes a deep brown, the color of liver. Cormen knew her well: Nilufer Emeksiz.

Cormen said to the mirror, "So you have moved a portable unit out in the garden for today's calls!"

The woman nodded and smiled, and touched a control beside her, causing the image to zoom in closer. "Yes! I always make my best calls from the garden! And there you are at home, shut up like a hermit, when all sorts of Sobrany are either in progress, or anxiously anticipated."*

Cormen always felt dull and superfluous before the ebullient Nilufer, an inveterate party-goer and attender of Sobrany. He smiled back, and said, "I haven't been shut up all day. I took a stroll this morning, and plan this very evening to wander over by Embara Park to see what might turn up. You know how I am. I prefer to be . . . well, not quite so intense."

"It's true! You are a hermit! A veritable anchorite! A mis-

---

*Sobrana, pl. Sobrany, Literally, a meeting. This is a social function very much like a restrained party, in which things of value are exchanged and rendezvous arranged.

anthrope! But people are always asking for you, do you know that? They say, 'please ask Cormen to come, please do, he always adds such substance to a Sobrana.' I don't know how you do it, really. I have to do exercises, stay in fighting trim all the time. And yet you perch up there in Crithote Hills, now and again to sally forth with another astonishing display of viewpoint-indeces, or some marvelous production which *everyone* wants to subscribe to.** Well," she said, turning down the corners of her soft mouth. "I suppose searching them out as well as you do does take some time."

Cormen smiled back at the image of Nilufer and said, "Everyone must search out their own best work. Besides, my vice is curiosity, as I am often reminded. It is true."

Nilufer asked, seriously, "Are you pursuing that thing you were worried about, about . . . what was it? The city is shrinking. Yes? Why, that's like saying, 'the sky is falling.'"

"Yes, that was what I was working on, just now. I am sure of it; but I need confirmation, of course, and it is a most difficult thing to get out of MEC. You know, you can work it in view-mode one of two ways: City-now, or Open. In City-now, there's no time reference, so you can't trace things. Also, the movement program is very slow, so it is hard to move about. You don't have the space coordinates available to move about much. Fly it manually, as it were. And when you go to Open mode, you can move about more, but you can't find the City."

"Cormen, there's a lot of Time and Space to look in in Open mode."

"But no one, to my knowledge, has ever found it."

"Give them time, dear. They are not looking for it. And besides, you do so have Time in City-now."

**Viewpoint-indeces . . . productions. A Viewpoint-index is a set of time-space-angle-of-view settings, referring to a specific event, nominally in the past, although this is not absolute. Productions are, in essence, works of art arranged by the citizen, combining many media, often transforming the originals into unrecognizable forms. Cinema and music are the most popular modes. An original may be a true-original, as done by the original artist, or a meta-original, a work which could have been done, but wasn't; for example, Beethoven's Tenth Symphony. MEC arranged all these transformations. All Viewpoint-indeces and Productions contained in their encoding set an address group which routed royalties to the arranging citizen. Trade in these items constituted the major income of the citizens.

"Yes, yes, but it's not scaled time, but reference-time—days-ago. I've tried it; you have to add them up one at a time, and as far as I've managed to go, it's just the same."

"You haven't gone far enough."

"If I do, it will take too much time. I know you'll call me a hermit, and I won't have time for anything else."

"Who could live that way, Cormen? But for now, you must give up your search!"

"How so?"

She continued, breathlessly, "You must drop your plans to cruise Embara Park! Those are low-class atavisms anyway. And do come to Brasille Sobranamest; Corymont Deghil is hosting a fine soiree and I have been asked to insure your presence. There! It's done! You must come."

"Deghil, is it? I'm honored, but how does he know of me."

"You are by no means as obscure as you might like to think. Just think, Cormen, cruising Embara Park! For shame! But They've heard of you—some have subscribed. That last one you floated out did it, I think."

"Which one?"

"Well, *I* didn't see it, but I heard it was strange . . . something about a masked king . . ."

"The King In Yellow?"

"Yes, that one."

Cormen demurred, "I would be surprised at that. You know the Original doesn't exist, except in fragments of another Original. The Prime author only referred to it, and included some poems, which were supposed to be scenes from an imaginary play which had the ability to cause dire events. I simply had MEC synthesize a real play, and then reprogram it as cinema, run as animation, based on the style of Virgil Finlay. It was an experiment . . ."

"Well, word has gotten around. And so far, it hasn't caused any dire events, except that Deghil and his associates have been looking up some of your other productions, and he wants to meet you. You have something up your sleeve, I trust?"

"Well, yes, I do have one . . . part of a series I'm working on. This is the first. I haven't had it out yet, but . . ."

"Oh, no! No cold feet! Do it! Be revolutionary and daring! And tell me about it, so I can smile knowingly and leer when you tell him. I have implied I am much in your confidence."

Cormen smiled. "This is a fairly literal version of Robinson

Jeffers' *Roan Stallion*, performed as a live Rock Concert by the group Genesis, then filmed. The music turned out particularly good; I specified that they use their full tour regalia, and they used both the old and new lead guitarists. Got their famous light show, everything. It was done in an auditorium in Paris, Metadate supposedly around 1980. Of course this had to be simu-assembled, but I think it looks very good."

"You said it was part of a series?"

"Yes. If this went well, I planned to do all Jeffers' major long dramatic poems in this way, with Genesis. They seem particularly well suited to Jeffers, and no one else had used the combination before."

"I wonder why you didn't do it as cinema, with the music as accompaniment? I mean . . ."

"Nilufer, that's what everyone would do. But in some intense kinds of music, the performance of the music itself becomes the drama. This has been noted in several periods. And so . . ."

"Yes, yes, I know. I work the Rachmaninoff Era myself. But I didn't know that this had appeared later."

"Oh, yes, perhaps even stronger."

"Amazing! You are perverse, but a wonderful perversity it is! And now I must tell you that the day is today, or rather this evening, at the usual time, and . . ."

"And?"

"And, I have another . . . I have a new friend, very recently emerged, who has somehow come across your name and wishes to meet you in person. Oh, you gigolo! She is really very nice, a sweet girl, if a little boyish in the figure, you know. Quiet and polite. One of your second-glancers, I believe." Here Nilufer was alluding to one of Cormen's habits, of preferring girls, whom he said, only showed their attractive qualities on the second glance. Most other people didn't quite understand the concept; meaning well, they might bring forward girls who were merely plain, or perhaps some who could uncharitably be described as being aggressively ugly.

"That sounds suspicious . . . but I know you would not sell me to some awful creature."

"But never!"

"But you are always meeting them, aren't you? Well, I like intrigue as well as the next. Does this marvelous creature have a name, or is she to be a woman of total mystery?"

"Faero Sheftali is how she calls herself. And she's a cool one, she is. I offered her your call-code, and she refused it. And she doesn't give hers out. We have been out a couple of times, and she got plenty of offers, but to my knowledge she did not give hers out once. In fact, she said so, to me."

"Well, one doesn't need codes, after all. And the ones in which you get an arbitrary one-time call-code get billed as doubles, you know. If she got so many requests, she could be thinking to do it that way . . . if that is so, she's not plain, no matter what you say."

Nilufer thought a moment, and said, "That's true. But I still think she's a bit plain. But to do it without handout codes,* you have to use that dreary headset, and the damn thing— pardon my emphasis—gives me a splitting headache, and then I don't want to do it when the Simula comes, so the evening's shot. But! I promised Faero I would ask you to come for her, if not for Deghil, and now you must tell me you will come."

"Tonight, is it? But who am I to come for?"

"Both! Corymont, for your advancement and your credit balance, and . . . whatever may transpire with the other."

Cormen laughed. "Very well. I will come. Since I know so few in that circle, and the new girl—Faero?—not at all, I shall look for you. What will you be wearing?"

"Something from the closet! Good-bye!" And the image, clear as if there were no device there at all, shimmered and became a smoky, swirling plate, and then a plain mirror again.

Cormen spent the afternoon's remainder in a nap, knowing that in all probability, he would have to be up late, and that he had a work-shift to perform the next day. It was important to appear at these things fresh.

---

*Each person had a call-code, by which one could request the company of that person. What actually appeared was called a Simula. It was known that what came in response to a call was not the real person, called a Prime, but it was not known how this was done. Simulas were indistinguishable from Primes in every way. The purpose of these calls was generally, but not exclusively, erotic gratification. In addition, the MEC transferred funds from the citizen's credit balance from the caller to the callee, and so great store was set upon good appearance and manners. Failing to obtain the desired person's code, one could derive a one-time number through the Master Entertainment Center, but it cost double, and sometimes caused unpleasant side effects as well, although these could be overcome.

On the way, walking along the gracefully-curving walkways of the city, Cormen considered that this invitation had been a rare piece of good fortune for him. The circle of which Corymont Deghil was the nominal head was adjudged the most influential and successful of all, and admission into it could be considered a token of a long and successful life. He did not feel a sense of apprehension, but an elation, as if his chance had finally come. And as for the unknown girl who had asked for him? Such things were rare, extremely rare, what with all the possibilities there were for selecting a night's partner. Still, it hinted at an unconventional flavor he preferred as much as he could find.

Cormen reflected again on Deghil: according to rumor, Corymont Deghil was considered extremely knowledgable about the most productive areas, media, periods and eras in time in which to derive the best programs in Viewpoint-in-deces, music, cinema, and all the arts. Not only strong in matters of refinement and taste, he was also known to do programs for the commons, popular programs that enjoyed wide subscriptions and acceptance. And he was reputed to enjoy an enviable credit balance by remaining attractive and dynamic. Indeed, Cormen thought that this was the correct way to proceed. He could feel his own life going that way, in subtle feedbacks, such as the deference Nilufer now used with him, as if he were becoming someone to know. At any rate, going to this Sobrana could not fail to be promising. And in any event, he could allay his pet project for a time, a thing which had gradually come to occupy his attention more and more, sometimes emitting tantalizing glimpses of a sense of something utterly wrong, completely astray.

Cormen passed a shop and observed his reflection in the glass of the window, checking for correctness of appearance. He saw in the mirror a young man of slender physique with a narrow, rather intense face, dressed in suitable attire for the occasion: soft grey pants and tunic, with a maroon night-cape. Everything seemed correct.

On the way, he passed Embara Park, where they were already beginning to gather for the evening's exchanges. Here he himself had begun, and he frequently returned. Of course, it wasn't as it had been in the old days, and he missed the flavor of that time, several years past. Things had seemed to mean more then; people made hard committments and stuck by them. Nowadays, they seemed to rely more on what Cormen thought was cheap sensationalism in their productions. Some built up a repertoire of morbid works, others specialized in works depicting violence or bizarre and ritualistic sexual practices. Despite the reproaches, however, he still came, now and then, to Embara Park, to see and be seen, to trade in productions, to talk and to meet new faces. Here were his roots, so he felt, however tawdry and perverse they might have become. Such encounters still had the power to energize him. And besides, what did it matter where the city was? Here it was real and vital and showed no signs of going away.

Brasille Sobranamest was located towards the center of the city, among larger structures, but tastefully set. In appearance, it resembled the outdoor cafes of long ago, with an exterior partially roofed against the heat of day and the chill of night by an extended arbor of grapevines, this type a wild breed that produced small, black, very tart grapes, whose taste, eaten fresh, was unsurpassed. Now they were past their peak, but still leafy and green. A low planter set off the pavilion from the avenue. It was filled with an inner and an outer planting, the inner being soft billows of English Boxwood, the outer tiny-leaved Yaupon intermixed with Pfitzer Juniper, which had been carefully trimmed into grotesque and contorted oriental shapes. The junipers and boxwood lent to the air a subtle, foxy odor full of exciting pungencies.

Cormen walked casually along the outside of the planter, as if passing by, and turned in as if struck by a sudden whim, the best possible way to come to such a place. Looking about, he could see no overt attention paid to him, but he sensed, rather than directly perceiving that he was already spotted, and was being evaluated. Here, now, there was a distinct air of the highest levels: gestures were refined and subtle, and one did not hear loud guffaws and sudden brays of laughter. Clothing was plain and unrevealing, but to a person it was uniformly understated and quietly elegant. He was pleased to be here. It was entry into the highest levels.

Some had already arrived, and others were quietly helping arrange the refreshments. Guests, of course, were expected to help out, since there were no servants or waiters. At first, as he looked, he did not recognize Nilufer out of the assembly, but after a moment, he found her chatting animatedly with a small group. She had her back to him, but soon she turned to leave, and caught sight of Cormen.

Once again, Cormen reminded himself that Nilufer remained stunning, a figure of commanding attention at any gathering. Tonight she wore a simple woven gown of a darkish blue-aqua color, but beneath its subtle color, a reflecting layer had been woven into the fabric, for the gown rippled about her body like flowing water softly shimmering. It concealed everything—and nothing at all. Underneath the fabric, Nilufer's ripe body moved, swaying and gliding. And her wonderful long black hair fell over her shoulders in cascades, a waterfall of darkness. She came to him quickly, as if they had been separated for years, and embraced Cormen warmly, so that he could feel the varying patterns of softness and hard muscle beneath the gown. Cormen returned the squeeze, brushing his lips lightly on both her cheeks.

When Nilufer spoke, her entire body spoke with her mouth. She said, in a low voice which she seemed barely able to restrain, "At last! You are here! I almost thought you weren't coming!"

"Of course I am here. You asked me, didn't you?"

Nilufer looked to the side, coyly. "You only came for Corymont and his friends."

"No."

"Then worse! Only for Faero, the new girl you don't even know."

"No."

She turned her face back to him, on a level with his, breathless. "Then you must tell me."

"I came solely to be captivated by your matchless animal magnetism. Corymont? Some moping aesthete. And another girl? Nilufer, you are absolutely unique, and tonight especially so. You are gorgeous, do you understand? The subtle citizens of the higher orders may not be accustomed to such things."

She gave him another quick hug, pressing her breasts against him. "You are a dear, always one with the right things to say. You know very well that I did not emerge from the House of Life yesterday, and that I am no longer the gawky girl who came out and who was all legs and a flat chest like a boy . . ."

"The legs remain, and as for the rest, let the change be praised."

"No! No, but it is true, that you said I might be too much for these. They are subtle ones, that's a fact." She glanced down along the curving lines of her voluptuous figure, luxuriant and ripe. "I have seen some here that I'd wonder what they were, you can hardly tell the men from the women!"

Cormen laughed and said, "Never worry, Ni'. I'm sure the distinction can be ascertained for those who are interested."

"Yes, they'll find a way . . ."She paused. "And as we speak of finding a way, now you come along with me! First to Faero, and then Corymont, that moping aesthete, and then some others, equally interesting. This is a good night for you and I— we must circulate and be seen! As we are new in this group, we can expect a better cred after tonight, if we do not ourselves spend it first. Ha Ha."

Nilufer took Cormen's hand and led him towards the back of the pavilion where a solitary girl was standing by one of the serving tables alone. At first glance, she seemed plain and unassuming, and was dressed similarly: a loose, full skirt, a flowered peasant blouse covered with a thin wool shawl, and sandals. She was nibbling absently at one of the tidbits and looked rather out of place.

Nilufer swirled up to the girl and switched sides, standing by the girl, announcing breathlessly, "Cormen Demir-Hisar, you meet Faero Sheftali, a newcomer to our city who would need a guide in the ways of our world." She added, to Faero, "This is Cormen. He is inventive and well-balanced, and I mean the double entendre. One of my protegees."

Now Cormen took the second glance, for which he was so well known. And indeed was it worth the look: seen closely, Faero was indeed a girl of a remarkable, still, subtle beauty. She was somewhat shorter than Cormen and Nilufer, yet not small, or petite. Her figure was slight, the lines of her body firm and slender. The skin was a soft pale amber sand color, and shadings along the lines of her neck and collarbones, shoulders and arms, suggested a recent slight suntan over a paler original color. She had a small mouth, thin-lipped, and a rather sharp nose that lent her face an intent, predatory look. Determined, but graceful and well-formed. Her hair fell artlessly to her neck, but very thick and full, also a pale sand color. She had tied a flower in her hair, and this seemed to catch something about her. Something innocent, yet adventurous. She also seemed a bit older, more advanced, than the usual recent emergee, late in adolescence, but she did have the tentative questioning air of one. Cormen took Faero's hand. It was cool and dry, small-boned but firm. She was, all things considered, possessed of an extraordinary natural beauty such as one seldom saw.

Before Cormen could speak, Nilufer said, "Stop! Now you

know who you are, and so you can have all evening to know each other. You are already moonstruck, both of you! Stop it! You will turn to stone! And now I will borrow Cormen for others—just a bit!" And she tugged his arm and they set off towards another group. But as they left, Cormen managed to look back at the girl, and she caught his eyes and looked back with what he thought was a glance of the same meaning and the same intensity. Yes. He would definitely return.

Nilufer circulated Cormen around, making sure that he met everyone who was anyone, including the redoubtable Corymont Deghil, with whom he had an interesting, if, for the moment, inconsequential talk. They traded some request-numbers for some small pieces, nothing serious, but all the same it went very well.

A byproduct of the evening's touring and circulation was that Cormen was asked for his own request-code several times, and of course he reciprocated. One would never know whether he used it or not. All in all, a fine evening in a new group, especially one so restrictive as this one. Nilufer agreed, having entertained herself a considerable number of requests for her code, which seemed to allay her fears that she might be too much for the high-class gentlemen of the Deghil circle. And at last satisfied that Cormen was well-oriented and off on his own, and had learned a decent number of names, she released him to wander about as he would.

As soon as he could do so with the minimum of flurry, Cormen moved off through the crowd, looking for the girl, Faero. After some searching, he soon found her talking to an older couple who seemed to know each other well. Cormen joined in, and after some perfunctory introductions which they all soon forgot, the couple drifted away.

Cormen secured a flagon of Bernkasteler Riesling and a pair of glasses from the dispenser, and conducted the girl to a quiet corner of the pavilion where they might talk more privately. She took the wine he offered her shyly, and he began first, seeing that she seemed somewhat backward and reticent.

"I can't say I'd blame you for feeling a bit out of water in this group . . . but thank you for waiting for me. This was necessary, you know."

"So Nilufer told me. Did it go well?" Her voice was soft and pleasant, but also very clear.

"Yes, I think so. The next few days should show some

evidence of it . . . all seems well."

"I am glad you decided to come."

"It should be me who says that."

Faero looked aside, shyly. "I thought I would need to meet someone curious. I want to do as well as I can . . ."

"You make a better compliment than Deghil asking for me, I think . . . and I will do what I can. It helps to have someone to show you things."

"Yes. Nilufer doesn't do much, herself, except, of course— herself. But she seems to do well at that."

"She is well known and moves about a lot. Tell me, is it true that you have not given out your number to anyone?"

"True. The idea seems strange . . . that someone should be your lover and yet you wouldn't know it."

"Not knowing it, it is no experience at all, except that such events appear in the Periodic Accounting Register."

"She told me about that, at least. Well, I will wait. Perhaps I won't hand it out at all."

"Double or nothing?"

She smiled, softly, but knowingly. "Yes."

"But what would you do, for yourself?"

Faero looked coy for a second, then herself again. "I might not."

"What a thought! Hardly anyone denies themself the least thing, in requesting company. You would be with us far too short a time, and I would not get to know you nearly as well as I would like to. Every thirteen weeks PAR is summarized, and if you are below the line, showing negative . . . then . . ."

"I know. Back to the House of Life."

"I hope you will not."

"Nilufer has done well so far in introducing us . . ."

Cormen said, "I hope I will not change your mind."

"I imagine not . . . and now you must tell me something about the real things you can do with MEC, besides order lovers of your choice, and food and clothing."

Cormen chuckled. "You are knowledgable about one part of it. I dare not ask . . ."

She smiled broadly, exposing perfect teeth. "And I would not dare answer, for then you would know my innermost secrets. We don't ask, and we don't answer."

"There are many other things you can do."

"How do you find the index to do them?"

"Easy. There isn't one."

"There isn't one?"

"Exactly. At least not in MEC. Even with the Originals, such a list would be impossibly long. Its very size would deter one from using it."

"Tell me then."

"People have their own pet index listings they collect. Basics, they are called. Much trading goes on in these, which are traded outside MEC, as it were. Tonight, for example, I obtained a reference to a Briullov, a Russian painter of the 19th Century. I traded Michael Whelan for it. One for one. Tomorrow night, or the next day, I'll have MEC make me up a catalog of his works, and then we'll see what we can do with it. I can reproduce Originals, and if no one already has the code for them, I can use it. Also, I can order Projections, things he could have done, but didn't in the real world. While the number of Originals is limited, the number of Projections is endless. From the style of the painter, we can have cinema animations."

"MEC fills in the motion?"

"Yes. Here a word of caution from an old practitioner of the art: stay away from the best artists, because the best ones, animated, become so dazzling that they erase consciousness of the story line. It's called Media-swamping. Beginners often do this. They select styles too intense for the story. Beautiful, but too bright, so we say. Be subtle, wary. Balance counts for a lot, because you want people to subscribe to your works often, and perhaps again and again."

"MEC takes the credit from the viewer, and posits it to the producer..."

"Right. And of course the same thing can be done for music, drama, many things. It works the same way. And then you also find Viewpoints, which are interesting or beautiful incidents in space-time, and they are credited the same way. You learn which coordinates give the best results... I can help. I won't give you all my secrets, but I will give you a start."

"Then I will have to carry a notepad about!"

"Of course. Everyone does. And you work to find the best of all, and have others use them, and your future is assured."

"What if I don't do any of this?"

Cormen felt a dizzy coldness wash over him. "If you do nothing, at the end of thirteen weeks you would show a negative

balance, and that would be all ... You would not be anymore.
It would be a loss to me to have you do that. Please don't, at
least for me."

Faero touched his hand lightly, with hers, cool and damp
from the wine-glass. "I will try because you ask it. What good
fortune I have had, to find someone so interested from the first.
I will try to live up to this."

"I need to know something about you to begin properly.
Tell me about yourself, what do you like? Did Nilufer show
you anything?"

She paused for a moment, looking off into space, as if
thinking, or musing. Then she said, "She showed me how to
request things and the formats, and gave me some samples to
use, using her number. She offered me some things, but they
don't fit." Here she gestured shyly at her modest figure. "And
if they did, I couldn't wear them; they are much too ...
flambouyant. She is a good person, a heart of gold. Really,
she is, but she is much too extroverted, too exotic." She indicated her own modest clothing, which accented her remarkable, still, clear beauty. "Something is missing, and Nilufer
doesn't have it."

"Music?"

"She plays dancing music. It's exciting at first, but
then ... there seems to be no depth to it, no ... vision. I don't
know."

Cormen retrieved his notebook, and removing a sheet, wrote
a list on it, and handed it to her. "The first part is guides for
how to search and command assemblies. Also, how to get
summaries. You have to limit them in time and place, and try
to be fairly specific, because there are really too many Originals. The rest are examples, some by me, some by others.
They have program notes which are instructive. Use them spar-
ingly—they cost credit."

She took the list and read for a moment. "Tell me."

"Extended works, Metamusic, are always the same, taken
in general, although when an Original's work takes an abrupt
turn, one can splice from that point—or start with it. What is
done then is to discover the best 'eras'. The search is endless,
of course. Beethoven, for example, projected forward, past his
Original 9th Symphony, produces generally mild pieces
throughout the remainder of the Nineteenth Century, until after
the Great European Wars. The Symphonies rapidly improve

after the thirtieth or so. With popular artists, it's harder. Often you have to splice on from a particular single work, or from a work onwards. Jim Morrison is an example of this. Then, try the works on the list. Pink Floyd's *Sacco and Vanzetti* is a good introduction to it, as well. The painters are Kuniko Craft, Jeff Jones, Kelly Freas, Albert Feldstein. You can get small Original Reproduction catalogues for free. Notes go with them: use them. 'Cycle one 5/4' is an arbitrary, random selection of jazz pieces in 5/4 time by the Brubeck Quartet. You order something like that by simply specifying the number of pieces you want to have. By the way, I will add that 5/4 time sounds extremely odd the first time you hear it, but it grows on you. There is also an enormous catalogue of rock done in 9/8 time, which is very disturbing emotionally, very commanding. And of course let me help you get started. Basically, you must find pieces no one has a claim on and popularize them yourself. Then you grow into more complicated assemblies, combinations. The more basic units go into it, the greater the reward."

Faero said, after a moment, "This is enormous in scope ... give me an example."

Cormen pulled his chin and said, "Very well. *Dune*, Frank Herbert. An Original novel. Then done as animation, cinema, 93% adherance to the text. You can't use 100%, by the way. Style of animation stills from Spain Rodriguez, color, music by Lou Reed, circa 1974 + . The music and the art style emphasize an element of violence present in the Original. Not for the squeamish, but excellent and deservedly popular. Not one of mine, by the way. It's an old one, the producer long since gone back to the House of Life. It's free. You program it in your View-window. Do it when you have time, because it takes about six hours to see all of it. Or *Lord of the Rings*, Tolkein, animation from N. C. Wyeth, music by Bo Hansson. There are a lot of those, but that seems among the better."

She said, "I see, you listed those, here. I have ..."

"A lot to do."

She looked at Cormen, bravely. "I will start ... tonight."

"You know, of course, how to request the companionship of persons towards whom one feels warmth and affection?"

Faero again looked coy. "Of course."

"It is considered desirable that people who meet and strike a responsive chord exchange call-numbers."

"I understand that . . ."

"Could we do this?"

"Let it be different with us. I mean that we could do something unconventional, extraordinary: we could see each other in person."

Cormen looked owlishly at her until she started giggling at his too-sober expression, and he realized it. He looked away, then back, and said, "Are you serious?"

"Of course. I think you are very nice. Why shouldn't I wish to see you."

"Nobody does it!"

Faero asked, impishly and impudently, "Is there a rule against it? Will we be punished?"

"No rule, no punishment. But everyone uses MEC; it has removed all the pretenses of the old times. What we do with it is what people really want . . ."

"And you are the famous citizen who floated *The King in Yellow* out on a world, most recently, which has everyone gasping at its subtle horrors, when the fashion is raw power-violence and impossible barbarians? And are you the Cormen who is preparing to resurrect Robinson Jeffers from the centuries with a baroque, theatrical rock band?"

"Who told you? Nilufer?"

"Who else? But you have an unconventional streak in you, and I have few habits in the life I now lead. I asked, and she gave you to me. She is terribly fond of you, and wishes you well in all things, and I thought we should do something different while I learn."

Cormen admitted that she was bold, to go so far. But that, in itself, did not seem a vice. She was quick and alert, and he felt that she was definitely a cut above the neophytes one met prowling about Embara Park and other public meeting-places. The idea intrigued him. He said, "All right, Faero. We will not exchange numbers. . . . when shall we start?"

She shifted her mood again, now sliding imperceptibly into a pensive, distant state. She said, as if thinking aloud, "You said that people get what they really want. I have an idea, with all the traffic in the arts that we have, that gratification of the senses, sweet as it must be, is not the sum of what we really want, but that we miss the anticipations, the uncertainties . . . yes, even the disappointments."

"And so you think that we search for it in the arts, in our productions."

"Perhaps. But tomorrow I must do my work-stint."

"I also, by chance."

"Can we meet tomorrow evening, here?"

"That can be done. I will." He felt lighthearted. "And then we will start."Cormen reached for a piece of cake on the tray, but as he bit into it, a piece caught at the corner of his mouth. Faero stepped close to him before he could brush it away, and gently took it in her lips. Cormen felt a warm, nibbling sensation, and a sudden hot flash along his spine. It was an intimacy he had not imagined.

For some reason, she stepped away, her eyes shining with mischief and delight, and said nothing, but the message was clear enough, he thought.

After that, they began to walk about together, sometimes talking to each other, sometimes to others, conversationally. During the course of this time he mentioned the problem he had been working on; he thought she had asked about it. No matter, that, for she could have easily heard of "Cormen's Problem" from Nilufer, or even others. It was not a secret. But when, in a group, he was with some success interesting several of those present to subscribe to *Roan Stallion*, she quickly whispered in his ear that it was late and that she would have to go. He broke off with the group, and went aside with her for a moment.

She said, "I ask you one thing, a small promise we shall make each other."

"I will listen, go on."

"Do not call for my Simula with the headset. I will not call for yours."

"Why?"

"That we should be surprises to each other, that is all. But I would know it if you did, and would never see you again."

"How could you know?"

"I could see it in your eyes when you came to me. You would know me, but I would not know you in the same way."

"I see. Well . . . so it shall be. But I hope you will take it as a compliment that I asked."

"Oh, I do . . . But there will be better. Good night." And she took his face in her hands and kissed him, quickly, lightly, as one would kiss a child. A quick brush of her face, the scent of her hair, and she was gone into the night, to wherever she lived. Cormen realized that he did not know. But of course there was tomorrow, as improbable as it seemed to him.

Before the evening came to a close, *Roan Stallion* was well on the way.

At home, Cormen prepared for bed. On the view-window he set in Everest By Moonlight, and left most of the lights off. It was one of his own View-points, so it cost him nothing to use it. And after a time, he thought about this most curious evening, and one who had made it so. Odd, that one. But tantalizing. He watched the image of the mountain in the window, following with his eyes the billowing of the snow plume off the blue-black mountain. The speakers in the walls faithfully reproduced the roaring of the icy winds that blow above 8,000 meters along the blind slopes of the highest mountains of the world . . . or whatever world it was they saw in the views. That was another part of his problem, which he kept mostly to himself, but which bothered him the most of all. All that they saw in the views—everything—the armies, the great pulsing cities into which a score of their own tidy little city might be dropped without a trace, the charging machines—and here, in the world they walked and ate and lived in, there was no trace whatsoever of those energies, those artifacts, those millions. No aircraft streaked the sunsets along their quiet sea with vapor trails; no ships plied the seas. Nobody came to visit. Nobody left, either, but that seemed easier. He knew why he wouldn't leave: they had everything. Everything but a connection to all that they saw on their viewscreens. Cormen had read some Science-Fiction, an art form that had appeared and tenaciously hung on no matter what had been done to it. Perhaps they were a forgotten colony somewhere, waiting . . . but for what?

But this world had the same wild animals that one could see in the Views, if one could be patient enough to steer the view in City-Now mode out to the edges, past. But they did not come, either. Something kept them away from the city.

He got up and walked about the reception-room, nervously. It always bothered him to set upon this train of thought, for there seemed to be no hard answers, anywhere. Others sensed it. He knew. But they carefully avoided pressing it. It was uncomfortable. *Where* were they? *When* were they?

Cormen consulted the bookshelf in which he kept his references, his careful compilations that enabled him to make up the productions for which he was now becoming well-known. Among the volumes there would be a listing of request-codes for a number of girls, many now absent, somehow still as lovely as the first time he had seen them. He thought about Faero for a moment, and her simple, unadorned loveliness, her slight, supple figure, the warm tone of her skin, the charming expressions and gestures. And his promise. Very well that was, but he wished for company, and the nepenthe of a warm body, too. He reached for a volume that had no markings.

Inside, there were no pictures, but lists of names, codes, and brief, acrid descriptions. He smiled. The descriptions were not of bodies, or faces—he knew them well enough—but rather of personalities, of psyches, of the innermost of them. This one: *Kavaklidere, Kerim, K-10019.* A handwritten note beside the name read: *Difficult and bitchy, intense, opinionated and athletic. Inventive, high-strung, arty, likes to argue politics, although specific ideology may shift.* Cormen smiled again, and noted the number. He replaced the book on the shelf in the darkened room, and dialed the number on the request-console: K-10019. Kerim would do.

She would clear his head and purge his soul. She was good for that. Cormen returned to his chair, and sat down to wait.

Some came early, some came late; some came uncaring, some came breathless. One could never be sure with Kerim. Time passed, and more. Late, this time. Cormen shivered a little, thinking, *when she's late, she is wild; may even want to argue first, over something absurd like who's on top first. One never knows.*

The bell for the door chimed softly, and Cormen got up and went to it, opening it. On the doorstep stood a tall, thin girl with an angular but pretty face, with long, straight blonde hair. She said, "Do I have to stand out here all night? It's cool this time of year!"

Cormen opened the door further and let her in. Kerim strode into the house as if it were hers and looked about as if expecting to find something repulsive lying about. Finding nothing, she looked at the dimmed lighting and the icy wilderness of the highest mountain on earth. She placed her thin arms on her hips and stared at the picture for a time, and then turned to Cormen, "Here it is autumn outside, damp and chilly at night, and you have snow at your window, and hurricanes! Do you know how impossible you are?"

"It's just a picture. We can change it. What would you like?"

"Something hot! I really am chilled to the bone. Be a dear

and order something hot, please."

"Something jungly?"

"Ugh! Brightly-colored disgusting creatures full of parasites!" Kerim was as lean and nervous as a starved panther.
She had a long, intense face of sensitive, full features, and in
some lights there was a suggestion of equine lines. Indeed, she
hovered on the line between uncompromising homeliness and
unique beauty. She added, "Cormen, you keep the same visuals
on the wall like tabards of a moribund dynasty." Her voice was
slightly nasal. "And Constantine Yuon pencil drawings! Academic Formalism! I suppose you have a Modigliani nude in
the bedroom."

Cormen answered, "Why, no, although I have a *Salome* of
unsurpassing wantonness, done by Frank Frazetta, and a very
wild thing called *The Apotheosis of Jimmy Carter,* by Abdul
Mati Klarwein."

"Really? A Klarwein? Now this might be interesting, after
all. And of course Salomes are always entertaining..." Here
she leered wickedly at Cormen, caricaturing lust and producing
an image of anger, or frustration. She continued, "Well, I have
an urge to be a desert woman, a Zenobia, a Delilah, a Sheba."

Cormen laughed and took her shawl. "Judith was also a
desert woman, but she took the head of the great general,
Holophernes, for her people."

Kerim shook her head. "No heads, and I won't cut your
hair." She turned about as if dancing, stepped, glided, and
made a short leap that looked much longer, a motion of surprising grace. And she said, "I might perform a lewd dance.
Just to warm up!"

Cormen nodded and dialed a change into the View-window
controls. It went dark, and then cleared again to a desert of
rock and sand. In the distance were eroded buttes, outcrops,
stark empty mountains, a truly desolate place. In the middle
distance the ruins of a city could be seen, its columns and
porticos and ruined avenues sharply etched in the reddened
light of a low sun. The slender columns were abandoned and
eroded by time and fortune. There was a sensation of dull heat
through the window.

Kerim went to the window and gazed thoughtfully into the
distances, slowly relaxing as she luxuriated in the light and
heat. She said, softly, now, "This is very good, Cormen. Tell
me what it is. It is better than I expected of you..."

He said, beside her, "Persepolis, an evening in August around the year 700 + . In the time you see, it was almost a thousand years old. Unspoiled by nomads, who fear the place, or restorations. I have other desert scenes, but this one I especially like."

Kerim visibly relaxed, and she faced the window, letting her thin shoulders sag, turning her face up, slightly, tensing the tendons in her slender, graceful neck. Then she stretched, breathing deeply, reaching for the ceiling with her fingertips; she could almost touch it. Letting her arms fall, she sighed, an oddly peaceful sound from one usually so combative. Cormen joined Kerim before the view of the hot desert, and stood close beside her, half facing her. He touched a strand of the silky fine hair falling past her ear, stroked it lightly. Kerim continued to gaze into the distance, but the hard, intense focus of her eyes faded and she looked pensive and a little sad. He could sense the warmth of her body through the thin dress she wore. He touched her ear, tracing the line of it, her temples, lightly brushing the backs of his fingers along her cheeks, the lines of her jaw. She relaxed, tilting her head back. Cormen traced with his fingertips the outline of her nose, her lips. And Kerim reached for his face with hot hands and turned to him, pale eyes bright.

When Cormen awoke in the morning he felt stiff and groggy, and for some time did not move from the position in which he awoke. No one was with him—as he expected—although there was a slight trace in the air and the bed of the pungent, aromatic scent Kerim used. He reflected, yes, this was the right way, the old way, the way we know. He had needed this. Not that Faero wasn't something special—she certainly was—but he felt as if he had re-emphasized his own personal reality. True: Faero was something out of the ordinary. In fact, she was fascinating. Equally true was the fact that his life had been composed of incidents with Kerim and Nilufer and others too numerous to name; they shaped him, tuned him, and delineated his sense of who he was.

From the other room, his musing was interrupted by the soft chime of an incoming call. Struggling with bedcovers that suddenly seemed uncooperative and unusually tangled, he made his way out of bed and into the living room to face the elliptical communicator. Running his hand through his hair to straighten it, and hurriedly fastening his robe, he waved his hand before the mirror. The mirror went dull and opaque, and then cleared.

Cormen recognized the caller: it was Corymont Deghil. Deghil was thin and aristocratic in manner, at once conveying the impression of effortless langour combined with a microscopic precision of thought. Grey hair showed at his temples, and his face, sharp-featured and hawk-like, was as impassive as that of an idol.

Deghil began, "Please forgive my rudeness and accept my apologies! I always assume that everyone lives as I do, up at dawn. It was not my intent to awaken you, but I recalled that you mentioned a duty-day."

Cormen answered, "No matter that you called. I was awake, indulging in the recollection of a late revel. I should be about getting on my way shortly."

Deghil said, "Exactly so! Of course, all must strive a little, all the same I endeavor to forget mine as much as is possible. I dimly recall that on certain days I have something to do with the lubrication of unspecified machineries. I believe I have heard that you have the honor of performing quality assurance at the main flow nexus of the Nutriment Division."

"That is so, impossible as it seems on days like today."

Deghil continued, "Thus, I will be on to the matter. I wished to convey my appreciation, and those of members of our little association, for the insights you provided us at Brasille Sobranamest. Indeed, much of last night was spent evaluating, and the verdict is unanimous: *Roan Stallion* performed by Genesis is a production of superior merit. I know the Originals by Jeffers well, and was pleasantly surprised by the combination. They turned out rather more musical and less loud than the usual sort of practitioners of rock, but equally startling. I trust you have reserved the remainder of Jeffers, else I would claim them myself."

"I have claimed them for this combination, but there are still details to be worked out before I release them."

"Excellent! We plan to have another gathering of our circle and wish to extend our invitation . . . and, of course, bring your most prized production numbers with you. You have a sure touch for it, my boy, and I feel certain that this will mark the beginning of a long and profitable association for us all. Day after tomorrow, at Sofiya Sobranamest. I might add, this will be a special meet, not so many folk there, and we can be — ah, more ourselves, that is the word."

"You may rely on me: I will be there."

"Who was the girl you spent the evening with? Never mind—surprise me. But bring her, too."

"That seems able to be done, although I will say she is a bit shy about her request-number, that I can tell."

"No matter. We have ways around reticence, do we not? And now, good day." The image faded, went opaque, and was just a mirror again.

Cormen began pacing about the living room, suddenly awake and alert with excitement and plans. The long project had worked! The preparation, the study, the research, the cunning slow buildup by Nilufer, all had finally worked. Now he was in the highest circles. All he had to do was to mind his manners and keep his ears open, and a long lifeline was assured. There would be plenty of time, now, to attack and unravel all those problems in which he had maintained a secret indulgence all these years. And of course, his Problem . . . But in this new light, the Problem seemed to have lost some of its edge—not so important any more, somehow. Cormen stopped and smiled. It might be possible to ignore it entirely. Perspectives changed with circumstances.

He headed for the kitchenette to program a breakfast, but on the way something caught his eye lying in the message tray attached to the mainframe console. A long printout, folded. He stopped and stared at it with a sinking feeling of fear. No! Not now, so close! He recalled with a sinking feeling that it was time for his Period Accounting Register to arrive. He had forgotten it. He swallowed, hesitating to even touch it. And he found himself wondering, just how was one called back to the House of Life? Did they know? Were they called upon by assassins? Was there fear, pain? He had heard rumors that there was not—either. Yet he did not wish to find the solution to that mystery; it could wait . . . indefinitely.

Cormen reluctantly picked up the PAR and unfolded it. It showed the Final Summation on the top line, and he read with a lightened heart: + 4,217. He was, as of this morning's sunrise, 4,217 units ahead. Safety, safety, and a good increase over the last report. Nevertheless, he stopped now and read carefully through the category listings included in the report, observing which areas were strong, and which were weak. All seemed reasonably well-balanced, although "Real-life Adventure Narratives" seemed especially weak. It was an area he would have to bring up to speed. That fitted in well with some sketches of plans he had been working on: he had tentatively titled it "The Circumnavigation of Antarctica in a 7-meter Sailboat by Robert Pirsig, Ken Kesey, and Hunter S. Thompson." Of course, he was sure that they hadn't actually done it, although they were contemporaries, but that was a trifling detail MEC could resolve. What was crucial here was the style in which such an adventure might be presented.

In the area discreetly titled, "Erotic Diversions", his credit side reflected a healthy number of requests, and especially so in the doubled rate of blind, one-time calls. There was no way to determine by whom the calls were made, of course, but it certainly seemed that he had some admirers, somewhere. Well enough!

In an expansive mood, he considered the recording of his own requests, which was quite specific in names and dates and numbers. He knew already, but was pleased to see in print the fact that he had restrained the impulse to select from the ranks of random passers-by, as some did. No headset calls in this period! There were twenty-nine items tallied to his debit, and he noted that Nilufer's name occurred five times, and his most recent adventure with Kerim had also been dutifully reported. He smiled at that, and at the recollection of Nilufer. There was nothing in her appearance that belied her performance and manner in more intimate encounters. He glanced at the list, and smiled, absently, and then frowned, looking sharply at the list, particularly the last five items:

R25: Emeksiz, Nilufer, E-77092, 818 ....DB100
R26: Pervane, Kim, P-44699, 822 ....DB100
R27: Velet, Palisandre, V-31225 ....DB100
R28: Ariamne, Lunette, A-82150 ....DB100
R29: Kavaklidere, Kerim, K-62556 ....DB:N/C

There was no billing for Kerim. This could only mean that she had returned to the House of Life. Persons so designated were carried as no-charge items for requests during the PAR period of thirteen weeks immediately after their redline report. After that, the request number was voided and double-billing was used, with one-time request codes furnished by MEC.

Of course he hadn't seen her for some time . . . But it gave him a momentary sense of chill, almost a shiver, to think of it. It was almost as if he had slept with a ghost.

Cormen thought the news sufficiently disturbing to have it confirmed with Nilufer, who would have an idea from the talk she always heard. And it would be good to speak with her, too, for this was a circumstance which Cormen had not experienced before. He felt empty: with all her flaws, Kerim had meant something to him, once. He even felt a little guilty. Perhaps he could have requested her more, in place of, say, Kim, or Lunette, or some of the times with Nilufer...

Cormen dialed the number for communication, and expectantly waited for the screen to clear. No worry she wouldn't be in. Nilufer was a late sleeper, and however many beds her simula cavorted in in the throes of love last night, the Prime Nilufer was at home in her own bed.

The mirror trembled and faded, but did not clear on a scene in her house or garden. Instead, the screen stabilized to a dull grey and the following legend appeared on it:

THIS NUMBER IS NO LONGER IN SERVICE - PLEASE CONSULT YOUR DIRECTORY FOR APPROPRIATE ACTION OF CORRECTION AND/OR DELETION.

The letters faded as they had come, gradually. At a moment in which Cormen could not be sure they were completely gone, the screen trembled, and became a mirror once again.

Cormen stared at the mirror, seeing only his rumpled reflection in it. For another moment, he was completely at odds for any action. This was insane; of course Nilufer was in. She was always in in the mornings. And there was never a malfunction.

Cormen turned to the request console, approaching it warily, and dialed in a request for Nilufer Emeksiz, E-77092. There was a way to test this, something he hoped most fervently wasn't so. The receipt light illuminated, then went out. Pulling the keyboard out of its slot, he typed in, "EFFECTIVE IMMEDIATELY." Waiting a moment, he then sent, "CANCEL PREVIOUS REQUEST. ACKNOWLEDGE VALID BILLING." Another pause, and he sent, "TRANSMIT CREDIT SUMMARY OF LAST REQUEST FOR E-77092."

Cormen stood back, sliding the keyboard back in its slot.

Then he waited. After a moment, a small piece of paper slid out of the message slot and into the receptacle. He picked it up, noticing a slight trembling in his hand as he did so. It read:

R01: Emeksiz, Nilufer, E-77092 ....DB:N/C

He forced himself to think rationally. A cancel after a request for immediate service was charged in full. No exceptions. It was just as if she had come. And the paper in his hand said it: no charge. Nilufer, properly speaking, did not exist anymore.

Towards the end of day, Cormen emerged from the Nutriment Distribution Center into the magic fading light of evening. There had been a transient hotness during the day which now the buildings and pavements gave up, putting out a glossy warmth. But the air was cool and bracing. He felt a fatigue, and thought about retiring early, perhaps with a text of the Real-Life Adventure he was working on—*Antarctica*, Pirsig, Kesey, and Thompson. Cormen always faced his problems squarely. He had the parameters for the basic text already drawn up, and it seemed ready enough, at least for checking. His plan was to make it a narrated cinema account, with some music in parts, most probably by Anton Bruckner. But the narrator was still a problem that would be decided by the tone of the text.

At the foot of the broad stairs flowing down from the building, the way was guarded by a pair of sculptured winged horses, the product of someone's private project long ago, for to his knowledge they had always been there. The horses were slightly larger than life-size, and the spread wings were proportionally large. In fact, they were immense. Sitting by the hooves of the left-hand one of the pair, childlike and innocent, Faero waited, her face illuminating in a warm smile when she caught sight of him coming down the stairs.

Now she wore a gauze blouse, off-white, and a brown, loose skirt which fell to her knees, leaving her brown legs bare. On her feet were light thong sandals. She stood and came up the stairs to meet him, full of animation and gaiety.

Cormen took the hands she offered, and touched his cheek to hers. "This is a fine surprise! I had been waiting for your call, but I would not have expected that you'd come in person."

She looked at him and blushed. "I know I left too soon,

and I didn't leave you a way to call for me. I was rude. So, since I insisted on real contact, I thought this might be the best way."

He said, "I am glad you came. You are a welcome sight after a workday."

"I had one, too!"

"I never asked you what it was."

She said, as if proud of the fact, "I am a technician of the Master Memory Section."

Cormen's eyebrows rose. "By now you must know that this is an extraordinary position. That is a most restricted area."

Faero said, thoughtfully, "Perhaps in where I go. Yet what I do there seems ordinary enough; repairs and checks. Someone has to crawl in there and inspect and remove things, clean corrosion. I know that the position in fact is not exercised continuously, but only as needed."

Cormen asked, mock-incredulously, "Is there much wrong in there?"

Faero laughed her marvelous throaty laugh, full of bubbling mischief, and said, "Yes, yes! Oh, MEC is well into incipient senility!"

Cormen frowned. "Not so! My Mainframe was prompt enough about billing me!"

She laughed again. "That will be the last section to fail!" Then she added, more seriously, "Not so... There is remarkably little wrong there, and so my work is as tedious and exigient as everyone else's. Still, it needs doing, I suppose, else I would not be here."

Cormen said, "To real things. How are you progressing with your studies?"

"I worked on it last night. Stayed up late, I did, Cormen, and I have some tentative things, but I don't know if they are worth seeing or not."

"Nonsense! You have to start somewhere. How will you learn, otherwise?"

"So I thought last night, but today... I found out what you said about lists was true. When I didn't restrict the category in either time or substance, MEC would send me a funny word on the screen, the small one by the Mainframe: Googol. Then it would start transmitting."

"Googol is a very large unspecified number, not infinite, but too large. What did you do?"

"I would stop it. And then start over, limiting. But you

miss so much!"

"I know."

"But more by accident than anything else I found some things and put a little bit together. You can tell me what I have done—rightly or wrongly."

"Where shall we view this?"

"At my house, of course."

"Lead the way. I will do my best."

"You are kind to a newcomer. Perhaps you are more strict as a teacher."

"Not so. Every student needs some warmth, too..."

"Yes, that. So far, I have much missed that as well. That is a disadvantage of meeting this way."

"It is true I have some for you."

"And so to my house!"

"Why not before?"

"It was recently inhabited, and the former tenant left much that was hers..."

"Hers?"

"It seems so, although I have guessed. But I wanted you to see me reflected there when you came, for we are the only people in the world doing it this way, you know."

"Ah! That I know—or suspect, at any rate."

Faero said, eyes enormous, all pupil, "Yes, tonight! We will play games and tease one another!"

"You are an incurable romantic."

She looked off in the direction of the sea, to the south, and quoted:

> *"What other consolation remains us than wine,*
> *And three nights' moonlight on the Bosphorus*
> *divine?"*

Cormen asked, "And wherever did you find *that?*"

Faero looked back over her shoulder, and said, mock-snob-bishly, "Yahya Kemal Bayatli, Istanbul, early Century Twenty +. He was a poet. I had it translated. Showed up in another context. It's marvellous, isn't it?"

"How did you arrive at Istanbul and twentieth-century Turkish poets?"

"It takes longer to tell than it took to do, I can tell you that!" She started off down the steps. "But it is lovely. The light of it was beautiful; it was always so."

"Always?"

"Whatever date I selected. The shape changed, but not the quality of the light. But now, Cormen, let us walk a bit, and see the people at their pleasures, at their entertainments, their desires. It is evening, and the Sobrany begin, and all the informal meetings in the parks and plazas. To see and be seen!" Her grey eyes glittered for an instant, and then faded. "Come with me. I would we walked by the sea; then I will show you."

Cormen offered her his arm. "Lead on. It is your evening."

By the time they had reached the suburbs adjacent to the sea, it was near dark. Far off in the west there remained a luminous indigo glow in the sky, but to the southeast, over the palm-fringed islands far out in the bay, the stars were out, even near the horizon. There was a soft, sea-fragrant breeze, and small, lazy waves stroked the beach without sound. Faero had removed her sandals and carried them, wading in and out of the water. Behind them on the shore, a few houses in stucco, red tile, and grey-weathered wood, climbed a sandy rise back to the city, hidden among palms, Zamias, and fragrant groves of Chamaecyparis and Ilex.

They had kept a silence between them along the way. Cormen ventured, at last breaking the mood, "I thought you were full of joy and enthusiasm, back there. But here you are subdued and somber."

"Try as I will, I cannot rid my mind of thoughts . . . I have not been able to find Nilufer, and her house is empty."

"You know where it is?"

"Yes. She found me wandering when I came out . . . and took me to her own place until I could find my own. But she was troubled. She thought she had problems with the Periodic Accounting Register and she told me some practices to avoid, like excessive charges. I know no more, but . . . Cormen, I think she was called back, and I feel a melancholy spirit in me because you and Nilufer are, were, the only people I know well—know at all. And I would lose neither of you. It makes me worry, that is all."

Cormen said, "No worry about me. Mine's good. But I also know Nilufer is missing . . . This morning I tried to call her, but the number was invalidated . . . I thought I knew her well enough. We have been friends for years, but she never mentioned she was worried about her balance. Still, I knew little about what she did . . . I suppose we knew each other hardly at all."

"That was why I have asked you to meet with me in person, and not through simulas."

"Perhaps you may be right in this, although it would set a novel precedent, you know."

"I will not worry . . . except about those trips you make along the edge of the city."

"I do not make many of them any more. How do you know of them?"

"She told me. Nilufer. Knowing that gives me an anxiety for you; prowling the edges, actually going outside it. How far out have you gone, Cormen?"

For a moment, Cormen felt an uncertain and alien element present in this girl who seemed all charm and surprises. The questions came naturally and were voiced in the mildest of manners, but he felt an edge behind them. Still he could find no fault in answering them, for they were valid ones at that. "I'd say, for the most part, they have been short excursions of a few hours' duration, in sight of the city. Once, mind you, I crossed the river—it's shallow and full of gravel on the bottom—and walked a whole day eastwards and actually spent the night in the open, camping. Roughing it."

Faero placed her fingertips to her lips and her eyes grew round. She exclaimed, "What did you see?" And she added, "You fool, you might have been eaten by some wild thing."

Cormen reassured her, "Nothing! There simply was nothing. Some small animals, the natural noises of birds and insects. And as far as I could see, the experience was disappointing. At least I could understand why no one goes to the east. Who knows how far the dunes extend?"

Faero added slyly, "You could have used the View and set in City-Now mode; it would be slow, but less dangerous."

"It is slow and tedious. And I could see for myself that there was nothing there. The land is empty . . . just wilderness. I don't understand this, but I can at least accept the fact."

Faero seemed to relax, and dragged her feet in the water, making pleasant splashing sounds. "It didn't whet your curiosity?"

"Did then. It took me a time to see it, but that was the question I should ask: not, 'where are the others?', but, 'why are there no others.' I never found the answer. It all has shifted now priorities, and doesn't seem to matter so much, anymore."

She stopped and looked directly at him. "How so? I know you to be deep into mysteries others do not know exist, or care."

"Thanks to Nilufer's aid, I was able to rise to the Circle of Deghil, and that process was complete at the Sobrana at which you and I met. An omen, if you will. I arrived, and I met you. Nothing could be clearer to me. And so there is change. I am in the place I worked to be in, and for the time, the old private project can be put aside. Perhaps indefinitely, because I will have to really dig hard now. So, I foresee no more trips outside for some time."

"Are you serious?" Cormen could not help but note an element of agitation, even alarm, but he could not see why, and so he ignored it.

He stopped for a moment, and then answered carefully, pausing often. "The great freedom of being nobody is that you can do as you please. But when you become part of desirable and influential circles within the world you have, then you pay a price. I saw it coming and agreed with open eyes to pay it. I chose, and now I will endeavor to fit. I may look back and wonder. It may color the way I make up my works, but I know what I must do . . . And I hope that this new direction would include you in it too, however unconventional you would be now. You will go through the same changes I did; you have much promise." He added, "And Deghil asked that you come tomorrow night, too. You should be able to make it on your own, with this introduction. And I will do what I can."

Faero bent and, wetting her hand, dampened her face with salt water. She said, "This is the way?"

He answered, "That we help those whom we love and admire join the success we find, as much as we can. What else can we offer?"

"Indeed. I understand how priceless it is . . . But you know me so little. How could you know I would succeed as you have?"

Cormen shrugged. "I don't know, but I hope, from the evidence I see, and . . ."

"Yes?"

". . . I would not have one I am becoming fond of slip from me the way Nilufer did. She did all for me. I could have done for her—the same. But I assumed she was fine on her own, and so let her go on, and now . . ."

Faero turned to him suddenly and clasped him tightly, pressing wet kisses on his face, kisses that tasted of salt, a genuine expression of something, but not particularly desire. And she stopped and turned away, concealing her face. Cormen turned so as to see her, and saw that her face was streaked and flushed, and that her eyes were wet and shiny. "What is it?"

She splashed salt water on her face again and said, her voice unsteady, "Nothing. Nothing. A passing fit, if you will. You have a strange effect on me. I suppose that is what we are." She added, softly, "Or at any rate, soon will be."

Cormen ventured, "Lovers? In person, as Primes? Ah, there we enter a land no one has trod for uncounted years."

She took his hand and came closer, brushing her hips against his as they walked. After a moment, she said, "Would Cormen the curious wonder how many years . . . How long that really is?

"No. I would not have it different, though others all did the same around us."

She skipped a little dancing circle around him, spattering the warm water. And coming to face him she turned and took his hands, and whispered, "Then we will go to my house now, and you will be my lover, yes, and I yours, yes, and the first time we lay together we will dedicate that to the memory of Nilufer."

"And then?"

"Then we must go as far as we can, for the world is a firefly shadow, the memory of a passing cloud, and we know only that we are here and now and that the real thing we will make with our bodies will be a sweetness that will never come again in this world."

"We are unique."

"Everyone is . . . but they don't know it. We do, now."

She now walked gravely out of the water, as if reluctant to part from it, still holding Cormen's hands tightly, leading him away from the sea towards the seaside gardens and cottages, the intangible neighborhood in which was her house. It was not far, only a few minutes walking, which they now prolonged, sometimes stopping for a time to exchange light, teasing, tantalizing kisses, touches.

She led him into the garden of an inconspicuous house which evoked echoes in Cormen's mind, but he could not place them. Somewhere he had seen this house, but where? He couldn't place it; nor could he think clearly enough to make much of an effort. Faero opened the door. Inside, she left the lights off, but quickly programmed the view-wall. Cormen waited. Faero tossed her sandals in the corner, unwinding her skirt, letting it fall off her hips. The view came on: a peaceful dusk in the country with a small pond bordered by tall pines whose branches were high up overhead. The pond was glassy smooth, over which swallows darted, slooped and skimmed. To the left, there was a darkened cabin, old-fashioned and rustic, plain wood and a screen porch. The sounds of night-things could be heard, crying off in the distance. The fading daylight in the View was soft and full of warm tones; in this light Cormen could see the smooth supple shape of her hip and thigh on the illuminated side as she came to him, and her skin was cool to the touch when he gathered her into his arms. Faero quite forgot to remove her thin blouse. In fact, it did not occur to either of them until much later. They also forgot to cry out in memory of Nilufer.

And much later, they returned to the sitting room, which also seemed to have some of the strange familiarity Cormen had noticed in the garden outside. Familiar, and yet strange. Faero scattered cushions on the floor and ordered, through the kitchen unit, bowls of fresh fruit, which she cut up for them with her own deft hands: apples, pears, tangerines, quinces, grapes of several shapes and sizes, including wild grapes, almost black. There were also tart wild plums, apricots, wild cherries, wafers of cardamom oatmeal bread, and carafes of scented tea. They sat on the floor by a low taboret and said meaningless things, smiled at each other, and placed bits of fruit in each other's mouths.

During a quieter time when they were concentrating more on the tea, and such thoughts as they had, Faero retrieved the handset controller from its slot in the wall and brought it back with her. She settled herself, and said, "I want to show you at least one of my inventions, to see what you think . . . if we should present this to the regard of the worthy Corymont and his friends, among whom are you, now."

Cormen arranged his cushions and lay back, pulling a plaid lap-blanket over his spare frame, relaxing. "Tell me first. What's it made of."

Faero moved her cushions so they lay side by side, and borrowed part of the blanket. She began, "This will be cinema. I queried to see if anyone had done it this way, and they hadn't, although there are several other versions, and a lot of queries.

The base plot is *Romeo and Juliet*, Shakespeare, but instead
of the Italianate background I set it in a so-called 'modern'
style, very bare with a lot of pale surfaces and climbing plants.
The presentation is full animation, art by a commercial artist
called Rosamond. The musical accompaniment is metamusic
based on the early woodwind compositions by Dmitrii Shos-
takovitch. This amounts to about a 20% edit-out on the original,
with a slight addition in the music. Are you ready? I am very
nervous about this."

"Yes, yes! Do not lose your nerve now: run it."

Faero keyed a coded sequence into the handset, and the
view-wall faded out the cabin scene and, fading it in, replaced
it with another that was at once strange and disturbingly familiar. There were buildings of whitewashed stucco, vines
trailing over walls, sunlight, and an odd, faded-out background. Somewhere off-screen was a pool that reflected light
onto the wall in ripples and dancing patterns of half-shadows.
The bright lines of the rippling reflections pulsed and shimmered into the letters of the titles and credits, and then this
faded out to the story proper. During this, there was a soft trio,
half-heard, playing tenor saxophone, English horn, and electric
bass, at the lowest possible dynamic level, painfully tender but
also with an undisguised slavonic melancholy.

Cormen was already impressed. He whispered, "Who are
the musicians in this passage?"

Faero whispered quickly, "Yusef Lateef on English horn.
He's a Jazz figure. Dick Parry on the saxophone. He worked
with the group Pink Floyd, and Michael Rutherford on bass—
an eight-string, by the way. Shh. Now, watch and listen."

The scene was now a street in some city, a severely modern
city, machine-like in its perfection, along which two bullies
were swaggering, talking loudly and crudely swearing...

...And the last scene ended in a section given over to the
dead of the city, the view focusing on a single tear in the eye
of the Prince, now zooming in close, close, picking up the
refraction of the Sun in the tear, glittering, while a fading
Saxophone played out the last fragments of melody and died
out in echoes. With the silence, the reflections fell to the edges
of the View and the View-Wall was blank and pale. Then it
went neutral.

Cormen took a deep breath and stretched. "I have been
completely oblivious of the passage of time. Of this piece, I
could say little more."

Faero asked, softly, "You don't think it's too much? I mean . . ."

"I know what you mean. Well, it is extreme in its own way, but I also know . . . that good art is an indefinable mix which lies on the ground between Harmony and Invention, between 'good taste' and bad, as it were. I like that spare treatment very much. You could use it in a lot of ways, a lot of things. It's a long way towards an abstract starkness, but also very lovely in execution . . . piercing. I would subscribe. You are better than you know at this. And with so little time."

"I did not stay up all night. There was little time, so I worked as fast as I could, and made fast decisions."

Cormen poked at her ribs. "Apparently it is part of your nature; you made up your mind fast enough about me."

"Not so!" She said, indignantly. "There was no decision to make. I made straight for you, and I caught you, too. Was I too early or too late?" At the last, her playfulness faded into a genuine sadness, a regret. She did not answer her question, nor did she give a clue to Cormen to understand her meaning.

She turned from them, to her works. "I also made up some Metamusic: *The Day on Fire*, an adaptation of James Ramsay Ullman's biography of Arthur Rimbaud, a triple set by Blue Oyster Cult. Also a Bartok cycle based on a deceptively simple piece he composed called *Two Portraits*. Here, instead of one girl seen two ways, are five I found at random in the Views. It's called *Working Girls*."

Cormen looked up at the ceiling. "Bartok's damn difficult, so I understand."

"I found a good splice-on by luck, as it were."

"You might instead, by fortune, have happened on *The Miraculous Mandarin*, or some of his more impossible works. This happened to a friend of mine, once. It so distressed him he couldn't work on his productions for weeks."

"Well, this isn't difficult . . . True, it's a little subtle, but it is really very pleasant music. Very relaxing. And if you listen very closely, you can almost get a fuzzy image in your mind of the girls, and that disturbs me. It somehow shouldn't be."

"Richard Strauss was said to believe that he could compose music from which the listener could tell the color of hair of the actress who might play the heroine."

Faero clapped her hands, like a child. "When was this Strauss?"

"Early century Twenty + ."

"Oh, wonderful! Then they were at this before we had the MEC to do it for us!"

"Deghil says that a machine is only a standardized method of doing what everyone already wants to do. First people do something, in a lot of ways with some overlap, and then they come together, and when the images overlap to a certain degree, then they can make a machine to do the job—whatever it is."

"Just like that."

"Yes."

"What about the knowledge? How do they know how?"

"They cut and fit and use what they have to, and they think up all sorts of tricks to get around the things they can't do— but do anyway. And the knowledge is just a byproduct of the activity, which is nothing but the expression of dreams and desires, some not very well-formed, and most poorly integrated and controlled."

"You understand this view?"

"Yes . . . it makes some sense."

"What happens when people achieve what they really want?"

"They do that to the exclusion of all else."

"That is more disturbing than you worrying about the size of the city, or where it is in relation to the Views. I could become frightened by that, I think."

"No need of that."

"And you are giving up your project, after learning this?"

"Yes. The more so: in essence, we have what we want. What I want, I suppose. Yes. And you complete it. Perhaps there is something to this—to have a lover, in person."

Faero reflected a moment, then said, "There are differences. I will be here in the morning, and we will have to make adjustments and allowances for each other . . . changing circumstances. And you would turn away from it, just like that?"

Cormen was puzzled by her insistence. "Yes. No hedging. This event with Deghil is timely. You see, we have no evil, no bad mischance, no malevolent will here, such as we can all see in the Views. *There*, they were all unhappy most of the time. They had fear, apprehension, worry, dissatisfaction, resentment, envy. They distrusted nature, each other, everything. Well, we all have our little vices, which we cultivate like herbs in a pot, but we commit no crimes, no violences. In a sense we live in paradise."

straighten things up a bit before he left. He was also enjoying the strange experience of being in another's house, and he wished to savor it a little longer before he left. There was, too, the disturbing element he had noticed before, a weak *deja-vu*, which he still seemed unable to place. He hoped to catch a stronger hint by looking about.

Somehow, he imagined that he would find pictures about that were somewhat like their owner, an expanded image, perhaps more work by Rosamond, which he liked, or perhaps David Hamilton Photographs, which had been on the list he had given Faero. He found none. The bedroom they had been in was really more of a workroom, and had several pictures, but they surprised him. One large canvas, an oil, was a metapainting by a projected Rembrandt Van Rijn, called, according to the title plate, "Richard Nixon and his Advisors Hear a Disturbing Report by G. Gordon Liddy." The atmosphere was one of intense emotions and dim lighting, and to a man, the faces glowered with emotions Cormen could only guess at. On the other wall was a group of prints, presumably photographs, of a costumed figure grasping a microphone under garish lighting which lent a ghastly quality, an unreal effect, to the performer. Always straining with heroic effort, the figure baffled Cormen. In one print, he wore an enigmatic angular prism of a headress and a loose black robe, and leered at the audience from eyes circled with fluorescent paint. In another, he wore a Nehru jacket and was made up in blackface. In yet another, he played a flute, but wore a headband that supported a pair of gauze batwings behind his head. One showed him suspended from a wire harness above the stage, exhorting the audience to unimaginable emotions. Cormen looked closer. The fine print at the bottom of each identified the performer as one Peter Gabriel.

Through the rest of the house, he found another series of exquisitely-detailed, slightly surrealistic drawings of multi-armed wizards, giant birds in riding harnesses, and machines that looked like insects . . . or perhaps insects that looked like machines. Cormen remained uncertain. These were works of Roger Dean, and a surprising number of them were, apparently, originals. Most, however, were metaworks. Again, he felt, as with the handwriting, a discontinuity, a subtle variation. A curious person, this Faero.

In a secluded corner he came upon a heap of discarded prints, neatly stacked out of the way, obviously property of the former tenant. Cormen looked through these as well. These were commonplace and vulgar—waif children with enormous eyes and young animals in the same style, attributed to a Keane. There were also glittering ballroom or nightclub scenes by a Leroy Nieman, and groups of urchins playing, by a Ted DeGrazia. Cormen shook his head. He agreed with Faero that they must go. But the feeling of *deja-vu* was strongest while looking at the prints. Very strong. He had seen them before. But where, and in what context?

Cormen shrugged and left, walking back to his own neighborhood by way of a detour along the beach road for some distance in a fine, crystalline morning air. The wind off the sea was cool and refreshing, and along the way he reviewed the list of works he had in mind from which he would make the choices that he would take to Sofiya Sobranamest tomorrow night.

He spent the rest of the day reviewing possible combinations, collecting and pursuing references, checking out examples, and trying out trial pieces, using the composition program subset of MEC. And towards the end of afternoon, when the time was shifting imperceptibly from afternoon into evening, and yet was not either, Faero came, obviously tired and silent, but with soft expressions of affection which Cormen found reassuring and complete. They spent the rest of the evening alternating compositional work with bouts of what Faero referred to as "flowery combat", a most entertaining and exhausting evening.

Cormen was pleased and surprised to find that her ardor and loving-kindness had increased, if anything, but he did note that at times she seemed distracted and preoccupied. More than once he looked up from his work and saw her lips moving soundlessly, as if she were talking to herself.

And very late, she excused herself, promising to return and meet him at his house. Equally binding, she promised to return again after a few days' rest especially for them alone, arrayed as he might wish. Cormen, having enjoyed Faero's slight, supple body to the utmost, sighed deeply, smiled weakly, and groaned. But he knew he would recover, and said, "Come to me in the moonlight, radiant in pearls and Vetiver and hair-fine chains of gold. We will taste the rarest vintages to the dregs. *Saluté*."

She stood by the doorway a moment, looking pensive and perfectly innocent, although slightly rumpled and mused. "Pearls and Vetiver? And gold? The scent, Vetiver, I will wear, for I love its grassy sweetness, but the rest must be opals and platinum. Otherwise..." And with the faintest of smiles, she turned and left, walking back towards her little house, stopping often to look back fondly.

The next day Cormen prepared his productions and rested. The day outside was a good one to avoid through work, for it was brazen and sultry, sometimes almost clouding over. The sun sank slowly into a glassy sea the color of slate, floating and shimmering. It had been colored a dull orange far above the horizon. And in the still dusk, Faero came, dressed in a soft blue wrap-around dress with large, loose sleeves, and wearing enormous blue flowers in her hair. She looked rare and delicate, something tropical from an unknown jungle. For the moment, all her earlier moodiness had vanished entirely, and she was again as gay and innocent as a child.

They arrived fashionably late. A good number of people were already present, and to the side, tables were spread with delectables of every sort. Deghil and his friends certainly did not stint on the provender. Cormen noticed something about the group almost at once, however, which excited the sense of curiosity which he had pledged to suppress. It seemed that there were two groups present, two very distinct types. Deghil and his associates proper could easily be distinguished by their subtlety and restraint in manners and dress; indeed, they were hardly visible. The others, who were somewhat fewer, were very noticeable and in some cases rather bizarre. At any rate, they behaved well enough. It surprised Cormen. Aside from the worst of Embara Park, he had hardly known such types existed.

They were met and greeted by Deghil himself, accompanied by a girl-child of striking and original appearance: she was child-slender, almost to the point of starvation, and of a pale complexion that seemed to never have been illuminated by other than artificial light, a pallor. She wore a limp leather jump-suit, very thin, whose access was by means of an enormous neck-to-crotch zipper attached to a parachutist's D-ring, now pulled open to her navel. On her thin neck she wore a choker of some black fabric, ornamented with silver and turquoises. The girl managed to appear perverse, wanton, and as perilous as forbidden drugs and forgotten rites, all at once. Deghil introduced her as one Roxanne Doymaz, who usually preferred to be addressed as "Rocky". The girl mumbled a few

ill-said false pleasantries, and then excused herself to do some
serious nibbling. Faero declared herself hungry as well, and
joined the girl by one of the tables.

Cormen would have gone with them, but Deghil held back,
as if there was more that he wished to say. Cormen said, "I
would not be rude, but I do find it curious that a person of
your station would come to a Sobrana such as this with a girl
like Roxanne. Am I missing something I should know, or must
I feel my way along?"

Deghil smiled and said, "Well, you may observe, that many
of us are accompanied—by certain persons of perhaps dubious
sort."

"Indeed! Thugs, purveyors of every sort of vice, girls of
the night." Cormen felt somewhat emboldened, and spoke
frankly.

Deghil said, enigmatically, "The, ah, escorts, do not seem
part of the circle..."

"No. I don't understand."

"But you must. It simply couldn't be otherwise!"

"No. I am serious."

"You stroke me!"

"No—not a word, I swear!"

Deghil said, thoughtfully, "Perhaps, perhaps... Very well.
I will risk face, then. The ones who are different, the escorts...they are all simulae. We bring them out on certain
occasions, as it were, for purposes of mutual exhibition. We
all have, of course, many to draw on, but it never hurts to
repeat one's successes, does it? My Roxanne, for example, is
a most perverse half-child, half-woman, and half something
utterly unspeakable!" He chuckled. "We go searching for them
in Time. That, of course, was a major reason for bringing you
in. At Brasille, you were seen with that delightful, marvelous
creature, and all agreed that she had to be a simula and that
your taste was virtually perfect. Now you can't mean to tell
me that this Faero Sheftali is Prime! I would never have
known!"

"As far as I know, she is."

"Curious, curious. There simply is no end to the marvels
that MEC can reproduce through the House of Life, is there?
It's creations are sometimes more... vivid, than ours, however
hard we try. Then I ponder, I wonder, I consider: impossible,
but perhaps it is Faero who is real, and Cormen who is the
pet."

Cormen hid a slight irritation he felt, and declaimed, "Not so, Ser Deghil: I have a request number." Struck with inspiration, he added, "You may claim it of me, if you desire."

Deghil was imperturbed, and said, "Excellent. A most excellent fellow. And indeed, we may speak of this later. But now, I must greet more latecomers. Excuse me."

Cormen, left alone, looked to the buffet, and there saw Roxanne and Faero sampling things and talking animatedly, as if they had become fast friends, or already knew one another. Cormen joined them, sampling the tidbits with them, and trying to remain tactful and discreet in the face of what Deghil had told him. Simulae at home was one thing, but out in the open, like this? It was madness, although not terribly different when he thought about it.

He noted that Roxanne appraised him openly, not bothering to conceal her interest from Faero, who in turn gave no sign that she was interested at all. Cormen looked closely at the pale form of the girl, and caught himself thinking that perhaps in some circumstances Roxanne could be an intriguing diversion. But bizarre! He saw that she had chewed her fingernails to nubs, so at least she wouldn't scratch . . . And he wondered exactly how Deghil had found her. Obviously in the Viewpoints, somewhere in Time. She bore the look of someone from Time.

A disturbing vision caught at his flow of thoughts, a late response to Deghil's cynical banter: who, indeed, were Simulae, and who were real? Cormen had always selected his Simulae from those he saw around him, in the streets, at Sobrany, in the parks. They were no more, and no less. But there was something about those from Time . . . They seemed—what? More clearly defined, perhaps, better-focused. He felt his perceptual world shift a little, a tiny bit, after the fashion of a nightmare, and during this, he also saw that Faero too shared that vivid sense of sharpness, a quality that made her infinitely desirable. He shook his head to clear the vision, and the old way returned, trembling and tentative, and then he was caught up in the swirls and currents of Deghil's Sobrana.

Very much later, the ranks of party-goers began to thin out, and the earnest conversations slowed to tangents and hazy repetitions. Slightly drunk, Cormen excused himself from a conversation with a group of some of Deghil's friends, and went looking for Faero, who had been behind him but a moment ago, but who was now unaccountably gone. He looked carefully, but he did not see her among the remaining guests. He searched the rest of the Sobranamest: the buffet, the kitchen beyond, around the outer perimeter. He knocked discreetly on the bathroom doors; she was in none of those places. Cormen passed by Deghil, who was conversing tipsily but intensely with an impassive young man who, although generally Caucasian of race, had arrayed himself to suggest a mandarin of ancient China, with dragon-embroidered robe, flowing long hair tied into a pigtail behind, and a soft mustasche drooping only from the outer edges of his upper lip.

Confused and dulled by the champagne he had drunk, Modesto Brut '81, Cormen attempted to recall something, but nothing came. He could not recall any arrangements. But he did dimly remember something about Faero saying she was feeling bad, over-extended she had said. Yes, that. Perhaps she had gone home. In any event, she would be in no shape for any further adventures. Making the proper motions and excuses, Cormen left Sofiya and started walking home. As he left, he observed, half smiling to himself, that a few of the free-adventurers were still prowling among the shrubbery of Embara Park, still profiling, still posturing, trying their best.

But along the long way home, his head cleared somewhat, so that by the time he had reached his own neighborhood, he was more or less himself, if a little tired. And he thought, the Circle of Deghil —was that such an honor? All he had heard from those he had met that night were references to works of strange and disturbing outlines, dissonant music that produced hallucinatory states of mind and heart, exquisitely morbid styles and modes borrowed from artists best forgotten. Or of Viewpoints of questionable spectacles, tragedies, disasters. And were these the ultimate pinnacles? Did one have to choose between Keane and The Last Days of Pompeii, live? Cormen felt that his ambition had been shattered beyond repair. Had Faero suspected that this was coming?

As he walked into the house he found himself greatly missing the odd girl. For some time, he turned on the lights and walked about the house aimlessly, thinking. At last, with a resigned sigh, he sat on the floor by the MEC main console, and opening a small cabinet, removed a helmet-like device of complicated, assymetrical shape, and put it on his head without hesitating.

Under the headset, Cormen summoned every image of Faero

he could recall: thoughtful, gayly abandoned, flushed with innocent lust, with that odd, pensive smile seen only on the face of a woman joined with her lover. In truth, Cormen did not use the headset much, and he found the side-effects it induced to be most unpleasant. One's limbs felt distorted, the eyeballs felt furry, his scalp crawled, and strange half-visions crawled across the eye of his memory, some obscene, and others incomprehensible.

And as yet nothing had happened. It was taking far too long! He reached up and felt by his right ear, and depressed the interrogate button, sharply, as if to say, "Well? Get on with it!"

A ringing sound told him that the scan was finished. Cormen removed the headset, feeling drugged and distorted. With heavy eyes, he looked at the readout screen on the wall unit as letters swam into view as if floating up from the bottom of a pool of ink, flowing together to form words like some abstract ballet. The words said: IMAGE INVALID.

Cormen thumbed the interrogate button again, and the screen replied:

IMAGE INVALID. NO RECORD OF SUCH ENTITY IN REFERENCE STORAGE. STOP. NO CODE. STOP. REQUEST VERIFICATION, HEADSET NOW RE-SET. STOP.

Cormen spoke a soft oath in a forgotten language. This was an impossible situation. If you were a person, you had to exist. Existing, you could be found and a simula printed on you—even if you were a simula yourself. It was at this exact moment that Cormen, his mind overstimulated by the headset, remembered that Faero had asked him to promise he would not try to find her with the headset/simula procedure. And she did not give her number out. But she had to exist, he knew this. He could remember vividly the way the afternoon sunlight had fallen on them outside, on her brown legs with their faint aureole of golden fine hair, for she did not depilate her body, anywhere. She was the most real person he had ever known.

And without a comm number, he couldn't even call her. How could he find her? He thought, hard, and he felt that somehow there was a reason for him to see her, to go to her, immediately. And in the same moment, it also came to him where he had seen those pictures before, the ones in Faero's house. They had been Nilufer's! Faero lived in Nilufer's house, and Nilufer was gone, after they had met. Coincidence? Cormen struggled with concepts he had only known in viewing works of art. Suspicion, concealed motives; they were alien thoughts. They did not exist in the City-now. Only *there*, in Time. In Art, which was from Time.

He got up unsteadily and went to the communicator, where he dialed in Nilufer's number and followed it by an imperative command that the number of that house be called whatever it was now. After a moment, the screen tried to clear, but it flickered badly, and seemed unable to form a coherent image. But he did catch glimpses of the house, as if the pickup were jumping around erratically. Yes! There was the Peter Gabriel prints, and a quick shot of Faero, face blurred, on her knees on the bed trying to look at him, speaking, moving her lips. But no sound came, only static. And then the screen went blank, and returned to being a mirror.

He knew what to do, although there was no precedent for it. He turned from the communicator and left the house, pausing only to take a night-cape from the coat-closet as he left.

There was a heaviness to the night left over from the day, a tiredness to the air that the sea-winds of the evening had failed to clear; a sullen quality. Along the way, Cormen felt an odd emotion composed of excitement and foreboding. *One does not go to another's house*. He had. And now he was going again, likely into something unpleasant, a thing they did not face. He had no idea at all as to what he might do or what he might find at the house of Faero, the house of Nilufer.

This thought went through his head: *All the suffering, all the worry, all the passions and extravagent acts—those were the legacy of of the Views, which the Arts were connected with somehow, because they dealt with the same things, but with permutated weights and different priorities. But now that part of the Views was intruding into the City, which was immune. Had he and Faero somehow broken some unspoken commandment, by what they had done? It seemed like such a small matter. But now he hurried to her house.*

At the house, all the lights were on, while the other houses were dark, the ones he could see. Either their tenants were now asleep or else the houses were empty. Many were in this quarter, near the sea, in the southwest quadrant of the City. This would be the next place abandoned. Cormen hurried up to the door past the fragrant shrubs and saw that it was standing open and the bright light inside was pouring out. *Wrong, wrong*. He hesitated, but then went in.

Inside, in the living room, nothing. There were some things out of place, but no indication of anyone. He crossed the open space, feeling watched, open, vulnerable. The pile of old pictures was still as he had left them. Faero had not yet thrown them out. In the bedroom there was no one. The bed was rumpled in disorder. Likewise, the bathroom was empty. Cormen started back, perplexed. Something he expected. An empty house left him at loose ends, unaimed, unmotivated. As he rounded the corner, turning from the bath to go back to the short hallway, he saw an untidy scrawl on the wall which he missed before because of the angle. It was written in a pale lipstick and said only, "Tape". It was barely legible. Tape?

Cormen looked about; there was no tape to be seen among the disarray of the bedroom. He returned to the living room and glanced about. There was a reel lying on the floor by the mainframe, next to the composition-section. Normally, a work in progress would be stored by MEC, so there was little need for taped records, but sometimes people used tapes to record references when doing rapid-scans through a time or over an area—things to come back to. This appeared to be such a tape. It would play back through an ordinary reproducer without going through MEC Central. Cormen bent to pick it up and saw a mark on the plastic, a streak of the same pale pink lipstick. He wiped the mark off, and inserted the reel in the player.

The voice began shortly, and it was her voice, but somewhat distorted, as if by an effort to breathe. The voice said, "...I left this to explain....as much as I can. I have to go back to the House of Life, and I thought I could resist, but it is impossible. I know I am going. Only this."

There was a long pause. Then, "...You could not have my call number because I don't have one, and if you tried the headset, you will have found that you can't get me. But I exist! True. There is a way you could have found me, eventually, but it was adjudged my mission would be finished by then. So it was....We all come from the House of Life, all, whatever sort. All alike. Prime and simula. MEC populates the city according to the averaging trends it senses in the requests, and as the trends change, so do the newcomers it makes up and trains. But the Primes are drawn from an ancient repository of records about real people who once lived in the Views. You and I, we were before, perhaps many times. MEC is commanded to ease things, but that things not be too easy, at intervals it puts an odd person into the roster of Primes, to stir things up. Most of these are not successful and return early, causing some change. You are one who did not, but was succeeding, and moreover were on the edge of discovering . . . the true nature of things. MEC knew your requests for data, and had not faced such a situation before. It can judge us only according to the rules it has in it, which are as you told me.

"Primes are not, essentially, under control, so that it had no one it could refer to . . . it made me up to judge you, Cormen. It has a pattern for me, and it set me on life, only to find you and judge you, for outside its competence, only a human who has the knowledge can. This I did . . . and then rescinded my judgement, and said it was the other way. I loved you. And for this, it was rated a flaw, that I was a unit which had failed, and so I am called back. You are safe now, for the while . . . but I am certain it will send another like me to read you again, sometime."

The voice stopped, but he could still hear breathing, very labored. At last, it said, "I wanted very much to stay, but it has become too much. I have to go. But I wanted, I hoped to draw you to my house to find this, that you would know . . . And because Nilufer was so much your friend, I would also have to tell you that she went to make room for me, because the City population can only be so much, and the exemption period expired. I was only a simula, but it held me in status past the normal period of simulas because of what I was to do . . ." It stopped, again, and Cormen thought this might be all. But she coughed, and spoke again, "I wish I could stay to tell you everything, that I could stay and spend a whole life here . . . but I have held out against a Summons for a whole day; I thought perhaps I could beat it, that it might leave me alone . . . not to be so. The coordinates for my image are written in my work-log, above the Mainframe . . . please call for her. She is I, even though she will not remember the sweet things we did . . . do some more with her . . . I . . . It's now. Good-bye." The tape ended.

Cormen dumbly looked in the place she had indicated and found a list of coordinates, date/time, Lat/long. He put the list in a pocket in the cape, absentmindedly. He shook his head.

That was how she caught on so fast; she came into the world with more knowledge than he would ever log in his workbooks, or enough to make up a production, if it was demanded of her. Deghil suspected, sure enough, and also Roxanne. They shared some kind of empathy, perhaps. All that, and he felt a great ache in his heart. Not that he had been spied on, but that he had lost something priceless, forever. Cormen turned from the house and set out for the center of the city as fast as he could walk. He thought that perhaps there still might be time, and that if he could be there, that somehow his being there might help her be free. A sober part of him said in a cold voice that it would make no difference, that MEC would have to take her back because it had given her too much of a headstart. Under the rules that applied to them all, Faero would always prosper. She had too much to start with. No wonder she hadn't gravitated to Embara Park.

The House of Life was a building set near the center of the City, and was severely plain; a simple cubical structure without windows. A tall, narrow door under a plain portico seemed the only additional lines added to it. Most of the time, the people of the City avoided this particular location; one could always go in voluntarily, if circumstances were such. But no one ever came out. That was the way it was. You could only come out once.

Cormen approached the House of Life from its back side, and so could not see the door and the portico over it. At a half-trot, he rounded a corner, and thought he saw a dim figure walking up the steps. He called out, "Faero! Wait!"

The figure hesitated, looking about, but went on up the steps.

Cormen ran now, breath short. All around them, the night was still and empty. At the foot of the steps, he saw a slight girl standing in the half-open door. She looked back, across the City, the plaza, and at last, at him. With a wistful, sad look at him, she turned, and went inside, and the door closed after her, without sound. Cormen stood at the foot of the steps, one foot on the first step, staring at the blank face of an unmarked door which would not open unless he opened it. He was breathing hard, and thought one thought: *We did not even have a chance to say good-bye.*

* * *

The night was late, silent, and the city was empty. Ringing emptiness hung over the City in the still-heavy air. For a long time, Cormen stood at the foot of the steps going up to the House of Life, not thinking, hardly breathing, unable to act. Shreds of past projects and productions echoed in his mind, mixed in impossible conjunctions and now threaded throughout with his own thoughts. Now. Henry Cowell's Eleventh Symphony. An Opera, "The Transposed Heads", Peggy Glanville-Hicks, Moritz Bomhard, Director. Boris Blacher, "Studie im Pianissimo". Carl Orff's Carmina Burana, with Disney animation after the manner of *Fantasia*, matching script by Aleister Crowley (a note: "Dropped—much too demonic, especially the finale, 'Fortuna Imperatrix Mundi'—Cormen") and then, *when the door was closed, all the questions are answered, but the answer cannot be sent back. I could now go there, where she has gone, but it is the silence and the nothingness.* "Gulag", an opera, metamusic, by Modest Moussorgsky, based on Solzhenitsyn, George London, lead, conducted by Leopold Stokowski. (Too long: after ten hours the audience tends toward catatonia and delerium tremens—C). And, *Of what use is it to return and act as if nothing untoward has happened? The best of all conditions, that we became, for a moment, that which we only see in the Views—reality. There is a pain to this that cannot be treated, ignored, or entertained away. An emptiness. If this is love, I do not wonder that we—whoever we are—chose simple lust. Eros can be anagrammed to sore.* (Research note: Even pressed hard by MEC, Moussorgsky remains intractable, producing two or three immense, impossible operas in bunches which tend to occur every fifty or sixty years. For example, "The Warsaw Ghetto", "Dien Bien Phu", etc. Hopeless. The man, even in metamusic, never learns that to create is to know when to stop!) *Aha: when to stop. I have stopped. Something in me has ended. This is—has been—nonsense from the beginning. What was real was us and what we gave freely. I was learning.* Wagner's "Rise and Fall of Adolf Hitler", libretto adapted from Dr. Goebbels' diaries, filmed live at Reichswahn, an open-air theater given over to musical legends of the raging demons of National Socialism. (Note: Must refer to Direct Views of referenced period. This material is so fantastic that it has to be based on some imaginative work of the period—C). Orson Welles playing Baron Harkonnen; Schwartzenegger as Conan. David Janssen as Gilbert Gosseyn. James Caan as Gully Foyle. Stop.

* * *

Cormen slowly turned away, a movement that felt centuries-long, never-ending . . . and began to walk away from the plaza of the House of Life. He did not know where he was going, only that he was going, wherever his steps took him. The clamor in his mind died away, leaving a silence as empty as the city behind it. Cormen walked on.

A soft pearlescent glow was streaking the lower skirts of the sky, but the stars were still shining overhead, Orion ascendant, when Cormen stopped and sat on a crumbled wall and looked back, south, over the city, flowing softly as carpet down to the gentle sea, the tropical waters of the bay. He could sense his favorite view emerging from the darkness—the distant palms of the bay islands—mere sandbars, far out over the water.

Beauty? Beauty was something secret and unknown that translated into exteriors. Now he knew it. A state of the inner person, a balance, an orientation. Desire they had had, but there had been moments of something else for which they now had no name. They shared, however small it had been. And she, the spy in the house of love, had tried to become free of the dream even though she knew the price. She knew. From the beginning.

He stood up. He saw the day spreading in light, the stars fading, the city waiting for him to return and complete what had been started. He felt a wry face forming, something between a grimace and a snarl, a tic that only lasted a moment. Yes—he would complete something. He would splice on the old track, the old curiosity line, and take it up, here, now. *Let it wait forever*. I can walk away from it, and there has to be a place where it can't call me back from. He felt regrets for the things he would not do again: food on request; a girl seen and enjoyed later at his leisure. The undeniable thrill of the forming of a new production. In place of these pleasant knowns he set unknowns: hunger, thirst, perhaps fear. Yes, there would be fear. Death. Not re-entering the House. Cormen shrugged, looked around once, and started out into the north, the future, without comment. It was the unthinkable choice, but something in him had stirred, and demanded that he at least try. He would never know, otherwise.

* * *

But Cormen grew a lot hungrier before he found an answer, and that one did not really answer the question he wanted most to know. It was either a long day, or perhaps two short ones—at times he could not be sure. Leaving the seacoast lands of the city, he had walked some distance through a scrub-covered hinterland of sandy soil and occasional dense tangles of low trees or high bushes. After that, the ground began to rise and an open pine forest took over. He found water, but very little to eat. Wild animals avoided him, but apparently only for reasons of their wildness; there was no sign at all of men or their works.

As the night approached, Cormen began to see fugitive gleams of a single point of light through the trees. It did not waver or move, but it seemed weak and far away. At times he lost sight of it completely. But as it became darker, the light became more easy to follow, and Cormen followed it to whatever it might be.

After many detours, including wading and half-swimming across a sluggish river with a ripe odor of decaying vegetation, Cormen cautiously approached the light, which appeared to be emanating from a translucent fixture of no great size set atop a starkly simple small building. For a time, he remained in the forest and watched carefully, but here, as through the rest of the forest, there was no sign of men, or indeed any form of life. The building was a cylindrical drum supporting an ogive dome, made of a material that looked like plain concrete, but which seemed to have small prisms somehow set in the surface. The grounds about the building were bare: a sandy soil in which nothing grew.

He stepped out onto the open ground, and began walking towards the structure, senses alert. Behind him he thought he heard a low snort, and some motion in the brush, *moving away* and presently fading completely. As he walked onto the bare ground proper, he felt a prickling sensation on his skin, exactly like the feeling of a limb with returning circulation, and tiny bright spots arranged in a hexagonal grid appeared in his vision. He came closer. He thought the sensations odd, but he felt no danger in them.

On this side, there was no door or opening; the drum and dome appeared to be one piece. Cormen began a cautious circle about it, watching carefully all about him. He saw no evidence that anything approached the building. When he had completed half a turn, he found a simple portal on the side facing away from the city, or at least where he thought the city was. There was no latch or handle. He pushed it experimentally with his hand, and felt a sharp pricking, although it seemed smooth enough to the eye. Extending his hand again, now with fingertips extended, he pushed at the door, and it swung open with the least effort, soundlessly.

The inside was a single chamber, not large, as if the walls were extremely thick. Cormen went in. There was a dry, musty odor, a sense of stale air, long undisturbed. Behind him, the door slid shut again. He noticed there was a plain handle on the inside side of it. As for the rest of the interior, it was as bare as the outside, save for a small grille opposite the door and a shiny plate set into the wall material just below it. The ceiling as well was low and featureless. Cormen moved closer to the grille, and when he got within reach of the wall, he again felt the prickling sensation and the spots in his vision. He looked around. The light seemed to have no particular source, and lent an unreal, flat quality to everything.

The prickling stopped, and the grille emitted a single click, which sounded very loud in the chamber. Out of it, a voice spoke. It was clearly the voice of a machine—clear enough, but utterly without expression or variation of tone. It said, "Do you wish to leave the city? If so, depress the plate in the wall, pause, and depart the way you came in. You are authorized. Thank you." After a moment, it repeated the message again. And again. Cormen tried to talk to it, but without result. Whatever this machine was, it did not answer. Somehow he had activated it, which he did not find surprising.

Cormen reached for the plate, and then stopped and asked himself, if he did wish to leave the city. And there, he weighed many things. Still he hesitated; this was reality, so he felt, but it was also powerfully unknown. Into what would the door lead? He pressed hard. There was no sensation of movement to it. He felt a slight shock, and that was all. He withdrew his hand, and said aloud, "Well, nothing changed. The circuits have long since corroded out of existence. So much for this, whatever it is." He listened carefully. There was no sound, just as before. The air was still stale. Cormen walked away, a little downcast. Hungry, tired, thirsty. There was nothing in this empty building but shelter from the outside. At least that. He felt safe. But before he rested, he went back to the door, thinking perhaps to prop it open a little, to let some air in.

When he opened the door, he opened it wide and stared, standing as still as one turned to stone. For outside was no nighted forest, but an enclosed landing, covered by a transparent material, and beyond that, an enormous room, or alley, or canyon. He could not tell. To either side were galleries with safety rails, and rank upon rank of panels. People walked along those narrow ways, many of them engaged in working at the face of the panels, which were covered with lights, switches, knobs, meters and other things he couldn't make out. As far up or down as he could see, in a dim artificial light. Directly ahead, the tremendous open space continued indefinitely, although far away, there was a suggestion of something, a barrier, a series of crossovers. He couldn't see it clearly.

Hesitantly, he stepped into the small chamber. It was almost as bare as the building, but there were some chairs and a plain metal table. To either side there was a narrow door without windows. Cormen sat in one of the chairs, automatically. There was nothing else to do.

He became conscious of a low noise all about him, the hum of energy, of many people, of endless activity. Among the low noise, he heard approaching footsteps on metal, not hurrying, but coming at a good pace. The footsteps stopped at the door, and the door opened. Outside were a man and a woman, of no immediately distinguishing appearance, save that they were rather stocky and short, and also homely. Their expressions were curious. Perhaps friendly, in a neutral sort of way.

The woman spoke, coming into the small room, "Hello. I am Elit. This is Dant. What is your name?"

"Cormen." Her voice had an accent to it, something he couldn't identify, but she spoke confidently enough.

Elit said, "Have you come from . . . the city?"

"Yes. Where am I? What is this?"

Dant now said in a gravelly voice, "For practical purposes, you may think of this place as a sort of spaceship. It is also a . . . ah, a communications nexus, a switchboard device. Yes. Have no fears. You will only be here for a short time. Come with us."

Cormen stood up, and made to follow them. Elit said, "There will be a short walk to your next destination, which will be the world Mola."

"Who are you?"

She answered, "We are your monitors. There is much you will need to relearn. Things here are not as in the city. Does it really still function?"

"Oh, yes. Perfectly, so far as I know."

Elit said, "It would have to, I imagine. The chamber admitted you, and it won't do that unless you're fully human."

"How did you know I was coming?"

Dant said, "We did not know. We were alerted that you had arrived. It was unexpected. There hasn't been anyone for a long time."

They stepped out of the room onto a walkway connecting this section with the far wall. There were rails on the sides, but the drop to either side seemed to have no bottom. Something dim and far away, hazy. Up, it was the same. Cormen said, "You have met others like me?"

Elit turned back to him. "We? In person? Oh, no. Not in our lifetimes. The last one was . . . I think, about three hundred of your years ago, and that one was the first in a long time, too."

Cormen stopped, looked around, and said, "Which is real?"

Dant said, gruffly, but unmistakably warmly, "This is real; that was a dream. People made it, long ago. They liked it so much that they couldn't leave the city—there were others, too. But some left, and we have made a new life among the stars. You will find it hard at first, I think, but if you left on your own, you will survive here. You can go back, if you wish."

"Has anyone?"

"Not to my knowledge."

"What is Mola?"

"A planet, a world . . . a new world we are populating. You will be one of those who builds it. We will teach you what you need to begin."

"And after that . . ."

"You are on your own. Now, attend. We will translocate to Mola Terminal, and then we can begin. First we'll start with language."

"Language?"

"Yes. We speak yours well enough because we learn it just for this task. You speak a language that has been dead and forgotten for thousands of years. Are you ready, now? Then come with us." And together, the three of them made their way across a narrow catwalk towards the far wall, immense, endless, coming closer, and Cormen followed them, slowly at first, a little reluctantly, but with increasing energy as they neared the far wall, and by the time they stepped off the catwalk, they were all talking animatedly and sometimes laughing.

There was another Sobrana at Brasille, and everyone was out, as usual dressed in their most impression-casting clothing. This party was not sponsored by Corymont Deghil and friends, but by a less-subtle group. Still, the level of taste and manners was high. One could contrast this group readily with the amateurs and brash newcomers of Embara Park.

By the serving table, at a lull in the proceedings, two young women happened to meet over a selection of hors-d'oevres. One was tall and statuesque, with flowing dark hair. The other was small and slight, with sharp, crisp features and skin the color of beach sand.

The smaller girl introduced herself as Faero Sheftali, and told the other that she was new, but was learning fast, and that she had already met a number of interesting people and selected some works to review.

The other named herself Nilufer Emeksiz, and also spoke well of this particular Sobrana. She added, "I also have a work I will mention to you that you may view it at your leisure: *Babel-17*, by Sam Delany, done as cinema, animation, after Boris Artzybashieff. Music accompanies, by Spyrogyra. It's really very interesting..."

Faero removed a small notebook from a convenient pocket and wrote down the information, as well as a number which Nilufer gave her. She said, "Thank you. I will try it..." She gave Nilufer, in trade, the index numbers of several sculptors of the early twentieth century, and also Giambologna, specifically referring to his series on the labors of Hercules. And she said, "You look familiar; have we met?"

And Nilufer answered, "I don't think so; but perhaps we saw each other at a distance."

"Yes, that seems likely... And by the way, do you have the call number for that gentleman over there, the one with light hair, wearing the bush jacket and walking shorts? I haven't been able to get near him all evening."

Nilufer agreed and gave Faero the number. After that, they returned to the Sobrana, and not long afterwards went separately to their own houses to sample some of the things they had uncovered on this evening, and to reflect and be thankful that the world never suffered change, that these pleasures, innocent enough, might not ever end. And they also thought that they both were doing extremely well for newcomers who hadn't yet received a billing.

Arsen Darnay

_____ became a writer because he was fed up with all
that crap. Literally. "I started writing Christmas 1973," he
explains, "a desire born of frustrations with my life as a reasonably high-ranking federal bureaucrat; in those days I ran
the nation's solid waste management programs at the federal
level with the Environmental Protection Agency."

Once he began putting words on paper, Darnay was an
almost immediate success. His first effort was a novel, The
Siege of Faltara (Ace, 1978), but the publishing field being
what it is, it was some years before the book was sold and
published. When he had finished it, he reports, "My wife,
Brigitte, demanded that I write something short—just to test
whether I could get something published quickly. I wrote 'The
Splendid Freedom' in something of a rush, enjoying the shift
to a shorter piece. I remember writing it in hotels, on airplanes,
as well as at home. I mailed it to Galaxy for no better reason
than that I viewed Galaxy as the 'best' of the magazines; my
judgements were formed during my science fiction reading peak

*in the later 1950s. The story sold out of the slush pile, and
from then on I've been going at it more or less steadily and
more or less productively."*

"The Splendid Freedom" was published in the September,
1974 issue of Galaxy; Darnay's first appearance in professional print, but hardly his last. From 1974 through 1976, he
was a regular in both Galaxy and its sister magazine, IF, with
the stories that would ultimately earn him his place on the
Campbell Award ballot. When Galaxy and IF fell on hard
times, Darnay had no trouble making the transition to Analog,
the field's leading periodical, and he became a semi-regular
there in 1977 and 1978. More recently, he has been concentrating his efforts on novels. In addition to The Siege of Faltara,
he has published A Hostage for the Hinterland (Ballantine,
1976), and the complex and inventive Karma (St. Martin's,
1978). A Darnay short story collection is long overdue.

The man behind the work is in his mid-forties, and lives in
Hopkins, Minnesota with his wife and three daughters. "We
live on an acre lot with fifty trees, most of which are ancient
oaks." Born in Budapest, Hungary, Darnay came to United
States at the age of fifteen. "I spoke Hungarian, German, and
French before I said my first words in English," he comments,
"but now I consider English my real language." Darnay was
educated in history and political science at Rockhurst College
and the University of Maryland, and dabbled a bit with writing
in his college years, but gave it up for more than a decade
after graduation. "I worked most of my life as an economic
analyst and as a research manager with stints as a federal
bureaucrat and as a corporate middle manager."

Darnay does not consider himself a science fiction writer
per se. "Much of my work has had to do with the future—
forecasting economic and technological events five to ten years
out—which has given me the necessary minimum of understanding to make my writing seem like science fiction to the
casual reader. I am not properly speaking a science fiction
writer at all because my interest is not in science or its ex-
trapolation but more in the human condition today. The science
fiction genre permits one to comment on life and the institutions
into which society is organized without revealing directly where
one's specific inspiration comes from. Like most writers I write
about the things I have experienced in some form or another,
and I find it easy to disguise the experiential skeleton in a
science fiction or futuristic cloak.*

"My interests are in the metaphysical: human development toward higher states, the struggle to awaken from the hypnosis of social programming, the mindless battle of bureaucracy against bureaucracy, ideology against ideology. I am fascinated by the depths of the past and can explore them by transposition into the depths of the future."

All that, and more, is to be found in the tale that follows, which is part fantasy and part SF, a fable of sorts, either from the past or the future, hard-edged and pointed and metaphysical and surreal and . . . oh, forget the labels. Read the story.

GRRM

THE PILGRIMAGE OF ISHTEN TELEN HARAGOSH

HARAGOSH

A Tale from the Pentessence

by Arsen Darnay

I

In my seemingly endless wanderings amidst the timeless documents of antiquity, I have come across another story from the System Demirius, mother of so many records and of such charming tales. This one concerns a successful yet unsuccessful punitive expedition launched from the famous planet against one of its satellites. The central characters are a priest and a patriarch, his superior. Both men were victims and victors at one and the same time—a fusion of concepts which is rather alien to our one-sided culture these days . . . Which prompts me to re-tell the story in translation, basing myself on the incomparably beautiful epic by the poet Abu Bakir Chandra, a number of related historical fragments, and—where details are missing but where telling demands it—the use of my own knowledge of men and times . . .

II

Legends about Demirius abound, but there are only a handful of antiquarians who know anything concrete about the place. The system has been lost from view although it still exists. Numerous agencies claim to be searching for Demirius and other lost realms; scores of volunteer exploration societies are raising money for fleets to find the planet; but accurate information, although available, is not often published. I make no apologies, therefore, for a brief introduction.

Demirius broods somewhere in the galactic Pentessence. By definition the region has an enormously high stellar density; the common laws of astrophysics there are sometimes unaccountably set aside or disturbed by other and still murky rules; travel to Pentessence from the Rim has ever been a risky undertaking promising little profit in the usual sense. These days the motives for rediscovery are dormant and displaced by practical concerns. Hence the agencies search by small, unmanned craft and the benevolent societies, despite fervent appeals for money, seldom raise more than the cost of the appeals themselves.

Demirius' sun is Korizon, a yellow dwarf of the type Pi-4. The system has twelve planets, including Demirius, but the others do not matter particularly in view of Demirius' size and unusual features. The planet is enormous, in girth just shy of a Pi-1 sun. It is a mildly radiating, irridescent sphere of gas of very low density and, upon cursory review, totally unsuitable for human habitation. But Demirius came to be explored and populated, and at the time of this story supported in excess of 1,500 billion people, not counting those perched on its moons.

Demirius has floating islands of enormous, continental extent complete with mountains, oceans, and rich biospheres. Thirty-nine such islands were known, a score or so more suspected, at the time when the Tri-ester wars drew us in and caused a severance with realms in the Pentessence. The islands floating in the higher stratosphere are bleak, empty, unhospitable places. The islands deep within the atmosphere are water-rich but frozen wastes and bathed in a deadly radiation rising outward from the tiny, hot core of the planet where Demirius gathers density and heat in preparation for becoming a sun in its own right and a companion to Korizon in glory.

It may be well at this point to insert reference to an occult doctrine used for symbolical purposes by the poet, Abu Bakir

Chandra, throughout this story. According to the doctrine, Demirius, in the Fifth Dimension, was said to be a conscious personality in process of development; the islands floating in its atmosphere were said to be its still unruly faculties, loosely related but not yet obedient to its hot, radiating core; the monumental storms that rage within the atmosphere of Demirius were said to be the planet's unruly thoughts and emotions; and so forth. According to this doctrine, Demirius itself attracted humanity to live within its gaseous boundaries because it needed the influence of a conscious biomass in its own development—as man needs certain vitamins to grow . . .

But to return: the theories attempting to explain how tectonic plates could float in gas had not advanced very far by the time we lost contact with the system. The islands had stupendous weight and should have fallen in, imploded, to the center. They did not. They floated. And those in the median layer of the planetary atmosphere swam in a peaceful band of gases, rich in oxygen, that separated two zones of extreme turbulence. These islands had paradisical conditions and climates, and it was on these that ships first landed; here it was that colonization began.

One theory advanced to explain the islands of Demirius had to do with the planet's seemingly innumerable moons. There were more than a hundred of them, all sizes, nearly all properly spherical. Forty or so were dense enough to hold various types of atmospheres. A few would be viewed as giant planets in their own right if they were in a system in one of the Rim quadrants rather than in the Pentessence. According to this theory, the islands floated because the moons exercised a gravitational attraction upon unconsolidated structures of a once larger planetary core. The theory stipulated that Demirius had "encountered" what must have been a shepherdless herd of planetary bodies wandering in the Pentessence and had captured them. But the new tides of gravity set up by this meeting had torn parts of Demirius loose from the core and now caused them to sink and float in complex cycles in response to changes in satellitic orbits.

The occult doctrine called the moons "distractions." Demirius had "lusted" after planets of its own and had turned from the eternal contemplation of blazing Korizon to bathe instead in the worship of its hundreds of new admirers. It had thus lost its way in pride and vanity and had interrupted its own development. But the pain of pride had slowly chastened

Demirius; it wished to consolidate itself again. Man's coming introduced a new element, a discontinuity, a measure of consciousness destined ultimately to break Demirius' fascination and thus to help its evolution toward light... But let me now conclude this introduction.

Demirius had an enormously stimulating effect on the people who struck root there. Much the same can be said for other points of settlement in the Pentessence, but Demirius was unique. A dozen great cultures sprang up on as many islands and then spread outward to the moons. These cultures collectively made a sound, a song whose melodies and rhythms still echo hauntingly even now, now that we no longer hear the source. Our own literature, music, thought, religion, fairy tales, and customs carry innumerable traceries of Demirian influence no longer recognized as such. The magnetic power of the cultures, however, was vastly greater before the Tri-ester war. Great waves of migration over several thousand objective years helped to populate the planet; the migrants went to Demirius attracted by its rich, cultural aroma which wafted in dizzying waves throughout the Milky Way.

III

At the time of our story, the Demirian civilization was in full bloom. The planetary cultures on the several floating islands had begun to crystallize but had not yet lost their charm or power of attraction. The greatest of all waves of immigration had yet to roll across space to crash against the planet causing all manner of disturbances (...which some historians claim indirectly caused the Tri-ester war). But at this time cultures were also beginning to germinate on a number of Demirius' moons which had but lately been occupied during a span of a couple of objective centuries. And the story of the priest and of the patriarch is in part the story of a moon and of its planet.

The priest lived on one of Demirius' smallest but most powerful of islands, Tarikafuna, a name which translates into "Suspended in the Grace of Righteousness." The island was ruled by a Directorate of Three, a Committee of Seven, and a Council of 2401 (seven committees of seven squared). The real power on the island, however, was exercised by indirection by a theocracy without official status of which the priest of our story was a relatively low-ranking but disturbingly influential member.

His name was Ishten Telen Haragosh, and his predominant trait was strength of will, an obdurate determination to realize God's will in the realms of manifestation.

He had no sense of humor and hence no tolerance. He lacked all subtlety or suppleness of mind, understood everything literally, and treated all matters as equally important. He felt no pain and hence had no sensitivity to pain in others. He drove himself in matters large and small and knew no boundaries: if the Law said ten, he said one hundred.

He was thin, pale, and his eyes glittered with one-pointed zeal. As a youth he had had contact with a wandering saint, and since then he had been on fire and ceaselessly at work. He seemed never to rest. He never approached but always stormed each task. Others wearied just from watching him. His determination to find and to uproot evil frightened even those secure in virtue and terrified his superiors—men inclined by social role to compromise. All of his opinions—and he had opinions on all matters spiritual and temporal—were based firmly on the most literal interpretations of the scriptures, and he had memorized the scriptures while still only an initiant.

Ishten Telen Haragosh was now thirty years of age, ten years a full-fledged priest, ten years active in the public life of Tarikafuna, and from the viewpoint of the religious authorities he was a growing menace.

His voice could not be stilled; nothing could curb his actions. He had been banished to the continent's remotest reaches only to cause pilgrimages by zealous followers, only to disrupt distant economies. The most onerous assignments had only fed his strength. He had been buried in the kitchens or laundries of monastic orders that practiced perpetual silence, but his writings had continued to screech and his mute protests—including self-flagellation and other extremities—caused anger and conflict in otherwise peaceful havens of prayer. He had a number of small civil wars to his credit. He had burst in on high-level councils of the Brotherhood and of the civil government. Mobs impelled by his oratory had toppled buildings, dug up and reburied corpses, flung his enemies into rivers from high bridges by the score, etc. On one occasion Ishten Telen Haragosh had caused a monumental train wreck by leaping into the path of an approaching express to protest the violation of an obscure dietary rule in the composition of a meal that would be served on board. This is a very partial list. Abu Bakir

Chandra, the poet, goes on at much, much greater length.

The continued actions of the priest, at any rate, threatened the effective, indirect rule of the Brethren of Righteousness on Tarikafuna. And if the hierarchy lost its influence, the secular power would gain preeminence. And if the secular power grew, virtue would tend to wane; and if virtue waned, the people would suffer. The people's suffering would fall most heavily on the children: they would turn hard, cynical, and dissolute. And if the children failed to bloom, the race would become extinct. All this, of course, might take centuries of objective time to come about, but the Brotherhood thought about the welfare of the world in very long frames of time.

IV

Among those who thought about the future was the ancient, venerable Patriarch of Righteousness, a frail, fading man whose shrinking frame seemed as if lit-from within by piety. The Patriarch was patient, long enduring, and filled with an abounding strength of faith. A long life of devotion and spiritual practice had transfigured him in the eyes of others but not in his own eyes. Although he had seen the Creating Ray unveiled, or some claimed that he had, although miracles were common around him, the only gift he truly prized was the power of his prayer.

Prayer so rarely failed to yield answers that the Patriarch had come to fear its efficacy. Whatever the problem he lifted up to the Almighty for solution, a solution was forthcoming forthwith. But the answers to his prayers sometimes took peculiarly novel forms that he himself did not anticipate and sometimes did not wish. He feared to pray fervently because he knew that later he would feel responsibility—and even guilt—for the hard, abrupt, and unsentimental ways in which the Unseen Power sometimes chose to intervene.

"Deep down at a level I cannot reach," the Patriarch was once heard to observe, "there is still a residue of the violent person I once was, and my prayers are sometimes colored by that still unreformed tendency." People smiled when hearing this because no one could recall even a hint of violence in the Patriarch's gentle life and manner.

Fearing his own prayer, the Patriarch had thus sadly watched the havoc wrought by Haragosh over the years. He had *hoped* that the willful, unruly priest would change, but he had never once *prayed* for the priest. The Ray might choose to solve the problem, as It had done on other occasions with other men, by squashing Ishten Telen Haragosh as one might squash an irritating, buzzing insect. The priest might jump before another train and the train might roll right over him this time; he might lead a mob carrying licentious nuns onto a bridge and the bridge might just collapse . . .

The Patriarch also hesitated praying because he viewed the angry priest as the well-deserved scourge of the Brethren of Righteousness and the society the Brethren guided. To pray that the Mighty remove the scourge might be presumption.

But the time came when at last, thinking of the bored and violent children of some future time, the Patriarch decided to pray. He withdrew to a solitary stone hut above the monastic fortress in the side of Mount Battu where the Brethren had their headquarters. Frail and already failing, the old man went up alone, carrying a few days' provisions. And there he prayed for wisdom to know whether to pray for Ishten Telen Haragosh. Some days later he descended again and began to wait.

Tarikafuna spun slowly for some weeks without an omen. Then came news that Haragosh had begun a new campaign. He was causing the slaughter of a species of birds kept as pets by old people. The priest made use of an obscure verse in the Book of Har as his justification.

Hearing this, the Patriarch sighed. He waited for a clear day, gathered provisions again, and once more took the narrow path up amidst crags and mosses to the solitary cell high above the land. Beyond this, Abu Bakir Chandra is silent on particulars. He tells us only that the Patriarch "took the priest between his hands and lifted the sinner up into the presence of the Creating Ray."

V

Whether prayer is believed to work or not is largely a matter of cultural climate. In our own gifted age, those who should know and routinely tell us what to think frown on the practice and link it to a feebleness of mind or a failure of education. Hence I do not urge anyone to believe that the Patriarch's prayer had the desired effect. But quite coincidentally, some days after the Patriarch's return, a man from off-planet visiting

Tarikafuna on some business or another came to Mount Battu and asked to meet with the Brotherhood's senior council. He presented a singular proposition.

The role in this epic of Chief Peerosh Rowka—the visitor's rank and name—is a curiously hazy one. Abu Bakir Chandra emphasizes the fact by describing Rowka as indistinguished and difficult to remember. The clothes he wore, a drab wool suit and a leather hat, suggested some provincial owner or operator from the fringes of civilization somewhere—on or off Demirius. In manner, Chandra says, the chief was "deliberately obscure," but no further explanation for this statement is offered.

His name raised no echoes whatever in the memories of the well-informed senior brothers. But when Rowka said that he was chief of the Nagitta Bandi tribe on Bolond, they listened to him with more keenness of interest.

The brothers knew Bolond as a moon of Demirius politically under the sway of Tarikafuna. Bolond engendered ambiguous reactions. On the one hand it was the world where a one-time Patriarch of great saintliness had been buried at his own request; his tomb had become a site of miraculous events and the destination of occasional pilgrimages. On the other hand, Bolond was the home of certain sects and groups whose doctrines were suspect. "Discords," as they were called, arose on Bolond and clashed with the theological "harmony" the Brethren tried to maintain on the island. (Among these "discords" were the occult interpretations of Demirius' meaning in the cosmic order.) The region Peerosh Rowka claimed to govern was one of the hotbeds of such discords, or so at least the high officials had been led to believe. In practice it was almost impossible to trace these peculiar "influences" back to their source.

For these reasons, Bolond stood in disfavor with the civil authorities of Tarikafuna. The moon had an enviable environment (although its atmosphere was a bit lean on oxygen); it orbited Demirius in a manner that would have made it an ideal trading point with the outside world. (For a number of highly technical reasons that need not concern us here, Time Collapse liners could only land on Demirius with difficulty, and most of the off-system trade took place on moons.)

Despite its advantages, Bolond was closed to trade and tourism. Its population subsisted on agriculture and animal husbandry, its only export being wool. Infrequent contacts maintained a semblance of communications between the moon and Tarikafuna: the occasional pilgrimage to the tomb of Appa Alpha Kom, the occasional supply or trading ship, a tax commission that came to visit every other standard year. But Bolond was isolated by the usual standards of the system. The Brethren of Righteousness made sure that no great mingling between the people of Bolond and the people on the island should take place lest discords overcome the harmony.

It was precisely this matter that Peerosh Rowka came to discuss. His singular proposition came in three parts.

He wanted Bolond's isolation broken and the moon opened up to interstellar trade. If the Brethren consented to arrange that, he promised to undertake the taming of the troublesome priest, Ishten Telen Haragosh.

"But once you have decided to deal with me," he said, making his third point, "you must give me all of your trust. You must believe that I won't do anything unseemly: you mustn't try to interfere with me or with whatever steps Haragosh might take."

The senior brothers heard this and sat in silence for a moment. They were stunned by the novelty of the proposal and Peerosh Rowka's boldness. They thought about the peculiar phrasing the chief of the Nagitta Bandi had used: "taming" the troublesome priest . . . At last the eldest of them roused himself to speech.

"You must understand, Chief Rowka, that we are simply a religious brotherhood. We have nothing to do with bans on trade. For that you must apply to the civil authorities."

"Your prayers are powerful," the chief said. "I ask only for your prayers."

The eldest said; "You have described Haragosh as a 'troublesome' priest. We do not view him in so harsh a light. On the contrary, we see him as a pillar of righteousness, as the conscience of the Brethren, the prod to virtue, the guardian of our morality . . ."

"I am sure that you are right," Peerosh Rowka said. "I have long observed the priest's actions from a distance with wonder. We do not have anyone of his exemplary piety on our little world, and we have in mind attracting him to live on Bolond for a while."

The brothers had a vague sense that they were beginning to comprehend the provincial chief who stood before them. One or two of them nodded sagely.

"You said that we must trust you . . ."

"As my plan unfolds," the chief said, "many rumors are likely to begin circulating on Tarikafuna. Some of these rumors might trouble you greatly. I ask you not to give credence to them and to believe regardless of what you hear that I shall do nothing to dishonor the Brethren of Righteousness."

After the chief's departure, the hierarchs sat together in silence for a while, eyeing one another. At last an inevitably long and sometimes heated discussion began. The brothers were tempted—and troubled. They weighed the risks and benefits of Rowka's proposition. Opening Bolond to intercourse with Demirius threatened the intensification of theological discord. But the "taming" of Haragosh, nay, even his removal from the island—nay, even his temporary absence seemed worth a very high price.

But what guarantee did the Brethren have that Peerosh Rowka would succeed where so many other worthy men had failed? And what precisely would the odd chieftain do? None of these elders wished to purchase the assassination of the troublesome priest under some guise of words. They were all serious and responsible men with much experience of the world, but they were more concerned, ultimately, with the Ultimate. They decided to lay the matter before the Patriarch for his decision.

The Patriarch received them propped up in his bed. A slight fever had put him low. He listened distractedly, seeming absent and in pain. At last he lifted a very limp, pale hand and gestured.

"Let him go ahead," he said, speaking of Peerosh Rowka. "Do what he asks you to do."

He said this long before the entire matter had been laid before him and long before even a portion of the argument for and against the action had been presented. In the corridor outside the patriarchal bedchamber, one senior brother said to the other as they were leaving side by side:

"Alpha must have prayed about the matter."

"So it appears," the other one said. "So it would seem."

VI

Several weeks later, Bolond's isolation was lifted by the combined action of the Council of 2401, the Committee of Seven, and the Directorate of Three. The moon received a trading franchise and permission to build an interstellar spaceport at an ap-

propriate location; "appropriate location" was not further defined. The legislation passed rapidly and without fanfare. The
secular authorities had long ago identified Bolond as a very desirable trans-shipment point; they had kept the moon in isolation
only in deference to the Brethren of Righteousness; when the
Brethren hinted that Bolond might now be given more freedom,
action was swift.

The mad priest Haragosh heard nothing about this action.
The transaction was buried in small print and the Press Lords
were asked to keep the matter as obscure as possible. Quite
independently of the Brethren of Righteousness, the Directorate
judged that Haragosh might disapprove of the action and might
be tempted to make Bolond into the center of yet another of
his virulent campaigns against the worldly authority. At present,
fortunately, Ishten Telen Haragosh was still preoccupied with
birds.

And, indeed, he was. Haragosh travelled from town to town
these days accompanied by a small band of fanatic disciples
preaching against certain species of colorful birds older people
kept in cages as pets. He used as his justification two verses from
the Book of Har—4:18–19—which stated:

> They sigh and roll their eyes in illusory preoccupation with
>   winged creatures and miraculous effluvia from tombs,
> Neglecting all the while the most rudimentary of practices of
>   justice, hope, and kindliness.

Now these verses had been written by Malamati Vagyok
Har some hundreds of objective years earlier. He was chastising
a popular religious movement of his time centered around the
worship of angels and pilgrimages to the tombs of men and
women reputed to be saints. The last thing the inspired Har
had had in mind when writing of "winged creatures" was caged
birds, of course, but Haragosh believed that the Creating Ray
personally spoke through the scriptures; Its sacred words were
for all times, not for a particular time; they had to be applied
to whatever sin had established itself in the public. Har might
have meant angel worship, but the Ray meant all winged creatures.

You must imagine Haragosh on his current campaign. He
travelled on foot, and barefoot, leading a small caravan of old
buses and jeeps wherein his immediate disciples followed—
"crept" is a better word—at snail's pace behind. The priest's
reputation went ahead of him, and as he approached settle-

ments, villages, and towns, righteous citizens met him at the border carrying caged birds of all sizes, colors and species. The citizens were usually solidly middle-aged and grim in countenance, hoping to convey by their facial expression the outrage they had felt—still felt—at having discovered these dread, feathery creatures in their aged parents' or children's possession. They had already found these symbols of iniquity and held them now awaiting the great saint's judgment and orders.

Haragosh came, thin, dusty, wearing rough, canvas culottes and a canvas jacket. Suspended from a chain around his neck hung a much worn copy of the Book of Har. His eyes gleamed with the fever of his zeal. He almost always stopped, held out his arms toward the crowd, and cried: "Behold the tempters to iniquity"—or words to that effect. Then he sank to his knees and inclined his head down, gazing through miles of rock toward the angry, hot center of the planet Demirius where he tended in his mind to localize the Deity, and fell into silent prayer. Sometimes he voiced his entreaties and hence we know that he prayed for strength in the renewal of the great struggle he faced. It was a struggle against the demons in the birds, of course, not against social resistance: the people were firmly in his hands.

The great hush which fell upon the crowd and Haragosh's own disciples at this moment tended to be marred and polluted only by the innocent chirps and warbles of the stupid birds, which had failed in their life by being caught and caged in the first place and now faced their last ordeal.

Then came the spectacle. The priest's disciples chose the proper site for the holocaust: a large, square playing field, an appropriate pasturage adjoining the settlement. There the ragged, dusty caravan settled.

The exercise took up two nights and a day and was usually well attended. Haragosh's disciples erected tents wherein they slept. The priest did not need shelter because he did not sleep at all during these struggles of exorcism. Once a pyramid of cages had been built in the center of the playing field or square—the townspeople building and the disciples directing the action and counting (statistics had to be kept)—Ishten Telen Haragosh mounted a narrow platform on top of a pole (the item was carried strapped to the roof of one of the buses during transitions). From that peculiar perch, neither eating nor drinking, but shifting his weight from left foot to right foot and back again at half hour intervals, the priest spoke unceasingly for a night, a day, and another night. His endurance was legendary, and even those who were in no way moved by repentance for the settlement's unholy traffic with winged creatures came to see him and then returned again, having eaten and slept and eaten again, and marvelled that the saint, all this while, had stood there preaching and shifting his weight on that sliver of a board above the crowd.

What Ishten Telen Haragosh said is no longer preserved, but those very few who in every village drank in the entirety of his immensely long sermon became his lifelong disciples and professed to have had their lives changed at the root.

The last night saw the greatest of crowds, because at the midnight hour, when the priest's harangue reached its hoarse climax, the disciples pushed toward the pyramid of cages a small trailer with a tank on top (a part of the caravan). Then a volatile liquid was hosed over the panicking birds—disciples working a large manual pump with handles that moved up and down like a seesaw. At last a torch was handed up to Ishten Telen Haragosh. And the priest, delivering himself of curses and commands against the demons still presumably harboring in birds, with a magnificent gesture—long afterwards remembered and recalled in every community—threw the torch (see it arching, sparkle-shedding, turning end-to-end) to ignite the pyramid. A whoof as the ill-smelling, volatile liquid exploded. A ball of flame and a blast of heat subsiding into a raging conflagration. Ishten Telen Haragosh, near collapse but still up there, swaying, silhouetted against the fire . . . Thus ended each struggle in this slow, hard, and bitter war.

It may be remarked in conclusion that every now and then an old woman, sometimes two or more, would in a frenzy of grief run into the infernal pile of burning cages to rescue some beloved pet; and sometimes relatives were not quick or courageous enough to prevent the ultimate sacrifice.

VII

The above rendition of the priest's crusade understates his impact by portraying the struggle in a slightly humorous manner. There was much more to it—there is always much more to everything than an account can ever encompass. The crusade was divisive, fanned all manner of delusions, and reverberated darkly in the collective memory of each settlement. And so forth.

The cultural background needs also to be covered by a footnote for readers of our time. It is no longer popular to maintain that a planet's own life and personality influence the cultures that take root on its surface. We have again returned to the comforting but, to me, untrue belief that planets and suns are mere aggregations of mindless energy and that we live on and among such bodies essentially free of other than their gross manifestations of gravity, radiation, atmosphere, pressure, etc. But the culture of Tarikafuna—which swooned so readily under the tongue-lashings of a Haragosh—can only be understood by understanding Demirius itself, a dark and moody planet engrossed in the passionate enjoyment of its seemingly worshipping moons. It vainly believed that the splendid light of its satellites was the reflection of its own, hot core.

The people who had initially settled Tarikafuna and the other floating continents had been urban sophisticates all, distinguishable from the masses of our present-day cities only by a longing for the adventure attending the conquest of "new" planets. It required only a matter of a year or two before those landing on Demirius became quite other women and men. And those who doubt me have never changed planets but are mere readers of books.

VIII

Ishten Telen Haragosh campaigned in the plains of Tarikafuna in what was conventionally defined as the western extent of the inhabited portion of the island. His plan called for an eventual turn to the cities of the east, but this plan he never carried out.

It came about that on the first day of the priest's crusade in the small town of For-du-lat a young man appeared amidst the crowd assembled in the town's market square. Outwardly he resembled the man who had sent him. He wore a baggy woolen suit and a greasy leather hat. Unlike Peerosh Rowka of Bolond, the young man had a sparkling personality, lively eyes, a ready tongue. He came bent under the weight of a long pole to one end of which had been nailed a narrow platform. Around his neck hung a seven-stringed, deep-bellied instrument called the ballazat.

The young man soon made known his intention. He wished to entertain the people from the top of the pole he had brought along. The people tried to ignore him at first, but there were in the crowd some young people who thought it might be fun to oppose the grim preacher on his pole. They ran off and came back with a posthole digger; they set to work energetically even as Ishten Telen Haragosh continued to preach while observing the disarray in a portion of the crowd.

The priest's disciples left off collecting money and rushed to the scene of disturbance. They tried to stop the raising of the rival pole, but the young people of For-du-lat had already taken a liking to the cheerful stranger with the ballazat. There were some arguments and, at the end, some shoving and pushing, but the town's inhabitants prevailed, the pole was raised, the young troubador climbed up, stood on the platform, and after tuning his ballazat began to sing a funny ballad in a clear voice that carried far.

The crowd was not sure how it should react. Some were angry and tried to shush the singer. Others laughed at the song. The disciples yelled protests from a safe distance. The birds in the pyramid of cages chirped in alarm. Ishten Telen Haragosh continued to preach as if nothing had transpired, but his spontaneous harangue now faltered a bit because he did not have the crowd's whole-hearted attention.

Now the young troubador was a very able entertainer. Before much time had passed, he had gained the crowd's allegiance. His songs were funny and caused feet to tap. He was there to poke fun at the priest and did a good job. When he imitated the priest's manner, especially the priest's shifts of weight from one foot to another, the crowd rolled with laughter. Gradually those few who still felt attached to Haragosh separated from the rest and formed a grim-faced circle around the priest's pole. Haragosh addressed them only. The rest of the assembly turned toward the troubador like iron filings around a new and more powerful magnet.

The priest now had an attentive audience again. It was much smaller, but nonetheless all his. And consequently his oratory again became more fiery. The zeal that had been temporarily cooled by the troubador's disruption once again blazed into flame. He preached against the sinfulness of For-du-lat with an eloquence fed by anger, and as he grew more heated, he singled out the troubador for verbal thrashing. It must have come to him that no young strummer blown into town by the

ill winds of karma could possibly command attention as long
as an old, seasoned campaigner like himself, and so at one
point—waiting first for a lull in the troubador's singing before
he spoke so that all could hear him—he cried out:

"Let the young cur strut and strum and poke fun at a man
of God. I shall be upheld and justified as you shall see. It may
be easy to turn the heads of the thoughtless and lascivious for
an hour's spell or so, but I shall stand here witnessing to the
Creating Ray long after that young dog slinks off to his corner
with a tail between his legs."

"Oho!" cried the troubador. "I think I hear a challenge from
the mighty killer of birds. Well, people, you deserve an answer.
So long as the preacher can preach, I can sing. And I shall
stand here and warble like a bird an hour after that scarecrow
has fallen from his preaching perch."

Then the troubador proposed a wager. If he could stay up
on his platform longer than the famous priest, so well known
for his saintliness and powers, then let the birds yonder be
saved. And if he fell from the pole before the priest, let them
be burned. Haragosh did not respond to this proposal, but the
crowd assumed that the bet was on. And thus began one of the
most interesting contests ever staged in the small settlement
of For-du-lat.

IX

The contest lasted six days and the nights between, and in the
end the priest collapsed and fell from his perch into the arms
of his disciples. The troubador stayed up for half a day longer
and sang like a bird. The pyramid of cages was taken apart
again and each pet returned to its owner. Haragosh cursed For-
du-lat on leaving the settlement with his diminished band of
followers. After a long and animated celebration of his victory,
the troubador vanished, and those of Haragosh's disciples who
had thought to attach themselves to the troubador's cause were
left without a master.

It would be fun to tell the story of the contest, but it is not
of central importance to the tale. But there was one episode
during the fifth and last night that needs relating. The two
contestants still stood atop their poles, each doing what he had
been doing all along. Five or six people remained below, those
men of For-du-lat who had made the largest side-bets on the

outcome, waiting and watching. Then the troubador seemed to rouse himself from sleepy plinkering on his deep-bellied ballazat; in a clear voice he announced that he had composed a ballad to the great priest Haragosh and would now sing it.

The priest had been in a sort of trance babbling an incoherent mixture of scripture and exhortation. Hearing his own name aroused him and he began to listen to the song.

The ballad was a scurrilous recounting of the priest's long career of causing mayhem in the name of righteousness. The troubador revealed an uncanny knowledge of the priest's activities, but he portrayed them in the most unsavory light possible. Anger roused the priest to a high state of alertness so that he distinctly heard and understood the final stanza.

In that final stanza the troubador let it be known that Ishten Telen Haragosh, in spite of his devotion to the service of Righteousness, had the brain of a *tagad* (a large but very stupid Tarikafuna reptile). He attacked the people's minor pecadillos while great crimes against the Ray and its prophets were nurtured right beneath his nose. The last two verses of the ballad, translated freely, ran as follows:

> While birds he burns in dusty towns on this fair island's western plains,
> Heretics are desecrating Appa Alpha Kom's good grave on far-away Bolond . . . on far-away Bolond.

X

After his humiliation in the town of For-du-lat, Haragosh marched directly to the next town on his route intending at that point to continue his crusade. He had rested only briefly after his ordeal, and the full meaning of his defeat had not properly penetrated his awareness, or so we must assume.

But when in the next town along his route the people not only failed to greet him but actively opposed his crusade—a young woman of his following received a broken collar bone for her troubles—the priest awoke to his dimena.

He reasoned, we assume, that the Creating Ray was trying to send him a message, and the time had come to listen, at last. He sent his caravan east again and withdrew with a few of his disciples into a nearby area of wilderness to ponder his problems.

Nothing is known about the priest's thoughts or actions during this withdrawal. The area where he stayed is volcanic and pestilential; fumes rise from fissures in the ground and the region is always covered by a nasty smog of Tarikafuna's own making. Korizon's light plays odd tricks in the spumes and columns of stinking steam and fume. It is a region well suited to the contemplation of the satanic forces which had suddenly interrupted the preacher's career. He communed with Demirius, no doubt, praying with his eyes down to the ground as was his habit.

Two or three weeks after his withdrawal, Haragosh sent his most trusted helper east, a young lady whose observations of a later episode we shall recount. We do not know what impelled the priest to seek information from the Capital, but it is safe to guess that the troubador's ballad had struck him, especially the last two verses of the final stanza quoted above. Was it really true that heretics were desecrating Appa Alpha Kom's tomb on Bolond? The trusted helper went to get an answer to this question, or so the poet Chandra claims.

XI

Let us now shift our perspective to the capital and the time to some weeks hence and observe how Ishten Telen Haragosh burst on the scene again with his new crusade.

His disciples came ahead with a marvelous story. An angel had visited Haragosh in the town of For-du-lat. The angel had chastised the preacher for neglecting his duty before God and Man. Haragosh had preached against small demons while a grown-up devil stalked the land with opposition. But in Its grace the Ray had seen fit to warn the priest. He was on his way now; he came on foot, wrapped in great chains to the ends of which were welded huge weights symbolizing the world's iniquity. And he vowed to carry those weights until the current evil was totally and ruthlessly eradicated.

The disciples would not divulge what the current evil was. And since they spent a standard month preparing the preacher's way, the people were consumed with curiosity by the time Haragosh appeared at the outskirts of the capital complete with chains and weights. A large crowd appeared to greet him, but he stared right through the people with his blazing eyes and said not a word until he stood on the steps of the Parliamentary

Palace. Beneath him stood a mob greater than any yet assembled; the people were a tide covering the ground, filling the park, spilling from the windows of nearby buildings, even hanging in clusters from a crane some distance from the palace that stood above a half-completed structure. And Haragosh waited, waited . . . watching the waves of excitation pass over the people. And doubtlessly this great assembly, making a rushing sound as great crowds do, reassured him. He was on the right path once again. How could it be otherwise?

At last, with tremendous effort, he raised an arm heavy with the artificial weight that hung from it by a chain. Then he opened his mouth and launched his last campaign.

Abu Bakir Chandra paints a frightening, confusing, and violent picture of the pandemonium the priest unleashed. Haragosh's crusade coincided with a time of economic depression on Tarikafuna and the people were ready for distraction. They embraced his cause by tens of millions, demanding that a war be launched against Bolond, the desecration of Appa Alpha Kom's tomb be stopped, and the saint's remains be transferred to Demirius immediately.

We shall not attempt to recreate the picture—mob scenes, ritual burnings, funerary marches, the burning of certain trading centers, the stoning of the homes of certain members of the Committee of Seven, etc.—and merely say that the government was sorely pressed and turned with unusual anger to the Brethren, demanding that they curb the priest. During several secret meetings, the senior brothers managed to suggest to the embattled government how the problem might be dealt with. The civil leaders promised to cooperate one more time, promised to endure the riots and disturbances for the last time, promised to see this crisis through to conclusion despite the very high political cost, but they strongly hinted that any subsequent outbreak of trouble would inevitably lead to a severed relationship between church and state.

The Brethren were chastened and humbled, but they had succeeded in arranging for the priest's departure.

The idea for a private expedition to Bolond came to the priest in due time—either by his own inspiration or by way of indirect suggestion spread by agents of the government. Once the idea surfaced, Haragosh found it astonishingly easy to implement. Money poured in, much of it from very rich, anonymous admirers of Appa Alpha Kom. Volunteers with the right training came in droves. Surplus military and other equipment came on the market as needed. It seemed as if the Creating Ray itself favored an invasion of Bolond by a mercenary army under the generalship of Ishten Telen Haragosh.

And so it came about that a bare three standard months after he marched into the capital chained to several stupendous weights, the priest's crusade against Bolond stood ready to launch.

XII

The expedition was composed of three craft. Two of these were large military landers capable of carrying troops and equipment. One was a small, fast command vehicle. All three ships were hermaphroditic in design, able to fly both in space and in atmosphere. In other words, they were not very attractive in appearance because each carried levitron jacketing for gravitational buoyancy. The levitron technology has long passed into obsolescence and the reader may need help visualizing this small punitive fleet: the ships were sausage-shaped. Girding each sausage was a huge doughnut of levitron tankage filled with the distillate of the levitating flower, *Lacrema veni*. These craft in no way resembled the Time Collapse liners of either our time or theirs.

After some weeks of lumbering travel, these ships landed on a large, flat plain of Bolond, amidst an ocean of sheep, not far from Rabia, the stronghold and settlement of the Nagitta Bandi tribe. Tribal shepherds presumably carried news of the invasion to Rabia and the chief's court.

Bolond was a tiny world compared with the nearby and gigantic Demirius. Demirius was faintly visible even by day, and for more than half of every standard month its huge, brooding visage occupied nearly the entirety of the sky, jealously watching the moon, its shadow hiding the splendor of Korizon, its faint luminescence providing reluctant light. But Bolond, like Demirius, circled in the Pentessence where there is never a shortage of solar radiation from some source and where, during Bolond's two kinds of night, ten thousand stars shone not like the pinpricks of light to which we are accustomed out here in the Rim, but like huge, brilliant wheels of glory.

As the punitive column set out toward Rabia, it moved exceedingly slowly. Haragosh led the way on foot, as was his habit, and his movements were hampered both by the chains and weights he carried and the unusual atmosphere of this moon which was heavy with helium and light with oxygen. Troops, officers, and disciples, of course, wore supplemental breathing gear, but Ishten Telen Haragosh refused all artificial aids. He was resolved to face Chief Peerosh Rowka—long since pinpointed as the enemy—as an equal in every way.

The chief of the Nagitta Bandi thus had ample time to prepare his defense. The troops and unit leaders soon grew anxious. Tribesmen came and went, observing the slowly creeping column. They used small, fleet vehicles, some wheeled, some floating on levitron; they came sometimes on foot and sometimes riding peculiar, six-legged beasts that carried two tribesmen each and ran more sideways than ahead. The tribesmen kept their distance but came close enough to the column so that the troops observed the hard, fierce faces of these scouts and also saw that the enemy was well armed with modern weapons.

Despite urgings that he ride a jeep so that an attack could be launched before all tribesmen on Bolond had assembled at Rabia, Ishten Telen Haragosh kept walking. He made a pitiful picture, forcing and dragging his emaciated body along, sucking great draughts of air from Bolond's deficient atmosphere, his face distorted with pain. But his eyes burned with inner certainty, and he promised to all doubters a great victory.

The invading fleet had landed imprecisely so that five days passed before Rabia appeared on the horizon, a flat sort of settlement in this flat sort of region, nothing to look at, at least from a distance of some kilometers, and noticeable from afar only because a communications structure—all wires, cables, and such—hovered above the town and stronghold supported on a grid of levitron piping. The structure brought to mind an empire of cobwebs and reflected light.

Another day's march brought the party to Rabia's edge. Here the priest ordered a halt, awaiting Rabia's surrender, one supposes. At close proximity, neither town nor the walled but flimsy-looking stronghold in its center appeared in any way threatening. Surrounded by its dome of ionic shielding, the invading army felt secure. The settlement was evidently not engaged in preparing a defense, and there were no signs that any large bodies of tribesmen had assembled and waited.

The following morning Haragosh rose from the worn blanket which, laid on bare ground, constituted his only concession to luxury. Then he ordered his officers to attack Rabia, to take the stronghold, and to capture alive the chief of the tribe presumed to be within.

Now this battle turned out to be a curious affair. Technically speaking it took place in daytime, but in fact Korizon was not in the sky that day. By reason of the moon's orbit around its planet, Bolond fell into Demirius' shadow that standard day. The scene was bathed in a peculiar twilight of reddish hue—Demirius' normal emanation—but according to reports of eyewitnesses, the planet glowed that day with an unusual intensity, hot and bothered, as it were. And according to the poet Abu Bakir Chandra, whose accounts I've followed closely all along, unusual weather systems on Demirius conspired that day to lend the huge rotundity of the planet the semblance of a face; clouds and storms formed a grim mouth, flared nostrils, and a single glowing eye by which Demirius witnessed events below.

(Abu Bakir Chandra hints that these outer signs of the planet's participation in the battle depicted in his poem are but symbolic of a deeper reality. He means that Demirius may have had a perfectly ordinary appearance that day but nonetheless was consciously watching. A kind of mysticism, this, which exercises on me a strange fascination but which I would not think of urging on anyone except parenthetically.)

The scene, at any rate, was murky with a reddish tint; a scene, as it were, illuminated by a conflagration. The priest's small army deployed for the attack, a hundred or so armored, shielded, heavy but levitron-lifted and jet-propelled combat cruisers. They ringed two thirds of Rabia, beam-guns aimed at the outermost row of houses, it having been decided to vaporize these at the outset as a sign of serious intent and then to move in, converging on the stronghold. And in the event of resistance, the plan called for merciless and full-force ionization of the enemy provided that the opposition lacked shielding, as seemed the case. And if shielding interfered, the cruisers' chemical and mechanical weaponry would be used to dig the tribesmen from their nests and to roast or choke them as they fled.

Growling over the radio channel, Haragosh at last gave the order to commence the action.

Although there had been ample time for such things, the army had undergone no training either on Demirius or on Bolond. The mercenary officers hired for the expedition were all of junior rank and had not pressed Haragosh to order exercises.

Thus neither equipment nor troops had been tried in simulated combat. The order to attack was promptly obeyed nonetheless, but it was followed by shocked surprise when all but half-a-dozen of the beam guns failed to fire, illustrating either that the tribesmen were lucky or that it's hazardous to go to war with untested surplus equipment obtained at bargain prices.

For a moment panic reigned as thought of betrayal and disaster flashed through the minds of the invaders. The reputation of the Nagitta Bandi tribe for gifts of sorcery, and the Demirian mentality's proneness to accept such rumors at face value, did not help much either in that moment. Several cruiser leaders broke from the encircling line ready to flee to the security of the spaceships and rapid orbit. Elsewhere men scrambled frantically on top and beneath cruisers to pinpoint and to fix the malfunctions. Most cruiser crews simply sat in frozen expectation of *something*.

Then Ishten Telen Haragosh growled curses over the radio. "Move out, faithless scum! Attack! Do you think we need the beams when the Ray itself's our weapon?"

His voice broke the spell of panic. Rabia lay silent and inactive in the shifting red light with but a few gaps in its first line of houses. Cruisers with functioning beam guns levitated and moved forward; the rest of the army followed. All cruisers had quickly articulated chemical guns and fired shells wildly in all directions creating an infernal din, bright explosions, and soon fires, and this continued until Haragosh ordered the firing to stop.

The vehicles sank to a halt outside the flimsy stockade-style walls of Rabia's stronghold and gate. His voice amplified electronically, the priest thundered a demand of surrender at the unimpressive three-story structure beyond the wall. And when this demand did not suffice to cause the gates to be thrown open, Haragosh ordered the stronghold taken by force.

Now we come to the most curious part of this battle, if a battle it may be called. On entering the courtyard, the attackers found but a handful of silent tribesmen, but great stores of very sophisticated weaponry of all types, including formidable beam guns mounted on platforms on the inner side of the flimsy stockade. Those few among the mercenaries who knew weapons well blanched at the thought that these light cruisers had attacked an objective so well defended or at least so well equipped. These guns, had they been manned and used, could each at a single burst render five or six of the attacking cruisers into pools of smoking metal despite the shielding. Truly Har-agosh fought with God's connivance and support. Why else had the tribesmen abandoned such military treasures and shied from an engagement with so weak an attacking force?

Let me now wind up the account of this battle. Chastened by the display of weaponry yet encouraged by the absence of defenders—the few tribesmen on the premises were soon in chains—the soldiers ranged over the stronghold until they found in a half-hidden loft room the man Haragosh was sure had fled—the chief of the Nagitta Bandi, Peerosh Rowka him-self.

The priest learned of the chief's discovery in the courtyard. He forced his chain-and-weight-laden body up three flights of stairs to the tower where his enemy had tried to hide from the wrathful eyes of justice. He found Peerosh Rowka in a room filled almost entirely with songbirds in cages.

XIII

Now Ishten Telen Haragosh was not a man much given to doubt, but the battle for Rabia had not been what he had expected. His officers explained to him the significance of the guns found in the courtyard, which made him uneasy. He felt a sense of disappointment and dissatisfaction and harbored perhaps a faint suspicion of ridicule somewhere, somewhere hidden; a feeling no doubt suggested by Peerosh Rowka's birds.

Be that as it may—and at this point we have no documen-tation to support our speculations about the priest's thoughts and feelings—Haragosh sent cruisers to roam all about the region searching for large assemblies of tribesmen, armies, castles, fortifications, whatever. Patrols of men on foot went into Rabia itself to search houses and to interrogate the people. And a strike force stayed behind to act as seemed appropriate.

Nothing.

The people of Rabia acted—well, as friendly as might be expected from a population that had been subjected some hours earlier to haphazard bombardment. Damage there was, but no one seemed to have been killed.

Out in the land, the searching cruisers found many, many flocks of sheep under small groups of fierce shepherds.

Nothing. The region appeared calm, pursuing what seemed

to be its usual pursuits. Only Demirius glowered suspiciously, shedding an unusually red light.

In their patrolling, the cruisers failed to notice the almost total absence of any activity that might have shown a spaceport under construction.

In a word, nothing.

XIV

It appears that Haragosh was angered by the news that his scouts and patrols brought back. His attack had not been taken seriously. Presumably he might have accepted either of two rejections by the enemy—active opposition or abject surrender. But it did not please him to find the Nagita Bandi tribe engaged in simple living and in what appeared to be hostile indifference to the armed visit from the father planet. He could not believe that he was seeing all there was to see. Something was hidden, but there was no sign of what. His patience evaporated by evening, and he ordered Peerosh Rowka brought to him for questioning.

Why had he waited so long? Perhaps he had an intuition that Peerosh Rowka wouldn't talk.

The priest's most trusted disciple left behind an account of the interview between the priest and the tribal chief; one of the very few records that give some hint about the nature of Rowka's character. Rowka was a short little man, described as "dumpy" by the disciple. He wore a rumpled, lumpy, woolen suit patched carelessly here and there. The disciple—writing years after the event—was still troubled by Rowka's seeming stupidity; the chief struck her both then and in retrospect as a very unlikely tribal chief and altogether the wrong man for winning an intersystem trading franchise. He had about him none of the poise, bearing, aura, or "magnetism" the disciple apparently associated with a saint. Peerosh Rowka struck her as a "fool"; he spoke in a blubbering, peculiarly incoherent way so that he seemed always to be saying something intelligent and profound, but his listeners, after an initial sensation of having understood, were left uncomfortably empty and uncomprehending—a "maddening" experience for the disciple and also for her master, Haragosh. Rowka also seemed to be hard of hearing. He constantly caused the priest to repeat his questions, saying, "Eh? Eh?" and cupping a hand behind his ear, and at these times the chief's face took on what the disciple recalls as an "astonishing depth of stupidity."

The interview took place in the light of improvised torches; there had been an electrical failure that took a long time fixing because none of the captured tribesmen seemed to know anything about the utilities of the stronghold. At first the room was filled with the priest's mercenaries and disciples who formed a circle around the priest and the chief. Later, as Haragosh failed to get meaningful answers from the chief, his rage turned on his audience, and he sent the people out, chased them angrily from the room cursing their whisperings and constant movement. The disciple whose record I am summarizing was permitted to stay only because she held one of the torches.

The absence of onlookers did not improve results. Not that Rowka refused to talk. He answered every question—at length. But as the sound of his voice faded, so did the meaning of what he had said, leaving behind that sense of frustrating emptiness already mentioned.

Ishten Telen Haragosh lost his temper time and time again, began to shout, tried to gesticulate (but found, of course, that chains and weights restrained him). Then he forced himself back into a semblance of control and with an icy tone repeated his question. "Eh? Eh?" the chief would counter, his face a bottomless mirror of imbecility. The question again. "Eh?" Hand cupped about the chief's ear. Haragosh trembling in an effort to curb his rage. The question for the third time. Then came the answer at last, a blubbering of words that satisfied something deep within the listener ("I was never quite the same person again after that bizarre interrogation," the disciple writes), but with a meaning so unstable that the hungry intelligence, having seemingly fed, found itself again starved when the answer was done and only the uneven sputter and crackling of improvised torches could be heard in the room full of jumping shadows.

And so it went. At last came the point which the disciple describes as "the turning point of my life." Haragosh lost all control over himself. His thin, long face chalky and rigid, his zealot eyes took on an altogether insane intensity, and with a sound which was a scream like canvas rending, he raised his chained and weighted arms, and with fingers spread for choking, he threw himself toward the chief. But now the chief— and it was his action that plunged the torch-bearing disciple into another style of life—gave forth a very peculiar whine of fright, fell to his knees, and then on all fours scurried swiftly past the disciple—so swiftly and with such animalistic movements that the disciple recoiled in terror and in the process singed her hair—and hid beneath a large, heavy table. And from there continued to issue spine-chilling whines and snarls and growls, so lifelike and so very suggestive of a dangerous but indistinct wild beast that no one in the room dared to move until, suddenly, and without the agency of any of the expedition's electricians prowling in the basement, the lights came on again.

XV

Much, much, much later that night, Ishten Telen Haragosh awoke from a sleep of utter exhaustion. A wind had risen, a strong, persistent wind. It whistled eerily as it passed through the electronic spiderweb structure levitating above the stronghold. Then steps stumbled up the stairs in haste, the light burst on the room, and in the door stood one of the disciples with shock on his face.

"He has escaped," the disciple said, whispering. He whispered because he had ascended the stairs so rapidly that his breath was gone.

"How?" the priest asked. "How is it possible—"

"Come and see."

The priest rose, lifted his weights, and forced his body to follow his will down.

On the bottom level the odors of hydrocarbons, burned feathers, and roasted flesh still lingered. The loft room had been emptied; the "winged creatures" of the Book of Har would fly no more. The two men did not linger. They went down farther to the bottom-most level of the basement where the prowling electricians had discovered a jail full of barred cages the evening before and where Chief Peerosh Rowka had been placed after his interrogation.

Down below they came upon a busy, crowded scene. Four of the five mercenaries who had been assigned to guard the chief in his cell lay side by side. Next to them squatted the expedition's four medical experts taking readings with bioenergetic instruments and aural probes. The four guards were well enough, but blind. The cell where Rowka had been locked was surrounded by a clump of soldiers and disciples. They parted when the priest arrived to show him a gap in the bars just wide enough to let a small, dumpy man step through. The heavy metal bars seemed to have been vaporized by very high-intensity energy. Inside the cell two disciples, including the lady whose life had reached a turning point, stood staring at one of the cell's stone walls. Scorched into the stone in an attractive script stood the only message from the chief that thus far seemed unambiguously comprehensible. "See you at the tomb," the message said. "Come there alone."

What had happened? Seeing a bright light inside the cell in the middle of the night, the guards had awakened. A voice within the light had told them to look away, but only one of them had done so soon enough. The guard who had turned aside heard the metal of the bars cracking and then, momentarily, bubbling. The light then disappeared, and the electrical illumination in the room now seemed like darkness by comparison. Turning toward the cell, the guard saw Peèrosh Rowka just as the chief stepped through the bars. "I made a move to stop him," the guard reported, "but he smiled at me and said something. I thought I understood him, but by the time I realized I hadn't, he was already gone."

The guard then searched the cell to find the object which had been the source of light, but the cell was as empty now as it had been when the chief had been locked in.

XVI

"And now for the first time in his life, he was sore afraid."

With these words does Abu Bakir Chandra introduce the next segment of his narrative—although my rendition does not do justice to the Demirian original and, in our language and scriptography, the sentence also fails to convey a number of other meanings, not least of which is that the letters   Art serve as the common root, in two different arrangements, for both the words "fear" and "hope."

From Rabia to the tomb of Appa Alpha Kom was a distance of perhaps ten kilometers or a very brief ride by jeep or cruiser. Ishten Telen Haragosh could thus have followed the chief's invitation on an instance had he wished to do so. But perhaps the poet was right and fear—peculiarly mingled with hope as is only possible in Demirian—held the priest back from haste . . . and obedience. For he set out toward the tomb at once,

on foot, but not alone. His entire expedition came behind him,
tail to his comet.

The strong wind had brought a thin veil of clouds over the
region. Soon it was technically day, but the Father Planet
Demirius still shadowed Bolond so that the army marched off
in relative darkness. The light had changed again from the fiery
red of the attack to a sickly greenish yellow. And you may be
sure that Abu Bakir Chandra makes the most of that, squeezes
it dry of symbolism, turning Demirius into a greenish lemon
and professing that the huge planet seemed to have grown
longer in visage and smaller in extent during the night, ap-
pearing now pale and withdrawn through Bolond's thin clouds.

It is clear that a certain hysteria had come to grip the ex-
peditionary force by midmorning. Some members of the company had refused to go forward at all, including the torch-
bearing disciple and the guard with sense enough to turn away
from Peerosh Rowka's metaphysical welding. The lady gives
us a list of those who chose Rabia and adds that none told
Haragosh of his or her defection; each simply vanished into
the stronghold's nooks and crannies.

Many of those who mounted cruisers and set out seem to
have been possessed by a literary compulsion. We have fifty-
some-odd incredible travelogues covering the few kilometers
to the tomb, each more fantastic and incoherent than the next.
We are asked to believe that wolf packs ran beside the column;
that trees, vegetation, and even rocks trembled with such inward energies that those gazing out through the narrow observation ports of cruisers—some of them husky, hardened
adventurers and louts—burst into tears at an excess of beauty;
we have reports of sheep—and in one case of a "king of
sheep"—speaking in human language while lumbering along-
side the armored and shielded vehicles; some there had conversations with dead relatives who urged them to turn back;
some claim to have turned back; some claim to have turned
back and to have ridden sheep—in one case a "king of sheep"—
all the way back to Rabia; we have earthquakes to report,
apparitions of Appa Alpha Kom and of an army of other saints;
one man claims to have seen a burning candle and to have
heard a voice urging him to keep it always in view—whatever
that means—lest it go out and he die; a woman writes . . . but
why go on? The priest's army was badly spooked. I might add
parenthetically for the cynical and urbane readers of my time

that these visions on Bolond were not that unusual for that time
and culture; every pilgrimage produced a rash; unusual here
was merely the number of those affected and their urge to fix
it all in writing.

The plain around Rabia is a high plateau which ends abruptly
some kilometers from the town. The land falls off abruptly
into a wild, craggy, forested lowland. We have a picture of
Ishten Telen Haragosh on the edge of the plain hesitating for
a moment before plunging down by way of a narrow path.
There is the army deployed behind him; huge stars wheel blazing through the thin clouds ahead; Demirius is behind the
painter and present in the picture only by its greenish light.
Down below loom fantastic trees, waterfalls, and cliffs half
revealed and hidden by creeping fog. And everywhere, super-
imposed on the naturalistic scene, are luminous marvels and
apparitions natural and infra-natural.

The picture is memorable for one special feature. It shows
the priest surrounded by a greenish aura of light; his eyes seem
empty, unseeing, and the painting suggests that of all those
present only Haragosh failed to see the wonders and prodigies
that overlay the painting and fill the accounts of his followers.

XVII

In any case, we have it on good authority that the priest was
sore afraid. Abu Bakir Chandra moves in his epic poem from
an objective, external narrative viewpoint to an internal one
at this point in the story. Having presented Haragosh to this
point essentially from the outside and more or less in caricature,
suddenly he moves inside Haragosh and continues from the
inside out, viewing subsequent events from the priest's perspective. Nay, more. Chandra even shifts from a third person
to a first person narration: "he" becomes "I," "they" becomes
"we," etc. A poet of Abu Bakir Chandra's rank can get away
with so wrenching a shift in structural alignment. I cannot. But
in what follows I shall continue to stick closely to my original
to the extent of revealing more about the priest's inner thoughts
and feelings.

But before I describe the priest's descent into that wild and
misty valley, a question must be answered: how did Abu Bakir
Chandra know what went on inside the priest? *Did* he know?

Or did he invent it all for lack of any better source of information... seeing that Haragosh went down alone, unaccompanied by witnesses...?

Those familiar with Demirian literary matters are doubtlessly groaning now, anticipating a partisan discourse on the *real* identity of Abu Bakir Chandra. It is true that Chandra's identity is uncertain and that the scholars are not in agreement on even so basic a point, but I intend to sidestep that controversy. My purpose will be quite adequately served by pointing out that *some* scholars claim that Abu Bakir Chandra *was* Ishten Telen Haragosh, while other scholars, equally cogently, argue that Chandra only *met* the priest many years after the events to which I now return.

XVIII

At the point where Rabia's high plateau abruptly ends and falls off into a wild, craggy, forested valley, the mercenary army came to a halt and refused to go on. This collective act of disobedience seems to have come about spontaneously, although each of the fifty or so fantastic travelogues reports some different marvel or apparition which induced the specific witness to turn back. The painting above referred to is a record of the moment when the cruisers stopped and Haragosh hesitated momentarily before he lifted his chained weights, lunged forward desperately, and disappeared down over the edge.

Such was his inner state, so great was his exhaustion, that he tottered on, trembling like a wind-pressed birch. His bare feet, though hardened by uncounted kilometers of penitential wandering on Tarikafuna, soon bled from the sharp rocks and thornbearing roots covering his path, and though skillful walking might have spared him, he had his weights. His chains impeded his movements, and he still breathed only Bolond's oxygen-deficient air, gasping, working, sounding like a leaky bellows. He could not concentrate on walking, he staggered beyond control, and his innards were in great turmoil.

Fear had invaded him in the small hours of the morning when he had seen the gap in the bars of the cell where Peerosh Rowka had been held. And he realized then that his busy thoughts—seeking and instantly finding an explanation for the chief's escape (a laser torch in some secret compartment in the cell's stone wall)—had to be wrong. He understood in a moment of painful lucidity that the blinding light was sophisticated psychic power, the very power he had sought throughout his long, arduous years of mortification. A power that had eluded him and still avoided him.

Staring at the gap in the bars and listening to the report of the sensible soldier who had looked away, the priest recalled vividly, sharply that episode of his youth which had impelled him toward the Brethren of Righteousness. He had been eight or nine years old. A wandering preacher had passed through his village and had asked for lodging at the Haragosh household. They had made a bed for him in the barn, and late that night after the adults already slept, young Haragosh furtively went to the barn to look at the preacher. He was eager to have a private look, entirely his own, at the man who had entertained the village that evening with incredible, haunting tales.

That was the scene: a dark night on Tarikafuna, a dark yard filled with the sharp, familiar smell of livestock, a young boy tip-toeing toward a barn.

He moved carefully. A faint light issued from the barn. The preacher was not yet asleep. The boy squeezed himself between the doorpost and the door almost without a sound, moved forward stealthily over straw, peeked around a post, and saw the preacher seated at prayer and—aglow. A shimmer of light surrounded the man; it came from the man and no common lamp. The boy held his breath, astonished and mesmerized. He could not or dared not move; he could not avert his eyes from the luminous preacher. Then, gradually, the glow intensified until the boy could stand it no more and covered his face with his hands. And at that point a voice spoke in his head— the preacher's voice, but in his head—saying, "Boy, you should be in your bed asleep."

After the preacher had left the village, the boy collected some halms of straw from the spot where the wanderer had sat in meditation. He kept these for many years, but they grew ever more brittle with time and were mere shreds and tiny bits and pieces by the time he joined the Brethren as a young man.

Haragosh remembered the light and fear then invaded him. Until then he had been sure that only true saints could command such powers. But now, looking at the empty cell, he realized that one of Satan's brood had brandished the same weapon. Spinners of heresy, befoulers of saint's graves! And he, himself, God's loyal servant, still waited, long-suffering, for his first miracle. Was there justice in the Cosmos? Had all the years of pain and work and deprivation been for nothing?...

The question left Haragosh hollow, empty and disturbed. He controlled but did not overcome his shock. He ordered departure, but he acted no longer from unquestioned certainty but from years of habit. He was a man of action, and therefore he acted. He had been challenged by the Creature of Inertia, and he had never yet refused a challenge. But all across Rabia's high plateau he struggled more with the yawning darkness that had opened up within him than with weights, chains, exhaustion and breathlessness combined.

As he descended into mist, passing moist faces of rock and fantastic trees, his numbness gave way to an internal argument.

If God was a trickster, the scriptures lies... If good and evil were equally rewarded... If he had wasted all his years... Yes, even then he would continue as he had.

Yes, he would go on. But why? Because... because Ishten Telen Haragosh felt rising in himself, out of his very desperation, a naked, hopeless, hard, forbidding, but nonetheless reassuring conviction that he was right even if God disagreed, that he was right and God was wrong, that in the end, having fought men and their sinfulness on every front God at last revealed Itself a sinner. And Ishten Telen Haragosh now had to carry the battle to God itself, the last enemy. And Peerosh Rowka, God's own mercenary and armed with God's own luminescence, would have to be faced even at the risk of near-certain annihilation.

That naked, hard conviction... Chandra says that it was the very feeling which through years and years had driven the priest from excess to excess. He had lost the feeling for a short while only, in front of the empty cell and on the march across Rabia's plain. Now it was back again as strong as ever, but no longer colored by hope or expectation of anything on earth or heaven. It was naked conviction translated into unadorned intent.

The poet adds another note which I too must include in order to stay true to my original. Concerning the planet Demirius.

It isn't clear from Chandra's epic just how we are to understand his account, whether literally or figuratively, but he claims that at this time were recorded on Demirius and on several of its moons sudden and unanticipated changes in Demirius' planetary mass. Disturbances began in the planet's hot inner core; vast quantities of gaseous matter are said to have evolved. Tumultuous explosions and implosions moved matter outward and inward, the explosions causing spurts of hot but rapidly cooling matter outward into space. Chandra tells us that as a consequence of the inner phenomena on the planet, the moons of Demirius were "loosened"—I am translating the very word he uses—and although they continued in orbit with little or no change, they were no longer quite so "attached."

And finally, the poet tells us that for the immediate future Demirius' emanation became bluish-white.

And yet one more and absolutely final footnote. I have not been able either to confirm or to deny Chandra's poetic observations. Some kind of planetary changes *did* take place in this specific period, but they are not much discussed in our technical literature. The scattering of descriptions that survive label the changes as examples of "anomalies" associated with systems in the Pentessence.

XIX

He walked—trembling, staggering, gasping—for more than an hour down into the valley through successive layers of mist, past thundering waterfalls, through groves of dripping forest. When at last he reached the immediate area of the tomb, there were the birds.

He knew that he had reached the region of the tomb because a semblance of man-made order appeared. His path straightened. The land was flat. Confusing walls of rock and trees and hurtling water, of foaming and of drifting mist hedged him in on two sides and behind, but the way ahead was clear. A rapid stream passed to his left between banks of round rock that seemed to have been placed by human hands rather than the chance and circumstance of trickster God.

The farther he dragged himself the wider the valley and the more park-like his surroundings. The strange trees with cobweb-like foliage stood now in rows and patterns. Bushes marked what seemed like paths leading to pilgrim encampments, although there were no people or animals anywhere—only the birds.

He failed to notice them at first because they were all silent—and when at last he noticed them their silence shocked and frightened him. They covered the trees, they weighed down the branches. The valley was dark, shadowy, bereft of all but pale colors, but the birds were bright, brilliant with color, like dabs of luminescent paint added as an afterthought to a black-and-white photoprint. And Haragosh could not understand how he could have overlooked them from a distance. Now the more he stared at them, the brighter they seemed—and silent.

He shouted. With supreme effort he waved an arm. He wanted them to chirp, to fly away in fright, but they would not. They sat on the trees moving every now and then, enough so to indicate that there was life in them and that they were no mere artificial decoration placed on the trees by some eccentric and wealthy pilgrim's wish. Their strangely cold, beady birds' eyes stared steadily at the priest so that he recoiled from them and looked down on the path now paved with flat stones. But he could not thus avoid the message the birds tried to convey: the air grew thick with acrid but invisible smoke; it smelled of hydrocarbon fuel, burnt feathers, and roasting flesh. The priest began to choke. He hastened on, nearly suffocated. His eyes burned and watered from the invisible smoke, and when he looked up to see the birds from time to time as he advanced, he saw them as bright, blurred blobs of color.

At last he reached a point where no more birds perched in the branches. He stopped then and wiped his eyes and looked up into the nearest tree just to make sure. And there seated on branches he saw a dozen old ladies with smoke-blackened faces; they grinned down on him with frightening expressions on their faces.

Haragosh closed his eyes in horror and repeated to himself a prayer of exorcism over and over again, his bloodless lips moving without sound. Thus he groped forward blindly. He did not dare to open his eyes to see whether or not his prayer had been answered. He had no faith in prayer any more. God was now allied with Satan. He prayed from naked intention, because he could do nothing else.

XX

The tomb of Appa Alpha Kom sat astride the valley at a narrow point. A grove of trees obscured the building. The area directly in front of the grove was flat and empty park, a grassed expanse of perhaps five hundred meters square where during pilgrimages the people sat in prayer awaiting their turn to enter the tomb itself.

From a distance and through moist eyes still burning from the smoke, the park seemed empty to the priest. A faint mist hung over the grass and the branches of the trees before the tomb reached out toward him from the fog gnarled and bent, and not altogether friendly. Somewhere a waterfall thundered. The light was peculiar. Korizon had at last succeeded in peeking past Demirius for the first time in days, and sunlight bathed a portion of the valley wall high up to the priest's right hand. A little of that light found its way by multiple reflections into the valley, oddly diffused. The fog behind the grove of trees glowed and faded and glowed again without regularity, like a faint smile coming and going on a face enthralled by dreams.

The priest was heartened by the sunlight. It restored his fading sense of reality by a reminder of more objective worlds—huge suns and planets majestically marching through the void. Thus he moved forward for the last time, gathering his inward concentration for the meeting and the clash with God's adversary and mercenary, the incoherent Peerosh Rowka.

But then as he painfully waded into the mist of the grassed expanse, he saw that he was no longer alone. Pale figures loomed ahead, at first in clusters of two or three and then in masses, tightly packed, and seeing them the priest was suddenly overcome by an overwhelming sense of shame and remorse. It came to him by reason of the eyes—thousands of eyes. They seemed like lights in that mist, like stars in a heaven. They looked at him with incredible depths of compassion and pity. He recognized some of these people; some he knew to be alive, some he knew to be dead. Others he could not recognize, but he knew nevertheless that they were in some way victims of his many crusades, harmed by his zeal. They had assembled here to pay him the homage of pity, conjured up by the satanic art of Peerosh Rowka or the lingering power of the sanctity of long dead Appa Alpha Kom. And the brightness of compassion shining in the eyes of this assembly cut deeply into Ishten Telen Haragosh. He felt an excruciating pain, unlike any he had ever inflicted upon himself in his unceasing self-mortifications. Lifting his weight-bearing arms without sensation of effort, he covered his face with his hands. Inwardly—in his chest and stomach—he felt a searing heat which the poet likens to the hot core of Demirius. Before his mental eyes passed fragmented memories of passionate violence.

Then, in the midst of this inner state of turmoil, came suddenly and quite surprisingly a cold realization. He stood in close proximity to Appa Alpha's sacred tomb, had in fact approached it for several hours. Nowhere had he seen signs of construction. This misty ground of pilgrimage had not been visited by earth-moving machinery. If Bolond constructed a spaceport, it was not in this vicinity. The rumors and whisperings he'd heard and had readily believed had been a pack of lies. On the strength of lies he had inflamed large masses of people, had attacked a settlement with beam guns and artillery. He had exposed disciples and soldiers to retaliation by a strongly armed tribal government. He had at last placed himself thus in the hands of God and God's agent and adversary—for Peerosh Rowka seemed to him to be both at once.

The sense of his own incredible stupidity and sinfulness was now so strong that despair arose within him. The grim conviction of his own righteousness once more gave way to a feeling of his worthlessness—but why elaborate. Let me merely say that Ishten Telen's world, secure though nasty as it had been until his premature awakening that morning, was now splitting apart; now this and now that aspect of the angry priest's painful personality took charge of him. Fear and doubt, grim conviction and rebellion, now despair, and immediately thereafter rage. He was not entirely himself, but then he had never been himself through most of his life.

Despair, then rage.

He could not sustain the shock of conscience. His conscience was raw and overwhelming energy, and it flooded him. He could not accept what he saw and deflected and projected it outward.

He had been tricked, deceived! The trickster now waited inside the tomb, over there, hidden by trees with gnarled, arthritic, beckoning branches!

A sharp outcry of frustration and impotence—then Haragosh lifted his weights and moved forward again, oblivious of the crowd around him. He passed right through them, not even very surprised that they were insubstantial and could be walked through like holograms.

XXI

The tomb was a circular structure with a domed roof formed of many large quartz crystals faintly suggesting the eye of an insect immensely enlarged. The outer walls were formed of marble with delicate patterns; the marble was so thinly cut that it seemed translucent when viewed from within, provided that the light outside was strong.

Inside the tomb were seven chambers arranged around the periphery in such a manner that each had to be passed through in succession to reach the eighth room in the center under the quartz dome. Each chamber was slightly larger than the one before it in the sequence. Each had associated with it a special grace, a special color, and a specific meditative practice. Pilgrims were admitted in groups of seven and spent an hour in each chamber, and by the time the seeker came to the final room where Appa Alpha Kom's remains rested beneath the marble floor, he or she had reached a state of deep collectedness; most had experienced peculiar graces, insights, healings, inspirations, or at minimum a sense of peace, and no one reportedly left the inner room (connected to the outside by a narrow corridor known as the "Canal of Birth") without being profoundly changed. Although, again reportedly, the change was not always long lasting.

At the risk of boring the reader—but this too must be said—let me report additionally that the tomb was said to have within it a quite objective and measurable field of energy. It emanated something subtle and powerful, and the emanation was experienced by everyone in a different way. This has bearing on the priest's behavior inside, hence my insistence on reporting it to a modern audience.

And yet one more aside: the scientific methodology for the measurement of such subtle fields of force as were cast like webs over saints' shrines *did* once exist. The art was developed in the worlds of the Pentessence but has been lost since the Tri-ester wars.

XXII

Ishten Telen Haragosh entered the tomb's first chamber in a rush, wild-eyed. He stopped short and looked the place over with angry, jerky glances. Fatigue and pain had left him moments before when the energies of conscience flooded his being. He would not likely sit or kneel in meditation for an hour in this small room nor in the larger ones beyond. He was looking for the enemy, and a glance told him that he had not yet found his man.

Now by coincidence (as Chandra tells us coyly), Korizon succeeded in rising high enough in Bolond's sky so that its rays angled down and struck the skin-thin marble walls of the tomb. The small room suddenly turned luminous. The red, green, gold, and amber traceries of the marble outer skin began to glow like arteries through which fresh blood had been released.

This moment also coincided(!) with the impact on Haragosh of the tomb's above described emanations. He both saw and felt the presence of Appa Alpha Kom, but in the state in which then he found himself, the state to which he had developed or degenerated, he felt the saintly vibrations and Korizon's accompaniment not as a grace at all but as an overwhelming irritation. He felt goaded and laughed at. He suspected Peerosh Rowka's invisible stage management. And more: he felt just then that Appa Alpha's tomb was no real shrine at all but suddenly knew, with an "Aha!" of suspicion borne out, with a sense of grim discovery, that this place was an invention and concoction foisted on the world by the Nagitta Bandi tribe in order to attract a heavy tourist trade to inconsequential Bolond.

And yet more: he felt that he had been tricked by Peerosh Rowka and his agents—oh yes, now he understood where that troubador had come from—into publicizing this place of pilgrimage by his personal fame and his crusade.

And finally, he felt that now he would be subjected to a faked, concocted revelation from Appa Alpha Kom—cheap telepathic trickery and light effects, of course—so that on returning to his planet he would lead his considerable following in a great pilgrimage.

All this came to him swiftly. Equally as swiftly he formed a plan, and thus moments after entering the tomb, he began destroying it.

Ah, yes! His mind was luminous with insight. He had been inspired weeks ago when in penitential fervor he had wrapped chains around his body and had hung huge chunks of metal on the chains. God loved him. No, he had been wrong to doubt the righteousness of the Creating Ray! God had foreseen all this and had induced him to carry the very tools he needed to do God's holy work. And God now gave him the energy to lift and swing the weights as if they were mere hammers rather than being, as they were, veritable anvils.

And swing the weights he did. They crashed against the sheet-like marble walls and caused the delicate luminous screens to collapse.

His fury grew as he moved on to the next and successive chambers. He left behind wreckage, sparing only the stone columns that supported the roof. These he planned to deal with last. The work of destruction took a fair amount of time, but surely not a standard hour per chamber as Abu Bakir Chandra suggests. But time it took to do a thorough job on walls and floors both. Gradually Haragosh grew weary. The tomb's emanations fled outward now that they were no longer subtly held by veins of gold in marble. They fled "like random thoughts, like winter's breath," says Chandra, and no longer gave the priest the superhuman strength he needed. He was a bent, exhausted, grey, gasping figure when at last he reached the final door leading to the eighth chamber.

XXIII

He stood there, bent, gasping, gasping, trying to recover the wondrous power he had felt earlier. Through his body still coursed blood with decaying residues of adrenaline, but the glands no longer felt stimulation and had consumed all power in their chemical storerooms. Haragosh looked at the door out of hollow sockets. Despondency was creeping back over his mind. Korizon hid behind clouds.

The final effort. Haragosh tottered forward and pushed the last door.

It was murky and yet luminous within. Light fell through the diffracting crystalline structure of the roof above. The chamber's walls were made of solid rock and would need a new surge of power to demolish. Later. After a little rest. But first he wished to face the perpetrator of this hoax. If the man had not already fled, he and his laser torch.

Haragosh could not see properly. Thin clouds stroked Korizon's underside in passing. The light changed constantly, and the crystals turned it red and lilac and yellow.

At last he made out the figure seated with his back toward

the priest in the center of the room, quite near, in fact, almost overlooked. The lumpy wool suit, the shape of the man generally, assured the priest that he had found the enemy at last. What was the chief about? Had he not heard the crash, the crack, the rend, tear, and shatter of destruction? Did he feel himself safe inside his fake sanctuary? Or was he in a trance of terror, a catatonic dissociation from reality? And where, by the way, was the laser torch that he had used to cut his way from imprisonment? Best to take no chances. Weary though he was, God still stood by him and ensured opportunity. No need to kill the chief, but he should be incapacitated lest he interfere with the completion of God's holy work . . .

The chains rattled fearfully as Ishten Telen Haragosh lifted his weights on high, above his head, but the chief did not move.

Three steps brought the priest staggering to the seated figure. He was about to drop the weights on his adversary—on the shoulders, not the head, no need to kill—when the figure turned.

The figure turned slowly and deliberately, but with perfect timing so that the weights were still on high and still supported by the priest's trembling arms. Thus Haragosh had time to recognize the face turned toward him and to arrest the action on which he had been intent.

XXIV

At this point in the story, Abu Bakir Chandra makes use of a literary device which, I confess, always irritates me when I meet with it: he abruptly changes time and location. One moment we stand with Ishten Telen Haragosh, his chained anvils uplifted, staring in shock down between his trembling and emaciated arms at the face turned up towards him. And without the slightest apology (not counting the adorned capital letter which marks transitions in Chandra's manuscripts), we are in a spaceship hurtling through the void, the priest at the controls and no' one else on board. We are outward bound. Demirius and its herd of moons is left behind.

Readers will recall that the punitive expedition arrived on Bolond in three ships, two large transports and a small, fleet command ship. It is this small vessel which has become the priest's transportation.

Chandra digresses at length explaining how the mercenary army and the priest's disciples met at Rabia to ponder what next to do—racked by guilts and split into factions—even as their leader emerged from the valley again in haste, no longer encumbered by chains and weights. While his people debated, and they did so for days, the priest caught one of the six-legged beasts of Bolond grazing near the valley's edge—peculiar animals that ran more sideways than ahead—and rode it to the place where the spaceships had been left. He bypassed, skirted Rabia on the way.

The poet also gives a rather lengthy, elaborate—and probably true if improbably sounding—explanation of how Haragosh had learned to pilot space-going craft years earlier. These details, however, do not greatly add to the narrative and hence can be left aside.

What does need establishing is that the priest came out of the valley a changed man. No one enters Appa Alpha Kom's room unchanged. He had shed his weights, and generations of pilgrims in later times scraped rust from chains and anvils and carried them far in specially sewn little sacks. But he had acquired in their stead a total desperation which only his purposeful actions masked. He was bent now on self-destruction. His destination was Korizon. He meant to extinguish his sorry existence in a blaze of thermonuclear explosions even as part of him survived and stayed behind on Bolond. But now we begin to skirt mysteries which only some nodding acquaintance with the cultural dynamics of the Pentessence can make intelligible, so let me move on slowly and circumspectly.

XXV

What had the priest seen, experienced? Unlike the poet, I see no reason to delay the telling by long diversions. When the figure seated right above Appa Alpha Kom's mortal remains turned to gaze up at the priest, Haragosh expected to see chief Peerosh Rowka's all too indistinct, pudgy face, of course. Instead he saw himself, but not as in a mirror but in the flesh. It was none other than himself—better fed, in expression serene, the eyes lit up by an inner blaze, cool yet warm. It was his nose, his mouth, yet without the bloodless severity and the downturned corners.

Shock passed over Haragosh, and he forgot the weights he

held uplifted until the trembling of his arms grew uncontrollable and the anvils threatened to fall on his own head. Then he broke his gaze and dropped the weights down, one on each side. A cunning hope arose in him as he looked away, the hope that the man before him would be Peerosh Rowka when next he looked at him. But he was disappointed. He glanced at the figure. It was still himself.

"Why do you persecute me?" the man on the floor asked. The voice was his own voice.

The priest did not answer the question. Rattling like rodents over litter, his thoughts rummaged in search for an explanation but found none that satisfied. Twin brothers? Illusion or vision or hallucination? Trickery, makeup, hypnotism? Any one or all of these might serve the purpose he sought—reassurance. But he felt now within himself that the man, his double, was not only real but really himself, always present but only now shockingly separate and visible. Nonetheless, with a feeling of curiosity he had not experienced since childhood, he squatted down before the man, reached out, and touched the face. It was tangible, real; the flesh was warm. Haragosh traced the features as if they were those of a statue. The familiar stranger suffered these actions with good humor, faintly smiling. Then yet cloud moved over Korizon above; the lights shifted oddly from bright to dark to bright again, and Haragosh found himself squatting in an empty tomb, his arms and fingers extended, tracing something in the air.

XXVI

Up ahead Korizon filled the world. The spaceship had no self-emotion and hence moved obediently toward sure destruction, but even in those days and especially in the Pentessence ships were quite intelligent, even those sold as surplus by a conniving planetary government. The ship reported to its pilot in a voice not programmed for excitement the extremely dangerous prox-imity of a star. Its hull was boiling in its outer layers and soon the skin would peel off as so much ionized matter. Inner barriers of radiation were nearing critical temperatures. The drive coils had ceased operating and had begun to "sweat," the latter being a jargon phrase of that era corresponding to our own "soot", with the same unwelcome connotations. Emergency equipment dropped and popped and sprang and coiled from every compartment and crevice of the control room. Ishten Telen Haragosh paid no attention to any of this. He stared intently into the slowly liquefying screen of his console where Korizon— or at least that portion of it where they, two intelligent machines, were fated to "land"—sent vast, turbulent tongues of flame licking out or up toward them.

The priest welcomed the prospect of his impending incineration. His life had ended in that moment when the Other, so lately found and so briefly touched, had disappeared and had left him fingering the air in a half-demolished tomb. What followed was the empty rattle of dead leaves on a winter's tree (Chandra's image). The priest had at last seen the full portent of his life, unadorned, when the Other disappeared, and the picture left him with such a loathing that nothing seemed any longer worth doing except to exit in style. And now he also knew that his self-important, dramatic gesture—which would be noticed and recorded on Demirius by scores of observers— was itself the product of his pride. But he could not help himself, and longed only for annihilation.

XXVII

And here, but for a flourish or two, our story should really end, that of yet another hysteric who managed an unregretted exit. But this is a tale from the Pentessence where nothing is as it seems, and so for the moment I must forgo a well deserved rest. The poet and tradition assert unambiguously not only that Haragosh plunged into the sun but also what follows, believe it or not, and here I will gladly join those readers who confess an inability quite to disentangle the factual, objective aspects of this historical account from the symbolical cargo which Chandra carries so easily on his rolling rhymes, but which is so awkward in our humble prose.

In any event. We are asked to see Ishten Telen Haragosh in what would in normal space be his final moments. The ship has long since melted, and only the control capsule itself is rushing toward Korizon, a well-made compartment, a hardened kernel of a seed within a seed. It still withstands the unimaginable heat. Inside sits the priest, his hair on end and beaded by ten thousand sparks per hair, his emaciated body glowing through and through so that the organs are visible, his lungs breathing fire and his heart pumping lava.

And then comes a change. Some kind of barrier has now been crossed, a new state of matter has been reached. The heat abates, the glow continues. Korizon is no longer a nuclear fireball but a strange, space-dwelling being whose shape and character are undoubtedly beyond description, although the poet does his best: a web of light extended in all directions and joined, fused with other webs of light... a primordial, androgynous Man who lifts the priest up to his face so that the two of them—micro- and macrocosmic creatures—can have a face to face conversation... an angel who materializes inside the still intact compartment just as the vaporizing console screen explodes and a million incandescent atoms shoot in all directions...

For once even Abu Bakir Chandra fails. His verse grind to ...incoherently...halt a...Never mind. With an elaborately decorated capital letter, he goes on.

And on Demirius the hot planetary core—red and angry heretofore—bursts into fire. The people on the floating continents perceived only a changed radiance in the night-sky, but the change was welcome; the brooding planet shone. Moondwellers saw the red, green, and sometimes yellow planet now as a small and not yet matured sun in the making and saw themselves in the future promoted to planetary status. And all the while the priest conferred with Korizon, but what they said to one another not even Chandra tells. He lets it go by remarking that those who know do not say, and those who say do not know.

XXVIII

At the seat of the Brethren of Righteousness on Tarikafuna at this time, the saintly Patriarch, long ailing, called together the senior-most members of the hierarchy and in the faintest of whispers—his monks leaned down over his bed to hear him—gave his last will and testament. He wished to be buried on Bolond, he said, on the lands of the Nagitta Bandi tribe. Slowly, painfully, he gave precise instructions concerning the place and the manner of construction of the tomb. The elders carefully recorded his words.

Next he conveyed special blessings to seeming innumerable people and institutions. He whispered names for hours.

At last he made his wishes known concerning the man who would succeed him. The Patriarch did not mention a name but described a man and the manner in which that man, a wandering preacher and storyteller, would make his appearance, on such and such a day, at such and such a monastery, asking for lodging and food in such and such a way.

Then the Patriarch waved a hand feebly and dismissed his servants. That night, unattended, he crossed the border.

Two aspects of this portion of the story are curious and as yet not adequately cleared up either by my own or others' scholarship. One is that the circumstances the Patriarch described as marking the appearance of his successor were the very same circumstances used to recognize him on instructions of his predecessor.

The other is that in this portion of his epic Chandra insists on calling the Patriarch Appa Alpha Kom, which is either an inadvertent error or a deliberate mystification which Chandra thought humorous.

XXIX

And now we are essentially done. Ishten Telen Haragosh returned to Tarikafuna without fanfare or announcement, and all traces of his return, documentary or other, seem to have been lost. He no longer used the name by which he had been known and did not get in touch with any of his erstwhile followers.

Those with a technological bent may be interested to learn that he is said to have returned in a curious ship fashioned seemingly by a rank amateur in astronautical engineering on some airless rock somewhere. The drive was rudimentary, the hull badly formed either for space or atmospheric travel. But the welds were flawless and the control compartment was, for that time, of standard design.

He wandered over the continent Suspended in the Grace of Righteousness earning his keep by preaching and telling stories. Once in a village, we are told, a young boy observed him late at night praying in a barn and shedding some residual radiation left over from his contact with Korizon. The boy revealed what he had seen, and after that the preacher had to move swiftly and often to escape untutored adulation.

Then—months had passed—and it was such and such a day.

The preacher came to such and such a monastery asking for lodging and for food in such and such a way.

And his future, thereafter, of course, is history.

Joan D. Vinge

made her first sale thanks to a song.

Writers get their ideas from all sorts of places. Some stories are autobiographical in origin, no matter how much they are transmuted. Some derive from things the writer has read. Some concepts are gifts from editors like John W. Campbell. And sometimes the seed that blossoms into a story comes from music. From a song.

In Joan's case, the song was a popular Top-40 hit of the early Seventies called "Brandy," performed by a group called Looking Glass. "Brandy" was all over the charts for a few months, and no doubt it thoroughly insinuated itself into Joan's consciousness, where it began to transform itself into fiction. The story that resulted she titled "Tin Soldier." It was published in Orbit 14, *the 1974 volume of Damon Knight's prestigious original anthology series. Vinge (rhymes with stingy, I'm told) included a homage to the song in "Tin Soldier"—a principal character named Brandy.*

"Tin Soldier" drew a lot of attention when it appeared. It was a poignant, powerful story, romantic in the best sense of

180   JOAN D. VINGE

*that word. One of those whose attention was drawn was me.
I did not know Joan Vinge at the time, but when I read "Tin
Soldier" I knew that an important new writer had burst onto
the SF scene. Like many other readers, I became a Vinge fan
right then and there. Unlike the others, I went away mumbling.*

*I mumbled and muttered and swore because I recognized
"Brandy" within "Tin Soldier"—and because I had just written
my own story based on the very same song. My story, "Fast-
Friend," wasn't published until 1976, however. It too con-
tained a homage, in the form of a protagonist named Brand.
I told you that song was everywhere.*

*"Tin Soldier" was Joan Vinge's first sale, but by no means
her last. After 1974, her byline became more and more familiar
in all sorts of magazines and anthologies. She published in
Analog, in Galileo, in Isaac Asimov's Science Fiction Magazine, and in Orbit and other anthologies. Her stories were
regularly snatched up for Best-of-the-Year collections. She was
nominated for the Campbell Award in 1976. In 1978, she was
a Hugo finalist for the first time, with a story called "Eyes of
Amber."*

*The world convention was in Phoenix that year, and just
before the Hugo ceremony I was up in the Dell suite with
editors Jim Frenkel and Don Benson. I was eating a room-
service meal that Dell had provided, and talking with a per-
sonable, attractive, red-haired young woman that no one had
bothered to introduce to me. I talked for quite a while before
she finally said something that made me realize who she was.
I promptly set down my fork. "Joan Vinge," I said, pronounc-
ing it wrong. "Brandy! That's where you got it, right?"*

*Later that evening, Joan virtually soared out of her seat to
collect the Hugo for "Eyes of Amber," and I clapped as hard
as anyone, even though she did steal my thunder back in 1974.
Since then, Vinge has been a finalist for numerous other
awards: the Jupiter, the Nebula, several additional Hugos. As
I write, her blockbuster second novel, The Snow Queen (Quan-
tum/Dial Press, 1980) has just been published to enthusiastic
reviews, and it bids fair to collect her a whole shelf of trophies.*

*Other Vinge books include the novel The Outcasts of Heaven
Belt (Signet, 1978), and two collections, Fireship (Dell, 1978)
and Eyes of Amber (Signet, 1979).*

*Born in Baltimore in 1948, Joan Vinge has been reading
SF since junior high school. "I've been 'making up stories'
to put myself to sleep since before I was three years old," she*

says. "*I formerly wrote some poetry, though now I concentrate on prose.*" Educated as an anthropologist, she worked for a time as a salvage archeologist before becoming a full-time writer. "*Archeology is the anthropology of the past,*" she says, "*and science fiction is the anthropology of the future.*" She lives in Chappaqua, New York.

Of the tale that follows, Joan comments, "*The story is appropriate to this volume because it's about the characters in the first novel I ever wrote—starting when I was 17. It was a pretty awful novel, not one I consider to be a part of my official career as a writer, but I've always been very fond of the characters. Careers being what they are, though, I've recently sold a (heavily revised) version of that novel to Delacorte as a young adult book. The novel is called* Psion, *and this is a direct sequel to it, as well as being what I hope turns into the first in a series of stories about Cat.*"

G R R M

PSIREN

by Joan D. Vinge

I don't know why she came that evening. Maybe it was for
the reasons she gave me, maybe not. If I'd known her mind
like I used to, when I was really a telepath, maybe it would
have come out differently.

But I might as well have been a blind man, falling over
furniture in silent rooms, with just glimmers of gray to show
me there was still a world outside my own head. And so I
didn't even know she was there until I heard her voice, "Knock
knock." Jule never used the stairs, so I never heard her coming.
She didn't need to. She'd just be there, like some nightwisp
come to grant you a few wishes. I didn't mind that she came
in first and knocked afterwards; we'd shared too much for that.

I climbed down from the sleeping platform high up under
a constellation of ceiling cracks. "How're you?" There was a
time when I wouldn't have needed to ask.

"Lonely." She smiled, that quirky, half-sad smile. I stared
at her, my eyes registering her for my mind because my mind
couldn't see her: Black hair falling to her waist, gray eyes
deeper than the night; the bird's nest of shawls and soft formless

182

overshirts wrapping her long thin body. Protection . . . like mind layers. At least they were in bright colors now, pinks and purples and blues instead of dead black. She was pushing thirty standards, had more than ten years on me, but she was still the most beautiful woman I'd ever seen. Because I'd seen her from the inside. Nothing would ever change the feeling I had for her—not the future, not the past, not the fact that she was married to another man.

"Doc will be back in a couple of days."

"I know, Cat." Her forehead pinched, she was angry—at herself, for letting need show.

"Somebody's got to mind the mindreaders," I said. "And you're better at it than he is." She glanced at me. "I remember how your mind works," I shrugged. "So does Doc. You've got the empathy, he's got credentials. So he hustles the cause, you hold the fort." *And I sit up here pretending to be one of the healers, instead of one of the cripples.* "You're lucky you miss him . . . and so's he." I moved two steps to the window set in the thick slab of wall. Looking out I saw the building straight across the alley staring back at me, black ancient eyes of glass sunk deep in its own sagging face. I listened to the groans and sighings of the one we stood in; the real voice of buried Oldcity, not the distant music in the streets. I refocused on my own reflection, a ghost trapped inside the grimy pane—dark skin, pale curly hair, green eyes with pupils that were vertical slits; a face that made people uneasy. I looked away from it.

"Sometimes it feels like the Center is becoming my whole life, consuming me," Jule was saying. "I need to break away for a while and let my mind uncoil. I wondered if maybe you felt that way too." She wondered: Jule, who was an empath, who knew how everyone felt; who *knew*, who didn't just guess. Everyone but me.

It wasn't just the Center that was consuming me, even though I spent all my time here watching over it. It was the rotting emptiness of my mind. "I don't have anything to uncoil."

She looked at me as though she'd expected to hear that. But she only said, "You have a body. You ought to let that out of here once in a while."

"And do what?" I tried to make it sound interested.

"Go out into Oldcity, see the parts I've never seen . . . parts you know."

My skin prickled. "You don't want to do that."

"Prove it."

"Damn it, Jule, it ain't—*isn't* anything you want to see. Or I want to see again."

She nodded, drawing herself in. "All right. Then can you take me somewhere I do want to see? Give me a fresh perspective for a few hours, Cat."

I dropped the print I'd been reading onto the windowsill. "Sure. Why not?"

She picked it up as I moved away, looked at the title. "CORPORATE STRUCTURE AND THE DEVELOPMENT OF THE FEDERATION TRANSPORT AUTHORITY." She looked back at me.

"Not bad for a former illiterate. . . . Gimme a break, will you." She blushed. She was the one who'd taught me to read and write. I picked up my jacket from a corner of the floor, thinking, *Only a year ago. A lifetime. Forever.* "You know something?"

She raised her eyebrows.

"Stupidity is easier."

She laughed. We went down the creaking stairs, through the silent rooms of the Center for Psionic Research, and out into the street.

The streets of Oldcity were bright and dark: the bars and gambling places and whorehouses lit up like lanterns, the heavy glass pavements inlaid with lights that followed you wherever you walked, down the narrow alleyways between the walls of buildings almost as old as time. None of the light was real light, it was only imitation. Only the darkness was real.

Oldcity was the core, the heart of the new city called Quarro, the largest city on the world Ardattee. Every corporate holding grew on Ardattee after the Crab Nebula opened up and made it the gateway to the Colonies; when the FTA moved its information storage here and picked Quarro to set it down in, Quarro became the largest cityport on the planet by a hundred times. Earth atrophied, and Ardattee became the trade center of the Human Federation, the economic center, the cultural center. And somewhere along the way someone had decided that the old tired colonial town was historical and ought to be preserved.

But Quarro was built on a thumb-shaped peninsula between a harbor and the sea; there was only so much land, and the new city kept growing, feeding on open space, always needing more—until it began to eat up the space above the old city, burying it alive in a tomb of progress. The grumbling, dripping, tangled guts of someone else's castles in the air shut Oldcity off from the sky, and no one lived there any more who had any choice. Only the dregs, the losers and the users. It was a place where the ones who wouldn't be caught dead living there came to feed off the ones who couldn't escape.

I walked with Jule through the wormhole streets that tendriled in toward Godshouse Circle, the one place in Oldcity where you could still see the sky. For years I'd thought the sky was solid, like a lid, and at night they turned the sun off. I didn't mention it, as we pushed our way through the Circle's evening crowds of beggars and jugglers and staggering burnouts. But I looked up at the sky, a deep, unreachable indigo; down again at the golden people slumming and the hungry shadows drifting beside them, behind them, a hand quicker than the eye in and out of a pocket, a pouch, a fold. I felt my own fingers flexing, my heartbeat quicken.

I pushed my hands into my jacket pockets, made fists of them. Once a Cityboy, always a Cityboy. . . . I felt Oldcity's heavy rhythms stir my blood, dark magic in my head; my body filling with the hunger of it. Hot with life, cold as death, raw like a wound, it left its scars on your flesh and its brand on your soul. A hollowed-out dealer was oozing between us, selling the kind of dreams that don't come true in a voice like iron grating on cement. *It still shows. They can smell me.* I shoved him away, remembering too many times when it had gone the other way.

I turned off of the Circle into another street, not saying anything; my face stiff, my mind clenched, hardly aware of Jule beside me. The dark, decaying building fronts faded behind walls of illusion: Showers of gold that melted through your hands, blizzards of pleasure and sudden prickles of pain, fluorescent holo-flesh blossoming like the flowers of some alien jungle. The heart of the night burst open here in sound that took your sight away, hard and blistering, sensual and yielding, shimmering, pitiless. You could drown in your wildest fantasies right there in the street, and I heard Jule crying out in wonder, joy, disgust, not knowing her own emotions from everyone else's.

But it was all a lie, and I'd lived it too many times, hungry and cold and broke; seen the ones who went through the images, through the doors where the fantasy turned real, and left me standing there—all beauty, all pleasure, all satisfaction running through my hands. Reality was no one's dream in Oldcity. Suddenly I knew why I'd never made this trip, why I'd stayed like a monk in a monastery at the Center since I'd come back here . . . suddenly I was wondering why the hell I'd made it now.

A hand was on my arm, but Jule was drifting ahead beyond my reach. I turned, wanting to see a stranger; the past looked me straight in the face. The hand ran down my sleeve, a heavy hand with sharp heavy rings; the soft ugly mouth opened, showing me filed teeth. "Dear boy," it said, "you look familiar."

"I don't know you." Panic choked me.

"Boy . . ." wounded.

"Get away!" I jerked free, ran on through the phantoms of flesh until I collided with Jule.

She steadied me, staring at me and past me, frightened. (What's wrong?)

"Nothin'. It's nothing. I just—" I shook my head, swallowed, "Ghosts."

Without another word she took my arm and pulled me through incense and pearls: The nearest door took our credit rating and fell open, letting us past into the reality. And suddenly there was no floor beneath us, no walls, no ceiling; just an infinity of deepening blue like the evening sky, shot with diamond chips of light tracking away toward an endless horizon. Our feet moved over a yielding surface that didn't exist for my eyes, and with every step my body came closer to the dizzy brink where my mind swayed now. But we reached a low table, cushion seats like cloud; all around us other cloud-sitters watched us walk on air. The sound of their voices, their laughter, was dim and distant. Patternless music flowed into the void, a choir of spirit voices weaving their conversation into its fabric.

As we settled at the table a slow mist rose, curling between us; I felt it tingling against the skin of my face, rising deeper into my head with every breath. The pungent cold of glissen was in it, along with a flavor I couldn't name, that made my mouth water. You could get arrested for this out on the street. My hands were trembling on the transparent table surface; I watched the trembling ease as the glissen began to make me calm. "What is this place?" I took deeper breaths, letting it work.

"It's called Haven." Jule was still searching the room with her eyes. She sighed, as if her inner sight saw only peace and quiet. She looked back at me. "I thought you needed one."

I smiled, half a grimace, pulling at a curl behind my ear. "I didn't—didn't know it would—come back at me like this. Like . . . I don't know. I've never been in one of these places. Never." My eyes traveled. "Maybe that's the problem. Everything's changed for me, Jule, but I don't believe it. I could *leave* Oldcity—" My hand clenched on itself.

She didn't answer, only looked at me with her storm-colored eyes, until I almost thought I could feel her mind tendril into mine the way it used to. I felt it soothe me, felt her share without question.

"Cat, you heard me, outside."

The way she said it made me say, "What?"

"When I asked you what was wrong, I didn't speak it."

"Yes, you did."

She shook her head. "I never got it out of my mouth; you answered me first."

"But I—" I looked away, back, dizzy with infinity rushing at me. "It—happened? And I didn't even know?" I felt cheated.

She nodded. "That's why it did: because you lost control."

"The first time—" *since I killed a man*, "since we came back from the Colonies. More than a year." *Living in solitary.* I let my mind reach, trying to feel it, the unfolding, the opening out—

She frowned, straining. "You're cutting me off, Cat. Don't—"

"I'm not trying to!" I hit the table edge; my voice made heads turn. I sank back into my seat. My mind was like a knot.

"Sometimes I've felt you let go, for a second, sometimes you almost—"

"I don't want to talk about it."

"You can't keep it buried. You've got to start facing up to the fact that you are a telepath—"

"Not any more."

"—and you work with me, with us, helping others like us. But you're making yourself a martyr to the problems we're all trying to face. I've tried to help you, but you aren't doing a damn thing to cooperate!" The anger and frustration startled me; I couldn't feel them.

"It's not the same!" My own frustration fed on hers. "The

rest of them live in a hell made by other people, because the deadheads hate our guts. Nobody else made my hell."

Jule's eyes dropped. "I'm sorry. It's just that I can't help feeling—responsible for the way things are for you now. It's just that when I remember what you had—"

"You think I don't remember?" A silence apart from the music and the room settled on us. I remembered times we'd sat like this in the past, when I was a thief, and she was afraid; before we'd learned to trust each other more than any two human beings had the right to. Before I'd saved her life and Siebeling's by ending someone else's—and lost it all. The music and the awareness of unreal distances around us came back to me slowly, as the glissen numbed my memory. "What do you do in this place, anyhow?"

Jule lifted her head, tension still in the half-smiling corners of her mouth. "I don't know. Meditate?"

I glanced down at the data bracelet covering the old scar on my right wrist. My credit balance had dropped a hundred points. I looked at it again. "Whew. It better be more than sitting on clouds."

Jule glanced down at her own bracelet; her fist pressed the center of her chest. There must have been a time when a hundred credits didn't mean anything to her. But that was somewhere in another life, and now whenever she thought of money she thought of the Center first. "I guess you don't do anything in Oldcity without considering the consequences," rueful.

I nodded. "That's your first lesson. The second one is that most of the time you don't get the chance to think about it." She started to get up, and I thought about going out into the street again. "Wait—till we know if there's anything else. We're paying for it."

She didn't object. She settled back in her seat; we began to talk, but not about what had just happened. The glissen began to make our words slur and our minds wander. After a while the murmuring choir faded out of the air. In the blue distance ahead of me a dark opening appeared like a wormhole from another universe. A figure came through it, walking softly on air to a place in the center of the cloud-sitters. "We welcome you to the Haven." The figure bowed, wrapped in dark folds glittering with stars; I couldn't tell whether it was male or female, even from the voice. "We hope your time here has been one of tranquility and peace. To further deepen your experience we give you the Dreamweaver, who will open to you the secret places of your soul."

I glanced at Jule, rolling my eyes, but she sat half turned away watching the act as though it mattered. The figure raised its arms and folded in on itself, disappearing; the crowd gasped. I jerked, wondering whether we'd seen a teleport. But Jule turned back and said, "Just a projection."

I shrugged. All done with mirrors. As I sat watching, a light began to fall from above us, a captive star drawn down out of the night. It settled where the projection had been, and as the light faded there was total silence in the room. I waited for more cheap tricks, wondering how they ever got enough of the audience back to this place twice to make it pay.

As the light faded I began to make out another form inside it, a human body. I kept blinking, trying to clear the dazzle out of my eyes. It was a child . . . it was a tiny, fragile woman, lost in a shining silver robe. Her arms were bare, hung with bands and bracelets showing colored fire; her skin was no color I'd ever seen before, burnished brass. But her arms were as thin as sticks, and the bones stood out like a scream along their length; her face was a shadowed skull.

Her head twisted like a doll's head until she was looking toward me, at me alone. The touch of those sunken eyes was a blow. I shut my own eyes, not knowing what I was seeing, afraid to see it; kept them shut for a long minute.

It was the light—the light playing tricks on me. When I looked at her again there was no ugliness, no suffering in that face. But there was a strangeness—something alien about its flat planes, the coloring, about the way her body fit together. *Alien*. I leaned forward, trying to meet her eyes again. She looked at me, and they were green, impossibly, translucently green. Our eyes locked; in my mind I saw her seeing the same eyes, like jewels trapped in the matrix of a face that was too human, my face. . . .

I read confusion, a silent cry in her look. She twisted her head away again, searching the crowd as if she needed a hiding place. But infinity was an illusion, and the audience held her captive with its anticipation. I almost thought she shimmered, began to disappear . . . caught herself, in control again. Jule murmured something across from me, but I didn't listen.

The Dreamweaver put her hands up to her face, but it was

only a gesture, a sign of beginning. A feeling like a sigh moved through the crowd . . . something like a whisper formed in my mind. I felt it answered as fiery hunger burned my heart away. I shut my eyes again, trying to hear the image clearly; a soft, fragile-colored dream that echoed palely as a ghost in my mind-darkness. I strained toward it, trying to make it clear, to share what made even the blind, deaf, and empty deadheads all around me gape and dream and squirm in their seats.

"Cat. Cat!"

I opened my eyes again, blinking; whispered, "Damn it, Jule—"

Her face twisted with pain. "I want to leave. I have to leave."

I couldn't focus on her, the echoes wouldn't leave my mind alone, calling, promising—"I can *feel* her, I can almost—"

Jule put her hands to her head, and tears started in the corner of her eyes. "I can't stand it, Cat. Please!"

Laughter rippled across us and through us; the cloud-sitters, lost in another world, one I wanted to share so much it hurt.

"It hurts!" Jule gasped.

"Block it, then," trying to keep my voice down, trying to ignore hers.

And then she was gone. Into the air. "Jule!" The one or two people nearest me jerked and swore. I stared into the empty space across from me. She'd teleported, she'd left me behind; she'd wanted to get away that much. *Why?* Why would she run from this? But the whispers were smokey and seductive now, I couldn't keep my mind on her, couldn't keep it away from them. . . .

The Dreamweaver held the room inside a spell for what seemed like hours, but wasn't. A part of my own mind felt the passing of time, a dim clock marking seconds to the beating of my heart. My concentration and my need fell inward until I was as lost in seeking as the dreamers around me, all lost in fantasy inside themselves.

But dreams end, and the time came when the mindsong faded like dawn light, growing fainter, paler, farther away . . . until all that was left to me was my own mind lying. The light in the room was brightening into sunrise; feeling it through my lids I opened my eyes. The Dreamweaver was drowning in light until I couldn't look at her, couldn't see her, felt the light wash me with physical heat—And she was gone. The light imploded, left my eyes dancing with phosphenes.

The other cloudsitters began to shake themselves out, mur-muring and gesturing toward the empty center. There was no applause, no calling out for more. Dazed by glissen and drugged with wonder, they stood on air and began to drift toward the door.

Someone passed through my line of sight like a rainbow. I caught at his arm without thinking; felt the electric prickle of the charged cloth and let go of it again. He turned to look at me, seeing worn jeans and a leather worker's jacket, the only kind of clothes I felt comfortable in; seeing the plain tight curls of my hair, the flat half-homely strangeness of my face. He couldn't make me fit in. . . . I saw him figure me for some rich eccentric. I realized he was right in a way, and I grinned. He smiled, a little uncertain.

"Is—uh, is the show always like that?"

He nodded. "But the dreams are always changing."

"Is there anyone here besides us? I mean, who runs this place? Who owns it? Where are they?"

He shrugged. "I never see anyone. But I've no doubt they watch over us all from the other side of the sky." He waved vaguely at infinity. His eyes were glassy.

"What about the Dreamweaver? Who is she? Where does she go? I want to . . . want to . . . thank her."

He laughed. "She sees into our minds; no doubt she sees our gratitude there. Who knows where she goes, or who she is? It's all a part of her mystery. Knowing too much would spoil it." He leaned forward, sharing a secret. "Anyway, she's not human, you know."

I felt my face close. "Neither am I."

He half frowned. "That's not funny."

"I know." I looked back again at the emptiness where she'd been; feeling the empty place in my mind. He drifted away. The room was darkening around me, infinity reaching an end, walls closing in with almost a physical pressure. I followed the rest of them out into the street, not thinking about where I was this time, but only about tomorrow—about remembering this place, and coming back to it again, and again.

I walked back to the Center through Oldcity's night without seeing any of it. I climbed the ancient circling stairs at the rear of the quiet building to my room. And as I opened the door I remembered Jule again, remembered her coming here and how our evening had started; how it had ended, when she left me at the Haven without a goodbye. *Why?* But I wasn't ready yet to go to her and find out. Because it would mean sharing what had happened to me, and I wasn't ready for that; not even with Jule.

I stretched out on my sleep platform, staring at the ceiling with my long-pupiled stranger's eyes that could trace every crack, even in the darkness. *Alien.* She was an alien, the Dreamweaver—and that was why she'd been able to reach into every mind in that room at once and start them all into fantasies. Why she'd even been able to crack the tomb I'd buried my own mind in. No one else I'd met since I'd lost my telepathy had even come close—because I was only half human. The other half was Hydran, like she was, and that half came with psionic ability that no one I knew could touch. But she had looked at me and known, and even holding dozens of other minds, she had made a blind man see.

I rolled onto my stomach, pushing the heels of my hands into my eyes; seeing stars, *God, oh God!* feeling tears. I ground them out. After more than a year working with other psions crippled by human hate, proving to them just by existing that they could be worse off than they were . . . to have this happen! To feel alive again, to *feel* the presence of another mind reach into mine. The pain of returning life was the sweetest torture I'd ever known. The Dreamweaver . . . I had to find her; had to let her know . . . *let her know* . . . a heavy peace began to settle on me as I touched the memory again . . . *find her.* . . .

It was daylight when I opened my eyes again; another artificial day of Oldcity street-lighting. I blinked and squinted in the band of glare that lay across my face; sat up, feeling excitement hot and sudden in my chest as I remembered. I tried to remember how long it had been since I'd felt anything but a dim, tired ache, morning after morning. I pulled on a clean smock over my jeans and went downstairs.

I'd overslept. Jule was already there, passing out hot drinks to the day's first handful of miserable-looking psions who'd come in for their day's ration of human contact—something I should have been doing for her. She jerked as I came up beside her, catching her by surprise. I took the drinks out of her hands, keeping a mug of bitter-root for myself. "Sorry. Why didn't you call me?"

She looked at me with an expression I couldn't read. "I didn't know you were here."

"Jule, I want to take the day off."

Her face pinched. "Cat, not today. It's half crazy around here without Ardan. Mim and Hebrett can't handle it without you."

The hell they can't. I opened my mouth to say it, changed my mind. I sighed, and shrugged. "If you need me . . ."

She smiled. The smile stopped. "Yes, I do want to talk about last night. Later, at lunch."

I nodded and went back to work. The morning passed in a haze of going through the motions, setting up control exercises, watching them happen, listening to a new day's complaints from the 'paths and 'ports and teeks who were trying to come to terms with the freak mind talents that were tearing up their lives.

And then I was alone with Jule in Siebeling's broom-closet office, sitting on the corner of his perfectly organized desk and drinking soup. I watched Jule sipping at her own cup, sitting in his chair; watched the kinetic sculpture on his desk, afraid to let my own mind focus. The sculpture was lifeless, nothing more than a tangle of metal without Siebeling here to make it dance with his mind the way he did. You could tell what sort of mood he was in by what it was doing.

"Last night . . ." Jule said finally.

"Why did you leave?" The words sounded hard.

She leaned back, the chair re-formed around her. "Because it was . . . *pain*ful." She bit her lip. "I felt a—"

"It was beautiful! Everyone there, everyone in the room—she made them let her into their minds and love her for it! And she—she—"

"Touched you." Jule nodded.

"Yeah." I looked down.

"The strength of her sending—"

"She's Hydran."

"Yes." Jule's eyes traced my profile. "Even you couldn't resist her."

"You couldn't either." I leaned forward. "But why run away from it? It ought to make you happy to see a psion in control, strong, proud."

"She wasn't in control; she was afraid! She was there out of fear, need, helplessness, compulsion . . ." Jule's knuckles whitened against the cup. "All that and more, inside the pretty lies. Cat, I know what you felt last night, and how much it

meant to you. But inside she was screaming, she couldn't
stop it, and I couldn't listen any more." Her body shuddered,
and soup dripped.

I lowered my own cup slowly onto the desktop. "I don't
believe it." But Jule wouldn't lie—wasn't lying. I shook my
head. "Why?"

"I don't know."

"Then if anybody ever needed our help, she does. But she
appears and disappears—how can we reach her?"

"There is a way," meaning mind to mind. She took a deep
breath. "But I can't face it, Cat. I can't block her out. And
I'm not even sure she'd listen. There's something else she
needs more." Her hand moved in an empty circle through the
air.

"Does that mean you won't try?" My hands tightened.

"It means that I want someone else to try. Someone she
might respond to, who's protected from what's inside her."

Me. I was the one she meant. There was something I might
be able to do that no one else here could. . . .

There was a knock at the door. Jule called, "Come in," and
Mim came in. She looked from Jule to me and back again.
Mim was a telepath, a student psi tech; she could have told
Jule anything she needed to without ever opening the door.
But they did it the hard way, because of me.

"What now, Mim?" Jule looked tired suddenly.

Mim rubbed her hands on her pants, frowning. "There's a
Corpse out front, who wants to speak to Whoever Runs this
Freakhouse. He's going to ask us about corporate crime and
using psionics for brainwashing. He's also scared we'll rape
his mind while he's here." Her mouth twitched, her blue-green
eyes were as cold as the sea.

"All right: I'll make him feel like we're all angels." Jule
pushed her head into her hands, leaning on the desktop. "Corporate Security looking for blood, that's all we need. Damn
it! Why don't they leave us alone? . . . Cat, where are you
going?" She called after me as I started for the door.

"Hunting." I pushed past Mim and went out.

I spent the rest of the day, and as much time as I could steal
of the ones that followed, searching and asking around the
Oldcity streets . . . getting nowhere. I'd known all my life how
the information root system spread through Oldcity, thick and
tangled; sending shoots up into the light among the shining

towers of Quarro. Now I had money to back me, something I'd never had before; a key to Oldcity's hidden doors that had always been closed to me. But still I got nowhere. Whoever controlled the Haven, and the Dreamweaver, wanted it kept a secret.

And meanwhile I went back again and again, like an addict, to drop another hundred credits at the Haven's door and sit on clouds and needles, waiting. Until infinity would open once more and show her to me, let her reach out to me and into me, touching my need. And every night I tried to catch her eyes, complete the circuit, give her something in return—just my name, just my gratitude, *Ask me, ask me for anything*. But there was never an answer, never a sign that she felt anything. Her control was complete, and I was a blind man asking her to let me guide her. I wondered if she laughed at me, somewhere behind the inhuman peace of her face. If she was suffering there was no sign of it. Any suffering was my own, anger and frustration eating at me until it was all I could do not to get up from where I sat night after night and cross the space that separated us like the barrier of my mind. Always knowing that if I ever tried it she'd disappear, and I'd never see her even this way again.

There were other regulars in this place. I got to know them on sight, although none of them ever talked about why they came, or what they felt, sharing the forbidden fruit of telepathy. Some of them were corporation or Transport Authority officials, wearing power and arrogance like their fine upside clothes. I tried to find a little pleasure in watching their faces get soft and slack from glissen and psidreams. And one night, watching, I saw something happen I'd never seen before. At the end of the regular show, after the Dreamweaver had disappeared and the crowd was drifting toward the door, the hologram host came back through the crack in space and caught one of the guests with a word. The man nodded, lighting up like a lottery winner, and followed it back into somewhere else. I started after them as soon as I saw them disappear. But as soon as I did infinity went black ahead of me; a soft, clammy wall of nothing was suddenly between me and the place I was trying to reach. I turned back, disgusted, and went out with the rest.

The lucky winner was back the next night, as if nothing had happened; and a couple of days later I saw the same thing happen to someone else. Again I tried to follow, again I ran into a soft wall. Somehow, a few of the ones who came here were being chosen for something extra; but no one would tell me what, if I didn't already know. And no matter how I asked her with my mind, the Dreamweaver never answered me.

Siebeling had come back to the Center in the meantime. I figured when he finally called me into his office that it would be to tell me what Jule had begun telling me with looks and frowns, if not with words: That I was spending too much time and money and getting nowhere. That maybe I'd taken on something impossible, and was too damned stubborn to admit it. Jule was with him when I got there, standing, looking uncomfortable. Just like I felt. "Doc?" making it half a question.

He glanced up at me, his face the same as ever, only more tired. He was a plain-looking man, and the clothes he wore were even plainer—but there was something about him, a quiet determination that made you pay attention. "Jule told me about your experience with the Dreamweaver. I take it the two of you had very different reactions." He leaned forward; his hazel eyes searched my face.

I nodded, leaning against the closed door, running my fingers along the seams of my smock.

"You want to talk about it?"

"You've heard it all." I glanced at Jule, not able to keep the accusation out of it. She met my eyes; something darker and more confused than resentment was in her own.

"I've heard that the Dreamweaver is Hydran. That for Jule her sendings are a cry of pain. That you can't feel the pain—but you feel something. And so you keep going back for more. True?"

"Yeah." I stared at my feet, at braided straps of scuffed leather. Resentment was pushing hard inside my own chest, the sound of his voice taking me back suddenly; making me remember old times, bad times, before we'd seen the inside of each others' minds and our own.

"Why?"

What's it to you? I almost said, almost let my own doubt turn me back into a scared street punk. I took a deep breath and raised my head. "I want to help her. Jule says she needs help—and nobody else wants to try."

"*Can* try," Siebeling said softly. Jule's face was turned away, and I understood a little more.

"Then why do you want me to stop?"

"I didn't say that." Siebeling leaned further across the hard, shiny desk top, and I could see his tension. The kinetic sculpture was tumbling and ringing softly, constantly. I remembered his first wife, who'd been Hydran too, who'd died when he wasn't there to help her. "I just want to know what you're getting out of this for yourself." It wasn't an accusation. Only a question.

I shrugged. "I dunno, I . . . that is, it's what we're here for. It makes me feel like I have a purpose. A reason. It makes me feel alive—"

"Knowing someone exists who can prove that you are."

"Yeah." I looked down again.

"There's nothing wrong with that. You're only letting her help you." He glanced at the sculpture; it reversed direction. "But what's going to happen if you can't help her? If she won't be helped? Can you let it go, or is this thing an obsession?" I finally began to let myself believe that he only meant what he said.

"I can handle it." I let my hands hang loose at my sides. "If I have to forget her, I will." *But I won't have to.* My fingers twitched.

Siebeling smiled at Jule, who matched the smile without quite meaning it, because she knew he wanted her to. I wondered if we were all thinking about his first wife then, and what had happened to her. "Then I don't see any reason not to continue; at least until you've reached a decision. As you say, it's what we're here for." Several kinds of longing were in his voice.

"Thanks." I opened the door and went out, not wanting any of us to have more time to think.

But that night the Corpses came back; three deadheads in matching gray, looking more like businessmen than police. The Transport Authority had taken what had once been separate corporate police forces and made them its own. The Corpse who asked most of the questions was a Transport Special Investigator named Polhemas; his coming in person meant that the matter under investigation was making a lot of people upside sweat. . . . And it meant that even though Dr. Ardan Siebeling was a teek who didn't try to cover it up he was still Dr. Siebeling, who had a few friends Up There somewhere. But the Corpses were looking for someone who could pick the brains of important officials and researchers and sell what they found to the most interested party. Not just the usual corporate backstabbing, but something with underworld roots. They were looking for psions, and here we were in the middle of Oldcity, right where they'd expect us to be. We spent hours arguing the truth and our right to exist; the way we'd had to do so many times since we'd begun the Center, and probably would have to do forever. They didn't leave until the time of the Dreamweaver's show was long past. I went up to my room and stayed there staring into the darkness, like a burnout aching for a fix.

And the next night it happened again. Just as we were closing Polhemas showed up, his hired help pushing the door back into my face. And this time they'd come to pick on me. They wanted to blame their troubles on us, because that was easier than thinking; they were going to pry into the cracks until they could. And I had a past record that matched just about anybody's opinion of bad. Jule and Siebeling wouldn't leave me alone for the questioning, which meant that Polhemas was going to give us three times the grief; but I was grateful anyway. We stood together in Siebeling's office while Polhemas sat in his chair, daring someone to object; demanding to know what I was doing here, what I was *really* doing here, what I did in my spare time, whether anybody could prove that, prove I wasn't moonlighting, prove I was really a mental burnout and not a galactic arch-criminal. . . .

Some other time I might have enjoyed watching a Corpse on the wrong track making an ass of himself. But the questioning went on and on, he talked down to and over and through me, while I watched the minutes crawl past up on the wall until I'd missed the Dreamweaver's show again. Until I couldn't sit through one more insulting question, couldn't listen to Jule or Siebeling make one more civil answer in my place—

I pushed away from the wall. "Listen, Polhemas, maybe you never get tired of this, but I do. So I've got a record: if you know that, you know it's been sealed. If you've got anything fresh on me, then do something about it. Otherwise, try a different datafile. I've got a Corpse commendation on record too—just like they do," nodding at Siebeling and Jule. Just saying it made me stronger. "That means I don't have to—"

"Shut up, freak," one of the other Corpses said.

Polhemas glared at him. "Is that true?" He asked Siebeling the question.

Siebeling nodded, with a smile only I could see in the corners of his mouth. "Even we have served justice in our small way." The smile said we were still waiting for justice to give us something in return.

Polhemas glared at Siebeling; back at me again. "I don't like your attitude."

I opened my mouth, saw Jule stiffen. I closed it again, watched the sculpture clattering on Siebeling's desk.

"The matter isn't closed. I may still close this place down before it is." Polhemas gestured his clones into line and went out into the Oldcity night.

"He knew about the commendations," Jule said finally. "There was no surprise in his mind . . . he knew before he came here. But it didn't matter to him."

Siebeling grunted in disgust.

I looked up at the time again, and didn't say anything.

The third day was business as usual; I went through the motions, counting the hours until the Center closed and the Haven opened. But then Jule was beside me, her face drawn with a strange tension, as if she were holding her breath. "Cat, there's someone here to see you."

I followed her out to the front reception area, holding my own breath; knowing without knowing who it was I'd see there.

The Dreamweaver stood near the entrance, melting into the darkbeamed wall while the Center's regulars circled past, some of them not even seeing her, some of them staring and edging away as though they were seeing a crazy woman. My skin prickled. One of the telepaths across the room started to moan; Hebrett pulled him through into another room and closed the door. Jule's face was rigid when I glanced at her.

But I didn't feel anything except hope swelling inside me; didn't see anything but a tiny frightened woman holding herself together with her arms. She wore a loose cowled smock and pants, rich cloth, all in brown. Her hair that had been a haze of spun gold was buried under a heavy beaded net. Only her face showed her alienness—the color of burnished brass, with planes and shadows that were subtly different. Her eyes were waiting for mine, as green as emeralds.

We stood face to face at last, and suddenly my mouth was too dry for words. I nodded.

"This is Cat," Jule said, because something had to be said. She caught my eye, asked me, begged me with her look to *Go away, take her away, far away from here please—*

"What are you doing here?" I got the words out at last.

The Dreamweaver kept her eyes on my face, hugging herself, as if it was all she could do to hold herself here. "You didn't come. Twice."

I felt myself blush, hot and sudden. "I—I couldn't. I wanted to, but I couldn't. I would've come tonight."

She blinked, her arms wrapping her harder. "Truly?"

I nodded again. Jule turned and walked away too quickly. "That's why you came here? How did you know—how did you find me?"

"You told me. Every night I heard you. Showing your self to me, showing this place. Saying, 'Come, come please'—"

"You heard." I swallowed a hard knot of joy. "I—listen— I mean, do you want to go somewhere? Somewhere we can— talk?" *But talking is so hard, useless, when two minds can share the space of one and you only have to know.* "Somewhere else, quiet, away from here." I waved a hand, wishing that somehow I could make the whole Center disappear.

"Yes." Her face eased and turned eager to be gone all at once.

"Is there a place—?"

"Yes," almost impatiently. She led me outside and along the street to a cab caller. One of the upside bubbles was drifting toward us over the crowds almost before the silence started to make me feel like a fool. We got in, she said, "Hanging Gardens" into the speaker. I felt something I couldn't name, that almost choked me. We were going up—out of Oldcity, into Quarro. I'd never been upside in all the time I'd worked at the Center—hardly been more than a kilometer from the place itself, even here in Oldcity. I swallowed and swallowed again, as the cab carried us in toward Godshouse Circle and then rode an invisible updraft into the light of day, the real world. The air brightened around us as the shadowed, twisted underside of the city fell behind and below. The air got sweeter, clearing the stench of a thousand different pollutants out of my lungs. I only knew them now by the fact that they were gone. The corporate crown of Quarro shone around us, the silvered, gilded, blued towers mirroring endlessly flowing images of more reflecting more and somewhere the sky caught up in it, bluer-on-blue and cloud-softened. I thought about the first time I'd seen the city I'd spent my whole life inside of, out the window of a Corpse flyer, under arrest . . . not even two years ago.

The cab set us down again almost before I'd finished the thought; the Hanging Gardens were above Godshouse Circle, like the rim of a well whose waters had gone bad. We climbed out; the cab docked me for the whole fare, and I realized that she wasn't even wearing a credit bracelet. If I hadn't had mine on no cab would have taken us up from Oldcity.

The gardens rose and dropped away on all sides of us; man-made tiers of living land growing, flowering, spreading, shading. Islands in the sky, worlds-in-a-bottle, each of them a living miniature of a homeworld somewhere in the Federation. I followed the Dreamweaver along the curving walkways that spiralled through the air between one suspended island and another. The spring breeze was sharp and biting, the arch of sky above us was bruised with purple clouds. There weren't many other walkers on the paths.

Her silence began to get on my nerves until I remembered that a Hydran didn't need the useless small talk humans needed to bridge the emptiness between them. Words were an emphasis, or an afterthought—the contact was already, always, there. Knowing she didn't need the words when I did didn't make it easier. But she seemed to be moving toward something, not just moving for its own sake, and so I kept my words and my thoughts to myself.

We came out at last in a garden where the green of tendrils and crescent leaves was shot with veins of silver, the wind making them shimmer, fade, brighten as though reality was something always just beyond the limit of my eyes. I looked back at the Dreamweaver, seeing that she'd reached the right place at last. *The right place* . . . because there was something of this place in her, about her; something not-quite-seen.

"Your homeworld," I said. My own voice startled me. "A piece of it. Koss Tefirah," squinting at the plaque beneath a silver-skinned treeshrub.

She nodded. She sat down on a low bench sculptured out of stone, touching the crystal-flecked surface with copper-gold hands.

I stood a minute longer watching her, thinking about how small she looked, how fragile, cupped in the hands of stone; how much like a child or a flower or a piece of down carried on the wind. Nothing like Jule, who was tall, taller than I was, thin but with a man's kind of lean strength. . . . And yet everything like Jule on the inside, lighting my darkness and making me see hope again. Sharing a strength with me that she couldn't afford to give, but gave anyway because I needed it . . . even when her own need, her own fear, were more than she could live with.

I jerked out of the thought, not knowing where it had come from—from what Jule had said or from something lying deep in my own mind. The Dreamweaver looked up at me, her green eyes shifting like the green on every side, and I looked down into them, seeing the same healing strength that had held Jule together when the world was pulling her apart. Seeing the strength that had been my mother's once, too, and the eyes. . . . And seeing those things, knowing someone like this should never have to use that kind of strength just to keep herself sane, I knew that I would do anything for her, anything at all—My knees got weak and I sat down on the bench, keeping just out of reach, hers or mine, I wasn't sure. I looked away across the floating glade in a half-blind glance; seeing the swaying boneless treeshrubs and the flowering vines that softened the hard underside of the next tier above us. The air was sweet and musky with the scent of them, like the scent of a woman's skin—I swallowed, wondering if it was her doing this to me, or the place, or if I'd just gone a little crazy hiding from life down in my Oldcity room. "How—how long've you been gone? From Koss Tefirah, I mean?" still not looking at her. *Oh God, geezus, can she hear me? Stop it stop it you damn fool—*

"Many years." Her voice was suddenly small and dreary.

"And so you come here, trying to hold onto the memories." I twisted my hands on the edge of stone. "Doesn't it make you sad?"

She turned toward me abruptly. "Yes. Yes—" turning away again. "It makes me sad. But still I come . . . I don't know why."

"Because you think someday you'll find what you're looking for here. What you lost."

She stared at me, and out of the corner of my eye I could see that she was afraid.

"No. I'm not reading your mind. Just my own." I shrugged. She didn't speak but I knew she was asking. My hands hung onto each other in the space between my knees. "I—I miss a place, a life, a right, a—a—" hating my stupid, clumsy words, "—*belonging*. Me, too."

"How long are you gone?"

"A long time. A lifetime."

She frowned her confusion. "Where is your home?"

"I don't know." My hands fisted. "Here. Oldcity! I mean, I was born here. I lived my whole life here . . . thinking I was only human, and wondering why people kicked my ass all the time. But I went away, to the Colonies, and I met—some of our relatives. And they made me proud of what I really am—half Hydran." I looked back at her finally, letting her see my eyes that were as green as emeralds, as grass, as her own. "But that half of my life, I lost it before I ever had a chance to learn. . . . And now I've come back to Oldcity, and I keep waiting for some kind of magic to show me the way home. Only it never happens. Because it's not Oldcity I'm looking for, and it won't ever give me what I want." Every word of it was true, and I wondered why I'd never seen the truth before. "But it's all I've got."

She nodded, her face pinched, her eyes shimmering, drowning. I noticed something wrong with the eyes then—the pupils were open almost halfway, pooling endless black depths in the green. We were sitting in bright sunlight, and they should have been no more than slits, barely visible.

What are you on? I almost asked it. But no matter where either of us thought we belonged, we belonged to Oldcity now, and in Oldcity you didn't ask. Instead I said, "Why? Why did you come here, why do you stay?"

"Relocation." The smallness, the dullness, the loss came back; the single word hit me like a fist.

Relocation. One indifferent, empty word filling up with rage, suffering, loss, the grief of a life and a whole people torn apart. Once Koss Tefirah had been her own world, the way Earth had been home to humans. But Earth hadn't been enough for them; like roaches, like flies, they'd spread out across the galaxy to other worlds. Some of the worlds already belonged to another people, the ones they called Hydran; naming them for the system Beta Hydrae where first contact was made—and for an ancient Terran monster with a hundred heads.

The Hydrans were humanoid enough that they could even interbreed with humans; their only real difference was in having psi talents that made most humans deaf and blind by comparison. Some early xenobiologists even called the human race a world of defective Hydrans, psi mutes. It wasn't a very popular idea with the rest of humanity, especially when some megaglomerate wanted to strip the resources of a Hydran world. The FTA would oblige them, one way or another, and because the Hydrans' telepathy made them non-violent, getting rid of them was easy. They lost their lives, their rights, their homes...they lost everything. And they couldn't—wouldn't—fight back. I took a deep breath, and another, before I could say anything more. "I'm sorry." Something stupid. "At least—at least you're the Dreamweaver. At least you make them come to you hungry for the dreams they've lost themselves, and willing to pay. Even if it'll never be enough."

She didn't say anything. Her fingers traced the folds of her smock over and over. Twitchy. Mindless. Not in peaceful silence any more. Birds were calling somewhere far below us. I noticed again that she didn't wear a credit bracelet.

"How do you get here on your own?"

"I teleport." Her lips barely moved.

"Oh. Right." Pure-blooded Hydrans could do nearly any form of psionics there was a name for. Most human psions couldn't. I couldn't. All I'd ever been any good at was telepathy. But once I'd been *good*...better...the best.

"What happened to you?"

"What?" I looked up.

"Why is your mind like that? What have they done to you?"

I felt my own eyes drowning suddenly, blinked them clear. "Somebody made me see myself without illusions, once. I killed him for it."

"Murder?" The sound filled with thick horror.

I shook my head. "Self-defense." I made myself go on looking at her, knowing that no true Hydran could kill another being and survive. Their own empathy destroyed them. "I'm human enough to kill. But I was Hydran enough to pay for it." *And pay, and pay*...knowing I would never forget the white agony of death that had burned out my senses and left my mind a wound that would never heal. "Scar tissue. That's all I have now...except when you send your dreams out to me. I've been trying, wanting, for so long just to—thank you." It died in whispers. "Why...how...all those others and still you knew, you touched *me*." I almost touched her, but only with a hand. "Why?"

"You were different, you and the woman. Not like the rest—" I heard her disgust. "I looked at you, and I felt you different from all the rest, even from her; and so alone, more alone than anyone could be."

"It's not so bad," lying.

"But you came back, over and over. I felt you thanking me,

and calling me, and asking me things I could not answer. Until you stopped coming."

"You heard me—" I straightened, feeling the stone grate against my back, "and I heard you. Could we be that way now—talk mind to mind, not words?" *Please, please.*

"No." She shut her eyes. "You aren't like the guests, the empty minds. You focus sharply, clearly. But then your own mind's hand covers its mouth, and you make less than a whisper. And your mind's hands cover its ears, even though I am shouting. . . . Even to talk like humans with you is easier. Forgive me."

"It's all right . . . I shouldn't have asked." My hope curdled, and I was glad then that it wasn't easy for her to see my thoughts. We sat together without thoughts or words, listening to the wind speak and the leaves answer.

"You are called Cat. Why?" Change of subject.

"It's my name." I relaxed finally, smiled a little, settling into the seat.

"Is that all?" She bent her head; beaten-gold earrings winked at me. "Cat?"

"It's all I need." I shrugged.

"But it is an animal." Curiosity and protest.

"Have you ever looked at a cat, at their eyes? They see in the dark. Their eyes are green, and the pupils are long slits. Like mine; like ours." I laughed once. "I picked it up on the streets. It fits."

She nodded slightly to herself. "I see. You keep your real name hidden. The humans don't do that, because their minds are hidden already."

"Real name?" I shook my head. "I don't have any other. Maybe once . . . but not any more." I felt an old loss cut deeper. "I'm not hiding anything." *But you are, damn it, you are.* 'What about you? I don't know any of your names."

"Ineh. Call me that."

"Is that your real name?"

"No." Her hands stroked the bench, never quiet.

My mouth twitched. "Oh."

"I could not show you that name. You would have to see it in my mind's heart."

"Oh," again. I couldn't decide whether to get annoyed or get angry, so I didn't. "You're telling me that I'll never know you that well."

She didn't answer.

"Why did you come to see me, anyway?"

"You stopped coming to see me." She glanced up, her pupils wide and black. "And then I had a sending that you would help me."

I opened my mouth, but nothing came out. A sending ... precognition. The wild card power. Nobody who had it could control it; they could only learn to sift images when they came, try to pick the true ones out of the static. "How? How can I help?"

"I don't know."

"What's wrong that should be right?"

"Nothing." Her pupils like black pools of emptiness swallowing the sun said, *liar, liar*.

I laughed again, frustrated. "Is it the Dreamweaver, the Haven—do you want out of it?" I remembered what Jule had said. No answer again. "What is it, are you afraid to tell me? I owe you a debt. Let me pay it."

"I have no right." She looked away, searching the glade for enemies, or an escape.

"I want this. Ineh—". I caught her hand, like a handful of bones; jerked, but then it was only a hand, soft-skinned, pulling free. "Who owns the Haven? Have they got something on you, is that what you're afraid of?"

"Stop it! Stop!" She held herself rigid like a shield.

I stopped.

"I should not have to come to you. If they find out they would keep you from seeing me." Her face fell apart. "You can't help me, I was wrong to speak of it. Promise me that you will not ask me any more."

"It's drugs, isn't it?" It had to be the answer; how else could any human hold someone like her, and make her obey?

"No." *Yes, yes,* her eyes said.

"Yes."

She wavered, losing substantiality, going—

"No, no wait! Don't—" I reached out, caught her arm, felt it solidify into flesh again. I let her go, sitting back. "I'm sorry. I should've known better. We are what we are. It won't happen again." I kept watching her body still held like a shield, her closed face; my own face promised her.

She let herself loosen, nodding. "I cannot share with my own people, or with the humans. But you are both and neither. When I see you I will not feel so alone. Will you come in the evenings to my show?"

I moved against the bench, feeling uncomfortable. "Look, Ineh...this is hard to say, but I can't keep coming forever. I don't have that kind of money."

"No?" She looked at me as though she couldn't understand why not.

"No." I shook my head. "Do you even know what it's like to be poor?"

"Yes." She looked through me. "My people were poor when I came here. But that was a long time ago...." As if it didn't matter any more.

"And you're not poor any more. What about the rest of them? What about your family?"

"I don't know. I don't know where they are."

Anger rose in me again. I swallowed it, and said, "That doesn't seem to bother you much either."

"No. It is a long time...." She shifted listlessly. "Before my people came here we shared a life, we shared our minds' hearts. But the humans took our life away, and in this place no·one shares anything. There was nothing left for us. We stopped sharing. We stopped wanting to. Because what was the use? There are better ways to stop pain."

And you know the best. I grimaced. It wasn't hard to see where her life had gone from there; or to see the possibilities some Oldcity user had seen in her, that had put her into this trap. But I only said, "I know."

Her eyes came back to me.

"I'll come to the Haven when I can. But I can come here too, it'll be better that way. Just let me know, somehow. I'll get the time off."

She nodded. "Come to the Haven soon. I'll know then."

I stood up, not needing to be told that our time was ending. "Promise me that this isn't the last time."

(I promise.) The words whispered into my mind. And then she was gone.

When I got back to the Center Siebeling called me into his office again. Jule came with me, and together they asked about what had happened. And suddenly I didn't want to tell them. "We talked. About things—you know," shrugging. "What we are, who we are. She's lonely, she's lost her people."

"Where is she from?" Siebeling asked. I couldn't know what he was thinking, but he must be thinking about his dead wife, not about Ineh. He couldn't see *her*, he wouldn't understand her trouble....

"Koss Tefirah. She was relocated here."

His face turned down.

Jule said, "Did she tell you why she came to the Center?"

"She missed me." Somehow even that was too personal,
too much. I could imagine what I would have been getting
from her mind: she couldn't cope with this, she couldn't understand any more than he did, maybe she was even jealous
of me for doing what she couldn't...

"Is that all?"

"I guess it's something," resenting it. "It's a beginning."
I knew then that I wouldn't say the rest, the whole truth. This
was my affair, *mine*, and I'd handle it myself because I was
the right one, the only one who could. "I'll be seeing her again;
and not just at the Haven." Daring them to stop me. "I'm going
to help her, I know it. She knows it." *Everybody know it!*
wishing that everyone could.

Siebeling glanced at Jule and back at me. They didn't say
anything. The kinetic sculpture on his desk stopped dead in the
air.

I met Ineh in the Gardens more than once in the next couple
of weeks, and watched her at the Haven. Watching her now,
knowing that drugs fed her the dreams she was feeding to the
crowd, I hated the place; hated myself for still needing the
touch of them, even while I was trying to stop them. But
nothing else changed. When we were together she never let
me any closer.

Then one afternoon at the Center Mim came up to me with
a strange, glazed look on her face. "Message for you."

"Huh?" I straightened up from the storage cabinets. Her
hands were empty. "Where is it?"

She tapped her head. "In here. What are you, deaf?" The
joke had teeth and it bit me hard. "Somebody's screaming her
brains out for you, trying to tell you she wants you *now*. Make
her stop, damn it! And tell her not to use my head for a call
box in the future." She started to turn away.

"Where's Jule?"

"Out."

I let out the breath I was holding. "Mim—"

She turned back, still frowning.

"I'm sorry."

She grimaced. "Just find her before she puts every 'path in

the building into an epileptic fit. When I say this is a pain,
I'm not kidding."

"I'm going out." I left the uncalibrated meters lying helpless
on the table and started toward the door.

"Hurry!" She threw it after me.

I left the building and headed for the cab caller. Ineh was
waiting there for me. I hadn't expected it.

"Why didn't you come to the Center?" It came out sharper
than I'd meant it to.

She shook her head. "They don't want me there. So I called
you."

"Next time use the phone." I pushed the call button.

She stared at me, looking tiny and miserable and alone.

"I'm sorry." I bent my head. "It's just that when you call
me I'm the last to know, in a place like that."

She still stared at me. The cab came finally, and I was glad.

We sat together in the Koss Tefirah garden. I finally asked,
"Why did you call me away?" Hoping there was a good reason,
afraid of what I was going to feel like if there wasn't.

"I was unhappy."

My hand tightened over the stone arm of the bench. "About
what?"

She shivered like a plucked string. "Nothing." Her own
hands twisted, always moving.

"About what?"

She didn't answer. (Nothing.)

"Damn it, Ineh! You can't tell me 'nothing' forever! Either
you trust me or you don't and if you don't I don't know what
the hell I'm here for!"

"I can't. I can't tell you. I'm afraid—"

"For you or for me?"

"I'm afraid!" She crushed her eyes shut, and her fists, and
her mind.

I unlatched my data bracelet, let it fall into my hand. "Open
your eyes. There's something I want you to see; I want to show
you something."

Slowly her eyes opened, and her fists. She looked at me,
tensing.

I held out my wrist. A band of scar tissue circled it, naked
and alien. "See that?"

She nodded.

"A bond tag did that." I turned away from her, pulled my
jacket up and my shirt loose. The sun felt warm on my skin;

I remembered the feel of another sort of fire on my back. . . . I let her look at the scars. "That's what it means to wear one." I pulled my shirt down again, turned to face her. "I was shipped to the Colonies as contract labor. If it hadn't been for the people who run the Center I'd still be there. I've been somebody's slave, Ineh."

She touched my wrist with cold fingers.

"Tell me what's wrong."

"I must give a private performance."

The words hung in the air between us like crystal beads. I felt the answer to the question complete its circle before I could even ask. The strangers I'd seen at the Haven, disappearing after the show, going on to something more—a private performance.

"It's different than what you do in the show?"

"Different . . . the same . . . more." Her hands pressed her arms inside her long sleeves.

"When is this next 'performance'? After the show?" It was dusk already.

"Yes." Her fingers dug into the flesh of her arms. "I don't want to go. I don't want to—"

"Then don't go. Stay with me. We'll protect you."

"No, they'll come for me. They'll find me; nowhere is safe from them!"

"Ineh, that's what they want you to think. It's not true, not if you don't want it to be."

"It is! I see it in their minds."

I broke off, not sure whether she was fooling herself, or I was, any more. "What about the Corpses? We could go to them—" Even the word left a bad taste in my mouth.

"No!"

I could have argued it, but I didn't. Suddenly I was remembering Polhemas, and why he'd come to the Center.

Ineh stiffened where she sat, looking past me. There was no one else anywhere near us. "They're coming. They'll find us together. I have to go—"

"There's no one—"

"I feel them!" She stood up, and I knew that in another moment she'd disappear.

"Wait, where—" Where can I find you?"

"In Ringer's End. Thirty-Five—" She wavered, and was gone.

I sat on the bench alone, waiting for whatever happened

next. The stars were starting to show through, and a sliver of the lower moon. About five minutes later a middle-aged man and woman, upside gentry, came into the glade, walking slowly. They looked at me a little longer than they might have; but no longer than anyone dressed the way they were would look at someone dressed like me, in a park at dusk. They went on, murmuring something I couldn't hear. Thinking thoughts I couldn't hear. Were they the ones? Or were they just her fear showing; or just an excuse? I sat twitching until they'd passed, and then I went looking for a cab.

I got to Ringer's End as fast as I could. For Oldcity it wasn't a bad looking street; at least it was clean, and almost quiet. I could hear the sea. I found the building entrance, but no one answered when I buzzed. It was almost time for the Haven show; I couldn't make myself stay there waiting, with no proof that she'd ever even been there. I left Ringer's End and went to a weapon shop, where I got myself a stungun. Then I chased the hour across town to the Haven.

I went through the Haven's doors again, hiking across infinity, not even noticing any more that I walked on thin air. Time mattered, not space—and time was shrinking in on me all the time. I sat down, leaning back away from the glissen mist, not wanting anything to dull my mind. My fingers beat seconds on the empty tabletop, out of rhythm with the gibbering background voices. I'd never noticed before how much like a dirge the music sounded.

At last the usual show began, and I held my breath until I saw Ineh coming out of her cloud of light. As soon as she was a solid reality I started, (Where were you? Where the hell did you go? What's happening; tell me what to do!)

And in the frozen moment before she began, my waiting mind filled with an echo of numbers, a combination . . . I saw that it unlocked the secret of the invisible walls and would let me pass through. (Why? Why?) But she didn't answer, and I couldn't let myself wonder too much. . . . There weren't any answers now, only the soft whispering of her soul reaching out to me, the knowledge that in another hour someone might be using it for a private playground. The seconds crawled past me, space-time warped out of shape in this strange dreamland; her performance went on forever—and was over before I had time to realize it. The guests were on their feet, shuffling out, the room was darkening behind them.

I got up, stood trying not to look like I was waiting, until

most of them were gone. The invisible wall was moving up
on me, pressuring me to leave. . . . I said the numbers, and the
wall of darkness swallowed me up.

Beyond it there was nothing but a corridor—blank, gray,
empty. I blinked, shaking off the feeling that I'd walked
through a wet, open mouth. At the far end of the hall was a
door. I walked toward it, still not quite believing that I'd come
this far. I put my hands into my pockets, feeling the stungun
cool and smooth in my palm. The door at the end of the hall
didn't have a knob or a plate. I pushed it, and it swung open.
Beyond it was more darkness—an alley.

I turned, looking back over my shoulder. Behind me, the
entrance I'd come through had become a solid wall. I had the
feeling it wouldn't let me back again. And there were no other
doors; at least none that I could see. (Ineh!) I shouted her name
with my mind, but there was no answer. This time I wasn't
expecting one. I'd been shown the door, and Ineh—Ineh—
The door was still open. I went through it.

A heavy fist came down across my shoulders, clubbing me
to my knees. Grease and grit skidded under my hands, scraping
my palms, and then it was somebody's foot in my side throwing
me back against the wall. The hands on my jacket dragged me
up, knocking me against the cold peeling surface until my
brains rattled, pulling away and coming back to hit me again,
everywhere, and I couldn't seem to make any part of me work
well enough to stop them. . . . Until the hands let go again at
last and I slid down into the trash.

"Keep away from her, freak—" His foot in my ribs, un-
derlining the word. "Or the next time they won't find your
body." The foot came after me one last time.

Somehow I brought up my hands and caught his leg, twisted
under him with his own motion and jerked him off his feet.
He fell past me onto the pavement, coming down like a con-
demned building. I thanked God he hadn't landed on top of
me. I hauled myself up, the stungun in my hands; reversing
our positions and a lot of other things. "Hold it."

He was trying to get his feet under him. He stopped when
he saw the gun.

"Where is she?"

"Who?"

"You know who." I tried to stand straighter and not listen
to my body. "I ain't got much time. Are you gonna make this
easy or hard?"

He laughed, giving me the answer.

I could see the features of his face clearly now. It looked like he'd landed on it. I wondered how much he could see of mine. I grinned and spat blood. He knew what I was; if he was like most psi-haters—"Did they tell you what kind of 'freak' I am—did they tell you I'm a 'path, like she is? I can turn your brains inside out, read everything you ever thought of, back to the day you were born. It hurts like hell...I'll make sure it does." I grinned wider, hurting like hell. "You gonna give me what I want, deadhead, or do I rip it out of your skull?" I frowned like I was concentrating hard; watched his face turn to jelly.

"All right, all right!" His head dropped, but he was still staring up at me with white eyes from under his brows. "They took her to Kinba's."

"Where's that?" I knew the name; I tried to keep my voice steady.

"Outside the city."

"What's the co-ords?"

He told me.

"Access codes?"

He told me that too; his own voice wasn't too steady.

I spat again. "You sure about that? Maybe I should take a look."

"It's true!" He threw his hands up again, shielding his face, as if he thought that could stop me. "Geezus."

I nodded. "Okay. I think I believe you." I hugged my aching stomach with an arm. "Thanks, sucker."

His own arms came down, and already his face was hardening again. "You...you ain't no 'path! You didn't even sense me waiting. You can't—"

"I know." I pressed the button on the stunner with my thumb, and he went to sleep.

I went out to the street to find a cab. No one looked twice as I pushed my way through the crowds; a stumbling punk who drooled blood was business as usual in Oldcity. And the cab didn't ask questions when I shoved the woman aside and got in, just, "Destination?" I let myself collapse as it took me up over the crowds, heading for the world upside; heading for trouble.

The cab carried me out a long way beyond the southward limit of Quarro, on along the thin peninsula between pincers of sea gleaming like gunmetal under the light of the two moons. I tried to keep count of the wealthy estates winking like stars, hiding in the darkness down below. I remembered seeing mansions on the TD somewhere a long time ago. I ached all over, and felt lonelier than I'd thought I knew how to.

After a while the cab dropped down again, and the world came back at me in a rush. An estate opened out below, like a holo-still blown up out of all proportion: I couldn't quite make myself believe what I saw tumbling down the steep hill slope, layer on layer of broken crystal pulsing with light. The cab didn't veer off as it came down; the codes worked.

And then I was standing on the landing flat, staring at my own reflection haloed by the cab lights—tiny and shattered, repeating over and over in the crescent of facing walls. A lens opened in the smooth surface, and someone came through. It was the hologram host from the Haven. There was no cloak this time, and I decided finally that it was a woman. "Are you real?"

She smiled; her face cracked. "Real enough. But that stungun you carry won't help you. This house is weapon-sealed, of course. So why don't you toss it away." She flicked a hand. The words were all hard surfaces and sharp edges, like the house behind her.

I shrugged, and tossed it away into the dark, bloodstained-colored grass. I wondered how many other eyes were looking me over, all up and down the spectrum.

"This is a private estate, boy. Why are you trespassing here?" Her voice swatted me like a bug: not even worth a threat. I had to admire her ice.

I had to match it: "Ineh wants to see me."

The hard heavy line of one brow quirked. "Ineh? You've come to see Ineh? Then you're that one . . . ?" Her finger darted out at me like a snake's head. "All right. Come in and see her, then." Her smile ripped me to shreds.

I smiled back, tasted a little more of my own blood. "Thanks." I followed her in through the opening iris, jaws full of glass teeth; heard it ring shut behind me. She led me through room after room that probably made the Five Worlds Museum look sleazy. "You know, I used to be a thief myself. What did I do wrong?"

She looked at me; she didn't smile.

There didn't seem to be anyone else in any room we passed. This was the private estate of Farheen Kinba, one of the dark gods who ruled Oldcity's underworld. I thought about what it would be like to live in a place like this all alone . . . knowing all the time that alone was the last thing we were right now.

We took a lift down and down into a part of the house sunk deep into the hillside. And there were all the rest of the bodies, the rest of the eyes that weren't already watching me; there was even Kinba himself. And they were watching someone else, through a wall of mirror-backed glass: Ineh.

The room she sat in was almost empty of anything else; the walls were a silent gray-green, and so was the carpet. She sat in a hard, straight-backed chair, its arms and legs carved with eye-twisting tangles of vine until it almost seemed to be growing up and over her, holding her prisoner.

And across from her in a cushioned recliner, not touching her in any way, lay a man. They both wore long white robes, like shrouds; but from what I could see of his heavy face and his soft, thick hands, he was somebody who was used to having too much of everything. His eyes were shut, but he wasn't asleep. He was dreaming. . . . I watched his face, the expressions that stretched it, warping rubber; his body tightening, jerking once, shifting. Ineh's face moved with her own shaping and sharing of his dream, but the emotions that moved it weren't the same. Her body was as rigid as the chair that held it, trembling with strain. Her eyes were shut, and I saw the wet-silver tracks of tears lying on her cheeks.

I closed my own eyes, shut off all the outside senses I could—trying to reach what was happening out there with the one left inside. I felt whispers and mutterings, muffled cries, pressing my mind against the wall of glass that lay inside my own head. I held my breath, forgot my body and where it was. . . . Ghost images began to form, began to pull at me: Cold raw hands began to dig into my brain: This was a man with hungers that had never been satisfied, never could be. Hungers that had driven him to a position of power only a few others ever reached, given him all the pleasures that still weren't enough. And now he had the powers of the Dreamweaver to play with. She wasn't leading his dreams, she was following them, letting him fix the rules and being forced to play by them. The power he'd always wanted, to dominate and humiliate and use—the freedom that the laws of society kept him from ever really getting his fill of—all that was his now, his to dream about, with Ineh as his tool and his victim.

(Ineh! Ineh!) I screamed her name silently, trying to break through. But she was caught up in his nightmare; her mouth opened in her own silent scream. I pushed through the knot of watchers to the transparent wall, beat my fists against it. "Ineh!" But the surface was solid and impenetrable, the sound recoiled. Ineh didn't move.

Hands caught my arms, dragging me back into the real world. The group of watchers around me were suddenly all watching me, their faces half slack, half ugly. I realized they'd all been listening to what I'd just heard; a bunch of goddamn voyeurs peeping through the keyhole into somebody else's mind. Two or three of the faces I recognized from the past, Kinba himself and a couple of Oldcity's other first citizens, all looking businesslike and respectable in drapes of watercolor silk. There was a stranger dressed the same way, but looking uneasy. The rest I didn't recognize; but I recognized the type.

And there was someone else in the room, sitting to one side while the others stood, a remote on his knees. Right now he was leaning forward muttering some kind of message into it. He stopped, looking up, not at me but at Ineh again, and his eyes got glassy. He didn't seem to fit in with the rest, and I knew the look on his face too well. He was a telepath—a corporate telepath. Some companies used them to scan callers or party guests; but most were too paranoid to use a 'path who was good enough to really pick brains, including their own.

And this one was communicating with Ineh, getting messages that no one else here was getting. . . . I looked back at the stranger who was dressed for business, and suddenly it all fit. The Corpses were right: Somebody was using psionics to pick brains. It was happening right here in front of me, and the victim never even knew it. Ineh must have screened every crowd at the Haven, picked out the customers whose minds were crammed full of secrets to be sold to the highest bidder. And this was how she pulled them out.

Kinba turned to the woman. "Hedo, what is this?" He waved a hand at my face. He was wearing a sapphire as big as a cockroach on his middle finger. "Why did you bring him here?"

"It's Ineh's freak; he got past Spoode. I thought such determination ought to be rewarded. And I thought you might like to ask him how many others know he's here."

I saw Ineh slump over the far arm of her chair. I tried to pull free, but Kinba's bodyguards held me with no trouble. I felt something slip over my wrists behind my back and tighten, pinning them together. Kinba smiled at me, a tiny twitch pulling his mouth against his perfect teeth.

"You son-of-a-bitch," I said.

The hand with the sapphire ring slapped me. I shook my head, feeling fresh blood in a warm trickle down my cheek. "Mind your tongue or I'll have it cut out." His voice was white and cold like his face. "If you prefer to keep it, you half-breed abomination, perhaps you'll consider telling us who else knows you're here?" The rest of them had stopped watching Ineh, and their faces were grim.

I kept my own eyes on her, felt my body trembling. "The Corpses know. They know about the Haven and what you're doing with it—"

He held up his hand. I stopped. "We'll see." Some of the faces began to look worried; but not his. The corporate man kneaded his hands together. A door was opening in the next room. Two men were shaking the slug awake, hauling him off his couch. The woman called Hedo went to Ineh, helped her to stand, leading her out after the others were gone. The corporate telepath stared at me as if he'd just noticed I was there; glanced at his boss, who frowned. He looked back at me, confused, and I tried to make him react somehow. He looked down again at the remote in his lap, his shoulders hunching. Kinba's bodyguards led me out of the room.

We went back up in the lift, back into the main part of the house; into a room looking out on the night and the long ruddy slope of the hill. Ineh was already there. She sat gulping something from a cup, her robe soaked and stained, her movements jerky. And yet she was more beautiful, almost shining; not because of what had happened, but somehow in spite of it. I shook my head again, not understanding what I was seeing. She looked up then and saw me, froze as she saw what I looked like.

"Ineh," the woman said, "see who came for your performance."

Ineh still sat frozen. She didn't answer. Her mouth quivered.

"I'm okay," I said. "I've come to take you back with me. The Corpses know everything. If anything happens to me or you, they know who to blame."

"Ineh, is he telling the truth?" Kinba strolled past me to where she sat, ran his maggot fingers through her hair, massaged her neck.

I felt her touch me with her mind: A hard clumsy blow that tore the tight-woven defenses of my thoughts apart. I tried not to resist, holding out trust, hope, reassurance, not even bothering to hide my lie. Trusting her—

"He told no one." Her voice was flat. "He is here alone, no one knows what he's done."

Kinba's hands dropped to her shoulders, patted her lightly; all the hidden tension had gone out of them. His laughter was loose and easy. I was just exactly as stupid as he'd figured I was. "You see, good people, there was nothing to worry about," heavy on the *nothing*.

I looked down at the floor, twisting my hands against the hard edges of the binder.

"Ineh, I'm disappointed." His hands squeezed her shoulders. "Is this quixotic idiot really your idea of someone who's going to change your life?" She grimaced, but didn't answer. "Well, here he is. You did well enough for us just now. But you seem to detest it, you resist it so. That impairs your usefulness. I always said our relationship was one of mutual need, not slavery. You could leave any time you chose. Would you like to go away with him?" She looked up, her face caught in the middle of half a dozen different emotions. "You've given us years of loyal service. Shall I repay you now . . . let you go away with him? Of course if you do, you'll be losing the privileges of our partnership. Are you ready to lose all that? Or do you want to stay on, safe and protected, and . . . let us get rid of him?"

I couldn't believe that she was really listening to what he said, any more than I believed for a second that he was offering her a real choice. But she stared up at him like she was seeing God; looked at me for a long minute, without letting me through into her mind. She looked out the window at the empty night, and the minute stretched into two, into eternity. My mind ached, waiting for her to choose, even while I knew it was no choice and at least one of us was going to die.

I looked after her out the windowed wall at the sky . . . just in time to see the windows dissolve like a film of ice in the sun, the sun bursting in on me, my sight going redgoldwhite-black before I could shut my eyes. Then all hell broke loose—shouting and curses and noises I didn't recognize, bodies slamming into me, knocking me down. By the time I blinked my eyes clear, there was a Corporate Security cruiser hanging beyond the slagged windows and the room was filling up with Corpses.

And Ineh was on her knees beside me, pulling at my arm. Her voice was high and broken, I could barely make out what she said, "Cat, Cat . . . they come to arrest us, to take us away!"

I sat back, trying to get my feet under me. "Get out of here, Ineh! Now, while you can—" A Corpse had spotted us, was starting toward us through the shifting forest of bodies.

"Where, where can I go? I'm afraid—"

"Somewhere they won't be looking! Anywhere. Go on!"

"You—?"

"I'll be all right. Go on!"

She disappeared; I felt the soft inrush of air that followed. Neat gray legs stopped short beside me. I heard the Corpse swear, and looking up I saw Polhemas. I started to get up. He reached down and caught the front of my jacket, hauling me onto my feet.

"Where did she go?"

"Who?"

"Don't play brain-damaged with me." The polite official front was gone. "You're in enough trouble as it is."

"Me?" I jerked at my cuffed hands. "Come on, Polhemas, you think I did this to myself? You know I didn't have anything to do with them—" I bent my head at the rest of the room.

His hand was still clenched on my jacket front. "I knew you were lying when you told me you didn't know anything, back at the Center. That's why I had a tracer put on you. And it led us right to the answer."

"You think I didn't know you were following me? It would've been damn stupid to walk into this all by myself if I wasn't involved; that's what you figure, isn't it?" I tried to stare him down. I hoped he couldn't see my ears burning. "I'm not stupid," *just crazy*, "and I wasn't lying to you. But I was smart enough to see a few things you overlooked, while you were spending all your time trying to blame this on the Center. Face it, Polhemas, I'm the hero here. You can't turn it inside out."

His face turned redder than my ears, and his hand on my jacket jerked me forward. But then he grunted and let me go. He was going to be hero enough himself to keep him from making a case of proving I was wrong. I let my own breath out in a sigh. He looked me over again, looking hard at my bruised face. Then he turned me around and released the binder on my wrists. "Why didn't you just tell us what you learned? If you wanted to be a hero that would've been enough. Why risk being a dead one?"

I pulled my hands forward and rubbed them. "Why should
I do you any favors? What have you done for the Center for
Psionic Research lately?"

He ignored that. "It was the Dreamweaver, wasn't it? Where
did you send her—where is she?"

"I don't know. Somewhere you won't find her. You can
drug me all you want but I can't tell you more than that."

"We'll find her." It was a threat.

I caught his arm. "Why don't you leave her alone? They
made her do it, she didn't want to. That's why she came to
me, for help. She's suffered more than that mindfucker ever
did—" pointing at her 'guest' standing sullen and confused
while two Corpses questioned him. "He's the one you ought
to send up. If you'd seen the inside of his head you'd kill him
on the spot."

Polhemas looked at the slug and back at me without saying
anything. His eyes were still cold and empty.

"Look, you've got what you want. Leave it alone. . . . It
probably never occurred to you, but we're just trying to live
like everybody else. Give us a goddamn break! We gave you
what you want; we've earned it."

He didn't answer.

I let go of his arm and turned away. The corporate telepath
was looking at me from across the room, where his boss's
voice was getting louder and louder. His face was full of fear
and despair; I could see it, but I couldn't feel it. I started to
walk away.

"Nobody said you could go anywhere," Polhemas said.

"Try and stop me."

He did.

It was hours later before I was free again, walking back
through the streets to the Center, feeling the steel and stone
of all Oldcity weighing down my heart. Polhemas had asked
me a thousand questions about everything I'd seen, heard,
overheard, thought or guessed. I'd told him everything I could,
because it didn't matter any more and I only wanted to get out
of there. It was only after I'd left the detention center that I
let myself realize he hadn't tried to force anything more out
of me about where Ineh had gone. It surprised me, because
it meant that he must have listened to something I'd said to
him before. But either way it didn't really matter; because Ineh
was gone, and I didn't know where. How the hell would I find

her; what would she do—what would I do?

The Center was long since closed for the night when I reached it. But there was still a light on somewhere inside, so I went in the front entrance instead of taking the back way up to my room. Jule and Siebeling stood waiting for me in the empty front hall: I almost walked by without seeing them.

"Cat?"

I stopped, shaking my head; stood there without saying anything. They came toward me when I didn't move. Siebeling lifted his hand, and across the room the lights brightened. Their faces showed pools and lines of shadow, their tired eyes looked me up and down. Siebeling caught my jaw with his hand, gently, turning my face right and left.

"Did Corporate Security do that to you?"

"No."

"What happened?" Jule asked. The question didn't stop with my face.

"I fell down." I tried to pull away, but Jule held my arm.

"Wait a minute." She stood in front of me. "You've been trying to pretend that you're the only one who's involved with the Dreamweaver's problems; but you're not. You're not alone in this. You're not alone in the world—for better or worse."

"You weren't exactly killing yourself to help me out."

"That's hardly fair," Siebeling said. "You didn't give us any information. You didn't tell us the kind of problems that were really involved, the kind of people, the danger. You went off on a suicidal crusade against Evil, and you damn near got just what you were asking for! Didn't it ever occur to you that—that—" he broke off, shaking his head, "that we can't read your mind, Cat."

"I never thought about anything else. That's the trouble." I looked down, my arms hanging heavy at my sides. "I'm sorry. Maybe I'll start appreciating what I've got left, now." *Now that it doesn't matter any more, now that it's too late.* "How'd you know what happened? Were the Corpses here?"

"No." Siebeling leaned against a seat-back. "They haven't been here."

"They haven't? Not at all?"

He shook his head.

I laughed, a choked sort of sound. It meant there might be something decent in Polhemas after all, and I wasn't ready to believe it. "Then how did you know?"

"Ineh told us," Jule said.

Ineh? The word wouldn't form in my mouth. "Where— where is she?"

"Up in your room. I had to give her a sedative to help her keep control; she's sleeping now." He touched his head. "You know she's an addict, Cat—?"

I flinched. "Yeah, I know. What's she on, Doc? Did you find out?"

"It's called Trihannobin. It's—"

"Nightmare." I felt cold. "They call it nightmare."

He nodded. "And they say it takes you for quite a ride.... It's a kind of nerve poison. Most people don't use it for long. They generally stop when it kills them." His face was as stiff as my own.

"I went for a ride once." The images came without my wanting them to, "I thought I was in heaven. I didn't eat or sleep for three days. And then it wore off." I kept my eyes open, kept looking at their faces: proving that I was here in the present, that I'd really come through it. *Nightmare... that's why they call it nightmare*. I could still see the hospital ward through their faces, the nutrient bath shining on my skin, the straps.... They hadn't cared enough to try and make it easier. "Give her something to make it easier—"

He shook his head, looking down.

"Why not?"

"She's Hydran, Cat... I can't predict how it would affect her. She doesn't react to the drug the way a human does, or she'd be dead by now. If I tried to counteract it without doing an analysis, I could make it worse for her instead—" He sounded helpless; I wasn't used to hearing him sound that way.

"I guess I want to see her now."

He nodded, and the three of us went upstairs.

I was the first one into the room. Ineh sat waiting, watching, from my bed platform. Her arms were locked around her knees, her fists were tightly clenched. Her face was clenched too; I couldn't tell what she was thinking.

"We may need restraints," Siebeling murmured to Jule.

"No." I looked back. "If she needs it I'll do it; I'll hold her." I realized as I said it that I was going to do more—that I was going to do everything. Not because I wouldn't share it with them, this time, but because I couldn't. Ineh would lose control again, and once she lost it completely I'd be the only one left who could stand being near her. "The best thing you can do now is get out of range while you can."

They looked at each other, and at me. This time they didn't
argue. They left the room.

"Hello, Ineh." She didn't answer. I moved across to the
bed platform, climbed up and sat beside her, trying to keep
my face calm and easy. "Thank God you came here," thinking
that she had more sense than I did, to trust Jule and Doc when
I hadn't. "I just about went crazy wondering how I'd find you."
I reached out to touch her arm. Her body jerked away; I didn't
know whether she'd meant for it to or not. "Sorry." I looked
down at my hands, up again. A hard knot was forming in my
throat. "I know, it's already started. Don't be afraid."

Her eyes fixed on me, wild and glassy, as though she was
listening to a lunatic. She licked her lips. "I need my dream
tonic. Help me."

I shook my head. "Not that way. I've been through this,
Ineh, and I came out the other side. I'll help you. Let me in,
let me share the—"

Something blinding hit me behind the eyes, fed back along
the nerve-paths to the ends of my senses—all her power focused
on me and driven home by fear. I cried out, holding my head.
And I saw her—not the Ineh I thought I knew, but the Ineh
I'd seen in ghost glimpses when her concentration slipped,
when she couldn't make me see her the way she wanted the
world to see her, and I'd fallen through it into the way she
was. The nightmare Ineh, brittle bones, sunken eyes, wasted
flesh. *The nightmare*. The nightmare already beginning—Disgust and hatred filled me up like the urge to vomit: Ineh loathing
the thing she'd become in her mind, was becoming with her
body; a filthy, crawling, drug-infected ruin, born to pain, de-
serving pain, terrified of pain but trapped inside it with no
escape, trapped—

Trapped. I was trapped in her nightmare journey of pain
promising more pain, pain until you wailed, howled, beat yourself senseless against walls to get away from it. Your hands
ripped your own flesh, your legs wouldn't hold you up, your
body betrayed and humiliated you in ways you never dreamed
of and you didn't even care. . . . When I could sit up again in
the hospital there was a corpse in the mirror, I saw a corpse
and I screamed and I had two black eyes and I can't go through
it all over again I can't—!

I threw myself down from the platform, away from the sight
of her. I almost shouted for the others, almost started for the
door, almost ran—out of the room, away from her and the

power of her pain and myself. Instead I turned back and looked
at her. She hunched forward, burying her face in the stained
whiteness of her robe, dragging isolation over herself like a
shroud. There was no reaching from mind to mind; I'd shut
her out, and she wasn't trying to get back in.

And I was going to leave her that way. I was going to leave
her alone and prove to her that there was nobody on this world
who wouldn't betray her; that there was no one she could count
on; that no matter what she tried to do, because of what she
was it would turn against her. . . . That if she reached the other
end of this road through hell she'd only find that it hadn't been
worth the trip. I was the only one who could share the journey,
who knew the roadmarks, who could make her believe there
was a reason to survive it. But I was going to leave her here
alone and run from her problems, just like I'd done to myself,
just like I'd always done. . . .

I climbed back onto the platform. I kneeled beside Ineh,
put my arms around her huddled body, feeling her muscles
knot and quiver. "I'm here, I won't leave you. You can count
on me—" my voice broke.

A wall of blind hatred slammed into me, locking me out.
Hopeless pain was all that was left, all that was real to her
now, eating her alive from the inside. I had to break into it
somehow again, before everything imploded.

And there was only one thing still working in her mind—
one way I might be able to break into her fugue: If I could
turn the rage that was holding me out into a tool to let me
in. . . . "All right!" shouting it into her face. "You hate me now,
you want to blame it all on me for forcing you into this. But
you dragged *me* into this, you set me up to do this for you
when you didn't have the guts to do it for yourself! Then you
lost your nerve, you set me up with Kinba and I got the shit
beat out of me. If I was going to stop believing, that should've
done it. But I didn't; I didn't give up on you. I kept on until
you were free. You're *free*. Listen to me, listen—!"

"If you have to hate somebody, don't make it me. Remember why you wanted this—remember where you were before
you came here tonight! Remember who did it to you, who
chained your soul down and turned your gift into something
sick and dirty. If you want to shut somebody out of your life,
shut them out! If you want something enough to die for it make
it your freedom! If you want to hate somebody let it be Kinba!"
I shook her. "Don't let them win. We don't have to let the

goddamn scum of this world destroy us. Let it out, get it out
of your system, the hate, and the pain will go with it. Let me
in—" (*Let me share your pain,*) pushing myself aside, trying
to loosen my mind, to lose any other thought, and let the
emptiness go unguarded.

Ineh jerked upright, tears streaming down her face. She
opened her mouth. And screamed. The scream went on and
on, pouring out of her like blood.

My mind burst open as the images smashed into me, losing
all control as she lost all control. Not my own mind any more
but a stage in darkness for the Dreamweaver's nightmares:
Agony from a million neurons like live wires snapping . . . the
taste of gall, the stench of putrifying flesh, my ears screaming,
knives of light slashing my eyes, agony that filled all time and
went on and on and on. . . . Cancer flowers spreading, the face
of the torturer with a thousand faces, petals opening endlessly
changing out of control controlling body, soul . . . Kinba, white
yielding *inevitable* cajoling soothing *strangling striking tearing
destroying/*flash shatter* hot blades broken glass*/Hedo, ob-
livion's water food of gods of dreams *hands of ice edge of
knives/*screaming blackness* eyes torn from sockets*/ Body of
a slug mind full of worms bursting like a boil, endless floods
of diseased image that went on and on, no escape from ugly
minds, stupid, greedy, blind, empty empty minds—mutilating
her gift denying her self, suffocating her soul in their soul-
darkness until she was only a thing used by things. . . .

(*I know, I know.* . . . Struggling up out of her nightmares,
dazed, torn, falling back, into my own: In the mines breathing
poisoned air, beaten starved buried alive in the freezing guts
of an alien world. No rest, no hope, no night or day . . . no
escape, no end except a dead end. Warm bodies, cheaper than
cold machines. No one caring if you lived or died until finally
even you didn't care, betrayed, abandoned, a thing used by
things. . . .)

Hate them I hate them!!!/*Stars*/ Kinba, Hedo, an endless
wheel flickering changing *offering betraying humiliating tor-
menting* . . . no one in all the space of the living who was not
there to torture/*ripping forcing* violation death*/ Let me go
oh let me die! die! die! Ruined, infected, weak degraded cow-
ard!! No reason to live no reason no no

(*Her hands* from another world, the real world, flailing,
clawing, reaching for my throat; *my body* sprawled against her
own, holding it down, holding the hands away from her face,

226   JOAN D. VINGE

from finding a weapon. The false light of a new day breaking,
showing me the truth—life was the nightmare, and there was
no waking out of it. This was real, and reality was no one's
dream. They sang it in the streets . . . the streets of Oldcity, the
faces of a lifetime glaring down like floodlights, smothering
me in spit and blows and ugly laughter: City-boy, halfbreed,
bondie, scum. All *shouting* whispering thinking it . . . their
hands fists, their feet on my neck; taking what they wanted,
over and over, and never giving a word, a touch, no friendship,
no kindness, no reason—

("Let me help you." *Jule . . .* Jule, saying four words that
I'd never heard from anyone before, touching my mind with
gentleness, making me see the world in the mirror and not hate
it any more. There was a reason, there *was. . . .* Clinging to it,
forcing belief, *Ineh! Listen, listen to me,* fighting upstream
against the flood of two rivers. *It doesn't matter what happened, none of it, none of them. What they did to you, or me,
it isn't us, it hasn't changed the truth—* Repeating it, over and
over and over; getting nowhere, losing strength, losing—*You
have a gift, reaching out to the world,* reaching out to me, *so
many that need it, really need it. Not sick, only like you are
or I am, sick of hatred and pain—*)

Hatred pain/*nails thorns iron*/ nothing else real, no one
not evil ugly empty *human*! . . . herself, evil ugly human
corrupted . . . I want to die! let me let me go—

(*Not human! No, you aren't, you never will be—they'll
never let you be; be glad of it! Remember who you were,
remember your real people, everything you shared with
them—*)

Nooooo! wild anguish, denial, terror—

(*Yes! You belong to your people, you can help them, share
with them—*)

No no *gone* lost abandoned betrayed—! Herself, themselves, betrayed, lost. . . . Faces, loved faces torn away torn
apart by parting, minds torn apart families torn apart, lost in
the endless darkness of space lost forever, forever, pain going
on forever lost in pain. . . .

(Lost in pain . . . my own, my people lost to me, lost in the
endless darkness, lost forever . . . *No! stop* . . . terror, pain,
screams echoing in an alley-end—in a child's ears, in a child's
mind. . . . *Stop, stop it!*)

New world harsh ugly gray prison walls gray minds hunger
hatred fear . . . minds sharing *shriveling breaking sealing shut,*

closing out hunger hatred loss each other giving *giving less, giving nothing, giving out giving in* . . . *betraying, abandoning, surrendering—*

(*It doesn't matter! It doesn't matter! Find your way back, they'll take you back, they have to*— Only one thing, one thing could never be forgiven.)

Too far! Too long, too much shame filth ugliness! Never return, never forgiveness enough for so much shame! Only death only death forgives!

(*No! Not death—only death never forgives, only death is never forgiven!* . . . Choking, suffocating, fluid: my mind filling up with blood—no *no—No forgiveness*! No death for a killer no help for a cripple—*me, not you! My punishment, my guilt, my shame!* The weapon lying in my hands and the hatred in my soul and an enemy inside my mind showing me that I had no right to pride or love or loyalty, halfbreed scum I ought to be dead! Like my dreams my memories *my mother in an Oldcity alley*, screaming and screaming inside my head until I can't hear anything at all. . . . She died, and I couldn't save her. She died inside my head and I didn't, and that made me human enough to hate and kill. No matter that it saved a life, two lives, three—my own. . . . I could, I had to, I wanted to—*I did*.

(Mind inside mind exploding like a star, burning out circuits senses soul . . . lost in a rain of black ashes falling through silence. Silence and blackness—no light no sound no way back to the land of life . . . dead inside my own body—Lie down and die, murderer, betrayer, failure! black ashes to drown in, ashes blood death only death forgives, darkness, darkness soft and deep, drowning. . . .)

Light breaking like sunrise on every side, rays beams streaming through the choking fall of death. *See death*, see it for Nothing, absence denial loss fear escape—lifeless beautyless emptiness . . . *Light* growing stronger, surrounds crystalizes dissolves darkness—(*I remember, I remember* being wrapped in light, mind joining mind strong enough to drive out any pain) *Light* rising suffusing, golden, opening onto sky, endless rumpled fields of whiteness, clouds (*snow* the snowfields of another world, remembered world, spring green mountains rising impossibly from snow against a sapphire rainwashed sky: proving beauty still existed, trust, friendship, love. . . . Death destroys us, hate/pain makes us blind but those things still exist, still live and are true within us without us) True beyond us—true because of us, true between us, nothing

hidden now, my name written on my heart, read it, read it and
show me your own, let me in....*Light* growing stronger
brighter incandescent, dissolving pain, hatred grief loosening
bonds setting free, dissolving into the universal heartbeat promise refuge peace, peace, peace....

I woke, and waking was like a dream. I moved through
slowtime, the room flowed around me like honey as I lifted
my head. Ineh was beside me, eyes shut, barely breathing.
Nothing reached me now from her mind, but one of her hands
was locked inside my own like a double vise; my arm was raw
with scratches. Slowly I knew that my hand was aching with
cramp, my whole body was locked in a cramp, my skin burned
and the room stank of sweat and sickness. Ineh's face was
bruised and hollow, her hair snarled like weeds; her own genuine body lay beside me, wasted by drugs. There was nothing
hidden now; but I couldn't be sorry, only glad. Nothing was
hidden between us; nothing hidden from ourselves. She had
shown me the name hidden in her soul, and shown me my
own; we had shared the understanding that surpassed all truth.
I could see again—and everything I saw was beautiful. I let
my head fall back, my empty mind was full of peace, and I
slept.

When I came to again there was no one beside me. I reached
out with my mind, groping, and found nothing. Then I believed
it. I dragged myself to the edge of the platform and looked
down—had to shut my eyes. There was a sound like a sigh,
and when I opened them again Jule was standing there.
Jule . . . I kept trying to see Inch.
"She's safe," Jule said, and smiled. "She's all right."
I grunted, and let an arm drop down.
She squeezed my hand, helped me down from the platform
and into the bathroom. I drank six cups of water while she
peeled off my stinking clothes. Then she pushed me into the
fresher and disappeared again. I stood inside until it turned my
raw skin numb and tingling, until I could tell that I had legs
to stand on. It felt like a long time since I'd used them.
It was a long time. The readout on the clock said two days.
I pulled on a tunic and drank some more water, trying to sort
out my mind.
Then Jule was back again, with food. Eating it gave me a

little extra time. Finally I said, "Is she with you?"

She nodded. "With us, yes. Ardan's treating her; she's in bad shape physically."

"I know. It's all right? She doesn't—?" I touched my head, looking at her.

Jule shook her own head. "It was her suffering that I couldn't bear. The worst of that is past; I can protect myself from what's left. But it's going to be a long time before she believes she has any control—over herself or her life. She's going to need a lot of help, a lot of shared strength."

Do any of us really control anything? But I only said, "I know. Half a lifetime doesn't heal in a night. Nothing's that easy. But the worst is over, like you said. And I'll—we'll be here, to show her how much good she can find in..." Something in Jule's face made me stop. But I didn't ask; with my heart beating quick and sudden I let my mind go loose, trying to feel what was wrong. And got nothing. Nothing.

"Cat? What's the matter?"

"Nothing. I mean—*nothing*," feeling my face collapse; feeling my mind as tight and hard as a fist. "Did you—was there anything?"

She looked at me, confused. Then, "Oh." No.

"It didn't last." *Didn't last, didn't last, didn't....* Echoes, was that all she'd left me? (Jule, feel it, for God's sake, *feel* it!)

She blinked, twitched.

I leaned forward, tilting my stool. "Did you...?"

She nodded slowly, starting a smile. "I felt something. I felt something."

"Yeah?" I settled back; knowing I should have known that Ineh wasn't the only one whose healing wouldn't finish in a night.... "At least there's something. Hope." *A crack in the wall.* A beginning, now that I'd finally accepted the guilt that would only die when I did. I sighed, looking back at Jule. "What did I say wrong about helping Ineh?" Asking; just asking.

Jule stood up, turning away from me. "She doesn't want to see you again."

"What?"

"She doesn't want to see you." Her voice got weaker instead of stronger.

"Why? Why not?" I stood up, following her. "We shared—everything."

"That's why." She turned to face me, finally. "She isn't ready, she isn't strong enough to deal with what that meant to both of you. You saw things about her that made her wish she was dead, Cat. Things she'll be working to forget for the rest of her life."

"But she knows things about me—" *things that made me wish I was dead*, "things even you don't know. She doesn't need to feel any shame with me. What she knows about me—"

"Is more than she can bear. Not added to her own problems. Not right now." She frowned, not with anger, not at me.

"So she needs time, you mean. In time she'll want to see me again. . . . a long time?"

She nodded.

"I see." A long time before a Hydran could face a halfbreed who couldn't face himself. A long time before he'd ever be able to do even that. A long time, a long cure, a lot of memories like bandages . . . a lot of proving I had a right to be alive. "I can't stay here anymore." Jule didn't say anything. I went to the window, stared through the dark ghost trapped there in the dirty pane. "At least I know she's got you—at least she'll have the best friends anybody could ask for, to help her through if I can't." I traced lines in the dust on the deep sill. Glancing down, I saw that I'd written C-A-T.

"You've already done the most important part, alone. You saved her sanity, Cat."

I shook my head, wiped my name out in the dust. "You've got it backwards. She saved mine. I thought I could handle it, I thought I could make her believe in herself. But I couldn't. I was the one who broke. And she had to come after me and drag me out of my own death wish."

"But you showed her she could use her talent in ways that were healing, not degrading. And then you gave her a chance to prove it. You showed her that she isn't the only one who's suffered . . . and survived." Her voice touched me softly.

I glanced over my shoulder. "How much did you—did you—?"

She shook her head. "None of it. I couldn't. We're all afraid of something in our lives . . . of meeting the past head-on. But Ineh knows that, and I understand it, now. We've begun to find common ground. She showed me enough . . . she showed me how much you gave back to her."

I took a long breath, leaning against the casement. I could

hear Oldcity's voice through the window; feel it, gritty under my hands. I looked up and out, seeing nothing but walls. Somewhere up there was a garden where the sweet breath of spring moved silver crescent leaves; farther above two moons, hanging in the sky like lanterns. . . . "She's got a gift, Jule. For healing, for reaching even somebody like me. She could help her people here, the lost ones. Maybe she could give them back what they lost—not their life, but maybe their pride. Make her believe that, will you?"

"I'll try. And so will Ardan."

I remembered his own common ground, and nodded. "Yeah. That's fine. She'll do fine. . . ." I turned around, to look back at the room Ineh and I had gone through hell in together: Cracked, cramped, peeling; with a couple of cheap holos of somewhere better on the walls to make it even more depressing. Only one thing in the room that was beautiful, besides Jule; one thing that was beautiful and mine—a small Hydran crystal globe sitting on the bookshelf table, that Siebeling had given to me. An image of a nightflower bush, black petals striped with silver repeating like a starry night, lay inside it.

I went to it and covered it with my hand. It was warm, not cool; it always was. I closed my eyes and felt for it with all my mind, felt it tingle and stir with the psi-tuned energy I was calling. . . . But when I opened my eyes the nightflower was still there. Once I'd only needed to touch the warm surface and wish, to change the image inside. The nightflower had been there for most of a year, ever since Siebeling had given it to me. *A promise*, he'd called it. "Give this to Ineh for me. Say it's—a promise." I cupped the ball in my hands.

Jule came to my side, put her arm around my shoulders. Dimly I knew that she was trying to share with me. I held my mind open as far as I could . . . felt warmth belief hope sorrow trust love; a drop of nectar, a whisper of a poem where before there had only been the silence of the grave. Feeling what they had only been able to tell me, that they loved me, that they wanted to help me; that they were responsible for the way I was, and they would be responsible for making it right again.

"But it's not your responsibility." I moved away from her, gently. "It was my choice; I killed a man. I have to pay for it, I have to make it right with myself."

"You can't give up now, Cat, just when you've—"

"Jule," I said; she stopped. "You don't understand. You

want to help me; I know that. You tried—you did help. But all this has shown me that I'm the only one who can make the trip. You can't carry me; you don't need to: I'm not a cripple. I can walk." *Someday I'll run*. I looked down. "And I guess it's about time I got started."

"You're really leaving here, then." Not a question; a dim barb of dismay caught in my mind.

I nodded, not really sure of the answer until I'd made it; realizing then that I'd been certain all along. "It's better if I do. Better for Ineh. Better for me. Better for everyone."

She shook her head, but she didn't deny it. I moved back to her and put my arms around her. We held each other for a while, not saying anything. Her body was warm against mine, made real by the presence of her mind. "I'm sorry. . . ." she said finally; but I wasn't sure why.

I let her go at last and moved back to the window; looking out again because I had to.

"Where will you go?" she asked.

"I don't know. I don't care. Maybe it doesn't even matter." I shrugged. "I mean, what have I got to lose?" Up there somewhere two moons were hanging like lanterns in the sky; and beyond them were the stars.

Tom Reamy

was an incredible talent, a soft-spoken and gentle man with a wry, understated wit, and a friend. His career as a professional writer was brief but oh, so memorable. The speed of it all was amazing.

Tom was in his late thirties before he even thought to try his hand at fiction writing. But he brought to his first efforts such a store of talent, keen observation, and knowledge of humanity that he seemed to spring into being as a major writer full-bloom, without ever going through the agonized years of apprenticeship so common in the game.

In 1973 he made his first sales, two on the same day, a story called "Beyond the Cleft" to Harry Harrison's Nova anthology, and another titled "Under the Hollywood Sign" to Damon Knight for Orbit.

In 1974, a third story—more sales quickly followed those first two—became his first professional publication: "Twilla," in the September, 1974 issue of The Magazine of Fantasy & Science-Fiction.

In 1975, "Twilla"—Tom's first published story, mind you—was a finalist for the Nebula Award in its category.

In 1976, another Reamy story, "San Diego Lightfoot Sue," was nominated for both Hugo and Nebula. It finished as a runner-up in the Hugo balloting, but won the Nebula. The victory was startling and unprecedented for a writer so new on the scene. The same year, of course, saw Reamy nominated for the fourth John W. Campbell Award. He faced formidable opposition in the likes of Vinge, Darnay, Foster, and Varley. But he was formidable himself, and on Labor Day weekend in Kansas City, Missouri, he rose in a dazzlingly flashy light-blue tux, and accepted the award to sustained applause. From the stage, he said how glad he was to win the Campbell, since it was one award that you only got a few shots at. With the Hugo and the Nebula, there was always next year, but once your two years of eligibility have run their course on the Campbell, that's it. A few minutes later, he lost the Hugo for "San Diego Lightfoot Sue," but it didn't dampen his spirits. There would be more awards for Tom Reamy, we all knew.

And in early November of 1977, fourteen months after winning the Campbell Award as the best new writer in SF, Tom Reamy died of a heart attack in Kansas City while working on a new story. He was found slumped over his typewriter. He was 42. Only 42, with one unpublished novel and about a dozen stories to his credit, and so many more left to tell. He had been a professional writer for a bare four years, and already a Nebula and the Campbell sat side-by-side on his shelf. He was 42, a new writer, just beginning. And then he was gone. No words can mitigate that blow.

Behind him he left his novel, his stories, and a good many memories.

The novel, Blind Voices, was published by Berkley/Putnam in 1978. Reamy had intended to do one final revision of the book, one last polish to bring it fully up to the standards of his top work. The book never got the benefit of that polish. But still, still, it was a splendid novel. It bore some superficial resemblances to Bradbury and to Finney, and a deeper kinship to Theodore Sturgeon, a writer that Tom admired inordinately, but for all that it was an original, a powerful and affecting narrative that bore Tom's own stamp. It was published to much praise, and ultimately nominated for both Hugo and Nebula. I recommend it whole-heartedly.

The stories, just about all of them, were assembled in a

posthumous collection, San Diego Lightfoot Sue and Other
Stories *(EarthLight Press, 1979). Put together with love by
some of Tom's friends, the collection contains all of the Reamy
short fiction there is, save two stories; the one you are about
to read, and another forthcoming in Harlan Ellison's long-
awaited* Last Dangerous Visions. *Like all writers, Tom did
some minor work, some flawed work. But when he was at his
best, in "San Diego Lightfoot Sue," in "Under the Hollywood
Sign," in "Twilla" and "The Detweiler Boy" and "Beyond the
Cleft"—well, not many were better. He could evoke an image
or describe a scene in two pointed lines, rich with detail, the
right detail. He portrayed small town life as well as Larry
McMurtry or any other living writer. He could scare the hell
out of you, too, and often did. Some of his stories will be
popping up in anthologies for a long long time.*

But beyond Blind Voices *and* San Diego Lightfoot Sue,
*there was Tom the person. He had done a good many things
besides write. He had been a movie projectionist, a technical
illustrator, a would-be screenwriter. He was prop master on*
Flesh Gordon, *and assistant director on a few other low-budget
films during a couple frustrating years he spent in Hollywood.
He had been a fan of SF most of his life, and an important
one. He published a fanzine,* Trumpet, *that was nominated for
the Hugo several times and changed the look of fanzines for
good and all. He chaired a worldcon bid that failed (Dallas
in 1973), and did the publications for another that succeeded
grandly (Kansas City in 1976). He was addicted to both bridge
and cigarettes. He lived in Texas, California, and Kansas City,
and left friends in each of them.*

*As for me, I knew Tom's name before I knew Tom, when
I joined his worldcon bid, the one that never made it. Years
later I met him at a convention in Dallas in 1973, but it was
just a regional, not the world convention he'd hoped to bring
there. In 1974, on a trip to Texas, I was part of a writer's
conference held in his parents' house in Woodson, Texas, surrounded by coyotes and dust. It was a memorable weekend.
Tom's submission for the workshop was a story called "M Is
For the Million Things." I loved it. A year later, when he had
moved to Kansas City, he came up to Chicago to attend a
workshop there, and stayed in my guest room. A store on my
block had just gone out of business and was selling everything,
including the fixtures. I bought a huge section of wall shelving
for a bookcase, and Tom helped me carry it down the street.*

In 1976, I was there when he went up—in a short-sleeved sports shirt and tennis shoes—to accept his Nebula, and I was there when he went up in his fabulous blue tux to accept his Campbell. In between I was Guest of Honor at a convention in El Paso, the first time I'd ever been so honored, and Tom was the toustmaster. He roasted me gently, with anecdotes about our common roots in comic books and comic fandom.

The last time I saw Tom was in July of 1977, at a regional convention in St. Louis, Missouri. At one point we sat in my room and talked. Tom had been too busy to write for several months, and talked about wanting to get back into it. He was a partner in a small typesetting and graphics firm, and that had been eating up his time. My New Voices anthologies were already running a few years behind the award by then, but I reminded him that sooner or later I'd be coming after him for a story. He nodded and smiled, and I didn't need to say any more. When the time came, I knew he'd give me a hell of a story.

When the time came, Tom was gone.

A story remained, however: the very same story I had read in Tom's house in Woodson, back in 1974. Tom had put it aside, intending to revise it, as he had intended to revise Blind Voices. He had tentatively changed the title to "They Sleep So Poorly While They Live," but had never gotten around to doing anything more.

For all that, it is still a fine story, full of all the things Tom did best; the vivid small-town setting, the horror that comes out of nowhere, startling in its originality, the hints of dark humor, the people. Tom would have made it a finer story still, maybe something on a level with "San Diego Lightfoot Sue," maybe even better—but even as it stands, the story is strong enough, stark and well-wrought and memorable, and I'm proud to offer it to you here. You won't forget it easily.

I changed the title back. "They Sleep So Poorly While They Live" was more than a new title—it was a sign of intent, of the revisions Tom was going to make. It would have been a different story, longer perhaps, different in little ways or large ones. The story you are about to read was the one Tom wrote in 1973 or thereabouts, and called "M Is For The Million Things," so the original title is more fitting.

Normally, the story by the Campbell winner is the longest in this anthology. Tom's is the shortest. I did not want that, so I turned to our genre's leading critic, Algis Budrys, and asked him for an essay on Tom's work, on the Reamy contribution to the world of science fiction and fantasy. His afterword follows the Reamy story.

No doubt there are those holding this book who have never heard of Tom Reamy, or sampled any of his fiction. I hope that after you've read Algis Budrys' piece, and some of Tom's own work, that you'll go off and find Blind Voices *and* San Diego Lightfoot Sue. *In a sense, you are the lucky ones. You have yet to meet Angel and Tiny Tim and San Diego Lightfoot Sue and John Lee Peacock and Miss Mahan and the Detweiler boy and all the others. You have yet to meet Tom Reamy.*

G R R M

M IS FOR THE MILLION THINGS

by Tom Reamy

The evening before his wedding Ronny Huckaby was killed by the chickens. It wasn't an easy thing for them to do. Chickens are inadequately equipped for murder, and Ronny, who had turned twenty-two a month earlier, was strong and healthy. (He was also handsome, hung, and quite the local stallion, which did not affect the outcome of the situation one way or the other.) But the chickens managed. Through perseverance, dogged determination, a certain cavalier disregard for their own safety, and a great deal of surprise, they managed.

Ronny Huckaby lived with his widowed father on a small farm four miles east of Eolian, Texas. Just after sundown he went to shut up the chickens for the night. His mind was on his wedding—or, more accurately, his wedding night. Cheryl Stegall was an old-fashioned girl who didn't believe in *that* sort of thing until after she was married. He was going to show her a few old-fashioned things, all right. He grinned as he bent down to close the small chicken-house door.

In the semi-darkness he did not see a one-legged, usually

quite pleasant, white leghorn named Peggy crouched just inside.

She got his right eye with the first peck.

Old Mr. Huckaby, Ronny's father, who was a little deaf but wouldn't admit it, was watching television with the volume up quite a bit and didn't hear Ronny's screams. It's doubtful he would have heard anyway; the screams were quickly silenced in a writhing white mound of flapping hens.

In all fairness it should be noted that Lord Jim, the arrogant and self-satisfied leghorn rooster, was not involved. He watched with all the surprise his peanut-sized brain could produce and declared himself neutral in the whole affair.

Three-quarters of an hour later old Mr. Huckaby decided to check on his son's unusual absence and found him twenty feet from the chicken house surrounded by the corpses of eleven of his best layers. The surviving hens, once more as docile as they had ever been, were clucking contentedly to themselves while they scratched and pecked through Ronny's scattered entrails.

Carl Gene Tindal was awakened in the usual way. His mother opened his bedroom door and sang, "Carl Gene. Time to get up." She made two syllables out of "up" and flipped on the overhead light. Carl Gene, momentarily blinded, threw his arm over his face. He hated her turning on the light that way, but had long ago given up asking her not to do it. He sighed nasally and farted. It was a small, useless revenge for the light.

"Don't go back to sleep," his mother rattled on. "I don't want to have to call you again." The waking-up-of-Carl Gene ritual never varied from morning to morning. She went away and left the door open. He lay there for a moment listening to the sound of the radio. It was the Breckenridge station of course, the only one you could get without an outside aerial. Some woman was singing through her nose, feeling sorry for herself because she was having an affair and her husband might find out. It ended with a lot of sobbing steel guitars and the dj began stumbling over the local news, backing up every couple of sentences to read it again. Carl Gene threw back the covers and sat on the edge of the bed.

His depression seemed as deep as ever. The roaring and whispered words in his head, words he could never quite make out, had subsided since last night when he had gone to bed

very early to get away from the television set. He had lain for
hours before he went to sleep but, when he had, he slept as
if unconscious. The depression was worrying him. He couldn't
remember one of his spells lasting so long before. It had been
almost three weeks now.

"Your breakfast is nearly ready," his mother called from
the kitchen.

Carl Gene lit a cigarette and stood up heavily. He pulled
at the crotch of his jockey shorts, painfully binding his puffy
white flesh. Carl Gene was fat; soft, spongy fat like a balloon
filled with gelatin. He described himself (to himself) as a
beached whale lying belly-up on the sand.

He was almost forty-two years old, balding, and celibate.
He pulled on his robe and tied the sash around his waist. He
switched off the light with a vicious stab of his finger and went
into the bathroom to empty his bladder. He muttered when he
peed on the dangling sash of his robe.

"Your breakfast is on the table," his mother called.

The radio was off and the television tuned to the *Today
Show*. After that would be game shows until the noon news,
then soap operas until the 5:30 network news and the six o'clock
local news, then prime-time shows until the ten o'clock news,
then it was bedtime. They could only get the two stations in
Abilene. His mother didn't see any sense in spending good
money to get on the cable when they could get all the shows
she liked for nothing.

Carl Gene ate his breakfast of fried eggs, sausage, and toast
while his mother washed the dishes. "Isn't it terrible about
poor Ronny Huckaby," she sighed.

"What about him?" Carl Gene asked but he didn't care.

"I just heard it on the news," she said. "He's dead. Last
night. Something killed a bunch of their chickens and musta
killed him when he tried to stop it. Isn't that a funny coincidence, us having fried chicken for supper last night? The radio
said he was ripped into a million pieces."

Carl Gene doubted the radio had said exactly that but he
could summon only enough interest in Ronny Huckaby for a
grunt.

"Poor Cheryl Stegall. The wedding was gonna be this morning. Ten o'clock at the First Christian Church. Poor Cheryl.
Do you know her?"

"No."

"You know Ronny, don't you? He lived south of town close

to Eolian—on the old Horton place—with his father. His mother, poor thing, died three years ago."

"I knew him when I saw him," Carl Gene said and sopped the last bit of egg from his plate with a crust of toast.

"Must've been a bear," she said.

"What?"

"It must have been a bear that killed Ronny."

"There's no bears in five hundred miles of here. Nothing bigger than a coyote."

"Poor Mrs. Stegall. All that money spent on the wedding and nothing to show for it. Well, at least when you get married the bride's parents will have to pay for it."

"I'm not getting married."

His mother chuckled. "That's what they all say. One of these days the right girl will come along and you won't know what hit you. Better get your bath and shave while I finish cleaning up the kitchen."

The roaring began in Carl Gene's head, tugging at the corners of his brain, filling his limbs with lead.

Lynette Bingham was eight months pregnant and had a headache. It came on suddenly, during *Hollywood Squares*, and wouldn't go away. She couldn't understand it because she never had headaches, but she put it down to the pregnancy and tried to forget it.

She peeped out the kitchen door to check on four-year-old Tammy. She was playing in the playhouse with the little Mexican girl from down the block. Lynette wished they had enough money to move to a better part of town. The whole north side was filling up with Mexicans. George didn't make enough at the station to pay higher rent and he couldn't find a better job, times being the way they were.

The little girl's name was Elizabeth Sepulveda which Lynette thought was ridiculous. Why didn't Mexicans give their kids Mexican names—and she was always so dirty and ragged. She had tried to explain to Tammy why she shouldn't play with her, but her daughter had cried and didn't understand. Lynette sighed. She would when she was older.

She turned from the door and pressed her hands to the ache in the small of her back. If that wasn't enough she had to get a headache too. Well, this was definitely the last baby. She must have been insane to let George talk her into having another one.

Her whole life was made up of wrong decisions. This was just another one to add to the list. She should never have married George Bingham even if she was two months pregnant with Tammy. The last person on earth she planned to marry was a man content to work in a gas station. She only went out with him because he was good looking and had a trim muscular body. She had also been fascinated by the bulge in his blue jeans but she thought it cheap to admit it, even to herself.

Good lord, he was only nineteen when they started, two years younger than her. He was all right to go out with—he was crazy about her—and he satisfied her completely in bed, but you married a man with a future. If only something hadn't gone wrong with the pills.

The pain in her head was bringing back the memories. She thought she had resigned herself to her situation, but it was all stirring up again like sediment in the bottom of a pond. The old regrets mixed with the pain, and she felt sick.

She sat clumsily in one of the kitchen chairs and picked up a potato and the paring knife. George would be home for lunch in just over an hour and she had to hurry. She looked at the split vinyl covering of the chair where he always sat. It got longer every day, but there wasn't enough money to buy a new dinette suite.

The knife bit into the potato and sheared away the peel. She listened to the contestants winning piles of money on the game show but she couldn't concentrate because of the pain.

Tammy burst into the kitchen flushed from play and wanted a drink of water. Elizabeth Sepulveda stayed outside peering in with big black eyes, her grubby nose pressed against the screen. Lynette supposed she'd have to dirty a glass for her, too.

Tammy leaned against her thigh and grinned up at her. Lynette put the knife on the formica tabletop and caressed her daughter's cheek. The cheek opened and blood poured over Lynette's hand.

The child screamed and tried to pull away. Lynette put the knife down again and grabbed her. Blood swelled from Tammy's breast, spreading on the cotton playsuit Lynette had made herself. The little girl screamed until she couldn't catch her breath.

Lynette stared at the knife still in her hand. She opened her sticky fingers and let it fall to the floor. Tammy was going limp in her arms. She clutched the child to her and felt fresh warm blood cover the hand she had put against Tammy's neck, watched it run down her arm and drip off her elbow.

This time she threw the knife across the room. Tammy collapsed across her lap and blood made little trails down her legs. She struggled to her feet, holding her daughter. Tammy's head flopped from side to side. Lynette's hands were slippery and she couldn't hold on. The child slipped to the floor like a boneless rubber doll.

The pain in Lynette's head was unbearable. She leaned against the wall and closed her eyes. She put her hand on her stomach and felt a fresh flow of blood. Her eyelids were almost too heavy to open, but she did it. She looked down at herself.

She didn't bother to throw away the knife this time. She just kept plunging it into her swollen abdomen until she passed out.

Carl Gene Tindal's mother sighed. "What's the world coming to?"

Her words broke his concentration, which was tenuous at best these days. He looked up from the IBM Executive and switched it off. She was watching the six o'clock local news. He didn't know what had prompted the remark. He had finally, after a day of game shows and soap operas, managed to tune out the incessant sound.

"What?" he asked, trying to get it over with.

"Didn't you hear it? They just talked about it on the news."

"I was working."

"George Bingham's wife. You know him. He works down at the Sinclair station. He married that trashy Timmons girl."

"I know him when I see him and it's not Sinclair anymore."

"I don't care what they call it now. His wife, what's her name? Lynette?"

"I don't know."

"Anyway, she killed their little girl with a butcher knife and then tried to kill herself. She was expecting again, you know."

"No."

"She lost the baby but she's gonna be all right. 'The wounds were only superficial and the knife struck no vital organs,' they said." She snorted. "Poor George. He always cleans my windshield and checks the oil without being asked to, not like most gas stations. Never should've married her. She's a lot older than him. I heard they had to. Them Timmonses never were no account."

Carl Gene's father sat in the other chair but said nothing. Carl Gene had for some time thought of his mother as the Widow Tindal, though of course she wasn't. His father was a vague, ghost-like figure in the house mornings, evenings and weekends. He was seldom noticed or commented on unless he for some reason varied his pattern. He had long ago stopped trying to do that.

He decided his mother was finished and turned back to the typewriter. He usually stopped work before supper but he was so far behind. He hadn't been able to concentrate in weeks and would suddenly discover himself sitting like a stone, staring into space, the IBM Executive humming to itself.

He worked for a religious magazine published in San Antonio. His mother had gotten him the job right after he quit college three months into his first year. It was quite a good job, he thought at the time. The editor (there had been several different ones over the years) came by the house once a month—as he visited the faithful and collected contributions—picked up the completed, neatly justified, pasted-up repro ready to go to the printer, and left the copy for the next issue. He didn't pay Carl Gene a lot of money, but it was enough, and the editor knew when he had a good thing going.

Carl Gene didn't care about the magazine. He thought they were all nut cases—even though his mother was one of them.

His only love was stamps. He was a philatelist, specializing in the rich and fertile field of Nazi postal affairs. He collected all of Germany, of course, but his passion was the postal paper resulting from Hitler's chaos. His collection was not a fabulous one, there was so much of it. And it grew progressively more expensive as the years widened since World War II.

"I wish you wouldn't buy so many stamps," his mother said whenever the postman knocked with an insured letter.

"It's my money."

"How much could you get for your stamps if you sold them?"

"I don't know. They get more valuable all the time, but I don't intend to sell them."

"What good are they then? You ought to be saving your money instead of spending it on stamps."

"Why, so I can die rich?"

"You'll need it when you get married."

Carl Gene flipped the switch and began typing, but the voices on television kept seducing his attention. He had always been able to tune it out before, but during the last few weeks the hysterical laughter on the game shows, his mother's comments on the miseries of the soap opera people, all of it worked into the crevices of his brain, poking and prodding, picking like a fingernail on a scab.

The roaring began in his head and spread like heat through his body. His fingers kept hitting the wrong keys and the television got louder and louder and . . .

Pete Rosser picked up a slop bucket in each hand and pushed open the screen door with his shoulder.

"Wait a minute," his wife said. "There's no point in keeping this little dab of gravy." She raked it into one of the buckets while he waited halfway out the kitchen door.

"Is that all?" he asked impatiently.

"Yes," she said and flipped soap suds at him. He grinned and went on out the door letting it slam behind him. She returned to the sink to finish the supper dishes. The intro music for *Adam-12* drifted in from the living room.

Pete balanced the buckets carefully, muttering to himself because they were too full again. If she had to carry them she'd be a little more careful.

The pigs met him at the pen fence, grunting and shoving. He set one bucket on the ground and leaned over the fence to pour the other in the trough. "Get back out of the way, you greedy devils!" he growled when the pigs clambered over the trough, not leaving him room to pour the slop. He poured it anyway, getting it on their heads, but the pigs didn't care.

He was pouring the second bucket when he heard the sound. It was a far-off rumble like a train—but there was no railroad closer than Cisco nearly thirty miles to the south. He emptied the bucket and rested it on top of the fence. He looked to the west where the sound seemed to come from but he couldn't see anything but the glare of the setting sun.

The chickens still milled around outside the chicken house. Some had gone to roost, but they wouldn't all be in until dark. He'd have to make another trip. He went into the barn checking to see that everything was secure for the night.

When he came out the sound was louder; much louder. He looked again to the west. The sun was down and the sky was blood red. He thought it might be a jet, but he couldn't see one. He turned toward the house. His wife was peering out the kitchen window.

He picked up the empty buckets and started that way still glancing over his shoulder toward the sound. He could hear it growing louder, and seemed to be able to distinguish harsh grindings and sharp reports like explosions mixed with the rumbling.

His wife was yelling something through the closed window and pointing. He turned and saw the dust. It was about a half mile away, faintly visible in the fading light, shooting into the air like a geyser, spreading a hazy pall across the horizon.

Pete's first thought was a cyclone, but that was impossible. The sky was almost cloudless; the weather was completely wrong for cyclones. He dropped the buckets and sprinted for the house. His wife came out on the back porch still holding a cup towel. She was yelling again but he couldn't hear her over the roar.

Then the ground trembled. Pete lost his footing and fell by the big mesquite half way between the house and the barn. He got up again but the earth was rippling and buckling under him. He clutched at the tree and wrapped his arms around it. The noise was so loud it made his bones hurt.

Pete hugged the old mesquite tree and hardly felt the rough bark digging into his cheek. The dust cloud was on the other side of the barn, rushing toward it like an avalanche. He hung there, unable to move, unable to look away.

The dust reached the barn and shot sideways. It missed the larger structure but angled through the feed lot. Then he saw what it was.

A fissure speared the earth like a slow-motion lightning bolt. It shot ahead of the dust, lancing this way and that, ripping the ground, a twenty-foot wide chasm with great agglomerations of earth and stone sloughing from the sides to tumble into unknown depths. The noise was like the end of the world.

The crevasse roared through the pigpen and the chicken house. The pigs flopped on the ground unable to stay on their feet and slipped squealing into the abyss. Chickens flew in a storm of feathers and dust and splinters. Some flew to solid ground and escaped; others flew over the grinding cleft and sank from sight.

The barn shifted. It leaned drunkenly, spilling a whirlwind of loose hay, but it didn't collapse.

Pete Rosser clung to the vibrating tree and watched the riven land. The fissure moved erratically and haltingly, pausing for a brief moment, shooting hundreds of feet in a split second, moving in random directions. It skirted the mesquite fifty feet to the north. The tree lurched, but didn't fall. Pete gasped and hugged it tighter. Dust swirled around him, stinging his skin and burning his eyes.

The fissure changed directions again. With a sudden burst of speed it hit the house dead center. Pete's wife had gotten back inside. She was halfway across the kitchen, staying on her feet by clinging to the cabinets, when the lights went out and the floor dropped from under her.

The house sagged in the middle. It folded in on itself and slipped into the chasm in an explosion of dust, flayed lumber and sparks from the broken wiring.

Pete slipped down the tree trunk and huddled on the ground. He listened to the crevasse move away, felt the earth under him calm. Tears made pale paths through the dirt on his face. Dust and quiet settled around him. The quiet was broken only by the startled cackling of the remaining chickens and an occasional subterranean hiss that sent steam drifting to the surface.

And then the new sound.

Pete thought the fissure was returning, but it was coming from the same direction, from the west. As he listened, as the sound grew louder, he could hear a difference. It was a softer sound, a hissing, sighing roar. He stood up slowly, still holding onto the tree because his legs felt like rubber.

He saw it after a while, in the moonlight, a dark line across the horizon, moving nearer, growing louder. "Oh, my God," he groaned. "The dam."

He waited by the tree for the wall of muddy water, watched it tumble and churn, flinging brush, trees, parts of houses and drowned cattle, watched steam billow as part of the water poured into the abyss.

He waited because there was no place to run.

Carl Gene Tindal's mother waited in line at the Safeway store. She had two baskets heaped high as did her next door neighbor, Lena Trimble.

"I never saw so many people in here before in my life," she said clucking her tongue. Lena sighed agreement. "You know, I was just saying to Carl Gene, 'What's this world coming to?' And barely an hour later, an earthquake of all things! You'd think we were in California instead of Texas. It was just after seven o'clock. I remember 'cause *Adam-12* had just come on. They were showing that Chiffon commercial, you know, the one where Mother Nature thinks the margarine is butter? You know how she gets mad and throws up her hands and there's thunder and lightning?"

Lena nodded.

"Well, when she did that, the whole house just trembled. Not much, 'cause the earthquake was out in the country. Wouldn't it have been terrible if it had come right through town? Anyway, I thought it was a sonic boom. You know how those airplanes fly over. Well, it like to have scared me to death 'cause I knew it wasn't a sonic boom when the house just kept shaking, not enough to do any damage though. And then Carl Gene, he was working at his typewriter, he just keeled over. Fell right on the floor in a dead faint! I didn't know what to do. Couldn't get a doctor, of course. They were running all over the place about the earthquake. I couldn't lift Carl Gene to put him in bed. I try to get him to go on a diet but it doesn't do any good. I just had to leave him on the floor. Then the electricity went off and the phone went dead and the house just kept shaking. I thought we'd been bombed by the Russians or something. The electricity didn't come back on 'til nearly eight this morning and then all they had on television was about the earthquake. Didn't get to see any of my programs. They said that big crack just made a circle around Breckenridge. Nobody can get in or out! They said the National Guard is gonna build temporary bridges on the main highway. 'Course the highway to Cisco is completely washed away. Don't know what we're gonna do about water. They say Hubbard Lake is practically dry! That's why I thought I'd better stock up on a few things, just in case. Would you look at Carlene Ellis over there? She's got a whole basket full of meat! No wonder we couldn't get anything half decent."

"It's awful the way some people act," Lena agreed. "Is Carl Gene feeling better this morning?"

"Oh, yes. Just fine. Doesn't even remember passing out."

"You've really been lucky with Carl Gene. My Franklin lives so far away I never get to see him."

"Well, ever once in a while Carl Gene says something about getting a place of his own, but I tell him it would be silly. He's got a nice job where he can stay home all day and keep me company, he doesn't have to pay any rent, or buy groceries, or pay for laundry, or anything. I just wish he'd save his money instead of spending it on stamps."

"Yes, I know. Franklin can't afford foolish things like that what with my daughter-in-law and grandchildren."

"I wish those stupid checkers would hurry up," Carl Gene's mother said, changing the subject. "I'm gonna miss *As the World Turns*—if they don't cancel it for more about the earthquake."

Dr. Mossman went into the waiting room and looked at the two men sitting there. "Mr. Dillard?" he said and the younger one stood up. The doctor went to him and spoke softly. "I'm sorry, Mr. Dillard," he said as sympathetically as he could.

"My wife?" the young man asked.

"Oh, no. Your wife is fine, no problems at all, but we lost the baby." The young man stared at him. "I wish I could give you a reason," Dr. Mossman continued, "but we won't know for sure what went wrong until there's an autopsy."

He went on, explaining some of the possible things that could have happened but Jerry Dillard wasn't listening. Jerry was only seventeen. He hoped his face was showing the proper amount of grief but inside he felt only a monumental relief.

Barney Helm overheard what the doctor said to the boy and felt bad. It was sad for a young couple like that to lose their first baby, but they were awfully young. He guessed God knew what he was doing. Well, he didn't have to worry about Brenda. This was their fifth and she had never had even a hint of a problem before.

Brenda was nearly as good as her grandmother. Grandma Burkett used to tell the story of her eighth child. She'd had it in the cotton field. She was pulling boles and when her time came she lay down on the half-filled cotton sack, dropped the baby, buttoned it inside her shirt so it could nurse, and finished the row.

Barney chuckled to himself. He didn't believe a word of it but he knew women hadn't pampered themselves back in those days like they did now. They had been very lucky, actually. The National Guard got the new bridge up just before Brenda was ready. They'd been afraid they might have to drive all the way to Graham.

Dr. Bellah came in and Barney Helm saw the look on his face.

Carl Gene's mother listened to Harry Reasoner tell about the stillbirths in Texas and exclaimed, "What's the world coming to? It's those pills, I know it's those pills. They're a sin against God. Can you imagine? Hundreds and hundreds of babies born dead in Dallas and Houston and all over. They say it's spreading. Some kind of toxin in the mothers' systems and they think it started right here. They said it might have something to do with the earthquake, but I know it's those pills."

Carl Gene sat at his typewriter, his fingers not moving. The IBM hummed to itself. His mother's words hit him like drops of water, wearing away at him, eroding gullies in his flesh, ravines in his chest, gorges in his back, canyons in his stomach, arroyos in his thighs, gulches in his arms. His head roared and it would never, never stop.

Afterword: Tom Reamy

by Algis Budrys

This isn't a memoir of Tom Reamy, or an obituary. Those are to be found in *San Diego Lightfoot Sue and Other Stories*, the excellent posthumous collection from Earthlight Publishers, a small but very capable press located at 5539 Jackson, Kansas City, MO, 64130. The trade edition is $14.95, a slipcased edition is $25.00, and the value is there. The memoir is by Howard Waldrop, who knew Tom very well. The obituary—the eulogy, to be strict about it—is disguised as an introduction by Harlan Ellison. It may very well be the most usefully analytical piece of nonfiction writing Harlan has ever done.

My essay here is an appraisal of Tom Reamy's work, which, whether good, bad or indifferent in specific cases, had a rare and masterly touch to it. I hardly knew Tom himself.

We met once, in my back yard, at a writers' workshop, to which he had submitted a manuscript that needed more work. After a while, the workshop degenerated into a picnic with beer, on into the gloaming and then the starshine, and details blur.

I met him for the second and last time at a Chicago SF convention. I was deathly ill with the flu until the day before I was scheduled on a panel. Weak as only a bear-sized kitten can be, I staggered in, and somehow my wife and I found ourselves eating lunch with Tom, whom I'd invited over to our table because he had struck me as a friendly person.

I remember nothing of our conversation; I can't recall the sound of his voice. What I remember from these brief occasions is a large, shaggy man who looked as if he'd been outdoors a great deal in his life; a weathered man who could fix your truck, break your horse, cook for a crew, and would always be careful to latch the door behind him when he left your property.

And that's what I know about Tom Reamy the individual, firsthand. Secondhand, I know he was an active member of the SF fan community for many years, doing excellent work as an amateur magazine publisher, convention organizer and artist. This is what makes his writing even more remarkable. Many fans graduate into professional SF writing. It can usually be seen in their work. They—we—tend to spend their first professional years in producing new versions of stories read in younger days, in one or another of the traditional styles.

Reamy's style, or, rather, his expression, has some antecedents in speculative fiction; not many, and almost none in genre magazine SF. R. A. Lafferty, I think, comes from where Tom comes from, but there is really no one like Lafferty, either. Here and there, other famous genre bylines have produced sporadic examples of work that might be tune-detectived to find "sources" for Reamy, particularly if the detective is tone-deaf. But it's not really there, in the magazines or in the paperbacks from magazine-trained writers.

Tom's novel, *Blind Voices*, is almost certainly the work of someone who has read *The Circus of Doctor Lao*, by Jack Finney—a non-genre writer whose other work betrays a youth spent somewhere where the railroads are single-tracked. I don't know any of the immediately preceding assertions for a fact. Even less surely, there's a tinge in *Blind Voices* of the Ray Bradbury who had left the SF pulp magazines behind and started selling to media like *Mademoiselle*. But that may not be true; perhaps both of them go back to Thomas Wolfe, more or less together, Bradbury from the Midwest of Waukegan, Illinois, and Reamy of Kansas, where the Midwest is not quite the same but both versions relate in a variety of ways to Asheville in the Carolinas.

Faulkner. Faulkner, too, with his ear for names and his penchant for listing them; then Wolfe, who loved lists, and then such Reamy stories as *Sting*—an abandoned, hopeless beginning for a novel made over from a dreadful, cheapo-horror screen scenario—whose first few hundred words introduce us to Aaron Hibbits, Elias Pinker, Lester and Ira Tidwell, Belinda Hancks and Callie Overcash.

But you see how quickly and inescapably we moved out of the SF milieu for Tom's precedents. Good, bad or indifferent—and like all good writers when he was bad he was horrid, and when you tried to guide him he became indifferent—good, bad or indifferent he was always as much himself as any artist can possibly be. Magazine SF—of which he must have read a great deal, and enjoyed, and taken some comfort in—had entertained and nurtured him in his youth, but it had left few marks on his writing.

He appears to have done that difficult thing which most writers eventually come to if they're any good—the breaking away from doing new syntheses of material in the existing literature, and the turning toward doing expressions of actual life actually observed. "Write what you know," they tell you in the academies. Most young SF writers know very little besides SF. Tom appears to have known so much about life at so early an age that no one ever saw him in an apprenticeship.

He was older than the average novice when he began submitting stories for publication; in his thirties. Old friends nevertheless assure us that he had been writing the same way for years, during a time when he was too diffident to mail submissions to the market. This appraisal may be objectively true. Tom was a remarkably easy person to grow fond of, and memories now will be fonder still. But there may be something to it.

In the *San Diego Lightfoot Sue* collection there's one story, "Dinosaurs," which reads as if its author were aware of the popular SF market, in a distant way; it reads more as if he were aware of E. M. Forster's "The Machine Stops," which has been in the literature of England since the days when Aldous Huxley was recruiting mobs to drum H. G. Wells out of town. The remainder of everything else we have preserved from Tom's prose comes from both before and after "Dinosaurs," and there just isn't any Huxleyan SF in it, nor any Wellsian, either, which means in the latter case that it steadfastly ignores all opportunities to have visibly sprung from American newsstand science fiction.

American newsstand science fiction, dominated by the neo-Wellsian visions of editor John W. Campbell, Jr., is what is usually referred to in popular American discussions of "science fiction," or "sci-fi," that pervasive false neologism which all good SF people despise. This requires some writers to deny they write science fiction, and to resent having their work sold in sci-fi media, because not all speculative fiction is Wellsian, or technological.

That's another discussion entirely, and won't be elaborated much here. But the fact is that, as Ellison points out, Reamy wasn't a "science fiction" writer, yet appeared consistently in SF magazines, had his posthumous novel reviewed in SF media and sold on the SF shelves in bookstores, wrote screenplays for what Hollywood at least considers mainline sci-fi, and is here in this anthology of science fiction. Furthermore, he won an award named for the editor with whom he is specifically not connected. Another award was the Nebula, from the Science Fiction Writers of America, for the novelette which is specifically singled out in *San Diego Lightfoot Sue*.

Why is he here?

In part, because he was beyond doubt a New Voice. In part because most of these categorizations are false. There is a thing called speculative fiction, which subsumes science fiction and fantasy, and all their sub-generic compartmentalizations, and is a branch of world literature coeval with nonspeculative fiction, which is the only other kind of fiction there is. Both kinds can be "realistic," or not, according to their authors' bent.

So the usual SF community label for the other kind is "mundane" fiction; generally, fiction in which characters move through a setting with an actual counterpart in the world, or in the known history of the world. The normal use for mundane fiction is to illuminate some aspect of humanity by moving an unusual character through such a setting. The usual use for speculative fiction is to illuminate some aspect of humanity by moving a reasonably familiar character through a social setting that never was, and perhaps never will be, and following how he reacts.

Well, now, you say, most of Reamy's stories are set in

Kansas, or the Carolinas, or West Texas, or Southern California. How are these places 'a social setting that never was, and perhaps never will be?'

Are they not, as Tom depicts them? They *seem* real; that's the good SF writer at work, playing on what little we actually know about such places. But in each case, Tom intrudes an element that never was; demons, stinging menaces from the sky, a traveling circus whose "freaks" are actual creatures from mythology, children transmogrified into an inexplicable new race which attacks and devours its elders. . . .

Think about it. Blatantly in some cases, subtly in others, Tom rummaged through the used furniture of conventional science fiction or fantasy to select analogues of the real fears of small town America, or, even more tellingly, the secret desires. Never was, never will be. But was true, is true, in a way that "naturalism" or "realism" cannot ever attain.

The "feel" of speculative fiction is unmistakable, whether it be couched in fantasy or in science fiction. This is so despite the fact that speculative and mundane fiction both can display large sections of material which, taken word for word or paragraph for paragraph, seems fully appropriate to their sister kinds. Editors and writers know the one from the other, and so do readers. The gap is rarely bridged.

There is no place else for Tom Reamy's work to appear except in the SF media. It is pure speculative fiction. If it appears in media labelled "science fiction," when in fact it has no recognizable 'science' in it, that's because publishers work in narrow categories but most modern editors, thank God, have a clearer idea of just how broad the main stream of SF can run. And exactly the same applies when it appears in media labelled "fantasy." Or, as happened with much of Tom's work, in a medium called *The Magazine of Fantasy and Science Fiction*, whose very existence and enduring prestige over the past thirty years ought to tell you something about just how restrictive these marketplace tags really are when it comes down to the intimacy between writer and reader.

An SF reader whose first preference is for technology stories will nevertheless, if pressed, read fantasy . . . sometimes when hardly pressed at all. An SF reader whose first preference is for dark, wizard-ridden fantasy will nevertheless, provided he can understand some of the vocabulary, read science fiction on a sunny afternoon. So Tom Reamy doesn't have to fit in any narrow spaces. He can just be, and we can let the marketing departments of the publishing houses grapple with exactly what to call it all. That's the level at which the problem belongs, and may it consume many luncheon conferences. The people who vote on the Campbell Award have a better thing to do.

All right—what is Tom Reamy's place in literature? Somewhere over there with the populists, I think; that rambling Steamboat Gothic hostel with the gallused gentlemen leaning back in straight chairs on the porch, puffing stogies and sending out for more bourbon and branchwater, generally ignoring each other's remarks but willing to get up a game of horseshoes at which surprising intensity will surface.

Over under the cottonwood is the Model-A Ford pickup with the leaky radiator and sagging doors; John Steinbeck drove up in it and just parked it there. I can't quite make out who that is sitting on the running board with his knees up near his chest, but he moved off the end of the porch where Erskine Caldwell started telling ethnic jokes, and he sits where he is now with his broad back up against the warm black metal and the silvery dust, chain-smoking.

By and large, Tom belongs away from cities. Cities are places where people pass a package around, charging fees at each step, and when the package has been painted red and gotten back to the person who first brought it in, its value has risen 500% and everyone has earned a week's pay. Out in the rest of the world, where the feed has to be spread and the manure has to be shoveled, everyone, no matter how intrinsically stupid, understands that much about how the world works.

Tom is of the people who can go to no city except Hollywood. City people don't know how to fix their own elevators, find the shutoff valves on their own plumbing, or distribute their own food. I.e., city people practice an insane dependency. In a sense, it doesn't matter if they get up in the morning on time, because if the grocer's warehouse delivery truck driver didn't, it's all over anyhow. Only in Hollywood, which doesn't exist, is this fact irrelevant.

The thing to understand about Tom's characters is that people named Aaron Hibbits or Callie Overcash know from childhood that they'll be immediately affected if the crops fail and, worse than that, only systematic, unremitting and essentially

repetitious work will affect the speed with which the crops fail.
But they might fail anyway, even though you always put more
work into each day than your body can make up for overnight.

The people of central Kansas and western Texas, like the
people of Waukegan or of Asheville, North Carolina, know
this equation. A life directly based on agriculture consists of
evaluating how much must be done, and also of how much
must be left to slide because while any damned fool can see
it needs doing, a smarter head can see it won't pay.

You talk about a Global Village, and in truth the people
out in the panhandles of this world see the same TV shows at
the same time city people do. But city people see life as a
series of transactions, while the people Tom knew see life as
a holding action. They know that people are rather simply
motivated.

American newsstand SF is city writing. It assumes you can
break even or perhaps gain; that there potentially is immortality. A personal immortality in which you, as you are, might
be extended indefinitely into the future, with time to nurture
and refine a great many elaborations of what the human nervous
system can come up with to keep itself entertained.

Out where the dust is full of dead earthworm particles, it
is understood that the only immortality is theoretical and in-
volves a complete metamorphosis. There are things to do on
the basis that they must be accomplished within a limited time,
because after that you have been translated, and will no longer
be in a position to affect your situation. Every moment of
temptation assumes great importance, because it's fleeting, and
the time may come when you will bitterly regret not having
given in to it. Similarly with moments of beauty and opportunities for love. And then there is the day-to-day business of
making life mutually tolerable; the sip, sip, sip in the juke joint
or the blind pig, with its rigidly structured chaffering among
the participants, or the churchly politicking and its rigidly structured gossip; either way, it's a means of keeping yourself
usefully busy.

The reason I can't make this more clear is because it really
has to be shown to you in stories, unless you were involved
in this sort of life yourself at some extended time. I thought
I might be able to do it in expository prose, but all I can do
is hint at it.

Fortunately, Tom has provided the stories; I hope I've provided some basis for understanding in what essential way they're realistic about a milieu not many SF people can assimilate, and how this makes them feel different . . . how it is that Tom's stories are of a rare sort, because the usual kind of SF rarely explores into that aspect of reality. Most "bucolic" SF is couched to be understandable to city people; most of its principal characters are city-oriented people who admire the sound of crickets in the hush of twilight and like to go fishing in the streams. They're tourists, and we tour with them through their eyes. To Tom, such people are aliens making a fundamental error.

Leaving the land is something that many country people have to do. It's a way of giving in to temptation, and it's also a way of acknowledging that the land life now requires a certain proportion of emissaries, to move among the city people and make sure that at least a minimal quantity of goods and services—such as encouraging messages—gets sent back. It's very difficult to decide, if you're one of those people, whether your decision is in accord with ultimately useful motives or whether you've just decided to make the ultimately futile move of opting out. In the cities, you quickly fall in with all the other sorts of people to whom life is a holding action; it's the only touch of home.

So Tom's "urban" fiction is country fiction in urban settings. The people in it can't be sure of why they do things they do, but they have a very clear idea of what must be done if it can, and they know that whatever they're doing can't be done forever. They are not a guerilla army with ambitions to seize the megalithic sprawl; they are a separate race who did not pile these stones but are bivouaced among them, who must be constantly aware of the running changes the proprietors are making, and who know that most collisions with the immortality freaks will be unfortunate.

The central thing to remember is that there are two kinds of action, and only two. One of them is the following of routine, which is routine because it has been proven safest and most effective in a dangerous and ultimately overpowering world.

Urbanized or still on the land, routine is one of the courses of action, and is the mandatory one. The other course is to do something for the hell of it. Under the pressure of the mandatory, the temptation to break out can become overwhelming. When that fleeting moment arrives, the need to seize it prevails.

It *is* a fleeting moment, and it must present itself. It's not possible to decide to break routine, or it wouldn't be routine. A fortunate chance must occur. And things being the way they are in the world, it may be a chance to do good, or it may be a chance to do bad, but it's essentially the same temptation. Furthermore, who truly knows the Ultimate Plan? Might it in the end be good to do bad now? Or might it be the other way around? So doing either good or bad are seen as incredible risks . . . and irresistible risks. Man is born to trouble as the sparks fly upward, the Good Book says; it says specifically that you just can't get away from that.

In certain cases, the awareness of all this produces maniacs like the James boys, Bonnie and Clyde, and John Dillinger. City people will tell you these rural folk heroes were nurtured and sheltered out in the sticks because they stole from the rich and gave to the poor. This is urban transactional thinking. They were sheltered for the same reason you let a dog come up on your porch in the rain; you know that in God's eyes you could just as well have been a dog, and that only almost unbearable attention to details of dress and roof-mending prevents you from being as a dog.

In all cases, this produces an underlying melancholy as well as a great deal of caution.

In a certain few cases, it produces a sweet gentleness that goes right down to the core of what you are, and is thus invincible.

That, I think, is the secret of Tom Reamy the individual as well as Tom Reamy the writer. He knew what people are, and he loved it. Not because he didn't know any better; he was a man full grown, probably full grown at an earlier age than most, and he knew all the sides of being human. He loved us anyway, and we should feel flattered; the verdict was rendered by someone competent to judge.

As for what literary history will make of his role in it:

No one can tell. He was more than average proficient; he would have gotten better. *Blind Voices* is a good novel, in a field which produces far fewer novels than it does book-length fiction. It's not a great one. It could have used another draft. His strength is not in his craftmanship, better than average though it is. His strength is in how he looked at the world and conveyed that view in his stories. But that view has been seen before in literature. The unique thing about Tom was that it hasn't been seen very much at all in any kind of SF, and never with such consistency and intensity in U.S. magazine SF.

I don't know who there is to follow him. If he had stayed with us, he could have made the mode viable all by himself, gradually attracting apprentices, inspiring others to produce variations—could, in short, have melded his kind of work into the continually evolving body which attracts new persons to SF fandom and then into professional SF writing. Then, looking back from a time when he was, say, in his late fifties or sixties, we would honor him for having accomplished the thing we now praise him for having avoided.

As it is, he may stand by himself for quite a while. What usually happens in such cases is that literary history doesn't render a verdict; it loses it in the files. The water may close over this person's work, though it might take longer for the man himself to be forgotten by those who knew him, or by those who have heard what's said about him by those who knew him.

But if there are any country people out there who have been thinking about giving it a whirl, please do. There are shoes to be filled. Not Tom's; your own.

Winners and Nominees

The John W. Campbell Jr. Awards

1973 – 1979

1973 Ruth Berman
George Alec Effinger
George R. R. Martin
*Jerry Pournelle
Robert Thurston
Lisa Tuttle

1974 Jesse Miller
Thomas F. Monteleone
*Spider Robinson
Guy Snyder
*Lisa Tuttle

1975 Alan Brennert
Suzy McKee Charnas
Felix C. Gotschalk
Brenda Pearce
*P. J. Plauger
John Varley

1976 Arsen Darnay
M. A. Foster
*Tom Reamy
John Varley
Joan D. Vinge

1977 Jack L. Chalker
*C. J. Cherryh
M. A. Foster
Carter Scholz

1978 *Orson Scott Card
Jack L. Chalker
Stephen R. Donaldson
Elizabeth A. Lynn
Bruce Sterling

1979   *Stephen R. Donaldson   *** denotes winners**
           Cynthia Felice
           James P. Hogan
           Elizabeth A. Lynn
           Barry Longyear
           Charles Sheffield

The John W. Campbell Award for the Best New Writer in Science Fiction was sponsored by the Conde Nast Publications, Inc., from its inception in 1973 through 1979. In 1980, sponsorship was taken over by Davis Publications. Nominees and winners are both determined by fan vote.

94

MS READ-a-thon—
a simple way to start youngsters reading

Boys and girls between 6 and 14 can join the MS READ-a-thon and help find a cure for Multiple Sclerosis by reading books. And they get two rewards — the enjoyment of reading, and the great feeling that comes from helping others.

Parents and educators: For complete information call your local MS chapter. Or mail the coupon below.

Kids can help, too!